A Note about Walter D. Edmonds's
Books for Readers from Eight to Eighty

The books for young people by the author of *Drums Along
the Mohawk, Rome Haul* and other fine historical novels
began with *The Matchlock Gun.* This story, the first in the
present collection, won the coveted Newbery Medal in 1942.
Five more are in this volume: *Wilderness Clearing, Two Logs
Crossing, Tom Whipple, Cadmus Henry,* and *Uncle Ben's
Whale.* "Water Never Hurt a Man," the seventh story, was
selected from Mr. Edmonds's book of short stories, *Mostly
Canallers.* His short novels, *In the Hands of the Senecas* and
The Wedding Journey, have been enjoyed by many young
readers, specifically for whom he has recently written another
story, *Time to Go House.*

SEVEN AMERICAN STORIES

SEVEN AMERICAN STORIES

BY

WALTER D. EDMONDS

ILLUSTRATED BY WILLIAM SAUTS BOCK

LITTLE, BROWN AND COMPANY

BOSTON   TORONTO

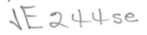

Published simultaneously in Canada
by Little, Brown & Company (Canada) Limited

PRINTED IN THE UNITED STATES OF AMERICA

CONTENTS

THE MATCHLOCK GUN

THE SPANISH GUN

EDWARD watched intently as his father struggled into the blue uniform coat that he had had made when he was elected captain of the Guilderland militia. It was a fine thing, he thought, to have Captain Teunis Van Alstyne for one's father, but he did wish that some day, just once even, his father would take the Spanish Gun to the muster.

It hung over the fireplace, its bell mouth pointing towards the front of the house, its brass-heeled stock towards the shed door. It was longer than a grown man, half again the length of the musket kept on pegs over the stoop door, and more than twice the length of Edward, who was ten years old, with long legs, dark hair, like his mother's, and serious eyes.

Teunis Van Alstyne often said that he had seen culverins that did not look so big as this matchlock gun. He used to tease Gertrude, his wife, about it, asking whether she had brought the gun with her to kill Indians. They were a young couple to have a ten-year-old son; they were handsome and high-spirited; he, lusty and thick-set, a true Dutchman; she, showing her Palatine breeding, dark, brown-eyed, with black hair braided round her head, her slim body limber and quick about her work. They had been nineteen and sixteen when they married; and she hated it when Teunis put on the militia coat.

All summer he had been going off on military service, into the hills and down to Albany; and every time, to Edward's disappointment, he took the musket.

This time, before Teunis could reach for it, Edward asked, "Aren't you ever going to take the big gun, Father?"

Teunis swung round to his son, looking down into the thin serious dark face. "Look, Edward, I'll show you." He lifted the long gun down. It was so heavy that a man could hardly hold it. As for Edward, when he tried, he could not keep both ends off the floor together.

Then, as though Van Aernam were not waiting outside impatiently in the gathering darkness, sitting his own horse and holding Teunis's mare, Teunis bent down to show the boy how the gun worked. "See, Edward" — he pronounced the name *Ateoord* in the Dutch manner — "it's a matchlock. It doesn't fire itself like the musket, with a flint. You have got to touch the priming with fire, like a cannon. It's a nonsensical, old-fashioned kind of a gun, isn't it?"

Edward felt disappointment over the lock. But he still thought it was a magnificent gun; and the candlelight caught the tracery on the brass bindings, making them look rich. He let go of it reluctantly when his father straightened up to replace it over the fireplace. Gertrude stooped down to pat her son. "Never mind," she said to him, "your Great-Grandfather Dygert brought it all the way over from Holland with him."

Edward brightened a little. "Yes," he cried, "he bought it in Bergom op Zoom to bring to the wild America."

Six-year-old Trudy laughed and said, "Bergom op Zoom!" and clapped her hands and jumped up and down in delight.

Teunis took his hat from his wife and looked at her over the heads of their children. Outside one of the horses jingled its bits as it shook itself. A northwest rain was falling, a real

November storm that had been blowing all day over the Helderbergs, with low clouds driving. At dusk, just before Van Aernam came, they had heard geese quartering the clouds, invisible and high. Winter was coming close.

"Where are you going, Teunis?"

"To Palatine Bridge."

"Did Van Aernam say whether there were any French?"

She was stuffing half a loaf and some sausage into his pouch, but she was looking at him. He had taken down the musket. He looked so manly and brave in his blue coat with red facings, his wide-brim hat and heavy boots. Now he seemed absorbed in examining his powder horn, then filling it from the big horn beside the chimney. He said to her, "I don't know. Indians, anyway. He said the settlers were running down from the north to the Flats. A horseman reached Albany two hours past noon."

He looked up then as he passed the thong of the powder horn over his head.

"Gertrude, you mustn't be worried. There's no real chance the Indians will carry so far as this. And, anyway, we shall have the militia at the bridge."

"I'm not worried."

"Good girl. If you get lonely, go over to the brick house. It's like a fort and Mother has guns for the Negroes."

"I won't go over there." She saw the look cross his face. "Unless there are Indians."

He knew how she felt about the Widow Van Alstyne. The older woman made no bones about telling him what she thought of Gertrude, either — "A black-haired Palatine wench with no 'Van' to her name."

"Give me a kiss, Gertrude."

He put one arm round his wife and kissed her mouth. She had both arms round his neck. The children watched them with interest. It was not usual for their parents to behave so.

Then Van Aernam's voice battered through the wall. "Teunis! It's wet as the ocean out here. Come on!"

"Coming," shouted Teunis in his great voice. He could roar like a bull when he wanted. "Remember, Gertrude. I'll send a man if the Indians go by us. But they'll never get so far."

He had opened the door now. The wind swept past his stout legs to set the candles swaying. Outside the noise of rain and wind-whipped trees was a living sound. The two horses looked all shining, like metal beasts, and Van Aernam, sitting one stoutly, dripped all around his hat brim.

"We're late already now," he said. "But I don't blame you. Here, get up." The children saw his eyes and teeth white under his hat. "It's been a long time since the French were in the valley. But they won't come this far. And if they do, we'll blast the breeches off them."

Teunis had mounted and swung the mare away from the stoop. The two splashed off through the rain. The darkness seemed to come down like the black cover of a closing book to hide them. Gertrude stood for a moment staring after them. Then she leaned against the door to close it, and the wind swept her skirt back from her legs.

Trudy said, "Indians don't wear breeches."

"No," said Gertrude, absently. "That's just a way of talking."

"I think they must feel cold in winter."

Edward said scornfully, "You talk too much, Trudy." He kept watching his mother. He wanted to say that he would look after her; but he felt shy of saying anything to her after the way she had kissed his father.

She said, suddenly, "Time for bed."

Trudy began her usual objections.

"I don't want to go to bed."

"Why not?"

"It's windy, Mama."

"That's nothing."

"I want to sleep with you, Mama."

"You go right up, now," Gertrude said evenly. "No non-sense."

7

❧ 2 ❧

IN THE LOFT

THE TWO CHILDREN slept together in the loft room, under the roof where the smoked hams made a scent in the darkness. On nights when there were stars or a low moon beyond the gable window, they could see the hams, white in their flannel wrappings, like French soldiers in white uniform coats, marching single file. But with the candle Gertrude carried in her hand to give them light the hams were hams only, and the dark bunches of herbs flanking them were not St. Francis Indians, but boneset, and camomile, and rhubarb.

The loft was warm from the all-day fire in the chimney that passed back of the low bedstead — rising out of the floor boards and penetrating the roof. Above the roof the wind hooted softly in the chimney mouth; the sound brought a sense of the cold and wet beyond the thickness of roof board and shingle.

The two children undressed quickly, scuffing off their shoes, one each side of the low bedstead. "That isn't neat, Trudy." But Trudy was already wriggling her plump body into the nightgown and dropping on round knees and rattling off her prayers.

Edward was slower, more methodical. He put an ending line for Father on his prayer, hoping his mother would take notice of it.

8

She said, "Poor Papa, he must be wet." She pulled the blankets over them. Her hands had a clean buttery smell from the churning she had done that afternoon. Edward smelled it when she came round to his side of the bed. She kissed him swiftly and hard, and then mechanically sang the familiar nursery rhyme as she straightened up to take the candle off the chest.

9

Trip a trop a troenje;
De varken en de boenjen.

(Up and down on a little throne;
The pigs are in the beans.)

Her voice under the low roof was soft and sweet. Her dark
hair took inky shadows from the candle flame, and the long
fingers, hardened by her work, shaped themselves to his cheek.

"Good night, sleep well."

"Mama, are the French coming here?"

"No. Papa is waiting. He will not let them get by, if they
come even so far as the bridge."

Trudy was already asleep, like a yellow-haired woodchuck,
round and fat, burrowing down in the feather tick.

"You aren't afraid, Edward."

"No, Mama. Are you afraid?"

"No, Edward."

"If the Indians come, call me, Mama. I'll come down and
help."

"Yes, Edward."

Gertrude went down the steps one at a time, softly. A
moment arrived when just her head and shoulders showed,
the smooth line of her throat disappearing into the wide neck
of her homespun dress. The light of the candle shone upward
against her face. She stopped for an instant to look back
towards the bed, brown-eyed and tender. Then the light grew
dim, picking out faintly a square of the roof boards. It went
out with a soft sound of her breath. Her feet passed over the
floor below.

Edward listened intently. Tonight her clear voice was not
answering his father; there was no reassuring laughter from

his deep voice to be shut off by the closing of the bedroom door.

There was only the note of the wind in the chimney and the feeling of it on the roof, like a hand pressed down out of darkness. It was easy to think of it passing through the wet woods, rocking the bare branches where only the beech trees had leaves left to shake.

The gable window remained dark, and the hams along the roof tree remained invisible, but Edward could see them in his mind's eye, like white-coated soldiers, in single file, marching towards the bed.

3

THE SMALL FIELDS

IN THE MORNING it was clear, with the wind still blowing, and white clouds in a blue sky moving loftily above the Helderbergs. The two cows, after Gertrude had milked them, lowed along the bank of the Hunger Kill, which had risen too high for them to cross. The land sloping upward from the low stoop was sopping wet, and the narrow road that led to the Palatine road by the corner of Widow Van Alstyne's brick house was a muddy brown brook. The bean vines, leafless, holding only a few ungathered pods, were like damp skeletons of the garden.

Gertrude looked northward as she came in with the milking pail, and the house seemed solitary in an abandoned world. She had had a restless night; it was seldom that her husband had been away overnight — three times since they had been married, she could name each one — but those times it was business in Albany that had kept him away, settling the rent with Patroon Van Rensselaer, or looking up a slave for his mother. He had never stayed out before on militia duty.

A line of smoke, snatched from the chimney by the wind, showed her that Edward was down and had refreshened the fire. She thought quickly that with a son it was not as if she were alone. There was Trudy also, of course; but Trudy was too young to notice things.

She wondered whether Teunis would get back that night. She wondered whether he had any more news of the French and Indians. There never was any definite word of them until the raid was over. Not even when they had burned Schenectady in 1690 had any word of the raid reached Albany until Simon Schemmerhoorn had ridden into town early the next morning. She felt afraid. Their fields were so small in all these woods. An Indian might walk onto the stoop before they were aware of his presence on the farm, if they were indoors at the time. She made up her mind abruptly to keep outside as much as she could all day.

She did not want the children to be frightened, so she talked to them all through their breakfast of corn mush and milk about how the cows were frightened by the water. Every now and then they could hear the distracted bellowing of the two foolish animals striding up and down the shore of the Kill. As if they did not have grass enough on this side! It made the children laugh. The sound of the laughing children made the kitchen seem secure and Gertrude laughed with them,

merrily, until Edward asked whether he should take the butter over to Grandmother Van Alstyne.

Gertrude said, "No," suddenly and firmly, so that he stared at her for a long time, and she made a lame explanation of wanting him around the farm to help her with the wood, since Teunis was away.

He said, "Grandmother will be angry if she doesn't get her butter, Mama."

"She can send Tom over to get it." Tom was the widow's head Negro.

Trudy asked, "Why haven't we any slaves, Mama?"

Gertrude explained that all the place really belonged to Teunis, so that Grandmother's slaves actually were theirs; but as Grandmother became so cross at the idea of leaving the brick house, they preferred to build their own house and live by themselves.

Trudy said she wished to live in the big house. "Why don't you make Grandma live here, then?"

"One has to be nice to old people."

"Anyone knows that," Edward said to Trudy. "Why don't we all take the butter over together, Mama?"

"No. I am going to stay here, and so are you, Edward."

She acted flustered again. After a while, Edward asked, "Are there Indians in the woods, Mama?"

"No, I don't think so. Papa would send us word if there were. There is nothing to be worried about, Edward."

❧ 4 ☙

INDIAN FIRES

JOHN MYNDERSE rode down after lunch, carrying his musket in his hands, balancing it on the withers of his bright bay horse. He called for Gertrude to come out, and she closed the door behind her so that the children, looking through the window, could not hear what was said. The sun was warmer now and the wind was dying down and the bay horse rested his hip while Mynderse talked down to their mother. She tilted her face up at him, looking young and small and worried.

"Teunis says to tell you everything is all right. But the French Indians are burning the upper settlements. People have been killed. They have sent a company from Albany to the Flats. The company will stop them all right, Gertrude."

"What are you doing?"

"Teunis wanted to let you know, that is all. I am riding over to Van Epps' and to my own place. But Teunis thinks maybe you had better go over to the big house." Mynderse looked down at her. "He won't get back tonight either, probably."

"Tell him not to worry about us. We are fine." He looked away from her as she squared her shoulders. "Tell me, does he want anything?"

Mynderse shook his head. "Yes, I forgot. He wants his schnapps in the wood flask."

"All right," she said. "Doesn't he want any food? Bread?"

"He didn't say, but we could use food. There are quite a lot of us."

"Just a minute." She flew into the house to get the schnapps. "Get the big loaf of bread, Trudy. And you get the ham, the big one at the end, Edward."

In a moment they had the food ready for Mynderse. He put the flask over his shoulder and the loaf in his bag and took the ham in his arm. "Just like my baby," he said, grinning at the children, and they laughed soberly.

They watched him clop away up the road, leaving deep tracks in the mud, and Edward said, "Mynderse does not ride like Father. He is like a flour sack sitting on a horse."

"You must not say such things about Mynderse. He is very kind."

Trudy clapped her hands and said, "The Indians don't wear breeches!" She sang it. "The Indians don't wear breeches. Oh, the Indians don't wear breeches," till she was hushed up and was sullen and went around muttering something. Edward finally asked her what she said, and she answered in a deep voice, "Bergom op Zoom!"

He looked up at the Spanish Gun at once. It seemed like a cannon with the afternoon light shining through the window along the whole length of it. He thought they need not be afraid with that in the house.

Gertrude said, "Let us go out for a little walk."

"Where to?"

"Oh, just for some air. And then we can get in the cows."

They went out, and to please Trudy, Mama allowed her to wear the old shawl, so that she looked like a comical dwarf woman with fat legs. The children chattered all the way along

and Gertrude had no trouble in leading them up the knoll beyond the garden. It was quite a high rise of ground. From the top of it one could see out clear into the north and east.

The sun was halfway down and the west wind, though it was much milder, was like a stream against their cheeks. The children saw the smoke as soon as Gertrude did. It was a leaning cloud, far in the north. They could see it plain against the pale horizon.

"Is it far away?" the children asked.

"Yes." Gertrude was straining her eyes. She tried to imagine where it came from. She thought it was much nearer than the north settlements. Near the Flats, she thought, since it showed so distinctly.

"Is it a big fire, Mama?"

"Yes, I think so."

"I want to see it!" said Trudy. "I want."

"It is too far. It is time to be getting back to the house."

Edward was silent. They walked down together with the wind cold in their faces and saw the cows by the creek.

"Come," cried Gertrude, "we must get them in."

"I'll get them," said Edward.

"No, we'll all get them. Hurry."

Trudy ran, waving a stick and screeching, "Bergom op Zoom!" but Edward kept watching his mother. He knew now that she was afraid.

"Are the Indians near?"

"Not very." She made her voice sound calm. Luckily the cows were eager to be brought in. They fastened them and went into the house. Then Trudy was sent to wash her face and Gertrude called Edward.

She looked pale and serious.

"I think the Indians are quite near, Edward. You must not go out any more."

"Why don't we go over to Grandmother's?"

"It is better here." She thought of an excuse. "If Papa comes back, he would want to find us at home, Edward."

ঙ্গ 5 ৯৯

LOADING THE GUN

SHE HAD THOUGHT out her course while getting the cows. It was better to stay. Their place was away from the main road, and raiders would be more likely to know and see the brick house. She knew that she could not help the grandmother, who would not want her help in any case, and she thought only of the best way to keep the children safe. To stay seemed the best way to her. Trudy's shouting had given her an idea for defending the house, for it seemed to her that if the Indians came they would not arrive as far as this except in small groups.

"Edward, I want you to be a brave boy and do everything I tell you."

"Yes, Mama."

"Would you be afraid to fire Great-Grandfather's gun?"

Edward looked up at the Spanish matchlock, all the great length of it, and said with a white, excited face, "No, Mama. But I can't hold it."

"I can fix that," she said. "But you must do exactly what I say."

She went over to the fireplace and mounted a stool and took down the huge gun. It was beginning to grow dusky in the Kill Valley already, and the kitchen had turned gray and shadowy. She lit a candle.

"Fetch the big powder horn."

She had no idea how much powder to put into the gun, but she doubled what seemed to her a musket charge. She wadded it down with a piece of writing paper, standing at the end of the barrel and pushing the rod, because of the length of the gun.

"It hasn't any bullets," Edward said.

"See if there are some with Papa's mold."

Edward found two. They rolled down the barrel with a faint rattling sound. Gertrude was not satisfied. She leaned the gun on a chair and told Edward not to let Trudy touch it. Trudy came in at that moment and as soon as she saw the gun she stopped dead. For once she was speechless.

Gertrude rummaged, finding some horseshoe nails and some small pebbles and two brass buttons. She rammed them all down and wadded them hard. Then she got Teunis's axe and chopped out a corner of the blind of the window at the left of the stoop door.

With Edward helping, she dragged the table to the window and then lifted the gun onto it, and with all her flatirons propped the gun so that it pointed to the missing corner of the blind, straight out onto the steps of the stoop. She bolted the blinds then, not only of that window but of the other windows also, and dropped the bar over the shed door.

She had become very silent in doing these things, and so had the children watching her. Edward trembled a little when she drew a stool up to the table and told him to get onto it. Then she primed the gun and set the candle beside it.

Seeing the whole thing complete, Trudy suddenly said with great acuteness, in a loud voice, "Bergom op Zoom!"

"Hush," said Gertrude. "Trudy, you must not talk. You must play on Mama's and Papa's bed." She made a doll out of a handkerchief and got a large lump of maple sugar and some of the silver spoons and put them and Trudy together on the bed, leaving the door open so that she would not be frightened. The little girl settled down in delight on the big bed and held her doll up so she could see, and whispered, "Bergom op Zoom," very softly.

❧ 6 ❧

EDWARD'S ORDERS

GERTRUDE WENT BACK to her son, thinking how young he was to have so much to do. "Edward, you must listen to me."

"Yes, Mama."

"I am going outside to look for Indians. If they come, I shall call your name, ATEOORD! Loud as I can. Then you must touch the candle to this place."

"Yes, Mama," he said eagerly.

"You must not do it before."

"No, Mama."

"You must not touch anything until I call your name. If I call Teunis, or Mynderse, or Uncle Sylvanus, you must not touch anything. But when I call ATEOORD, then what will you do?"

Edward reached for the candle.

"No, NO! You must not touch anything."

"I wasn't going to," he said in a low, indignant voice. He moved his hand through the gesture of touching the priming. She leaned down from behind and put her arms around him and kissed him.

"Good, brave boy."

He sat rigidly still. He looked small and white and dark-eyed. There was a hole in the knee of his stocking — she had meant to mend it that day.

"What do you do?" she asked again.

He repeated her instructions carefully and accurately.

"You are a smart boy," she said. "Do you know, even Papa has never fired that Spanish Gun?"

"Yes, I know." His voice shook a little. "Will it make an awful noise, Mama?"

"Yes, it will scare the Indians, and Papa will be so proud."

"Where are you going?"

"Just outside, Edward, to watch for the Indians."

"Not far?"

"No, I'll be near. Remember, you must not even move from the stool."

"No, Mama."

She looked at him once, then at Trudy; then, making her face serene as she could, she took up her shawl and a basket and went out of the house, closing the door upon them.

❦ 7 ❧

INDIANS ON THE FARM

SHE HAD TAKEN the basket to pick beans into. The pods remaining were worthless, but she wanted to have an excuse to stay out. Any raider coming must not be made suspicious. She had thought of picking the bean pods because she had noticed them early that morning. It had seemed to her as if the whole day had been made of pieces that had fitted together suddenly when silly little Trudy began screeching "Bergom op Zoom" after the cows.

Now, walking up to the garden patch, across the wind, she wondered whether she had not been acting hysterically. She had put Edward under a strain that no boy only ten years old ought to have. She had left him frightened, cold, with his resolution to be brave. She seemed to see him sitting there by the table at the end of the monstrous gun, listening and listening. But she knew that she could have done nothing else, unless she took them to Widow Van Alstyne's. As for that, she could still persuade herself that she had been right in considering her own house the safer place.

Twilight had stretched across to the Helderbergs when she came among the bean vines. She began picking pods into her basket, slowly, one at a time, fumbling with her hands in the cold wind, and watching the woods unceasingly. It would soon

be too dark to be able to see the woods. There was only a pale light to show the rolling tops of the hills. There was no light at all to the north now, and the night was a visible blackness in the sky.

So that Edward might not feel too deserted, now and then she sang, her voice carrying away from her lips along the wind. She hoped he could hear her.

> *Trip a trop a troenje;*
> *De varken en de boenjen.*

(Up and down on a little throne;
The pigs are in the beans.)

The wind seemed to be falling still lower with the failing light. Now and then she could hear the water running in the Hunger Kill below.

The widow's was a brick house, stout as a fort. As she thought of it, Gertrude turned in that direction and saw a rise of flames through the branches. She had been right, then. Van Alstyne's was afire. The wind was dying and the flames sprang high. Silence had come into their own little valley. She understood suddenly that the Indians had got by. They were in the Helderbergs. Where Teunis and his men could be she did not know. It was too late for him to help her now. But if she had been right all the way through, maybe she would not need him, after all. Maybe the Indians would not come along the Hunger Kill to find their house.

It was then that she saw the Indians.

8

"ATEOORD!"

THERE WERE FIVE of them, dark shapes on the road, coming from the brick house. They hardly looked like men, the way they moved. They were trotting, stooped over, first one and then another coming up, like dogs sifting up to the scent of food. Gertrude felt her heart pound hard; then it seemed to stop altogether.

She realized that they had not seen her. They were heading straight for the house, leaving the road now, so that their feet would make no sound in the mud. Her heart started to beat again. But her hands were stiff as she grasped the basket and stepped from the bean poles into the open. She made a pretense of seeing them for the first time. She stopped stock still, facing them, making herself count five. Then she ran for the house.

She must not lose her head. She must not run so fast as to outdistance them, for then she would have to wait on the stoop. They should be right behind her, only a step away from her.

She glanced back over her shoulder to see them loping along in long strides. They did not seem to cover the ground fast, yet they were already well up on her. She could see the feathers in the upstanding scalp locks of the leading three. She screamed "Teunis!" and ran for the house with all her might. She had not meant to let them get so close. The road was muddy and the footing treacherous. If they overtook her before she reached the stoop it would be no good at all. She would be killed, Edward and Trudy, the house burned.

She called, "Sylvanus! Van Aernam! Mynderse!" She had not thought before how utterly she had put her trust in Edward.

Coming down the slope of ground, the Indians closed in with unbelievable rapidity. Gertrude was a good runner. But she had never run as fast as this. She could hear the pounding of their feet over her own and the hammering of the blood in her head. But she kept her feet and ran up the steps onto the stoop, and shouted, "ATEOORD!"

Then a flashing pain entered her shoulder at the back and she was flung against the door. She knew the Indians had thrown a tomahawk at her. A second, missing her; entered the door beside her face. She turned about weakly to see them

springing onto the steps, their heads faintly lit from candlelight shining through the chink in the blind, their faces
painted red and yellow and white, and the silver rings swinging outward from their ears.

A tremendous flash, a roar that shook the stoop under her,

and a choking cloud of smoke removed them. She saw the leader cave in over his own knees and the next two flung back on their shoulders. She saw nothing else at all, but she knew that Edward had touched off the Spanish Gun.

◄ 9 ►

FIRING THE GUN

WHEN EDWARD touched the candle to the priming of the Spanish Gun he felt so cold that he could hardly move. He had heard his mother running down the road and had heard her shouts for his father and Uncle Sylvanus, now dead for a long time, for Van Aernam and Mynderse, and then he had heard the running feet of the Indians behind her. He could see nothing through the chink. Outside it was black dark. He did not even touch the candle then, but he fastened his eyes on the priming and moved his hand to the candle, ready to take it up.

Then she was calling, "Ateoord!" and he heard the toma-hawk drive into the door as he laid the flame down on the gunpowder. It fizzed for an instant, smoking out of the prim-ing hole. Then the gun roared, shattering the glass, and the butt, striking him fair in the chest, carried him backward off the stool.

He was not aware of it; he was not aware of anything till he heard Trudy screaming. That woke him up to the fact that he was lying on the floor of the kitchen with the Spanish Gun like

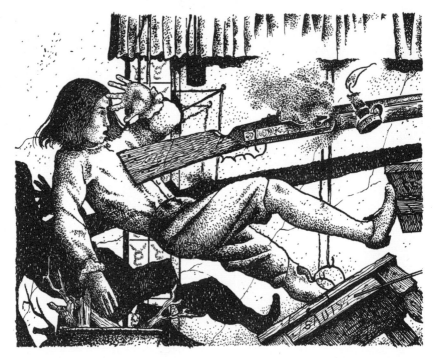

a log on top of him. He was puzzled to find the dead candle in his hand, for there was light enough to see Trudy.

He managed to wriggle out from under the gun, but the pain in his chest was so great that he could do nothing except crawl on hands and knees to the door. It was open. The light came from there. He crawled through to see the stoop ablaze, his mother lying on it like a dead person, and little Trudy desperately lugging at the handle of an Indian axe fast in their mother's shoulder. For an instant he could not take it in. Then he realized that the fire was almost to his mother's skirt.

He ordered Trudy to let go of the axe and help him drag their mother off the stoop. It was lucky she was so small. It was lucky, also, that the stoop was low, for they had to tumble her over the edge. In her fall the axe was dislodged enough for Edward to pull it forth himself.

"Is Mother killed?" asked Trudy.

Edward did not know, but he said she was alive. He made Trudy take off her shirt and he stuffed it into the open wound as well as he was able. There was plenty of light now. The flames from the stoop were already climbing up the walls.

The light went out into the yard, picking out the pools of rain water like shining eyes. They showed, too, the tumbled bodies of three dead Indians.

Edward tried to drag his mother away from them; but he could not move her. He sent Trudy inside to get blankets, telling her to hurry. She brought them from the bedroom, together with her handkerchief doll. She said gravely, "I didn't want it to get burned to death."

"No," said Edward. He thought Trudy had done well. He looked down at the dead Indians, thinking how big they were. Then he remembered the Spanish Gun.

He could not leave it there. Though he felt better, it was

hard for him to walk, and harder yet to drag out the ponderous gun. But he managed it at last, taking it out the back door and lugging it round the house. The stock left a furrow in the mud.

Then he and Trudy sat down together between their mother and the dead Indians, watching the house burn, and kept warm by its heat.

Trudy grew sleepy, after a while, and lost her interest in the dead Indians. She was no longer afraid of them. She teetered toward Edward and leaned down into his lap. Her head struck the lock of the gun and she said, "Bergom op Zoom."

"Yes," Edward said. "Great-Grandfather Dygert brought it from Bergom op Zoom to the wild America."

He was glad he had remembered to save it. Such a wonderful gun to show *his* grandchildren, maybe.

ᘔ IO ᗡ

THE MILITIA RETURN

Teunis, riding in with half a dozen militiamen, found them so: Gertrude still unconscious, Trudy asleep, and Edward sitting up with the gun across his knees, the bell mouth pointing at the three dead Indian bodies.

On their way in, the men had found the barns burned at the brick house and Grandmother Van Alstyne and her slaves barricaded, refusing even then to come out. And in the creek

valley they had found another Indian crippled and had killed him. But now while Teunis picked up Gertrude, the others just sat their horses and stared from Edward to the dead Indians.

"They sneaked by us," Mynderse said. "Who shot them, Edward?"

"I did. With the Spanish Gun," said Edward.

"You've killed more than all the rest of us put together!" Mynderse exclaimed, and he picked up the gun and hefted it. But before he could say anything more, plump Trudy woke up suddenly.

"Bergom op Zoom!" she said, pointing solemnly at Edward.

WILDERNESS CLEARING

GORDON'S CLEARING

War, and rumor of war, had not disturbed the heading of the wheat. Not a blade moved in the field. The crop had attained its growth; the ripening was finished; and now the grain was ready for the sickle.

The wilderness imprisoned the clearing in a green silence. There was no cloud, no wind, not even a stirring of air. The water in Black Creek seemed sluggish; on the rift beside the mill its voice was muted. The conical hills upon the barren, black-moss uplands stood as still as graveyard stones against the sky.

The beginning of the Jerseyfield road to Snyder's Bush and Little Falls was molelike, a small round hole in the leaves, and quickly lost. The house stood a short gunshot from the road. It was a one-story, framed building, the walls sided with new boards that had been sawn the year before at the little mill. Behind the house was the log cabin it had supplanted. The cabin was now the barn, with stalls for two horses and a cow. A fenced yard pushed out beyond the barn as far as a two-acre piece of Indian corn, which in turn was bounded by the wheat field. Among the corn, beans and squash and pumpkins were growing in the Indian fashion. There was no garden.

This, on the first of August, 1777, was Robert Gordon's place. No living sign of man or beast was visible on it anywhere. It remained so all through the day, until the sun, swinging westward, cast slanting arrowlike shadows through the stems of wheat. By then the heat haze had moved down from the northern hills and the sun, shining through it, had taken shape. Way off in the woods a woodpecker started drilling on a tree.

The bird had been at work only a short time when another sound entered the silence from the north. This was the slow uncertain clank of a cowbell. But it steadily approached through the woods towards the ford over Black Creek that led to Mount's place. A nondescript brown cow, limp-eared, and amiable, dawdled into the open and down to the creek, to which she dropped her muzzle. A moment later two people followed her.

They were a boy and girl.

The boy carried a rifle, and as he came into the clearing, his brown eyes quickly searched it from end to end.

"They ain't home yet, Maggie," he said.

Maggie Gordon shaded her eyes, and shook her head.

"They'd have heard Brownie's bell."

"The barn door's shut," he said.

He had a thick brown thatch of hair that grew almost to his shirt collar. His gray homespun trousers were frayed to the knee, and his bare feet and ankles showed cuts and bruises. His trousers were held up loosely by a single thong over his left shoulder.

He turned his thin face to the girl.

"I'll wait around for a spell, Maggie. They ought to be back most any time."

"You needn't, Dick," she said lightly.

"I wouldn't like leaving you alone."

"I don't mind now. I never was afeard of anything, except those two Indians coming around. But they've gone now."

"Hess and Cataroque was all right, for Indians. They've

taught me a lot of things. But Ma don't like them either. She says they smell too greasylike to suit her stomach."

"I'm glad they've gone. I never liked them. If they'd been friendly, they wouldn't have chased off to join the British."

"Shucks, Maggie, that don't mean anything. They told me any Indian showing up at Oswego would get a musket and a knife, and a copper kittle off the General there. You can't blame them for wanting a copper kittle."

He moved down from the bank and stopped beside the cow. The girl followed him. She also was barefoot, but her brown slim legs were smoother than the boy's. She wore a striped brown linsey petticoat that came halfway to her ankles, and a blouselike garment of blue calico called a short gown. She had opened it at the throat, during her hot walk home, so that the skin in the cleft showed startlingly white under her tanned throat.

"I wonder whether Dad and your Pa will get any news down there."

"Oh," he said with a slight start, "you mean the war."

"Yes, silly, what did you think I meant?"

"I hardly think about it."

"Why, Dick! Just yesterday you told me you wished you could go away and join the army."

"Well, I would, too. I'd like to get to be a drummer. They get better pay. Maybe I will go off this fall, when threshing's finished, if the war lasts."

"You couldn't join," she said. "You're too young. You're younger than I am."

"You needn't be so mighty, Maggie, just because you're a few days older than I be. I was sixteen last spring, and they're 'listing people sixteen years old. I'm big, too, for my age."

"You're most a man," she said with great gravity.

37

He turned suspiciously to look at her. She had put her forearms on the cow's back and was resting her chin upon them. Her gray eyes regarded him with huge solemnity, but the corners of the wide mouth, he saw, were twitching very slightly. The old cow, also, had lifted her head at him with bovine stolidity and a dribble from her muzzle into the smooth-sliding water in which all three were standing.

He jerked his head away again and did not speak.

The girl, however, did not shift her gaze, but studied him with a calm that slowly grew detached. The sunset took color in the sky and the creek began to reflect it, while shadows gathered under the western edge of woods.

The girl sighed, suddenly, and her voice was softer.

"Now, I've made you mad, Dick. I didn't mean to."

He did not wish to show too quickly that he was mollified. So he said, "You're always digging at me. I don't see why. Ain't it natural for a man to want to get ahead?"

"Why do you want to, so much?"

"You can't do anything up here, except work at the woods to make fields of it. Hoe corn, seed wheat, chop wood, and leach out ashes for money. We can't make much money, having to draw them so far. We can't do nothing here."

"Why, Dick, how can you say that, when you see everything our Dads have done? They cut the Jerseyfield road out, didn't they? And built Dad's sawmill and our houses. And now they're going for those millstones for your gristmill. Just think — we'll grind our own wheat this fall! That's more than they can say in Reeber's Settlement or Fairfield, and they're eight miles from Snyder's, and only ten from Little Falls. We're twenty miles," she said. "People are bound to settle where there's mills."

"You talk just like your Pa and mine."

"Why not?"

"Well, I want to get ahead. Just grinding flour ain't the whole wide world, Maggie. Your Pa's got some money. We ain't got anything."

"What's that got to do with it?"

"If I had some, I'd be as good as you."

"You're silly, Dick. What's that got to do with it?"

He swallowed and flushed.

"When I get some, when I come and ask you to marry me, then it will be all right."

"Why, Dick," she said.

He flushed still darker. She had leaned forward on the cow's back. He wanted to look at her, but he couldn't seem to, now that he had said something after so much bothering of his mind.

"Dick," she said. "Look at me."

Reluctantly he turned his eyes to hers. She was gazing at him as if she had never properly seen him before. But she wasn't laughing at him.

He felt a quick bouncing of his heart as he thought maybe now she realized that he had grown up.

"Why, Dick. Since when have you been thinking that way?"

"Quite some time," he muttered. "A man can't hardly help what he thinks, with you so pretty."

It did him good to see the color rise in her cheeks, too. Facing so, they seemed almost angry at each other.

"But we couldn't marry, Dick," she said.

"I know it. Not till I get money."

"That hasn't anything to do with it, silly."

"I know. Not between you and me, Maggie." He felt quite bold. "But what would your Pa say?"

He nettled her with his persistence.

39

"No, no. I mean you're younger than I am, Dick. And I can't leave Dad. I've got to look after him since Ma died."

"I wouldn't mind if he wanted to live with us."

"Can't you listen?" She stamped her foot, forgetting where she stood, and splashed them all. "You're younger than I am. A girl doesn't marry that young."

"Girls marry when they're fourteen, sometimes. You're growed enough."

"No, you. *You,* Dick. Don't you understand? When I do get married, I want to marry a man."

She had spoken in quick temper, but when she saw his dark flush, she realized all at once what she had said.

"Oh, Dick, I didn't mean to say it that way."

"You needn't say it at all."

"But, Dick. The trouble is, I never thought about it at all."

"Well, don't," he said. His face quivered so that she felt her heart bleed.

"I like you fine, Dick. You know that, don't you?"

"Oh, yes," he said. "That's nice."

They stared across the cow, each conscious of how miserable the other looked, and both feeling much more miserable inside themselves. It was just then that the old cow decided she had had enough palaver on this business. She didn't enjoy going visiting to spend the night; she preferred her own barn. Without ado she walked out from under Maggie.

The girl lost her balance and the boy was barely in time to catch her from the water. For an instant he held her in his free arm, feeling sentimental again. But Maggie was enraged at her own ineptitude.

"Let go of me," she ordered. "Blame that cow!"

He let her go, walked behind her through the creek, and followed her up the farther bank.

"Hadn't you better start home?" she asked over her shoulder.

"I'll wait, awhile."

He sat on the doorsill, digging gloomy holes in the dirt with his bare toes, while she started laying the fire for supper. When she had the supawn cooking in its pot, she came to the door with a milk pail in her hand.

"Dick." Her voice was timidly entreating.

"Yes," he said without looking up.

"Can't we forget what we said? I guess I hardly ever thought about such things. I guess I'm just not ready to."

"All right." But he would not.

He stayed while she took the cow to the spring, where it was cool to milk. The ground sloped up sharply there, and the water issuing from between two stones was led on a hollowed puncheon to a tub set in the ground. It made a steady trickling sound with its incredibly crystal thread of water; the flies seemed less insistent; the lengthening shadows crept in and quieted the cow; and the milk smelled strong and warm.

When Maggie returned to the house, Dick was still sitting in the door; but his face was turned towards the beginning of the Jerseyfield road. She also heard the creak of the loaded cart and the slow tread of both teams.

George Mount was jubilant. A great fat bear of a man, he leaned over the tailboard of the cart and patted the stones with thick hairy hands.

"Hello there, Maggie," he shouted when he saw her. "Come and take a look, will you?"

She set the pail down and with Dick went over to the cart. Both men were dripping sweat from their hot journey, and the horses drooped their heads towards their wet-streaked knees.

Maggie glanced at her father.

"Hello, Dad." His gray hair was mussed and his face tired. He did not show his usual amusement at Mount's boyish enthusiasm. She could tell by his eyes that he was troubled. But to please Mr. Mount she looked over his shoulder at the stones.

"Just take a look. I'd rather look at them myself than if they was diamonds. They mean flour, girl. Look, Dick. They didn't shift a hair. Ain't a scratch on either. And I'm saying right now it was a hard trip, too."

Robert Gordon began to unhitch his team. "Did you make out all right, Maggie?" he asked in his quiet voice.

"Yes, Dad." Without turning, she was suddenly aware of Dick's watchful eyes. "I had a real nice visit."

"You can tell me about it tonight. I want to get the harness off the horses. They aren't the only thirsty ones either."

She took the hint and ran for a bucket and went to the spring. Dick was helping to unhitch. As she brought the water, she noticed that all three were talking. Their faces together made a contrast: her father's looking old and gray and filled with worry; Dick's excited, tense, with just a tinge of fear; George Mount's red and round, mouth open and running over with his hearty laugh. Mount was a laughing kind of man and brash in his opinions. His eyes were small and clever, with immoderate self-assurance that made him quick at small things. He would give what he called his honest-to-God ideas on any subject at the shortest notice.

"Who'll want to come this way?" he was saying. "Honest, Rob, sometimes you make me laugh."

Facing him, her father, slightly built and slow to think things through, seemed ineffectual; but Maggie thought that if it came to a downright pinch, she would rather have her father to depend on. He was touching the stones with fingers

43

that were light and tentative upon the grooving, as if even now he were two thoughts behind the argument.

"Yes, George. It's surely fine to have them in — if we ever get a chance to use them."

George Mount's roving eye fell on her.

"Maggie," he shouted. "Come and listen to your Pa. He's all bothering himself about the war."

"Yes," she said, hurrying forward. She noticed that Dick was looking at her father, not at his, as if he put more stock in what Gordon had to say. "Did you get more news?"

"Yes, Maggie." Her father turned his head. "Burgoyne took Fort Ticonderoga on July fifth. He whipped St. Clair, and Schuyler's fallen back on the Hudson Valley. Burgoyne's threatening Albany."

He stopped. Mount cried, "That needn't worry us, Rob. You know that as well as me."

"Perhaps it needn't," Gordon said. "Here's what does. The Butlers and Johnsons are leading the army from Oswego that we learned about when those two Indians left here. They're down at Stanwix now, probably. Two thousand men. I saw Herkimer at the Falls. He says a thousand of them's Indians."

Dick broke in, "Then the Indians have broke the Albany treaty."

Gordon nodded.

"James Deane wrote Herkimer that the Indians are just invited along. But show me an Iroquois that can keep out of a fight he's watching. Herkimer's called the militia out. They muster day after tomorrow at Fort Dayton. There'll be a war as sure as shooting."

Maggie glanced at Dick and saw him pale and eager.

"I wish I was down there," he said.

"You'd wish you wasn't, if you was," George Mount

laughed. "Once I caught up with you with my bull whip, you would." He turned to Maggie. "I been trying to tell your Pa we're too far north for anyone to bother us."

"For a regular army, yes. For Indians, no."

"They ain't bothered us yet, have they?"

"No, but this changes the whole war for us. It means that the Johnsons have brought in the Indians. If they win, they'll run the Mohawk Valley like wolves running sheep. If they lose, George, I tell you every tree will have an Indian in it."

"You're crazy!" George Mount said with an oath. "Are you trying to scare the girl or what? Every tree? Why there ain't two thousand Indians in the whole mess of the six nations. And the Oneidas are safe on our side."

"Are they?"

"Dad," said Maggie. "Do you want to stay?"

She saw Dick look at her. Poor Dick, he's all mixed up, she thought. But Mount roared aloud.

"Stay? I'd hope so, Rob. Why, the war'll be over in a month. If it ain't, it's time enough to think of quitting. Either the British will put their foot in Albany or we'll hold them out till snowfall, and then they'll have to clear out. You can't manage an army from Canada, once the snow sets in. Any fool knows that much." He started laughing again. "Leastways, I'm telling you now, Rob."

Gordon said slowly, "I'd stay anyway till I got my wheat reaped."

"Sure, you stay that long. Tomorrow I'll come over for the stones. Dick and me can set them in. And in October we'll commence to grind. Come on, Dick."

Dick had unhitched the team. He forced himself to meet Maggie's eyes. His face got painfully red.

"Good-bye, Maggie."

45

She waved her hand cheerfully.

"Good-bye, Dick."

"What's the matter with Dick?" her father asked.

Maggie said, "I don't know." She didn't want to give him away. "I think he'd like to join the army."

"Dick's a good boy. Sometimes I think he's more of a man already than George is. But maybe it isn't just the army, Maggie. He's growing up and the way he looks to me, I think he's getting notions about you."

"Me, Dad?"

"Yes. Maybe he's falling in love with you."

"That's silly. He's younger than I am. Besides, I have to look out for you. I don't want to marry."

He smiled.

"Don't you, Maggie? Well, come along. I want my supper. We've got to start reaping tomorrow and I'm tired."

They went in and sat down at the pine-board table, facing each other, and dipping their spoons in the common bowl. While they ate the evening gradually enclosed the hills, the woods, the clearing, barn and house, and the voice of the creek, rising over its bank, made a small sound outside the windowsills.

Watching her father eat, methodically, not as if he had any taste for food, but as if he felt it was a duty to perform, Maggie saw how tired he was. She had never seen him look so old before. He was old to be her father, over sixty. Mrs. Mount had often discussed it with her — probably a love-match, late in life, for him. Maggie could not remember her mother at all. When she thought of her, it was through the possessions she had left; the white china teapot with the ivy leaves painted round it; the small looking glass over Maggie's bed in the loft;

and the little calf-hide trunk that contained a wedding dress of white with violets printed on it, and lilac knots and laces to the sleeves and front.

Last year Maggie had put it on, for fun, and it had fitted her so well that she had run out into the barn to show herself to her father. "Hello," she had said, half laughing and half shy; and when he had turned with his eyes amazed, she had thrown her arms round his neck. As he started to kiss her, she had felt his body stiffen and he put her away and smiled at her. His face had been so hurt that she had managed to understand that at first he had mistaken her for her mother. She must be very like her mother, she thought, but she had no idea how much.

Her father was thinking so tonight as he looked across the table at her. The odd little manners with which she ate and put her spoon down and lifted her whole face to look across at him, puckering her forehead slightly — the same dark hair, gray eyes, wide mouth in the small face. She catechized him, too, much as her mother used to.

"Did you get me those two yards of sagathy?"

"No. I couldn't get any of Ellice. I'm sorry. But he promised he would try from Mr. Paris down in Stonearabia the next time he was down."

"It doesn't matter, Dad."

"I got the flour, salt, and the balsam, and a pair of white-thread stockings."

"Oh!" she cried. He nodded to his bundle. She pounced on it, opened it, and pulled them out.

"Kind of a birthday present," he said. "But three months late."

"Oh, Dad. They're nice!"

He smiled.

She ran in to the shed, calling over her shoulder, "I'll try them right on, but I must wash my feet first. Please get my shoes."

He rose wearily and got the shoes from the loft. They were of black cloth with long red laces. She reached her hand through the shed door for them, then in a twinkling walked in with the gravity of a queen.

"You can't see them, half," she cried, and got a tallow dip and lit it at the fire. "Oh, Dad, they *are* nice." She lifted her petticoat nearly to the knee. "I ought to have my new petticoat on and the chintz short gown and my pocket to go with it. But I couldn't wait."

"They do fit nicely," he said.

She lifted serious eyes.

"I think lots of girls must have nicer legs than they ever know about, Dad, because they can't spend money to buy such fine stockings. Were they very expensive?"

"Not so very."

She leaned over and kissed his forehead softly. Poor Dick, she was thinking. He would be a long time making money enough to buy her any present like this.

"Well," her father said, "I got the other things, the horn-comb, the new kettle, the reel of thread you asked for, and two needles." Instantly she was burrowing.

"You couldn't get any tea?"

He said, "The price has gone too high since the war. Did you want it badly?"

"No. I didn't. But only today poor Mrs. Mount was saying how she fancied drinking real tea out of our china teapot. I think she takes a comfort in it. And I guess it does taste a little different, someway."

"Well," said Gordon, "it cost too much. But in that bag's a little present, too, you can share with her."

"What is it?" She was opening it, stockings forgot, sitting on the floor cross-legged like a little girl. "Oh!" she cried. "Loaf sugar. Two dozen lumps of it! Dad, you hadn't ought to spend so much."

He said somberly, "Perhaps it is extravagant. But the way things are, with prices rising, I don't know when we'll be able to buy things like that again. Even us. And I was thinking of Mrs. Mount, too. George is a good man, but he don't think of things."

"You always do, Dad."

He grumbled something and looked away.

"Do things look so bad, Dad?"

"Pretty bad, Maggie. It's the Indian business that worries

me the most. The war's hardly meant anything to us so far. But once they're loose, we'll all feel war. You can't provide against them like an army."

He paused to stare through the window at his wheat field.

"We're out of the way here. But Herkimer said it was foolish for us to stay. Of course, George wouldn't listen to him. George only listens to himself." Maggie sat still. A whippoorwill, late in the year to sing, began his calling somewhere out in the corn. They both noticed it, but did not mention it. "They're trying to gather people in that belong to the King's party. I hear they're going to send to Fairfield."

"What will they do to them?" Maggie asked.

"Send them down the valley, I guess. Near Albany they've been putting the men in jail. It's too bad. It's made the Scotch in Fairfield angry. I imagine they'll get out first."

"Get out, Dad?"

"Yes, to Canada."

"Isn't that a long ways?"

"Yes," he said. "But I'll be glad to have them gone. It's the worst part of this place, having them between us and the settlements."

"They wouldn't do anything to us, Dad, would they?"

"I don't know. I've never had any trouble with any of them. But George hates them."

"I know. Dick's afraid of them. He hates them, too."

"Down there," her father said, "everybody's afraid of everybody else. It doesn't matter who. The people at Reeber's Settlement are planning to leave, too. They say they'll go to Palatine."

She still had work to do, cleaning the dishes. She washed them in the shed in the light that came through from the kitchen door. Behind her back the clearing had darkened, bringing closer the steady calling of the whippoorwill.

The bird sang on and on in the cornpiece, making a small hollow in the dusty loam with the swelling of its breast. Beside the kitchen table she could see her father reading from a paper he had been given in Little Falls. He seemed a learned man to her, reading like that. Now and then he gave her bits of news: the army's in New Jersey; this has been a good season for lambing; the British King is trying to get 30,000 Russians to fight the colonies; the British tried to take Peekskill with a frigate and two sloops, but Colonel Marinus Willett drove them out with eighty men; they put American prisoners on hulks of ships in New York and take the clothes off them. . . . It was a paper of the preceding spring. "Willett's with Colonel Gansevoort at Stanwix," her father said. "He must be a good man."

The bird sang on. Maggie hardly heard her father's voice. There was no coolness yet to the night air; it was dark and close. She wondered what Dick would be doing at Mounts'. He had looked so miserable when he went away. She wished she had not said that thing about marrying a man. Dick was tall as a man. If he had on decent clothes, he wouldn't be bad-looking.

She could imagine the family crowded into the stuffy kitchen of the Mount house. It was not airy like their own, which had two glass windows. Mrs. Mount, she thought, would be uneasy over Mount's news. The three little boys would be playing the bean game with the Negro boy. Mount had bought him once at a bargain, using the money Mrs. Mount wanted spent on cloth. Mount took pride in having a slave; it was the one thing the Gordons didn't have; but the boy was useless. They said he was fourteen, but he was no bigger than ten-year-old Henry. He was terribly skinny to look at, with black sticklike arms and legs to which flat hands and feet were swivel-jointed. The only thing he was good at was playing the bean game which the two Indians had taught the smaller boys.

Maggie shared Mrs. Mount's dislike of the Indians, even if they were pleasant to the children, but she did not exactly hate them. To her they seemed two poor and rather dirty brown men — in some ways not very different from Adam Dingman who trapped up the West Canada Creek some winters. But Indians had that queer sweetish smell that Mrs. Mount said sickened her.

Luckily they didn't often come to the Gordon place, but Maggie had seen them at Mounts', sitting solemnly on each side of the hearth, their shirts hanging round their middles, their hairless torsos shining with sweat. They would sit there, alternately eating, drinking rum, and smoking for two days on end, sometimes, until Mrs. Mount was almost rabid with distaste. She didn't dare to throw them out. But once when Mount came home, after a three-days' absence, she had the

hysterics. Maggie was as glad as the older woman when Dick brought the news of their departure for the British fort.

The three younger boys were ten, nine, and seven. Henry, George, and Cobus. The first two looked like Dick, being wiry and shy; but Cobus took after his father. He didn't talk so much, perhaps, but he talked large when he did. It was almost comical to see him stand up, a small replica, with curly light-brown hair and freckled face, fat and fully stomached, saying to his mother, "Gosh a'mighty, you're a scary woman."

The Mount house was always overflowed with wrangling, bickers, shouts, and great opinions. In the midst of it, the mother seemed a washed-out figure, pale and thin, her hair already white. She had saved four children out of nine, but even those that died, she once told Maggie bitterly, had all been boys. And she had hoped so for a girl.

By contrast, their own house seemed to Maggie such a peaceful place. She took real pleasure in its ordering. Work out-of-doors was burdensome, though her father often said she did a boy's share in it, but indoors she was happy. She had never been afraid of the woods, either, like Mrs. Mount, or of the long-day silence, when all men were away from home. Mrs. Mount said she was too young to feel it yet. She would in time.

Maggie did not believe it. She glanced at her father. Would Dick, suppose a girl should marry him, be quiet and kind like him? She did not know. Poor Dick. If only there had not been this war, things would have been so peaceful. It was the war, more than all the work he did, that tired her father so. They belonged to the right party; Gordon had no use for Kings and Parliaments; but, except for the Mounts, they seemed to be the only people north of Reeber's Settlement that did belong to it. . . .

❧ 2 ❧

THE FAIRFIELD MEN

MAGGIE had finished her washing before she noticed with a sudden start that her father had stopped reading. The paper lay on his knees and his face was turned to the east window. For a few minutes she could not tell what was wrong. Nothing in the room, certainly. A few moths fluttered near the candle flame. Their shadows, large and vague, shifted noiselessly across the walls and ceiling. The sound of water flowing through the creek came in with articulate distinctness.

There was no other sound. The silence of the night was velvety, almost as if you felt it like a velvet cloth against your face. She shivered and quietly set down the empty pan. But even as she whispered the question, "What is it, Dad?" she knew what it was. The whippoorwill had stopped his singing.

"There must be something in the woods, Maggie," her father said quietly.

With a queer, quick sense of fright, Maggie saw his glance at the musket hanging with powder flask and bullet pouch from the deerhorns over the door.

She did not know why she should ask, "Shall I blow out the dip?"

He shook his head. Suddenly he put out his hand to touch hers, turned his face for a brief instant and smiled. He meant to calm her; but she felt the instinct of fear in his touch and her heart beat rapidly.

Outside the door the wheat field dimly showed its boundaries, like a spread of pewter-colored silk.

His hand tightened on hers. She heard it, too. A silver whistle in the woods.

"What's that?"

She was shivering now. After the thin silver note the woods resumed their quiet; but she knew that inside herself she would be afraid of the dark for a long time.

Her father said, quietly, "Some men are coming."

They issued from the woods, one by one, halting on the edge of the clearing, moving together into a single darker blot in the night. A voice roared out among them: "Gordon! Robert Gordon! Are you home?"

"It's the Fairfield men," said Gordon. "I thought they might come this way." He stepped to the door where they might see him. "Who are you?" he shouted.

The same voice answered: "It's Casselman. We're only stopping."

One after another men emerged from the dark blot and came at a quick pace forward along the wagon track. As she joined her father at the door, Maggie saw their individual shapes, black against the grain, with rifles on their shoulders.

The men crowded into the house. They stood round the walls, leaning on their guns, and looked curiously at Gordon and his daughter.

The kitchen was not large enough for them all. Maggie could see a few of them still beyond the door, faintly, in the candle glow, their leggings strapped at the knee, the dim shine of their rifle barrels. They were quiet, listening.

In the room the air thickened with their sweat smell. She began to feel that she and her father were being hemmed in. Suffrenes Casselman was sitting down. He said, "Those Dutch are sending up a patrol to herd us in to one of their confounded forts." As his head turned and he looked at Maggie, the light fell blankly across the surface of his eyes. "So this is your girl, Gordon."

Her father was standing at the end of the table. When he spoke, she realized that he did not like Casselman.

"Maggie's a decent girl," he said shortly. "You're making a long march."

"We're going to Stanwix. St. Ledger's there now, if he hain't put Gansevoort out already." Casselman's voice was flat. "The women have started north."

"North?" echoed Gordon.

"Yes. We sent them with some of the old men. They've got an Indian guide. My pop's with them. He used to know the trails in fifty-seven. They've struck across the Canadas; they'll hit Black River. The Indian called it Ka-hu-ah'-go. Go down it to the lake and strike along for Oswego."

"They went through Mount's?"

"Sure. We saw them past Reeber's Settlement and left them just below here. They hit the woods. We're bending south now. For Stanwix."

Her father said, "There'll be a fight at Stanwix."

Casselman gently patted the table.

"I hope there is." His voice was vibrant and low. "For two years we've been putting up with these here German farmers and their blasted committees."

"They aren't all Germans," Gordon said.

"They might as well be," said Casselman. "But I've got less use for Campbells and Clydes, turning against their own people. Who made this country anyway? Men like Johnson, and the British Army. Who's trying to grab the gravy now? The Patriot's Party, they're calling themselves. All they're after is the land. Profiteers of the French wars and now they've lost all their money and they want to sink the Johnsons and get an unlawful share of their estates. Congress! Committees!" He made a bitter oath.

A bit of laughter floated out of somewhere like a moth and then the silence fell. Casselman stared round with predatory eyes. His nose was hooked like a bird's.

He asked, "What's funny?"

"Ask Gordon," a young man said harshly. Maggie looked at him. He was someone she had seen before, named Empie. His eyes protruded slightly. They seemed to absorb the light. He looked like his brothers otherwise — tall, active, quick, with a good nose and strong, thin mouth. He shaped his mouth now, "I seen him at the falls two days ago, visiting with Herkimer, the son . . ."

"Whatever you think, you'd better hold your tongue," Gordon said. A thin flush had risen in his cheeks, but he looked frail and small in the candlelight.

"Who the devil do you think you are?" demanded Casselman, turning on the man.

Will Empie laughed easily, glancing Maggie's way.

"You aren't no brigadier, Suffrenes."

"I don't have to be to handle you," said Casselman. He swung back to Gordon. "Which party are you going with?"

"I'm staying here," said Gordon.

"Sure. I don't care where you stay. I've got to know what friendly houses we have in this district. Butler's orders. And mind you, Gordon, this is my last chance to find out."

"Are you threatening me?"

"Listen," said Casselman. "In five days we'll sweep this country from Stanwix to Albany."

Gordon leaned a little towards him.

"That's a threat."

"All right. Have it your own way. I've given you warning."

"What difference does it make which way I stand?"

Casselman looked puzzled.

"I don't know," he said. "I never had no trouble with you folks up here."

"Nobody knows anything," said one of his men. Several of the others thought that that was funny. Maggie found Casselman's expressionless eyes watching her.

"Gordon. This is no place to leave a girl when the Indians get loose."

"I know that myself," her father said. "I heard Sillinger has offered eight dollars for every piece of hair."

"What if he has? Congress has tried the same business." Casselman swung back to him. "Listen, man. You're just as British as I am. You wouldn't take orders from some German fool, just because he pulled a vote in some committee, would you? They haven't even got a flag!"

"I never did see what right they had to the Mohawk Flats," somebody said.

"They won't have it long," said Casselman. "How about Mount?"

"You'd better ask him," Gordon answered.

"No sense in you getting tarty now."

The lack of progress in the conversation disquieted Maggie. The men round the door had crowded closer, so that now she could see their faces and the sweat-soaked shoulders of their linen hunting shirts. She could tell by the way his underlip had drawn in that her father's temper was worn thin. He was looking down his nose at Casselman and Casselman had lifted his face, thrust far out from his neck, like a hawk's.

Then a cool voice broke in. "Say, Mister Gordon. Can we get a drink of water?"

Immediately the tension broke.

"I've always heard you had a real good spring, Gordon."

Casselman had lowered his eyes.

"It's fine soft water," Gordon said quietly. "It never runs dry."

"Not even this year? I'd rather have a spring like that than ten pounds English money in my pocket."

Maggie could have laughed. She spoke up from the corner where she stood. Her voice was fresh and light, and the faces all turned to her.

"Just a minute. I'll draw you two fresh buckets."

She stepped back through the door to the shed, and groped for the buckets in the darkness. It was incredibly cool and sweet there after the sweat-reek in the kitchen and she stopped to draw deep breaths of it. Behind her the voices started swimming back and forth across the candlelight. Outside, she was aware of the whippoorwill tentatively feeling out his song.

As she went out of the shed with the buckets, she bumped into a man. She could not see him. But she felt the cold touch of his rifle barrel.

"Don't be scared," he said. "I didn't mean to hit you with the gun. I just wondered if I could give you a hand, maybe." She thought it was the same voice that had asked for water.

She tried to make him out, but she could see no more than his vague shape against the night.

"I don't know who you are," she said.

"Do you have to know a man's name to let him carry a

bucket for you?" he asked, laughing a little. The laughter relieved her; it sounded natural; but at the same time it made her shy. She stood before him with a bucket hanging from each hand and said in a small proper voice, "My name is Margaret Gordon."

"My name is David Murray, Mistress Gordon."

She was aware that he had taken off his hat. In all her life no man had bared his head to her or called her *Mistress*. She wished she could see his face; then she was glad that the darkness hid her own. She had a sense of her own ineptitude. He didn't talk like the other men. Maybe, she thought, he was one of the high gentry from Caughnawaga way, cousin of Butlers or Johnsons.

"We're introduced," he said gravely. "Can I help you with the buckets, now?"

"Oh yes. If you want to."

"What do you think I asked for water for?" he asked.

She hadn't anything to answer that with. Besides, his hands were feeling for the buckets. His fingers touched her bare arm and slid down it to the wrist, and caught the bucket-bail. She felt herself flush up at the touch and was doubly glad of the darkness now. "He can't see me," she said to herself. "Out here I'm good as any fine girl friend he has."

"Here's the other one, Mr. Murray."

The buckets struck together.

"You better go ahead," he said.

"You'll have to follow me close. The path ain't straight."

"But I can't see you any."

"You'd better let me take them, then, Mister Murray."

"I won't. And look here. Nobody calls me Mister Murray."

"Esquire Murray?" she asked, with mingled curiosity and a sense of her own simplicity.

He laughed.

"Not hardly. Just David. Why don't you call me that?"

"But I couldn't and you call me Mistress Gordon."

"That's not hard. I'll call you Maggie. It's a prettier name than David, anyway."

She said seriously, "David's a fine name, I think."

"Lots of men have good names, Maggie. But there ain't every girl that's got a pretty face and name together."

He stumbled suddenly, crashing the buckets together. And Maggie recovered her breath, and asked, "Did you hurt yourself?"

"I'm blind as a bat," he said. "Who made this path?"

"Me," she said. "But I know it all right."

"Well, I can't see it at all. I can't see you except your short gown, and that hardly at all either. How far is this spring?"

"We're halfway there. But it's kind of stony from now on."

"Then I guess you'd better lead me."

"Why don't you let me have the buckets?"

"I'll break my neck first."

"Then I guess you'd better take my hand," she said.

She heard him set one bucket in the other, and again they fumbled in the dark.

His hand took hers in a firm grasp; as his fingers closed on hers she thought with surprise that she had never taken Dick's hand, though Dick wanted to marry her. She wondered what he would say if he could see her walking hand in hand with a soldier. The path was hardly wide enough for two to walk abreast; the man's shoulder touched hers and the stock of the rifle bumped against her back. She had to lead him as she would a blind man, saying, "Mind this stone." "Here you step over the water." And finally, "Here's the spring."

The half-barrel set in the ground confined the reflection of a star.

Murray let the buckets drop, set down his rifle, and kneeled at the edge. "Your father's right, Maggie," he said, after a moment. "It's cold, sweet water."

"It's a good spring and generally allowed so," she said with a touch of primness.

"I'm sorry!" he exclaimed. "I was so thirsty I forgot. Do you want a drink?"

Though Maggie had not been thirsty, she found it pleasant to have him fill a bucket and hold it up for her. A clumsy business, and she was splashed and her cheek wet. She laughed at his contrition, insisting that she was not wet at all, or only a drop.

"But you'd better let me carry the buckets back or you'll be sure to spill out half."

"Maybe you better," he admitted; but he still held onto the buckets. "It's quiet here, away from that houseful."

"But they're thirsty," she said. "They're waiting for us."

"They're no special friends of mine," he said. "Waiting a while won't hurt them."

Her breath came a little faster. From where they stood, up the slope from the valley, they could look down towards the lighted window on their side of the house. Twelve small panes of glass, and the back of a man filling them, the shadow of his head drawn out across the wheat. At the corner of the house another man leaned with his gun cradled in his arm. He wore a cap with a coontail hanging over his right ear. His head was lifted towards the east.

"Looking for the moon, I guess," said Murray. "Suffrenes says we have to start when it comes up."

Maggie did not speak. All at once, it seemed to her that she was detached from the house; as if she looked down on an invaded place, where the men had come in; where she herself was still standing behind her father, staring into their staring eyes. She made a motion to start back, but Murray said, "I hate to go."

"You mean you wish you were in our party?"

"Oh no. Just to go. We'll lose our reaping this year. I never liked reaping before. It's funny. Now I'm missing it."

She said gravely, "That's why Dad wants to stay here. To reap his wheat." Her forehead puckered, though he could not see it. "Dad says it isn't just cutting down with a sickle. It's finishing the work you started when you began to cut the land off with your brush-sith."

"I guess it is. But I had to come along, just the same."

"Why?"

"Dad went with Colonel Butler two years ago last spring. We had a message from him that John or I should come. We drew straws for it. The other was to stay and play the other party so we could hold our land. But Suffrenes said they were putting people into prison down the river. They've even got Mrs. Butler now; I think they've moved her down to Albany. Suffrenes said Mother and the youngsters would have to come along. It's a hard trip. John went with them."

"It is a hard thing," Maggie said softly. "What did you do with your house?"

"We put boards on the windows. I guess it won't do much good. We heard the rebels would probably cut our wheat. What we haven't cut already. It ripens earlier down there. We buried the silver spoons Ma had when she was wedded. We buried what we could and turned out the dry cows. Maybe they'll be all right. John took the horses along." He was silent for a moment. Then he said, "But Suffrenes says we'll be back down the valley in a week. All the Canada business meant nothing. Up there, once the real troops came in, the rebels ran like rats. You'll see how this Dutch militia pulls its feet. . . . I'm sorry. I forget you're the other party. It's too bad."

She had forgotten all about that: she felt so sorry for him.

"You aren't scared?" she asked.

"No. I guess not." He handed her the water. Her back straightened against the pull of the laden buckets, and she turned for the house.

Even in the darkness, he noticed how free her walk was.

"It's funny," he said, "I never heard about you before."

She flushed. She could hear him walking close behind in the darkness. As if he had forgotten everything, he began to hum a little tune.

"What's that?" she asked. "It's pretty."

"It's just a song."

"I never heard it. Won't you sing it for me?"

His voice was light and true and he sang the song softly as they went slowly towards the house.

> 'Twixt the water and the willow tree,
>   There stood I,
> When I spied my gallant gentleman
>   Riding by,
> And he looked to me so gaily on his
>   Horse so high,
> With his golden hair a-curling and his
>   Feather in the sky.

"Is that all?"

"No. It kind of suits, though. I hadn't thought."

> Oh, would a pretty lady give a
> > Guerdon gay
> To the comfort of a soldier on his
> > Lonely way?
> Yea, though he died tomorrow in the
> > Foremost fray,
> I would never love another, not till
> > Judgement day.

"It is pretty," said Maggie. "Did she never love another?"

"I don't know."

"She sounded as if she meant it," Maggie said softly.

"You think she did? But you see, according to how the song goes, he wasn't so nice."

"Why not?"

"I don't know. He just wasn't. You have to take a song's say-so, don't you?"

"I wonder . . ."

"What do you wonder?"

Maggie was bold.

"What color your hair is."

His voice was half-comic, half-serious, coming over her shoulder.

"Plain mouse-brown, if you want to know. It doesn't curl, either. It's cut short so I won't get ticks when I'm in the woods."

"Oh."

"But I'm not like him. I stopped to draw water with you."

"Oh, is there more?"

"One verse."

"Please sing it."

She noticed that the whippoorwill had hushed again.

The night is falling, bitterly the
   Lone birds cry,
'Twixt the water and the willow he has
   Passed me by,
With his gay and gallant feather, on his
   Horse so high.
He would not say a word to me — so
   What could I?

Maggie had stopped to let him finish the song. She sighed. "I feel sorry for her," she whispered, overwhelmed by a pity for women. She felt Murray close behind her.

"Do you, Maggie?"

His hand was on her shoulder. She turned her head. He put his arms round her shoulders and kissed her.

She stood stock still, and he said nothing for a moment after he had let her go. Then, with the inconsequentiality of all whippoorwills, the bird in the cornfield took up its song in a full tide of voice.

Maggie opened her eyes. "What could I?" she was thinking. She could see his shape, dimly, standing against her. He looked tall. It was a strange thing. She still held the buckets.

"You were wonderful," he said. There was something in his voice.

"Oh."

"You didn't spill a drop."

"Oh," she said again.

Then all at once she understood that he was laughing. Without a word she turned to the shed door.

"Don't go," he whispered. "Please."

She did not stop until she was safely inside the shed. But

there she had to wait a moment, to try to down her color. She felt ashamed because she had liked it; and she felt ashamed because she thought she must have acted queerly to him. No doubt he had kissed girls in plenty before her. But she did not know. Did he expect her to drop the buckets, or what in the world could he have expected her to do? And she didn't even know what he looked like.

Inside the kitchen the men were still talking round the walls. But her father was silent, and Casselman was watching his own finger as it tapped the table. He glanced up at her entrance and thanked her. "We won't trouble you long. We're just waiting till moonrise."

Maggie put dippers in the buckets and the men drank eagerly.

"Don't drink too much," Casselman cautioned them. "We've a long way to go and I don't want you sloshing like a bunch of churns."

Taking the second bucket through the front door for the men outside, she set it on the sill and leaned against the wall to watch them drink. She knew a few of them by sight, from passing Fairfield. Henry Davis, John McCaffery who was six-foot-six, and the three Ames brothers. They thanked her, except for Lame Hans. He had been born with a twisted foot and was a surly sort of man. The others were all strangers.

Now that her heart beat easier, she tried to see which one could have been Murray. At least it couldn't be the man with the beard whose leggings smelled of stable manure. He had said his hair was mouse-brown.

They did not talk much now; they kept watching the woods to the east of the clearing. When Casselman came to the door they made way for him.

68

He leaned for a moment on his gun, a looming figure, with broad, stooped shoulders and his small head outthrust. "Well, boys, she's about due." His voice wasn't threatening anymore. He looked as if he had put politics out of his mind and was thinking plain facts about their march.

A faint light began in the east, netted in the leaves of a high birch.

"She'll be up in ten minutes," a man said.

"There's not much light in her."

"Enough," said Casselman.

They were all outside the house, watching the sky. Maggie thought that most of them seemed young. A sense almost of pity invaded her, to think of them, marching all night in the shadow of the woods. They looked like a little band now, not the throng that had first crowded into the kitchen.

"Gordon," said Casselman, "I'd advise you to clear out. We've took your powder, but it's no more than the militia have done to us all over the valley." He paused. "If you'll come over to our side, I'll give half of it back."

He waited a moment for Gordon to answer. Maggie glanced quickly at her father. She understood the set look on his face now.

"Well," said Casselman, "you're a fool, but you're honest. And we ain't putting you in jail." His head turned slowly as his eyes went over the clearing. "You've got a nice place here. It would be too bad to see it burnt."

"You'll burn it?"

"We'll burn out every rat in Tryon County, before we're done."

"Beginning with Reeber's," one of the men added.

Gordon was silent. He stood in the doorway at Casselman's shoulder. Just outside the door was a young man Maggie had

not noticed before. He was looking at her, while all the others waited for the moon; he had his hat in his hand. Mouse-brown, he had said his hair was. It was newly cut, and not well cut — as if a mother or sister had taken the shears to him in a hurry.

"It's not mouse-brown," she thought. "It's a good color."

His eyes avoided hers, now that she had discovered him. He had not seemed bashful at the spring. Maybe he was shy in the company of the other men. Maybe it was not the same man at all.

Two days, three days from now, whenever it was, there would be fighting in the woods round Fort Stanwix. He might be shot, they might all be shot, and she never see him again. And she would have liked to know.

"She's up," said Casselman. "Come on."

A few said good-bye, but most went silently. The young man was the last to go. As he passed her she heard him humming,

> Oh, would a pretty lady give a
>> Guerdon gay
> To the comfort of a soldier . . .

The whippoorwill sang again, in the cornfield, and the men dropped into file behind Casselman. The moon found threads of silver on their rifle barrels. Only a few talked at all.

Gordon stood still in the door, and Maggie kept her place against the wall. For several minutes, father and daughter stared westward, until the sound of footsteps had faded away, the last shape had been swallowed in the night, the last voice hushed.

Maggie gave a little sigh.

"Did they take all our powder, Dad?"

He nodded.

"Casselman asked for it. There wasn't sense in trying to keep them from getting it. They're all of them feeling mean about their families going off to Canada."

His face was drawn.

He did not start, as Maggie did, when a step came down along the road.

"Dick!" she exclaimed.

Dick was bareheaded. He carried his squirrel gun.

"You all right, Maggie?"

"Why yes, Dick. Why?"

"There's a whole parcel of people camped down below us on our creek. We seen their fires and I went down. They were mostly women. Some little children and about six men, all of them old but one. I listened to them talking. One of the little babies was sick, I think. And I found out, listening, that they was the women of the Fairfield people and that the men had mostly come this way. When I got down here, I seen them all around your house."

"They didn't do anything but take our powder, Dick."

"Gee, Mr. Gordon! All of it?"

Gordon nodded. "They were nice enough about it. They said they'd give me back half if I joined their party."

Dick glanced up under his thatch of hair.

"You didn't say so?"

"I can't change opinions for a pound of gunpowder, Dick."

Gordon looked at him for a moment before turning into the house. The quiet of the night came in for a moment to the very door.

"Well, they've gone," Maggie said. She couldn't help comparing him, in her mind's eye, to David Murray. Poor Dick, he looked like some wild woods animal, standing that way, with his ragged hair, and his brown eyes quick in the candlelight.

"Does your Dad know you're over here?"

"I guess not, Maggie. He'd be mad, most likely." He flushed painfully. "But I had to come over and see you were all right."

His face looked up to her so earnestly that she said, with a little rush of warmth:

"That was nice of you, Dick."

She would have liked to see him in a decent set of clothes, with his hair cut neatly. It made her realize that she didn't know at all what Dick was, actually. And she felt curious. Even when he said, "Aw shucks," and shifted his bare feet.

But he had his own curiosity.

"Did any of them bother you, Maggie?"

"Me? What do you mean, Dick?"

"Pa says that some of those highlanders will raise hob, once they're loose." He looked away. "I didn't know."

"Oh, no," she said. "They were all right."

Poor Dick.

He asked, "What'll your Pa do now? Will he stay?"

"I guess he will, until the wheat's in."

"I'll be watching you," he said.

She smiled at him. Poor Dick, again. What could he do with his squirrel rifle? He was like a small boy, even the way he thought of things. But he looked so wistful to her, so helpless somehow in his promise to look after her, that she stepped down to him.

"I'm awful grateful to you, Dick," she said softly, and put her arms round his neck and kissed him.

He was too surprised to move. To see him so almost made her laugh. This afternoon he'd talked of being a man, and now even his ears were red. Then with annoyed humiliation it occurred to her that she must have seemed exactly like that to the Fairfield man.

They stared at each other like two young dogs, stiff to the tips of their toes.

"Maggie," he said. But he didn't know what else to say.

She recovered herself first.

"You'd better get back home, hadn't you? Before your Dad finds out you've been away."

"I guess so, maybe."

He cradled the squirrel gun in his arm and turned away. But beyond the feeble zone of light he halted. She heard a thickness in his voice out in the darkness.

"Good night," he said.

"Good night," she answered.

She waited till he must have reached the ford.

Then she heard his voice a little stronger.

"I'll be around again," he called.

She did not answer, but an instant after went in and closed the door. She still felt sorry for Dick.

❧ 3 ❧

ADAM DINGMAN

THREE DAYS after the departure of the Fairfield men, Dick Mount turned up at Gordon's house. He wandered into the kitchen, and, finding nobody at home, walked out again.

The same still heat that they had had for so many weeks persisted. Looking across the clearing, he could at first see no sign of Gordon or his daughter. But he saw where they had been reaping.

The stubble made a narrow border to the standing grain. Here and there the sheaves stood up neatly shocked on the ends of their morning shadows. Maggie was a first-rate binder, she enjoyed twisting the straw, and her shocks stood up securely. But as he walked through the stubble, Dick noticed that the sickle had made uneven slices in the grain, as if the hand wielding it continuously faltered. It also seemed to him that, supposing Gordon mowed every day, he had very little to show for his work. By now three acres should be down and bound.

He went quietly down the field to the far corner, and there, glancing through the heads of grain, he found Maggie as well as her father reaping. Both of them were unaware of his approach.

They worked bent over from the hips, their backs below

74

the kernels, their left arms crooked like cradles to receive the falling wheat. The blades of their sickles made dry shearing sounds through the straw.

He had never seen Maggie reaping before. He knew that her father did not like her to do heavy field work. But when he glanced at Gordon, he understood why she was working.

Already his face was dripping wet; but it had a gray tinge under its burn. The swing of his right arm was slow, as if he had grown tired by his first hour's labor; and he took each forward step deliberately. He seemed to be trying each foot before he set it down.

"There's something the matter with him," Dick thought. "He don't look well."

He turned his eyes towards Maggie again. She had pinned up her old gray petticoat to the level of her knees. Her brown legs were filmed with the dry dust that puffed up at every footstep. She wore an old short gown in which the pattern had faded to a sort of silver gray. It clung tight across her back and shoulders, showing their suppleness, and hung down loosely in front, where it was opened to let what air there was cool her throat.

Something in the posture, in the way her left arm caught and cradled the falling grain, as if she had an impulse to hold it to her breast, stirred the boy. His thin brown face grew sad. He set the stock of his squirrel gun in the dust ahead of his feet and leaned on the barrel, watching her. He had never watched her when she was completely unaware of his presence.

Doing so now, he could see little things about her. Not only the lithe way her body was put together, nor the manner in which she bent to the work, almost graciously, but little things that made for tenderness. His practiced eye quickly noticed that she could have worked away from her father twice as fast as the old man moved. But she did not. She held her head, round which she had coiled her braids to keep them out of her way, bent a little sidewise, so that she could see what he was doing without openly appearing to watch; and whenever he fell behind she slowed her own pace to suit his.

Gordon was working like a man in a stupor, who did not feel or see a thing beyond the motion of his hands. But when a blue jay suddenly became raucous in the woods down the creek, his hand halted at the beginning of a stroke, shook slightly, with a glitter of brilliance on the clean edge of the sickle. Then he straightened his back painfully and stared in the direction of the bird.

Dick felt at once that Gordon was uneasy. He could see that in the stiffening of the man's neck. But he saw also the slow stubborn setting of the underlip. It seemed to stick against his teeth. Evidently he found it difficult to smile and say to Maggie, "Jays are noisy birds, always hollering about nothing."

She had lifted her head at the bird's voice, with the wild quick gravity of a young doe, but she watched her father instead of the woods; and Dick saw her forehead pucker and the black brows lift slightly.

"Yes," she said, "they make a lot of noise."

Her father was not breathing as a tired man should. His breath came rapid and short. But he said, "We're getting along. If we can mow a little more than an acre every day, we'll be ready to move ten days from now. I'd like to thresh it, though. It would bring us better than fifty dollars, Maggie."

"We've got time enough." She spoke calmly. "Wouldn't you like some water from the spring?"

"Yes I would." He was mopping his forehead with his arm.

"It's not the work makes me feel bad. It's the heat. I never knew it to stay hot so long."

But he seemed to be unwilling to stop even for the few moments it would take her to walk to the spring and back. "I'll just finish out my swath," he said.

"No, Dad, you sit down in the shade."

"I'll sit down when you bring the water, Maggie."

"But look at all we've got done already today," she said encouragingly, and they looked back together and saw Dick there.

"Morning, Mr. Gordon," he said. "Hello, Maggie."

Her color had deepened as though she wondered how long he had been standing behind them.

Gordon said, "Good morning, Dick. How are things over your way?"

"All right. Except for Ma. She's acting uneasy lately, all the time. Pa sent me over to see if you'd heard of anything."

"There hasn't been a soul," said Gordon.

"That's what Pa thought. He thought it might make Ma easier though."

He still leaned on his gun, meeting Maggie's glance with diffidence.

"We were just quitting a minute, Dick," she said. "I want to get some water."

"I'll go along," he said.

"Yes. That's right," said Gordon. "You go along." He bent down painfully, sickle in hand.

Maggie and Dick walked a little way in silence, watching each other sidelong.

"Did you get licked t'other night?" she asked curiously.

"No," he said. "Pa was out himself, looking around. He wanted to know what was going on over here."

"What did he say?"

"He said he guessed Casselman was scared to start anything yet."

"Does he know you're over here now?" she asked. "Really?"

"Well," he said, "I guess he does. He's reaping today. We got the stones set into the mill yesterday. I told him I was coming over here and he said I wasn't to come till I got done with my half acre."

"Did you get done?"

"Me? No, I didn't."

"He'll be awful mad at you."

"Maybe he will. He keeps telling me all the time how he's got two years legal title to me yet." He scuffed his bare feet as he walked. "I figured I had to find out how you was coming on. After that night."

The color deepened in her cheeks, covered her throat. She blushed even behind her ears. He saw that from the corner ' of his eye. And when she found her voice it was uncertain.

"Dick. It don't always mean anything when a girl kisses a boy, does it?"

"What do you mean?"

"I mean, anything particular. I — I didn't mean it that way anyway."

He cleared his throat and scuffed some more sand with his feet.

"Shucks," he said. "I didn't take it that way. Not after what you said in the crick."

She turned her face to him with a pathetic kind of earnestness.

"Dick, did you notice Dad?"

"Yes."

"Did he seem queer to you?"

"He looked kind of sick to me."

"I think he is."

"What's he got? It's early for ague."

"It doesn't act like ague," she said. "I think he's awfully worried, but that wouldn't make him sick. I don't know what it is."

"He hadn't ought to work out there if he's sick."

"I know it, Dick. But I can't stop it. I tried to yesterday. He told me to hush my mouth, if I didn't want it slapped."

"He did?" Dick demanded indignantly.

"He doesn't know what he's saying. He's never hit me. He just didn't want me to help reap, not the first two days. But he said I could this morning. He seems to be possessed about that wheat."

"You hadn't ought to be working there."

"I don't mind it."

"You will by night, Maggie. It's the hardest work there is."

"I wouldn't dare leave him there alone."

"Well," he said, "I guess you'll have to help him then. If my Pa didn't keep me tied up so tight at home, I'd help you some. Maybe I could sneak away a while tomorrow."

"Thanks, Dick. But I guess we can get on all right. I wish we had some powder, though. We're out of pork. That's what troubles Dad the most."

"Why didn't you say so? I'll just step out and pick you up one with my gun. Where do they mostly run now?"

"There ought to be some up the beech ridge," she said. "If it wouldn't take too long and make your Pa too mad. I wouldn't want you to take a licking for helping us."

"If I'm going to, I might as well get licked for half an hour extra."

In the daytime it could be seen that the sunk half-barrel

into which the spring trickled was lined with soft green water moss. The water had a blue-green, deep-sea look, until one had it in a glass, and then, like a miracle, it was crystal.

Dick watched Maggie dip the bucket and lift it out. He didn't offer to help or to carry it back to the field. That was a woman's natural job. She didn't expect it.

She stayed with him a moment, her body slanting against the weight of the bucket, her free hand on her hip. With her blouse open and her hair about her head, her neck rose slender and free. The bones showed in her thin square shoulders. She made Dick think of a deer again. He remembered some girls he had once seen in Little Falls, going to a wedding the miller said, all in their best chintz clothes, complete with shawls and pockets. But it didn't seem to him that they compared to Maggie. And all these years he'd never noticed.

Her eyes seemed to come out of nowhere and see him again and she smiled at him. A person couldn't help loving her for her smile. It had a hesitant, half-shy beginning, but a wide and whole-souled finish.

"You do look serious enough to go to war yourself, Dick; not just to shoot a hog."

"I wasn't thinking of that," he said. "Do you want a big one?"

"No, get us a this year's one, if you can, well-grown. There's no sense in eating roasting pig now. But not too big." Her forehead puckered again. "I'll have to let the knuckles go to waste. Maybe I won't have time to try the lard out, either. And it's too early to salt the sides."

He nodded.

"It won't keep long."

"No. But I've got my flannel bags out in the shed to hang it in."

She turned away and he started straight into the woods to hunt the pigs.

Like all other settlers, Gordon let his pigs run wild. Even in winter they were left out on the back-bush farms, where there were neither threshing nor fold-yards to house them, nor food to give them if there had been yards. A settler brought a sow that had been bred and turned her into the woods. Herself and nature managed the rest.

Dick headed south, up the slope from the Black Creek Valley, towards the hardwood ridges. He half-hoped to spot a deer, but since the heat the deer had mostly gone back up the Canada Creek towards the mountains. At the crest of the first rise was a balsam swamp with sumach round the edges and moose maple and witch hobble. Beyond, the ridge rose up like a hog's back in shape and in the color of its brush-free carpet of dead leaves. He stopped at the foot of it a moment, staring upwards, but he saw no sign of any pig, beyond the last night's droppings.

Considering the drought and heat, it seemed more likely that they would be wallowing in the swamp, so he began to circle quietly along the edge, and suddenly, in a small clearing, he caught a fresh scent of them and, walking cautiously forward, found a litter with an old sow.

It must have been an early litter, for the young ones were half-grown, about the size that Maggie wanted. The old sow lay shoulder deep in her wallow, her small eyes unblinkingly looking his way. At his next move she grunted, jerked her shoulders out and left the muck with a long sucking sound in one swift rush. Her litter floundered up and squealed and then went bucketing in her wake. But the last one gave Dick a fair mark. He aimed behind the ear and fired.

The pig spun over on its side and rolled half a dozen feet
and then lay still. He went over to it, cut a stick and split the
hind legs, yanked the pig up onto a stub of a broken spruce
branch, bled, and dressed it.

When he was all through with the work, he looked round
for some ferns to wipe his hands.

"Well, youngster, what'll it weigh?"

Dick whirled on his heels. Afterwards he couldn't think
just what he had expected to see, but what he did see was a
smallish, thickset man in a dull green hunting shirt of home-
wove linen and deerskin Indian leggings. His bold blue eyes
looked humorously at the boy from under the narrow brim of
his hat; his heavy square red face was set sardonically, the thin
upper lip drawn down upon the lower.

"Adam!" said Dick.

"Hello, Dick."

"What you doing here?"

"Herkimer has me running a scout north of Dayton. Orders to go clear to Gordon's and see if there's anyone moving in from westward." He pursed his lips to spit a snuff-stained squirt. "I just come out on the ridge when I heard your gun go off, so I walked down this way. I thought I'd kill an Injun maybe. But I found you with your face inside the inwards of a hog and your gun twenty foot off against a tree."

Dick looked ashamed.

"Boys will be boys," said Adam. "I expect you're doing it for Maggie Gordon, ain't you?" As Dick nodded, the man stepped across to the squirrel gun and glanced at it. "Hain't even loaded." He handed it to Dick. "Now, son," he said, "you listen to me. Maybe nothing's happening in North America. Or then again maybe there's one or two people having words. You can't tell. But the first thing you want to learn after making a shot is to set still where you let the gun off, load it, and then look around." He sighed. "I could have

walked right down here and lifted your hair if I was taking pay from Sillinger. I could have got eight dollars for it without even laying out the powder for one shot."

Dick blushed furiously. "I'll remember after this," he mumbled.

"Good idee. But what's the matter with Gordon, he ain't killing his own hogs?"

Briefly Dick explained the visit of the Fairfield men, the taking of powder, Gordon's queer querulous condition. As Adam listened, leaning on his rifle, his bright eyes wandered the woods. His mouth was set in kind of a consciously intelligent expression. "Well," he said at the end, "I'll just mosey down his way and have a look. I ain't a complete fool, but I'm like you one way. I feel kind of fond of that girl Maggie. You load your gun and then we'll get along."

When Dick's gun was loaded, Adam reached up with one hand, grasped the stick between the hog's hind legs, and swung the carcass over his shoulder.

"Fifty pounds. Well growed. Must be good pickings round here for a hog. Better than for humans." He started off at a sturdy, easy stride of his short legs, going with a silence that Dick, for all his youthful lankness, envied.

Over his shoulder Adam remarked, "It's always seemed kind of interesting, the way the Lord provides for pigs, human or hog ones."

Dick said nothing. In spite of Adam's load, the little man went quickly. He seemed familiar with every tree in the woods.

Adam Dingman trapped the West Canada Valley. He said he had a cabin to summer in somewhere near the top of West Canada Creek, maybe thirty miles north of German Flats. He had trapped that way for years, he had his own trail beaten in; but after the Mounts and Gordons came, he used to make a detour to the Gordon clearing. He like to stop and ask a meal.

Gordon had great faith in Adam's judgment, and Maggie liked him, though she pitied him because he seemed so ignorant. Perhaps Adam felt that, for he used to say, "I'm just a timber beast. And I'm scared of a pretty girl. But up here I can get away to cover when the skitters catch me." He would roll his eyes at Maggie and add solemnly, "It's hell and all to be a skeery man."

Now he led Dick swiftly back to the spring, down Maggie's winding little track, and to the house. The Gordons were still in the wheat field. Down the clearing they could be seen beside the golden palisade of grain, small, bent, sun-beaten figures, painfully crawling in the heat.

Adam looked a moment.

"I guess I'll just stay here and scald this hog and cut him up."

Dick looked longingly in the direction of the Gordons.

"I ought to get back home," he said.

"I guess your pa is just the same durn fool as ever." Adam made it sound like a question.

"He thinks there's nothing to all this," Dick answered. "He laughs at Mr. Gordon."

"Well, I ain't seen any signs of trouble, yet," said Adam.

He grinned as he watched the boy shamble off to the creek and wade across the ford.

"Hain't got the nerve to say good-bye to Maggie with me round," he said to himself. . . .

He dragged the carcass of the pig quickly to the shed, laid a fire in the open hearth outdoors, selected wood, filled the big black iron kettle, and had the water boiling in thirty minutes.

He dipped the hog with a quick heave of his wrists, counted fifteen out loud, pulled back the pig, and started scraping off the hair. He worked handily. He had to dip the hog once more.

When the carcass was completely naked of hair, and white as human skin, he drew his skinning knife from its sheath, tested the edge, and cut the quarters out. He chopped the bones with single quick strokes of an axe. Then he went into the shed and found the flannel bags to put the fresh meat into. Outside again, he selected a tree where there seemed to be a faint drawing of air, hung up the bags, and called the job done.

By the time the Gordons slowly came up from the field, he had everything cleared up and was sitting on the doorsill whetting his knife slowly on Gordon's stone.

"Adam!" exclaimed Maggie. "What are you doing this way in August?"

"Walking round," said Adam. "Herkimer thought I ought to take a walk. I guess he thought I was skeering the militia. I told the boys the Russians was with Sillinger."

"Russians?"

Adam nodded solemnly. Gordon, he noticed, was not listening. He had slumped down with his back to the wall of the house, and Adam thought he looked sickly.

" 'Course," said Adam, "I just made up what I said about the Russians. I don't know there's any of them with Sillinger. I just wanted to occupy the boys." He said to Gordon, "Getting in your wheat?"

Gordon nodded.

"We're trying to get it all cut down and stacked before we have to move."

Maggie nodded wearily. "Dad's set on it. I tell him what's the difference — if we have to move."

Watching Gordon, Adam nodded. "Got to get it in though."

"Yes," said Gordon, his voice lifting with a little eagerness. "That's it. Got to get it in."

Adam met Maggie's eye. He winked his own in a knowing way.

"Dick Mount killed you a hog and dressed it. He had to go home."

"That was nice of him," said Maggie.

"I thought so, too," said Adam. "I left the liver of it in a pail. I thought maybe there'd be an end for me."

She smiled again. Her back ached. She was thinking with a kind of agony what a hot job scalding a hog would be after a morning in the field.

She said, "Of course, Adam," and went inside.

As soon as she had gone, Gordon turned to Adam.

"What's the news from the valley?"

"Nothing much. The militia's mustered at Dayton. It was almost all in when I left last evening. They expect to start for Stanwix tomorrow. I'm just running a scout."

"Seen anything?"

"Not a hair. I came up here because I was worried about you folks. But I guess you're all right."

"What do you think's going to happen?"

As he met Gordon's querying stare, Adam Dingman's eyes lost all their sharpness. They rolled a little, modestly.

"I reckon there's going to be some doings, Gordon."

"Do you think you'll drive out Sillinger?"

"If Herkimer listened to me, maybe we will," said Adam. He lowered his voice. "Anyway, you don't have to worry for a spell. The first place they'll head for, if they lick us, is right down the flats. If we lick them, you'll have plenty of time to finish up your work. I'm going to leave you my powder, all but a charge or two."

"That's too much, but I'll take it, just the same," said Gordon. "You're a good friend, Adam."

"Shucks," said Adam. "I'll come back for it after the fight. Let you know what happened. I'm a ranger, so I'll range a little when I want to. You and Maggie been nice to me," he added rather shyly.

"That's nothing. It's fun for us to have you visit. But aren't militia laws pretty strict about what you do with your powder?"

Adam rolled his eyes again. He heard Maggie coming quickly through the kitchen. "I'll just tell them a hedgehog ate it on me. I'll say the hedgehogs up here eat gunpowder to shoot their quills with."

"Adam!" cried Maggie, coming through the door. "You scalded and cut up that hog for me!"

"Me? Oh no. Me and Dick done that. And he dressed out the hog, too. I just wanted to practice how a hog would look with a Russian after it. I never thought of getting the rest done."

"Well you did. You and Dick both." Her face had brightened. As she looked at her father, it brightened further.

"Maggie," he said to her. "Adam's leaving us his powder."

"Oh." Somehow the woods had drawn away. She felt happier than she had at any moment in the past two days.

"And he's going to let us know how things are happening in the valley."

"Sure," said Adam. "You two ain't got anything to worry over. I'll let you know when it's time to move."

They had an almost merry meal. Before it, Adam had asked for some fresh soap to wash with. Woman, he remarked in thanking Maggie, was God's gift to man, but soap was woman's gift to man. An ignorant timber beast like himself found both kind of hard to come by.

But when he emptied the slop water for her, he said quickly, "What's the matter with Gordon?"

"I don't know, Adam. He's awfully worried. He's crazy to get in his wheat. But the work seems to make him sick."

"It wouldn't be a *de*cline," Adam ruminated softly. "It wouldn't be ague either. He's a healthy-living man, too."

"He seems much better since you got here," Maggie said.

"Well," said Adam, "you're a gritty girl. Don't get more worried than you have to. I'll be back some day pretty quick."

He left his powder and went away early in the afternoon, striking westerly through the woods to make a loop across the Canada Creek. His stocky figure seemed ridiculously squat and short in the shadow of the high woods.

◆❧ 4 ❧◆

THE WHEAT

ALL AFTERNOON the Gordons worked at the wheat. An hour before sunset, Maggie stopped reaping to bind and shock what they had mown. In one day they had more than equaled the first two days of Gordon's work.

He seemed even more encouraged than he had at dinner.

But he was utterly exhausted and just sat down in the kitchen by the window, where he could stare at the field.

"We'll get it in," he said. "We'll get it in. If I can get it threshed and drawn down to the Falls, we'll have enough to live on, even if we have to move."

Once she had come in out of the sun, Maggie could hardly stir her legs or arms. Her back ached so that it was difficult to stand erect. But gradually that wore off, and she went out to the barn and loosed the horses to let them go down to the creek. She watched them drink and then head off together for the beaver fly they grazed in during the nights.

Just at sunset her listening ears picked up the clank of Brownie's bell, and she went out to hurry the cow home. She milked, and the cow, relieved, went off after the horses.

They were alone, her father and herself. They were too tired to talk, more than to mention again Adam Dingman's visit and say it would be different, now that they were sure of knowing the news from the south.

It was only when she was cleaning up alone that it occurred to Maggie that Dingman might be killed. By then her father had gone into his room. She glanced into the dark room, making out his body, still as a dead man, lying along the blankets. She listened till she heard him breathing. It was a blessing that he could sleep.

She wished that she herself could sleep. But the thought of her loft bed, with the hot bark roof so close overhead, the two cowhide trunks for company, and the hams and flitches hanging from the rooftree like a row of felons, stifled her. Up there a person would feel trapped. Besides, her back semed to ache at the very thought of bed. She sank down in their one backed chair, where her father had sat, and stared unseeingly into the darkness beyond the window.

Now and then small thoughts and impulses towards thought stirred in her and vanished before she comprehended them — like bats, that one saw only after they had passed.

She thought of Adam Dingman making his long night march in the solitude of the woods. She thought of the Fairfield men; by now they would be in the British camp, and David Murray would be sitting by a fire. She wondered if it was as hot down there in the southwest as it was here in the clearing in Jerseyfield. She began remembering bits of her life before they came to Jerseyfield. They had spent a winter on Isaac Paris's farm while her father worked in the store and Mr. Paris went down to New York on business. Another time, when she was very small, they had stayed a while in the town of Schenectady. She had a longing now for the place, the stone houses along the river; the green wide pasture for the cattle; the square brown stone-and-timber fort where the gun thudded at sunset and soldiers beat on their drums, a comforting thing to hear when you looked across the river at the great north woods — the same woods where she, Maggie Gordon, was now alone.

She was ashamed to have thought that with her father in the next room. And then she was frightened. Suppose he was really sick; she did not know. There was no way for her to find out. The nearest doctor that she knew anything about would be in German Flats; Dr. William Petry was his name. But it was twenty miles by road to Little Falls, and then eight miles more westward, unless like Adam Dingman, you knew the woods and could cut cross-country. Even if one could send word to the doctor, he would be towards Stanwix with the militia. There was no earthly way for Maggie to find out what ailed her father.

She had a thought that she might ask Mrs. Mount about it.

But the idea of going to Mrs. Mount and hearing her worries, now that she herself was worried, was too much to bear. And Mrs. Mount had little learning in the matter of sickness. She purged her family twice a year with sulphur and senna, and let it go at that.

All the clearing was black. Maggie could not see beyond the nearer edge of wheat. She was conscious of the last calls of a thrush in the woods behind the spring. Then the silence came in.

She sat in a kind of coma, until the airlessness of the night became too much for her to stand. Her clothes stuck to her skin, her feet felt hot and dry. The small sound that the creek made brought the only coolness, and she got up slowly from her chair, thinking that, in spite of the risk of ague, she would go down and bathe her feet.

But when she reached the door and saw the pitch darkness before her, she couldn't summon enough nerve to step out into it by herself. It gave her a panicky feeling to think how often she had been used to run down to the tiny mill pond on just such nights. If there were only someone nearby to speak. Just to hear one human voice, one word, even. Yet she knew that if she heard one human word now out of the darkness she would be too terrified to move.

Perhaps she was understanding a little of Mrs. Mount's perpetual talk about the silence. While her father was well, all during their first years on this place, it had never occurred to Maggie to fear silence.

She had returned to her place by the window and was sitting rigidly there, when the moon rose at last. The final quarter — it made only a dim light through the clearing. It was too dim for her to see clearly, but light enough to show a thing that moved.

She saw it moving down beyond the wheat. At first she had thought it one of the shocks of grain; then she saw it pass into the shadow.

After a moment it emerged again and started on a slow patrol of the clearing.

Though Maggie was too frightened to call her father, she forced herself to get the musket down. She shook a little priming into the pan. Crouching by the door, she tried to discover what kind of animal it was.

At last it crossed between her and the bright water of the creek and she saw that it was a man. He turned opposite her and walked noiselessly for the cabin. Twice she lifted the gun, but each time her hands shook as if they were palsied. Finally she set it down to call her father. But then she saw the shape stop, as if whoever it was looked towards her. She sobbed suddenly as she thought at last who it must be.

"Dick."

"Maggie. You up?"

When he reached her, she was bent forward over her knees and crying into her hands.

"Maggie! What's the matter?"

He comforted her so by being there that she could not tell him. "I guess I'm tired," she said. "And Dad hardly talked and went right to bed."

"Yes," he said. "I guess you're tired. Girls don't know how big their notions are until they try them out."

"Men either!" she said, lifting her head. Then she laughed, with a sob in her throat. "Oh, Dick. I didn't know who you were, and Dad was like a dead person the way he slept. And I got the gun and aimed it at you but I couldn't pull the trigger. I tried twice."

"Let's see." He took the gun. "You didn't cock it," he said scornfully.

"I must have forgot." She shivered. "I was so scared. But thank God I did forget. I might have hit you."

He said, "I guess I would have been safe enough."

"How do you know?" she asked indignantly. "Adam says I'm a good shot for a girl."

"Good?" He was sarcastic.

"Oh, Dick! Let's not start arguing. It's too nice just having you here. How are all your folks over there?"

"Fine. Pa's up and mighty as a dollar."

"Did you have trouble with him?"

"Some," he said.

"What kind?"

"The same as usual. He tried to tell me I'd have to stay to home. We argued some. Tonight I told him I was coming over here. And he said if I done it again, he'd give me what for, and

I said I'd shoot him if he did. And then Ma cried and I lit out."

"Dick," she said seriously, "you mustn't quarrel with him about us."

"If it wasn't you, it'd be something else. It didn't used to be that way. I guess it's just Pa likes to be boss bullock in our family and don't like me setting up my own ideas."

"You'd better go back home," she said.

"No. I'll stick around, awhile." He paused. "But you'd better get to bed now. It's late. Past moonrise, and that's midnight now. I'll get along when you have got to bed, if you want, but I'd just as lief stay here."

He took her place in the doorway. She whispered "Good night" from the kitchen dark, and quietly mounted the loft ladder. It was comforting to sleep, knowing he was downstairs.

She did not know when he had left, but it must have been in the morning, for a small fire was burning on the hearth when she came down. She felt touched, even while she knelt down and rearranged the sticks to suit herself.

That morning, too, Mount and his wife came over.

George was sweating a good deal. He said, "We been having trouble with Dick the last little while. He stays away from home. He was out all last night. I had some time with him this morning and he said he'd spent the night over here." He wiped his forehead, blew his nose. His fat face got brick red. "I don't know what there is between him and your Maggie. I done my best to lick it out of him, but all he said was nothing. But I thought you'd better know about it."

He hawked and spat, and having said his say, looked at once defensive and relieved.

Maggie turned pale. She could imagine the scene. Mount

like a great burly bear; Dick white-lipped and rigid, his thin face with that look of hate it sometimes had; the little boys looking curiously on, the Negro with his eyes like popcorn, white and brown and bursting; Mrs. Mount in tears. Her eyes were red-rimmed, even yet.

Gordon answered, sickle in hand, "I didn't know he'd been over except yesterday morning. He killed a pig for us. We hadn't any powder then."

"Oh, that's all right. You have to be neighborly," said George. "I was glad he did when he told me about it."

("That's a lie," thought Maggie, staring at his big furred hands.)

"But when he comes over here all night, he hain't much good for working next day," pursued George.

Maggie said scornfully, "Dad was so dead tired, Dick thought somebody ought to be handy. He sat in the door all night, Mr. Mount." She drew her breath. "If you want to know, I wanted him to stay."

"Now why didn't he tell me?" demanded George. "Then there wouldn't have been all this business. But he's a pup for being stubborn." He laughed a little. "I guess he set there imagining war and Indians and such cock-ideas." He shuffled his feet. "Well, Maggie, if it makes you feel easier, I don't care. I just thought your Pa had ought to know."

Gordon said wearily, "Maggie's a dependable girl, George. You ought to know that."

"Yes," his wife said suddenly. "Hain't I been telling you?"

George Mount mumbled with embarrassment, flushed and walked down into the wheat.

The mother looked after him for a minute, then swung on Maggie. "Dick's the only one that cares for me. Do you love him?"

"Oh, dear," thought Maggie. She said aloud, her voice tired, conscious of the sweat in her eyes, "I told him, no. I like Dick, Mrs. Mount. But he isn't old enough for me to marry. He's younger than I am."

"Not much. A week or two. He's a good boy."

"I think he is, too," Maggie said helplessly.

The woman lifted her faded eyes, pushed back her gray hair from her forehead with one hand and held it there.

"Then why do you go leading him over here?"

"I don't. I told him what I just told you."

The woman stared away across the clearing, speaking in a toneless voice, as if it didn't matter.

"If you just go leading him, and teasing him, I'll hate you all my life."

Maggie's eyes grew large.

"Oh, Mrs. Mount."

"I mean it. Men!" she said, scornfully, staring to where Gordon had resumed his reaping while George looked on. "Any man ain't worth the thinking of — but once. Except Dick."

"Yes," said Maggie.

"They all dreen you except him. They take you into the woods and they shut you up for years there. They build you a house. You work all day alone. You look out on a lot of stumps. There hain't a thing to hear except the birds squawking. There hain't a thing to smell except the woods and manure heap back of the shed. When they come home, they ding your ears with talk of cutting trees, how hard it is to hoe, the way the plow got broke. They go to town themselves to get the flour. God help me, Maggie," she said quietly, "if I could only hear a church bell once a week. Just once a week."

Maggie said softly, "Yes, I understand."

"Understand!" cried Mrs. Mount. "You understand? You can't understand nothing till you've had your baby way out here. A woman don't know nothing till that's happened. Nine of them, one after the other. Wait till you've seen them pine or get the intermittent. All you can do is have another one. You know how old I am? I'm only just over thirty years and look at me." She turned on her heel, and said over her shoulder, "Dick's the only one that's been worthwhile. You're taking him from me. It's right for him. If you love him, you'll be happier than I be. He won't treat you this way. Men! They'll go to town and buy themselves a plowshare; but they can't afford a doctor. If you don't love him, though, and fool with him, I hope you'll be like me, just to know what you've lost. . . ." Her voice trailed off.

Maggie simply stared.

The woman suddenly turned back. Her eyes were wet.

"Oh, Maggie, I hadn't ought to talk to you like this. You've been nice to me, too. It's only I love Dick so well. And it was awful this morning."

"How is he? Did George lick him bad?"

"Not bad. I got him to leave off and come over here first." Her voice broke. "George ain't really bad-tempered. It's just his way. He's never raised his hand on me, the way some men do. I don't know what I'm saying."

George came up then, all his fat face embarrassed.

"Listen, Maggie. We got to go home. I see your Pa ain't very well. And I'll tell Dick he can do just as he's a-mind to about coming over."

"Thank you," she said mechanically. She felt as if she had been bled.

Neither she nor her father spoke of the visit till dinner,

when he said, "If you should want to marry Dick, I'd be willing. I leave it up to you." . . .

That night when Dick came over, she was kind to him. Not that she felt towards him any differently. The fact that he had had a licking because of her made him seem more like a boy than ever. She couldn't imagine a man like Murray being licked on account of any girl.

As for Dick, he said hardly a word. He seemed to be contented just to be around. And his presence did appear to take the deathly loneliness from the clearing.

As, day after day, they worked through the wheat, and the standing grain steadily decreased in area, Gordon's spirits picked up. He seemed to work easier, and Maggie began to think that he was getting well again.

Besides, they had had no word from the south and Dick had found no signs of anyone in the woods around Black Creek. Maggie grew used to the sense of danger; little by little, she began to forget her fear at night.

In two weeks she and her father had finished the reaping, and Dick came over for a day and helped them cart the shocks to the barn. They laid it up in two stacks, handy to the door to take in and thresh. They threshed out a little together that Dick might carry it home with him in a sack, and the next evening he turned up with their first home-ground flour. Even to Maggie that seemed a wonderful thing. Mount had sent a bill by Dick. It was written on a little scrap of paper. Two cents for grinding a couple of quarts. The heading said "Mount's Mill." They laughed together at the notion.

"Pa says you ain't to eat it. The wheat's a little green yet, he thinks."

Gordon nodded at Dick.

"Yes," he said. "We'll wait a week before we start real threshing."

Maggie spent the week stripping the corn leaves from the standing stalks. There was no grass to harvest in the woods, except on beaver flies, but they were used for pasture. So for the cow's green fodder, as soon as the ears had set on the corn, the leaves were stripped by hand. Later the dry stalks would be harvested also.

It was light work after the reaping, and Maggie did it by herself. She had persuaded her father to take things easy till the threshing started.

Sometimes Dick lent her a hand for an hour or two, but he came less regularly. He seemed more cheerful though, and they talked about what they would do if their families decided to move south for the winter. It was exciting for Dick to think of. He might get a chance to join the army for a three months' 'listment. . . .

The idea did not last; George Mount guffawed at the notion of going south. He came over one Sabbath afternoon with Dick and talked the business over with Gordon.

"Ain't I been right?" he demanded. "Whatever has become of that there Sillinger, we ain't noticed it, have we? We didn't notice it when the armies was in Canada. There's been two years of war, but we didn't notice them. Tea up? Sugar up? We make our maple sugar for ourselves and who needs tea anyway?" He rocked himself on the stool; his face tilted up, like a bear feeling funny. "North America is quite a good-sized country. What the devil difference does a war make to it?" His staring eyes seemed to say, "And I'm quite a good-sized man; and what the devil difference does it make to me?"

"That's right," agreed Gordon. "I guess you've been right. I guess I got my nerve up just for nothing."

"Of course you did," said George. "But you was sick. I could see that with half an eye. It's natural." He leaned over the table. "Know what I figure to do? Well, sir, I figure not to sell no wheat. I figure to grind it all in flour, and then I'll take it down in winter, when the flour's short, and sell it di-rect to Fort Dayton and army posts. I'll undersell Ellice. It's a government mill now. We can undersell any government concern, there's no gravy in our business. *And,* by then I reckon flour prices will be high!"

"It's a good idea," said Gordon.

Maggie was amazed to see them so, projecting projects just the way they used to.

"How'll you carry it down, George?"

"That's the trouble. I've got to find me barrels. I figure on going down tomorrow to get barrels. I'll look around in Fairfield. The folks at Reeber's can tell me which people went to Canada. Casselman used to lug in flour for the town, he might have had some. They're no use to him when he's in Canada. But if I can't find enough there, I'll have to go down to Snyder's and pick up some to salt our pork in. See?" He roared and rocked again.

"Salt pork?" Gordon laughed, too.

"Why," said Mount, "what's the sense of war if nobody makes nothing out of it?"

Next morning, sure enough, he came down through the ford with his cart and team and headed south into the tunnel of the Jerseyfield road. He was gone overnight, so Dick spent the night at home.

But the next afternoon Mount returned with a dozen barrels precariously loaded on the cart. He sat on the seat, hanging his legs over the horses' rumps and chuckled handsomely.

"Sure," he said, "I picked them up here and there. Some

was used for pork and other things. They'll need to be scrubbed out. There's plenty of good things in them houses. I found a mattock there, brand new. I took a share from Empie's plow. I got some little things for all the kids." He rolled his eyes. "Why it beat going to town. Variety and no expense, you might say."

Gordon looked serious.

"That's stealing, George."

"By thunder, you was willing about barrels."

"Yes. But barrels are barrels. We actually needed them."

"Now listen, ain't they threatened to burn you out? Didn't they lift your powder off you? Look! I brought Maggie a real nice crochet hook. I found it sticking down inside a crack of the floor in McGlashen's. Must have dropped it when she lit out at night. It looked like y-vory to me."

He fished it from his shirt and handed it down.

Gordon said, "Don't take it, Maggie. I won't have you taking stolen goods."

"Now, Rob." Mount flushed. But he was too pleased to take offense. "I reckon it is y-vory though." And they all looked at the yellow, slender little stick. They thought it must be ivory. Mount nodded solemnly. "That little tricksy article. Imagine. Once it was an elephant way off in . . . where do elephants live, Rob?"

"Africa," said Gordon.

"Africa? Well I'll be durned. I'm going to show this here to Turp. Being black, he ought to know for sure. I'll tell you later."

He gathered up his reins.

"Did you hear any news?" asked Gordon.

"Gol. Think of that. After I got to thinking this was y-vory I clean forgot. Boy, boy — it's just what I expected. They had a fight above Oriskany Crick. The militia took an awful lacing. Lost three hundred out of seven hundred men. But they dinged Johnson's men and gave the Indians all they wanted. I talked to Mrs. Ritter down in Snyder's. Jake had his throat cut there, she'd heard. He was dead anyways. She said she'd been told it was by Casselman."

"No," said Gordon. "I hardly believe that."

"Well you don't make money believing it. Do as you're mind to. It's a fact about the fight, though."

"Is Stanwix holding out?"

"Holding out?" He slapped his legs. "You got ideas. Listen. After that battle, Schuyler sent up General Arnold. Yes sir, General Arnold himself, with the Massachusetts Brigade. Learned's men, they say. A thousand of 'em. And Sillinger took such a fright, him and the Injuns, that he's high-tailed it clean to Canada. Down there they're out and working just the same way as they did afore the war. It's just about as good as over now. The Butlers and the Johnsons had their lesson, you can bet. Why they even got young Walter Butler captured and in jail. Old Ben Arnold would have hanged him, but Schuyler had him sent down to Albany instead. A good idea. John Butler's going to watch his step with Walter locked up that way. I call it cute, myself."

Gordon had gone pale.

"Is that all true?"

"True as Gospel and George Mount can make it."

Maggie thought for a minute she saw tears in her father's eyes.

"Why," he said, "we can go on and thresh and do our work the same as ever."

"Sure," said George. "Ain't I always said so?" And then he

added, "The folks at Reeber's Settlement have all cleared out. I bet they feel like fools."

He laughed and turned his team. As the horses splashed across the ford, the cart teetered and rocked and the barrels thumped and George yelled, "Hye! Hye! Hye!" to his horses. Like old times. For the moment it seemed as if the silence of six weeks was broken.

Maggie felt weak. She turned with her father to the house. "Look, Dad," she said. "There's rain coming, surely."

He looked.

Above the woods a long level line of blue-gray clouds hung low. They came from the southwest.

Rain. It was like Providence. There was an underscud of white. For the first time in almost two months they saw the leaves turn silver. Wind. A pine on a hill southward started waving its upper branches, as if it had volition of its own. The air was cool. It stirred slowly through the clearing. From far away a sound like rushing water came to their ears.

"Look!" said Maggie.

In the stubble, drops like bullets struck the dirt, making little clouds of dust. The rain fell at a slight slant. The woods turned green. One of the horses up the clearing arched his tail and kicked his heels and the old cow shook her ears at the unaccustomed touch of water.

"Rain."

Father and daughter felt it on themselves. They lifted their faces to the drops, and Maggie raised her bare arms. The wind came into the sleeves, soft and damp. Her breast seemed to fill. Her mouth relaxed and her eyes grew darker.

Suddenly she caught him by the arm.

"Come, Dad. We've got to run — or we'll get wet."

Her voice was gay; she let go of his arm and raced for the door. She ran with her elbows at her sides, her brown legs flashing.

When Gordon came in after her, she had closed the window.

"I had to. It was raining in already."

The roof ticked overhead, drops made a curtain off the eaves. A sigh, as from a thirsty world, filled all the air.

⋐ 5 ⋑

RETURN OF ADAM DINGMAN

MAGGIE WAS HAPPY. She thought of David Murray sometimes nowadays, especially when Dick came over, sullen and silent, because he now would have no chance to join the army.

"Cheer up, Dick. We'll all get rich as anything. With our mill."

"Our Pas maybe, Maggie."

"And us, too. You'll find a girl that's twenty times as pretty as me. Maybe there'll be war for a while in Jersey, where Washington is, and then the British will go home. People will come back again. He'll come back this way."

Dick lifted his head quickly.

"He? Who?"

She was so gay, she said unguardedly, "David Murray."

"I didn't know of him."

She told him then about the Fairfield man.

"There's no such man in Fairfield," said Dick.

"Well he was with them, Dick."

Gradually he made her tell him the whole business.

"That's why you kissed me that night!"

"I'll kiss you again," she said mischievously. "You're like my brother. Isn't it all right to try on you?"

"I'll not take them that way," he said sullenly. He could not see that at that moment Maggie loved all the world. In the barn her father was threshing. The sound of his flail thumped healthily.

"Oh, Dick," she said, "I love you, too."

"But you wouldn't marry me."

"Don't talk so like a little boy. The way you scowl down at your feet. They're muddy enough to frown at, too." And she laughed at him.

In spite of that, he came again. He couldn't seem to keep away, and Maggie was unaware of the dependence she took from his somber, brooding eyes.

He was there the afternoon that Dingman finally came back to the clearing.

Dick had been giving Gordon a hand and Maggie had been winnowing; but they had all stopped to come into the kitchen for a drink of birch beer. They were sitting there when they heard the sound — a queer deep moaning note.

"What's that?" Dick's head had lifted.

They crowded to the window.

A fine mist was driving over the clearing to a northwesterly wind.

Dick was the first to spot him.

"It's Adam," he said. "Over there."

Then the other two saw him, sauntering out of the woods, rifle on his arm. Even so far away, they could distinguish the deerskin patch over the lock of the gun, the bright blue of his eyes against the shining redness of his face.

He saw them all in the window and raised his left arm, and a little cascade of water ran off the brim of his sopping black felt hat.

Then, in a moment, he had come in the door, with a wet fresh gust of air, smelling himself of soaked deerskin.

"Hello," he said. "You've got in all your wheat."

He leaned his gun in the corner and sat down as naturally as could be, while the drops fell slowly from the thrums of his green shirt.

They just stared at him. It was odd to think that here in Jerseyfield they were in the same room with a man who had been in the actual finish of the war.

"You all look good," he said.

"And how are you, Adam?" Gordon asked. "We expected you earlier than this."

"Yes. I did myself. I got nicked down at Oriskany."

"Where?" Dick's face was narrow and tense.

"I hain't going to mention where."

Maggie's eyes sparkled and as for Dick and Gordon, they laughed aloud.

"I would have been embarrassed explaining it until I could set down," said Adam. Then he asked, "Did you hear my new conkshell horn?"

"Was that that noise we heard?"

"Yes, it was. I got to carry it now, though it's the devil bumping a man's ribs." From under his arm he took a conch shell. "All ranger lieutenants carry them. I'm in the Dayton company. Though I don't see what good it is for me to blow it. There hain't nobody to hear it."

He put it to his lips and blew softly, filling the room with the same hollow sound.

"You got to be an officer," said Dick.

"Yes, young man. I did. You'd better call me Mister, too, I guess." He put the shell on the table for them all to wonder at. "I got the northern section to patrol now. Just me to cover twenty miles in two directions. Ain't it wonderful the way those Congress bug-tits work it out? Down in Jersey they'd have a comp'ny of dragoons to do that work. Up here it's Adam Dingman. Down there a flea can't tickle a dog's ear without the county sees it, but up here you could put the whole British Army into a cup and saucer and nobody'd believe you if you told them."

He sighed and stretched. "Wet weather, folks." And he grinned as they fired questions at him.

Yes, the British had gone. Gansevoort even had took a vacation, though the plain soldiers had to stay at Stanwix yet. It was a nasty fight. Everybody for themselves and Herkimer setting in the shade. They were licked proper when a storm came up. Did that storm hit Jerseyfield? It was a dinger, sure. But it gave the militia time to get together. Then they mowed down quite a swath of Indians and Tories. Joseph Brant had found it too hot to suit him.

Adam's jaw got grim. He'd seen things. . . . Herkimer was dead: the best man in the valley. When Gordon finally got up to go to the barn threshing floor, Adam followed.

"Listen," he said, "I don't want to scare Maggie. You'd better plan on getting out of here, Gordon. Get Mount to go with you, if you can. And if you can't, let the dog-eared fool get ruined for himself. I know Indians. They're going to try and get it back on us for that fight. And so are the Butlers and the Johnsons and all their people. It's right there ain't going to be no regular army work awhile up this way, but what there is will be twicet as bad for people like you."

Gordon's flail hung limp from his hand, the threshing stave like a dead tail on the floor.

"You don't mean that."

"I didn't expect you to believe. You make up your mind, though. I'll be around a day or two and I can watch out."

He stopped as Maggie and Dick came through the door.

Gordon turned away from her so that she could not see his face.

"I just heard Brownie's bell," she said. "She's over against the ridge. I think she must be heading for the beaver fly, instead of coming home, and I thought I'd fetch her before it got too wet."

"All right," said Gordon. "Go along."

Adam grinned as he leaned on his gun.

"Dick's going with me," she said.

The two older men watched them pass out into the mist. Dick carried a switch and Maggie had a shawl over her head.

"I mean what I say, Gordon. There's times for everybody to hold out and there's times a man just can't afford to be a fool."

Gordon sat down.

"You must be crazy, Adam. Why, I felt that way a while back, but now they're licked, I'd thought everything was safe again. I can't quit. Everything Maggie and I have is here."

"I know that. Take out what you can." Adam's face was earnest. "I ain't seen signs yet, but I feel it's coming. You're an old man, Gordon. You're too old to stand up to what's coming."

"It's been so quiet. Just the way it is now."

Gordon stopped and listened to the rain. Adam listened with him. Through the mist they heard the cowbell ringing southward against the ridge. It went along steadily.

All at once Adam stepped to the door.

"Listen," he said.

"Listen to what?"

"That bell, you fool. Hush up!"

Again Adam stood stock still. His ears seemed visibly to stretch. His red face, atop his stocky body, was lifted against the mist.

Gordon stood at his side.

"It's just the cow," he said. "She wanders some in fall."

"Keep still," Adam seemed to count as the bell was silent for a moment. Then, without a word, he broke for the woods, running.

Maggie and Dick had gone only a little way when Adam caught up with them.

"Get back home," he said, staring beyond them through the trees, "and don't make no noise either."

He listened again to the bell.

"Why, Adam, what do you mean?"

"Go home." His voice was harsh. "Git, I tell you. You make her go, Dick. And don't talk."

Dick stared at him.

"Git, you fool. Quick! Git into the house and wait for me."

Maggie at last felt the wrongness in the rain. She did not know what. She pushed back the shawl from her face.

"Adam," she whispered, "where are you going?"

His heavy mouth grinned briefly.

"I'm going to fetch that cow."

Like a shadow he stepped beyond them. He seemed to drift into a growth of witch hobble, leaving them alone in the rain, the smell of wet leaves, the soft steam of the woods, in which the tree trunks rose like strips of satin shadow.

"Maybe we'd better go," said Dick.

"What do you think it is?" Maggie whispered back. Then, "Dick. He looked so queer."

"Come on." He took her hand.

Behind them they heard the steady sound of the bell. It

wandered past where the swamp should be and hung for a while almost still on the ridge, just giving a single clank from time to time. The note seemed to float over their heads. It had a mellowness in the wet air. It was gentle. It made one inevitably think of Brownie's amiable bony head and twitching ears.

Dick's hand was urgent.

"Come along."

Still Maggie did not understand.

They slipped down together by the spring, and stopped for a brief instant. The house and barn were gray in the rain, dim, homely shapes. Inside the barn they heard the flail strike haltingly upon the boards.

The two heard it; then again the bell sounding behind them. It was stilled once more. Then just a clank.

The noise of the flail ceased. It made a slight thud, as if Gordon had dropped it. Then the bell rang softly, once again, from the same place.

"Something's the matter with Dad," Maggie whispered. "Adam wanted to tell us. That's why he went for Brownie. Hurry, Dick."

She ran to the barn door with Dick at her heels.

Her father was standing in the beaten straw, his arms close to his sides, his wide-open eyes fixed upon the window.

Looking through the window, as she often did, was the cow. She wore no bell at all.

At that instant, all four of them heard the shot. Maggie and Dick spun together to face the sound; and at the same time, Brownie lifted her head and twitched her ears with bovine complacency.

It was nearly an hour before Adam Dingman returned to the clearing. By then the light had faded, early as it was, to a kind of dusk. The rain came harder, hammering on the bark roof and flowing down the windows with a dreary sibilance.

In the kitchen, where Maggie and her father and Dick Mount sat together, the candle she had lighted covered their faces less with light than a pale yellowness. The boy had taken down the musket, drawn the charge, reloaded it; and now he sat with his back to the chimney. His face wore a slight frown, as though he had a hope that somebody might turn up to let him show what he could do in an emergency.

Whenever Maggie shifted on her stool, causing the loose leg to squeak, his frown deepened. He would glance sidewise at her white face, compressing his lips; but he forebore scolding her. Then, in the renewal of silence, his body would hunch forward over the gun on his knees, and he would be utterly motionless, as if he listened with all his senses.

Maggie instinctively sat at her father's side. She wished to comfort him by her presence. At first she had been surprised by the way he had taken the sound of the single rifle shot. Less than a year ago she would have expected him to take command of any situation. But it had been Dick who brought them into the house and barred the doors. Gordon had come without a word, nodding his head a little, and he sat down and bowed his face in his hands like an old and brokenhearted man.

"Is he going to get sick again?" Maggie thought.

She could see his chin quivering from time to time, which made her suddenly afraid that he might be going to cry. She could not imagine what it would be like to see him cry; she had never seen a man do that; and if he did, she could not bear to think of Dick's being witness to it.

She remembered the times she had run to her father, crying herself, with childish hurts, when he had comforted her with the sense of unshakable serenity he gave her; and it did not seem credible that he should cry. She touched him with her hand, but got no answer. So she sat still, listening to the rain, and wondering what Adam Dingman was up to.

She thought of him as he must have slowly stalked the sound of the cowbell. But for him, she and Dick might have walked right up to it; and she tried to imagine what it would have felt like to see, not Brownie with the bell, but — she could not imagine it at all. She only shivered, shifted on her stool, and met Dick's intense frown. . . .

They heard the soft slopping of feet in the mud beyond the door and then Adam's plain voice hailed them. Dick took down the bar to let him in.

He entered, wet and steaming, laid the rifle carefully on the table and put down Brownie's bell, which he had been carrying by the clapper.

Maggie had risen from her seat, her eyes large with an unspoken question. Even Dick had not asked anything. But Adam merely shook the wet and sticking shirt loose from his shoulders and remarked that there was no fire.

"It makes me feel aguish coming in."

"I'll light it right off," said Dick.

Maggie, also feeling the instinct to serve him, asked whether there was anything he wanted.

"Well," said Adam, "if it ain't too much bother, I'd like a little hot milk."

He sat apologetically across the hearth from Gordon, his feet, shapeless in their wet heavy socks, stretched out to the blaze, and sipped his milk.

"I made a turn all round the clearing," he said. "I didn't see nothing but that feller's tracks. It's raining hard enough to wash them out afore tomorrow, I believe."

"How about *him?*" asked Dick.

"Him? Well, he was an Indian. Seneca. Had his paint on." He drank a little milk and eyed Dick over the rim of the cup. "Hain't much to say. I drug him down the ridge and sunk him in a waller. He was a youngster, probably running a lone trail. And that was a pretty cute idee, if I do say it. Ringing that bell." He glanced at Dick again, and grinned a little. "No, I didn't take his hair, Dick. It wouldn't be worth it without I went to Vermont. They pay cash there."

Gordon had raised his head.

"You think he really was out for trouble?"

"Well, if he wasn't, he took a lot of pains for nothing on a rainy day."

Maggie said, "I could feel kind of sorry for him. All by himself."

"Aw," said Adam. "It weren't a bad shot."

Maggie's wide-eyed stare embarrassed him, and he turned his eye to his conch shell. He treated it like a plaything, shook it, found that it had water in it, emptied it, and set it by the fire to dry.

"Do you think wet would hurt one of them things?" he asked.

Nobody knew.

Gordon asked, "What ought we to do, now, Adam?"

The trapper felt better to have the subject shifted.

"Well," he said, "there ain't much sense in running out blind. There don't seem to be any more of them in the woods right now, but I'd better look around tomorrow some. It's most likely that you wouldn't find a lot of them up this way yet. They'll probably go for Fairfield the first thing. But they're bound to use Black Crick sometimes coming down on the north side of the Valley. What I mean is, you can't stay here long. But there ain't no value in just running to the Valley till we know the road's clear."

Dick leaned forward tensely.

"Will you stay here tonight, Adam?"

"If it's all right with Gordon and Maggie."

"Then I might as well get home." He was plainly eager to tell his father.

"You cut along then," Adam said. "I'll look after Maggie the best I can."

It was strange how safe Adam's presence made Maggie feel, though. As he would have said himself, he wasn't much to rest a female eye against. But when she went out to the barn to milk the cow, she felt the darkness full of presences. The candle-lantern which she set down in the straw served only to bring the window closer, with its bright curtain of drops and sound of falling rain.

But she was spared what she most dreaded, going to the spring for water. When she finished the milking, Adam joined her at the door with two brimming buckets in his hands.

"I wasn't doing anything," he explained. "Your Pa ain't much company tonight, either."

"I hope he isn't going to get feeling sick again," she said.

"I don't see why he ought to, Maggie. But I guess when you get about so old, things mean a lot."

"Yes, Adam."

"I mean, your Pa ain't scared. He's just considering how bad he'll feel to move. He don't want to even now. When you're like him, it's pretty hard to make a new start, I guess."

She was grateful to Adam. And back in the kitchen once more, she tried to brighten things, as she got supper. She talked about how well the wheat was threshing out; she showed Adam her new white stockings that she hadn't worn yet; and then she got out the Book of Martyrs that was kept wrapped in heavy canvas so that mice wouldn't gnaw its pages.

Adam was filled with interest at the pictures. If the religious significance escaped him, other details did not. "I don't believe a fire ever burned like that right on the top of the pile," he said. His hand shook as he tried to turn the pages without damaging them. "They didn't stop at much, did they? But mostly they was partial to fire."

"Yes, mostly," Maggie said.

He closed the book with a sigh, handed it to Maggie, and remarked, "It certainly is nice to have a book to look at. But I never done no reading. Did you read it?"

"Oh, yes," said Maggie.

"Maybe you'd read some of it to me some time."

"I'd be glad to, Adam."

They ate their supper quietly at the table. Now and then drops of rain hissed on the burning logs. A draught from the shed door fluttered the candle flames from time to time. . . .

In the morning, Maggie came down to find Adam already out of his blanket, which still lay spread out on the kitchen floor. The weather had cleared from the northwest and long gray clouds were sweeping through the sky. The wind was cold and strong; when she went to the door she felt it through her dress against all her body; with a chill pressure, like forewarning of snow.

Looking across the clearing, she saw only the woods and the bending tops of the trees, and four adventurous crows who made a crablike progress under the clouds. The soil in the wheat stubble was dark and sopping. The leafless stalks of corn, with the filled ears like bunions, cracked as they rocked in the wind. The water in the stiller stretches of the creek was dark, metallic blue.

Of Adam there was yet no sign, except the footprints going from the doorsill towards the mill.

Maggie turned inside, with her hands smoothing her blown hair, and crossed the kitchen in order to call her father. The room he slept in was next the shed, making an L of the building. It had one window that looked out towards the spring and took in the end of the barn. There was nothing in the room but a row of pegs to hold his clothes, a shelf with his razor, brush, and soap dish on it, and the double bed, made of mahogany wood, and strung with hemp. He had often said it would be left to Maggie when he died.

He was lying in it now, quite still, sunk in the feather tick so that the blanket lay almost level across him.

"Dad. It's time to get up."

She got no answer.

"Dad. It's late."

She became conscious of the sound of her own voice. He must be sleeping hard.

She went round the foot of the bed to see his face. He was lying quite still, his eyes were open; but their expression did not change as she passed in front of them.

"Dad!"

He's dead, she thought. And yet she did not think he looked like a dead person. She forced herself to approach the side of the bed and put her hand on his. It was cool, and it wasn't rigid. She could not tell. Then she remembered that she had been told a person's breath would cloud a glass if he were alive, so she got the bit of broken mirror that he used for shaving and held that close to his mouth.

Two tiny films of fog appeared, and went as quickly as they came.

"He isn't dead!"

She seemed to hear her whole heart saying it, and she was conscious of the blood in her face and of an impulse to be gay. But he was so still on the bed, so pale, with the lines on his face printed as if in stone, giving an effect of being a statue of himself, that she was once more overwhelmed with doubt; and once more reassured herself with the mirror.

Then she went anxiously to the front door to look for Adam. She had a feeling that Adam might know what to do, being such a hardy self-dependent person. But when she failed to see him she was frightened, and returned to the kitchen and tried to occupy herself with laying the fire and cooking breakfast. Finally she milked and, heating some in a pan, took a cupful into her father's room.

She said, "Would you like some hot milk, Dad, before you get up?" in a purposely easy voice. But he lay as he had been, speechless, and unmoving.

On his return, Adam took one look and clucked his tongue.

"He ain't dead, that's sure. I think he's got some kind of stroke, Maggie."

"Yes, Adam. What does a person do for that? Do you know?"

He scratched his head, long-faced, his blue eyes troubled.

"Seems to me I've heard somewhere that you put a plaster on them," he said, roving the wall with his eyes, as if he expected to find a clue there to the proper treatment. "I don't remember where, though. I mean where you put it, Maggie."

She shivered slightly.

"Do people die of strokes, Adam?"

"I couldn't say. I expect you might die of most anything."

"What kind of plaster?"

"Mustard, or flax, or something. All I know is that they're hot and make you itch as if you had the crumbs."

She knew there was a little flaxseed in the shed, so she got that and she and Adam arranged a plaster with a piece of calico.

They finally laid it on Gordon's chest; then Adam, having had time to think of something else, found a piece of soapstone and heated it and put it to Gordon's feet.

"Now, Maggie," he said, "you keep ahold of yourself. I'm going to light out for the Falls and scout the road. I'll be back in two days. Maybe your Dad'll be all right then. Anyway, we'd ought to give him the chance before we lug him down in a cart. I've got to report this there to Dygert, and maybe get him to send up a bunch of men." He hoped he could persuade

Pete Dygert; he wished that Herkimer was still alive. "You won't get too scared?"

Maggie shook her head. But she could not say anything. It was like finding oneself back in the same nightmare for the second time.

She still felt so when she saw him leave. He waved to her from the entrance of the Jerseyfield road. Then he was gone.

She said to herself, "Two days. Once he's back, we'll be all right."

❧ 6 ☙

THE INDIAN DOG

AGAIN AND AGAIN during the morning, she said the same thing to herself. She even talked aloud to herself for company. "You've got to be sensible, Maggie. You can't get frightened with Dad so sick. He's always taken care of you; it's your turn, for a change."

And later, "They've always been our neighbors, Maggie."

"Yes, but that Indian."

"Adam said, though, that there wasn't any signs."

"Well anyway, he'll be back before too long. It would be nice if Dick came visiting with us today, don't you think?"

"Most likely he won't come. He said last time he was here that they were threshing out their peas."

She reminded herself when it was time to get lunch. First

she looked in again on her father and took the poultice and heated it. The pattern of the calico had come off on his chest, and she looked curiously at it on her father's white skin.

He still lay in his coma, saying nothing, unstirring, the next thing, as it seemed to Maggie, to the edge of death. He would have been amused to see the pattern on himself, in blue and red. But he couldn't, and somehow she did not care to tell him about it, knowing he wouldn't smile.

When she had replaced the poultice, she went to the spring. On the way back she stopped and talked to the cow. Brownie was lying in the shelter of the barn wall, lackadaisically chewing her cud.

"Do you think he'll ever come back to see us?" Maggie asked, and added almost crossly, "I mean David Murray, you stupid thing."

But Brownie merely altered the curve of her tail to twitch a fly away.

"You wouldn't care who came!" Maggie said scornfully. "You never notice anything. You wouldn't know the difference between him and Dick, I bet."

She walked quite stiffly back to the kitchen.

It was neither Dick nor Murray; it was George and Mrs. Mount who came. They had the team hitched to the cart, and they stopped at the house for a moment, the woman almost cheerful-seeming, and the man as full as usual of noisy notions.

"Hello, there, Maggie. Where's your Pa?"

"He's inside." Maggie looked anxiously at Mrs. Mount's pale face. "Adam thinks he's had a stroke. He doesn't move or say or see at all. Do you know what that is?"

"No, Maggie. Maybe I would if I saw him."

"Yes, let's look at poor old Rob." George Mount bounced

down from his seat on the cart, letting his wife make her own descent as best she could. He shook his fat head. "Too bad, too bad, about poor Rob. He ain't been like himself all this fall, I think. It surely is too bad."

He said the same thing when he had pushed his way into the bedroom. "Rob," he said in his heavy voice, then, "Rob! Rob Gordon!" until his voice seemed to shake the walls and Maggie felt her anger rise to see her father yelled at.

Mrs. Mount stared curiously. It was obvious to Maggie that she took a kind of satisfaction in seeing another person feeling poorly.

"No, I don't know what it is." She backed out of the room, and said more brightly, "I'll ask in the Falls what one ought to do. Somebody will know."

"The Falls? You're going down?" Maggie could hardly believe her ears. "Didn't Dick tell you about the Indian?"

"Sure," George Mount said as he rejoined them. "Crazy fool thing to do. Now somebody might think we done that. No Injuns ever would bother us up here. They like us. Why, look at all I've give to them."

"It did seem foolish of Adam, to me," Mrs. Mount observed complacently. Her mind was on her unexpected journey to the Valley. "George wants more barrels," she told Maggie. "And there's things I'd like to get and it seems like a last good chance afore the winter."

"Sure, sure." George was good-humored. "We'll be back in two or three days. I'll have to keep track of the price of millings, now."

He took his wife's arm in a hairy hand and pushed her out to the cart.

"But," said Maggie, following them with a pale face, "you're leaving the children all alone."

"Dick'll look out for them. I made him promise to. They're going to finish threshing the peas. But I told him he could come over here a couple of times." George winked.

"Oh."

"Why, Maggie, Indians ain't a-going to hurt you or them. They like the boys, and we always been nice to them, too."

"That's so," said Mrs. Mount.

One would have thought that in her excitement she had come to think the Indians pleasant people.

Maggie was getting supper all by herself when Dick came over. He had his three brothers and the slave in tow, or they had him. It was difficult to tell, for they ran about like young partridges, on their naked skinny legs — all but Cobus, the fat one, who had a kind of pompous wiggle to his round little rump, like his father. When they heard about Mr. Gordon they clamored at once to see so curious a sight as a person who looked dead and yet who wasn't.

"Get out, hush up," said Dick, flushing. "Ain't you any decency?"

"I wasn't going to laugh nor nothing," Cobus said, looking up with his fat, serious face. "But a man had ought to learn about things, hadn't he? Why goshamighty, Dick, ain't that the truth?"

"You shut your mouth," said Dick and drove them all from the kitchen. "And don't go yelling all around."

He closed the door, while Henry and young George and the little Negro, scampering a safe distance off, began to chant, "Dick, he's moony, Dick, he's moony, Dick he's moony for Maggie!" They shrieked and laughed and then George added in a treble squeak that pierced the clearing from end to end, "But Maggie don't love him at all!"

Dick, blushing furiously, with the sweat all over his face, found it hard to meet her eyes.

"I couldn't help bringing them, Maggie," he said apologetically. "Don't listen to them."

"No," she said, seriously.

They glanced at each other like grown-up persons, conscious of manners to maintain, and presently the boys gave up their shrilling to examine the sawmill.

"Is there anything I can do?" Dick asked.

"I don't think so."

"Pa was possessed and all to go. And Ma, too. I never seen a person act so possessed as she was."

"It's going to be a treat for Mrs. Mount," said Maggie.

They looked at each other again, not knowing what else to say.

"Well," Dick said at length, "I got to get them back 'fore dark. I hope your Pa gets better."

"Adam's coming back soon," Maggie said with stiff lips.

"The wind's south," said Dick. "If you want anything, you just fire your gun. I'll keep a-listening and I'll come right over."

"I will," Maggie promised.

She stood in the door, watching them troop through the ford. The water was higher since the rain, and Dick had to carry over his two smallest brothers.

They had been gone a good minute before she closed and barred the door. She lit no candle, either, that night, but she sat in the dark kitchen, and now and then, hopefully, she would go into her father's room and listen.

"Dad," she would say quietly.

But he did not answer her all night long; and dawn, coming

at last, discovered her with tired, shadowed eyes, still sitting in the kitchen. . . .

She had never seen him before.

He came walking down through the clearing, a tall shambling man, carrying a rifle and an Indian hatchet, and stood outside the door.

"This here is Gordon's clearing?" he asked.

"Yes, Mister," Maggie said.

She stood at the entrance, struggling to keep her face quiet. "Will you come in and sit down?"

She felt that she had to ask.

"No." He shook his head. He had a slight cast in one eye. "Where's Gordon?"

He had a sly, calculating face, and his eyes kept roving. She felt suddenly afraid that he might find out Gordon's helplessness.

"My father'll be here pretty soon," she said, wondering whether her face showed a lie as plainly as Dick's would. "Will you wait for him?"

The man ran his hand round inside the sweaty band of his hat. He had black hair on a narrow head, and his eyes never stopped their hunting here and there about the place. "You Gordon's daughter?" he asked.

"Yes, Mister."

"Maggie Gordon?"

"Yes."

"Know a man named David Murray?"

"Yes," she said again, wonderingly.

"I guess this is the place. I don't know the country very good." He seemed to mouth his words a little. "Seen airy Indian round here, lately?"

"No," said Maggie. "There's been nobody but yourself, Mister."

"That's queer." He looked sharply at her with his straight-seeing eye. "Murray sent one of his Indian scouts this way two days ago. Cataroque and Hess left him at the Canada Crick. He ain't come back."

"Is David Murray round here?" Maggie asked.

"Back north." He pointed a thumb. "Casselman and him have got a bunch of us. We're striking for a place called Reeber's between here and Fairfield." He grinned, showing brown teeth that stuck out slightly. "But Murray says to me, Ike, if you see Gordon's girl, you tell her not to be scared."

"Are you alone?" Maggie asked, the color rising in her face.

"Yes. But I was to tell Gordon to get out. Murray said so."

"Well, I'll tell him when he comes," Maggie said, not knowing why she continued to distrust him, because, after all, the man was from David Murray. Perhaps it was because she did not want him to know that she had misled him. Or maybe it was the furtiveness in his eyes. At any rate, she was glad to see him go, which he did, with a grin and a sidelong stare over his shoulder.

He passed down to the beginning of the Jerseyfield road and bent down over the tracks of Mount's cart, picking up some horse droppings in his hand. Then he turned suddenly and crossed the ford towards Mount's. Just before he entered the woods the sun glanced like a spark on the edge of the little axe.

Maggie returned slowly to the kitchen.

"Maggie."

She gave a glad cry, "Dad!" and hurried in to the bedroom. His eyes met hers as if he saw her.

"What was that?"

"A man called Ike. David Murray, he was one of the men with Casselman that night, sent him to say we weren't to be worried. Oh, Dad."

"What's happened to me?"

Her mention of Murray obviously made no impression on him.

"You've been sick, Dad. You'll be better now," she said. For the time it seemed to her that all her worries were coming to an end.

"I can't move my right arm," he said. "I can move my leg only a little on that side."

"You've been sick," she repeated. "Adam's coming back tomorrow. We'll move you down to the Valley where a doctor can look out for you."

He said, "My bed's in a mess," fretfully, and Maggie flushed with shame.

"Oh, Dad, I'll fix it right away."

She managed to get him off the blankets and onto the floor, where he sat with his head against the bed. He seemed exhausted by her labor, and just lay there, while she turned the tick and smoothed out the blankets. Then it took all the strength she had to get him back again.

He lay still for a while with closed eyes and she thought that he had gone to sleep. But suddenly he feebly put his left hand out, took hers, and squeezed it very faintly.

"This is a good time for me to get sick, isn't it?"

His voice had no strength, but the way he spoke heartened her immeasurably.

"You go to sleep," she said.

When she returned to the kitchen she saw with eyes that were amazed that it looked dirty, and realized that for two days she had not touched a broom. She smiled to herself, calling herself lazy. While she swept and sanded the floor, she hummed a tune. She was half through before she remembered what the words were that went with it.

> With his golden hair a-curling and his
> Feather in the sky. . . .

It came to her that all along she had been putting dependence in the hope that David Murray would look in again some day. And now he was in the woods to the north; even the fact that the looks of the man, Ike, had been so disquieting could not alter that fact. It was a thing no man could help in war, she supposed — the company he had to go with.

A little later her father woke again and asked for some food and drink. He grumbled when she brought him warmed milk, but he drank the cupful, admitting that it made him feel better. She promised to bring him some mush in a while.

She gave him the corn mush at noon. He fell asleep before she had finished spooning the stuff into his mouth; and it seemed to her that his face had lost some of its bluish tinge.

After she had fed herself on what remained of the mush, she went outdoors, carrying the musket, and made the circuit of the clearing.

There was nothing to see, beyond the place at which the man named Ike had entered the clearing on the western side. He had evidently been following the water, and she wondered where he had come from. There must be a camp somewhere westward; there was a trail, she knew, that struck from the West Canada ford to Black River.

Returning along the creek, she went as far as the eastern end of the clearing, opposite the ford to Mount's place. From that point a person could see their entire farm, the entrance of the road, the barn, the house, the hemlocks round the spring, the mill, and the length of the creek, the water dancing down the rifts with a bright spatter cresting the dark blue.

The woods on the hills showed a wind blowing, but in the clearing it was hardly felt. The sun had a clear, light warmth of September. The windy blue sky and the small sailing clouds were like bits of the vast white ones of summer.

The pattern of the wind in the leaves was the only moving thing that Maggie saw in all the woods. They gave no sign of life other than the swinging of the branches. They seemed aloof from all this business of war, as if in their almost limitless distances so small a thing as death could leave no mark upon them. Often enough Maggie had seen a hawk strike into that sea of green; in the first year of their coming she had heard wolves running late in the fall; once she had even seen one cross the western end of the clearing; but the wilderness always absorbed them and their business; always when she looked again there was the same unbroken sea of treetops, as if the wilderness were waves endlessly rolling down upon the clearing from the north and west. Now, as she turned her eyes back to the house, it seemed a tiny, new square box, set up in the fingers of the woods. Her eyes brimmed suddenly as she thought that a still smaller square, inside that box, was her father's room, where he lay helpless.

What had made her start along the creek path further eastward, she never knew; she had certainly no clear idea of fetching in the horses; and as soon as she had gone well into the woods she felt their stillness. The wind in the treetops was like a curtain shutting down the world. Underneath it anything might shape its being, unobserved of heaven.

When the fear first struck her, she stopped a while to listen.

It seemed to her that lately not her ears alone but all her senses had been keyed to listen with. There was a feeling in her that if she listened hard enough, she would surely hear the cowbell somewhere in the woods; and then she would know enough to turn and run for home.

But there was no sound. The cowbell, by Adam Dingman's advice, had been hung on the kitchen wall. She told herself that she was being silly. Adam would be returning tomorrow, perhaps even tonight, and they would take her father out, and if they did, they would need the horses. She had seen neither of them for the past two days.

The trail was a narrow path, kept open by Brownie and the horses, and meandering along the bank of the stream. Now and then it branched round little islands of undergrowth, as if the animals continually experimented to find easier going. Though there seemed no reason for these cranks and turns, for the most part they managed to seek out the levelest going.

Maggie scarcely expected to find the team in the beaver fly where they grazed for most of the summer. But on pushing through the dense wall of goldenrod and asters that fringed it, she saw both the horses peacefully feeding in the open.

They were, as a matter of fact, nearly at the far side from her, standing knee-deep in the beaver grass, under the shadow of a sailing cloud. As it passed them over and sprang up the distant wall of leaves and slid away, their hides shone with sudden brilliance in the sunlight.

The old horse was a black, with gray rims round his eyes, and badger muzzle; but the younger, which was her father's special pride, was a dark bay, a smallish, slat-ribbed animal, with straight forelegs, and a long neck and head. He was not as good a work horse as the other, but under saddle he was supposed to have a first-rate burst of speed. Maggie had always considered him a very handsome horse. She made a pet of him. Sometimes he would answer her when she whistled.

She thought of trying him now, for if he answered, she would avoid having to venture into the open. Then she noticed that he had lifted his head. He stayed like a statue watching over his shoulder. Suddenly, he snorted like a deer, gathered his haunches under him, and sprang away from the woods.

The old black skittishly caught flight, without ever glancing to see what it was, kicked up his heels, and whinnied as the two raced down the beaver fly. They did not stop for Maggie, but plunged headlong into the trail, obviously enjoying the run, now, in spite of their original fright.

Maggie was too surprised to try to stop them. She could not imagine what had set them off. There had been no panther for some time in their woods. Adam claimed to have shot the last one in Jerseyfield two years ago. And wolves would not be wandering down for at least another month.

Instinctively she crouched in the goldenrod. The impulse to follow the horses was strong, but she realized that to do so would show her presence to whatever had stampeded the team.

She had only a short wait before she saw it. It was a foxy-looking Indian dog. His ears were pointed as he came out of the trees, his sharp nose tilted upward. She had only a glimpse of his sandy-white coat before he vanished into the grass. Then in a moment he jumped up on an old stump and balanced himself to look across the meadow. She could see the hair on the side of his neck roughed by a puff of wind.

For a breath she thought that he must have scented her. But a whistle from the woods distracted him. He turned his head, looked back towards her once more, and then, at another whistle, dropped off out of sight.

As soon as he was gone, she scrambled up and ran into the trail. She followed the horse tracks at a run almost the full quarter mile to their own clearing. There, as she came out of the woods, she saw the team standing by the barn, each muzzling the other's shoulder, as peacefully as if they had been there all day.

She hurried to them, drove them into their stalls and haltered them. Then, at last, she leaned herself against the stable wall and fought for her breath.

The sound of the whistle, more than the horses' fright, or the sight of the dog, had unnerved her. It had made her think at once of the Indian ringing the cowbell on the ridge, waiting for one of them to fetch the cow. What the man named Ike had said that morning no longer comforted her. What he had said alluded to the Fairfield men, but it did not take in Indians, and she had, instead of George Mount's confidence, an instinctive fear of them. The dog had been an Indian dog, by the very look of him. The whistle must have been an Indian's.

✸ 7 ✸

CATAROQUE AND HESS

SHE forced herself to be quiet, and after she returned to the kitchen, when her father heard her and called out, "Where've you been, Maggie?" she answered in what seemed a tolerable voice, "Fetching in Prince and Blackie, Dad."

He said, "I heard them coming home. They sounded as if they were running."

"Yes," she said, "they're feeling frisky."

She went in to him then with some water.

"How are you, Dad?"

"I'm not much good, I guess. But I feel easier. I can't seem to move my arm at all, though."

"You will, soon, Dad."

"Didn't you say that Adam Dingman was coming back here?"

"Yes. I told you. He's coming back tomorrow."

Her father smiled thinly.

"Well, Maggie, I won't raise any more fuss about going." He let his head lie back upon the pillow. "We'll take what we can with us. But you'll have to pack, Maggie."

"Yes, Dad." She watched him try to smile. "The china pot," she said. "And the good cups in their box and my small loom."

He nodded wearily. "Whatever you think. And don't forget

the satchel I've got under the front of Brownie's stall. There's not much money in it, but enough to start us off down there. Pack it in one of the trunks, Maggie."

"Yes, Dad."

"I think I'll have another nap," he said. "It's about all I can do nowadays."

"Yes," she said. "You do. . . ."

Packing was something to keep her mind busy. She brought down the little cowhide trunk from the loft and set it in the middle of the kitchen. There were her own things to put in it, her shoes, and her new white stockings, her best petticoat and short gown, a lawn cap and a fancy chintz pocket, the locket that had been her mother's in a small rosewood box together with some silver buckles and a brooch, and last, her mother's wedding dress.

They comforted her; they were things that she knew; they had been before her time. She fetched the Bible and the Book of Martyrs and placed them in the bottom of the trunk. It was while she was looking for a place for the little bag of money that she heard Dick coming.

He walked in hurriedly.

"Hello, Maggie. What you doing?"

"Packing my things," she said mechanically. Then she rose quickly from her knees. "Oh, Dick," she whispered. "I'm glad you're here. Come outside."

They stood together by the door. The wind had strengthened, it blew about them both, fluttering her petticoat to touch Dick's legs.

"What is it, Maggie?"

Briefly she told him first about the man called Ike, and then about fetching in the horses, the dog, and the whistle. He watched her all the time with his steady brown eyes, then he turned his thin face eastward, so that she saw his jawbone, and the sensitive lean curve of his lips.

He said quietly, "That took nerve, Maggie."

She flushed all over.

"I was scared half to death, Dick."

"I would have been, too."

"Do you s'pose it was an Indian?"

"Maybe so. I'm not bothered about Indians. It's the notion of these Fairfield men."

"Why, Dick. How can you say so?"

"They hate Pa," he said. "And we hate them. We always have. If the Indians do anything, it will be because Casselman got them to."

He stood a long while thinking. And for once Maggie was not impatient with him for his slowness.

All at once it seemed to her that the world was going wrong entirely, she did not know why it should seem so, but it did; she did not understand the war or what made people fight or feel afraid. But she felt that whatever was to be done could be safely left to Dick. Standing there with his hair all tousled by the wind, he looked no longer like a boy.

"How's your Pa today?"

"He seems better."

"Is he fit to ride?"

"In the cart?"

"Yes, of course," he said shortly.

Feeling that she had said something stupid, Maggie answered meekly, "I think so, Dick."

"All right, I'm going back to fetch the boys. I'll bring them over here tonight. Then we'll decide. If Adam hain't come early, we'll maybe leave ourselves after dark."

"Dick, have you seen anything?"

"No, Maggie. But I get a feeling over there that somebody's been watching. I can't find the tracks. It's just the feeling. I'm scary as a girl about it. I guess it's Pa and Ma both being away just now that makes me feel so."

His eyes avoided hers.

"I know." She nodded her head, so that the two braids twitched on her back. "But maybe it's not so bad."

"You mean about the man called Ike and this feller David Murray."

"I was thinking so."

"I was myself," he said. "Didn't he say that that Indian was one of Murray's scouts?"

Maggie nodded again.

"But there's no doubt that Indian wanted to get you or your Dad out."

She realized that he said it without any malice; it made her heart warm to Dick. He wasn't trying to run down anybody; he was merely stating the obvious fact.

"Yes," she said timidly.

"You see, Maggie, I don't know this feller Murray. Maybe he's all right. No doubt he is. But there's people hate us, even if he don't. I'll fetch the boys."

"Won't your Pa get mad at you for that?"

"Pa's getting mad don't matter now," Dick said. "He told us to thresh out the peas. Well, George and Henry are finishing them with Turp right now. That's why I came over."

"Yes, Dick."

"You get all packed. What are you taking, by the way?"

"Just the trunk and some little things and my small loom."

"Don't take too much. We may have to travel fast." He

stopped for a last moment. "Maggie," he said, "that surely was a fine thing, getting in the horses."

He did not look at her as he left, and he went hurriedly.

By the time he had gone, the sun was low. With a last look out of doors, Maggie returned to her work. There wasn't much left to do. By twilight she had finished, had started supper, and was milking Brownie in the barn.

It was an odd thing to think that she might not milk Brownie again for a while. She realized that they would have to leave the old cow to fend for herself or follow at her own pace if she could. Knowing Brownie's lazy disposition, the last seemed unlikely.

As she helped her father with his supper she told him of Dick's plans. He nodded from time to time.

"Yes, maybe we'd better figure on meeting Adam. You'll have to help me dress, though."

She did that, holding his trousers for him over the edge of the bed. It was an awkward business. The right leg moved a little to his wish, but the arm was still useless. He said somewhat shyly, looking up at her, "You'll have to take care of the old man for a while, I'm afraid."

"Don't say so, Dad."

It was evident that he felt a sense of shame at having needed help to dress.

"I'd better rest while I can," he said.

"Poor Dad," she thought, returning to the kitchen. "He doesn't complain at all. Just imagine how George Mount would act if he was sick this way."

She went to the door.

The sun had set and a pale green twilight hung above the western woods, making the pointed tips of balsams wild and lonely. The wind was going down. The creek had a brittle sound, as if the banks were feeling frost.

Behind her in the barn the horses stamped the floor and shook their halters.

"It'll be cold tonight," she thought.

She went back into the kitchen and looked at the heap she had made of their possessions in the middle of the floor. She had not appreciated before how insignificant the pile would seem. The walls in the dusk had an odd look of bareness. There was a pathetic sense of emptiness in the house, as if already it were aware of their desertion; as if, the way some persons did, it had aged suddenly.

The sky darkened swiftly with the fading of the green twilight and the rounding surface of the moon changed color from its first full yellow to a chilled whiteness. With the cessation of the wind it seemed to sail surprisingly. The night became still.

In the bedroom Maggie heard her father's steady breathing.

> *Heavenly angels round my head,*
> *Please to watch me in my bed,*
> *If in sleeping I should die,*
> *Lift my soul to God on high.*

The words of the childish prayer popped into her head un-expectedly. The comfort of their recollection filled her eyes.

Maggie was still quiet from her thought of the prayer when she heard someone crying softly.

"Keep still." It was Dick's voice's voice. "That's a good boy. Keep still. Do you want Maggie Gordon to see you crying that way?"

"Dick!" she said and hurried to the door.

They came into the darkness together from the white dimness of the moonlight, their two figures like shadows of themselves. Dick, and the small fat shape of Cobus.

"Where's George and Henry and Turp?" she asked, closing them into the blackness with her. Then, hearing the sniffling continue and the heavy breathing of Dick, "What's happened? Oh, Dick!"

"Maggie, we've got to have a light."

His voice was unnaturally dry.

"Yes," she whispered, "just a minute. There ought to be coals left."

"No, no! Not yet. Have you got anything to hang over the window?"

She handed him a blanket which he draped over the pane. In another instant she was bending at the hearth, raking aside the ashes with stupid fingers, and blowing on a coal. The flame was born on the end of the candlewick, climbed feebly, and burned. She rose with it, facing the sound of Cobus's sniffling.

The little fat boy was standing on the floor, holding one arm across his eyes against the light. The other arm hung down stiff and straight in the tattered shirt-sleeve. Maggie caught her breath to see it sopping and dark.

Dick was already bending down beside his brother.

"It's only a small one."

"What happened, Dick?"

"They took a shot at us when we was pulling foot for the woods."

"Was it Indians?"

He nodded. "Hess and Cataroque."

"They did?"

"Yes," he said. "Got anything to tie this up?"

She stripped a piece of cotton from the cloth she had used to

cover the yet open trunk, and stooped beside Dick. Cobus, with blubbering lips, turned his face hesitantly and looked down his shoulder at himself.

"That's a good boy, Cobus," said Dick. "Don't you cry. You come along fine."

Maggie glanced at Dick. His face was drawn and still. There was only a kind of dull disbelief that still covered his eyes. At his direction, she held one end of the rough bandage.

"I thought they'd killed him, too," said Dick. "He'd sneaked out of the barn to lay down, the way he always does. I'd just got there when I heard Turp yell in the barn. Then Cobus got up from back of the manure pile and Hess come out with his axe." He stared at Maggie. "I knew then there wasn't anything to do. I yelled to Cobus and he came running to me."

"What happened to George and Henry, Dick?" Maggie, too, felt the same strange incredulity.

"I guess they must be dead. Turp, too, I guess."

Suddenly Maggie realized that little Cobus was trying to say something.

"What is it, Cobus?"

He was still looking down at himself, at the bandage that pressed into his plump brown arm.

His lips repeated the words, but she could not understand them.

"What is it, Cobus?" Dick asked.

"It's my own private swear," said Cobus. "I never tell it to no one at all."

Suddenly he began to cry.

"Be still," said Dick sternly, but his voice wasn't rough. "You're doing fine, Cobus."

"When did it happen?" Maggie asked.

"Just as quick as I got there. Cobus, had Hess and Cataroque been round before I came?"

Cobus nodded.

"Yes, they came in and set down, watching us thresh. They was asking about Pa and Ma and where they was. They asked where you was. I got tired talking and went out back. Then I heard Turp holler and I woked up and Hess was coming after me. And then Dick yelled."

His eyes were solemn.

"I was scared."

Dick stared at him, then turned to Maggie.

"I waited a while with Cobus. He didn't holler, in spite of the hurt. Then we seen a couple of white men come into the clearing from the west. They went into the barn. After that I cleared out."

"What are they going to do?"

"I don't know. I want to see your Pa."

He took the candle and went into her father's room. Maggie followed and Cobus crowded close to her. Putting her hand on the little boy's shoulder, she felt that he was still blubbering to himself.

"Mister Gordon," said Dick. "You'll have to get ready to move."

Gordon woke, looked up at the three white, staring faces, and said, "All right, Dick." Then he, too, asked, "What's happened?"

Dick told him in a few words. He still spoke with the dry disbelief in his voice, as if he were half-asleep.

Gordon listened quietly.

Then he said, "All right. We'll have to go right now." He smiled weakly at them. "I'm no good. No good at all. It's up to you and Maggie, Dick. Don't hurry too fast."

"I'll hitch the team now," said Dick. "Maggie, you get everything to the door."

With Cobus tugging nobly, Maggie dragged the trunk outside. "We'll leave the loom," she said.

"Gosh," said Cobus. He was becoming interested in the proceedings. He turned to Maggie with round eyes. "Say, Maggie, do you believe Henry and George and Turp got scalped?"

"I don't know."

She could hardly think. In the barn she heard the jingle of harness and the tread of the horses coming out. She heard the tongue of the cart being put into the yoke ring.

"I'll bet they did," said Cobus. "Hess showed me how to do it once."

"Hush up," she said.

He began to sniffle again.

"My arm hurts," he said.

"Yes, I know. You're a good boy."

They made no effort now at concealment. Dick brought the cart round into the light, before the door.

"We'll have to hurry," he said.

With Maggie and Cobus struggling at one end, the three heaved the trunk into the cart. Then she and Dick went in for her father. Already he had worked his feet off the bed himself. Putting his arms over their shoulders, he stood up between them.

"Now," he said, "we'll just take it easy. And we'll go fine."

Maggie's heart swelled at his voice. He was comforting them more than anyone else could have, sick as he was.

They helped him to the tail of the cart, where he stood with his good arm bracing himself. Dick bent down behind him and caught both legs below the knees, heaved suddenly, and thrust him forward into the cart.

"Get on, Cobus," he ordered.

While Cobus climbed on, Maggie drew herself up over the wheel and turned her father on his back on top of the blankets. Dick handed her his squirrel gun and the Gordons' musket, caught up the reins, and jumped onto the seat.

For one instant he poised there, looking north towards his home.

A redness that did not belong to the moonlight was spreading slowly above the trees. As they watched, it leaped skyward, and a great cloud of sparks whirled after it.

"They've set fire to the wheat stack," Dick said dully.

"Yes," said Maggie.

"Yes," echoed Cobus.

"We'd better start," Gordon said quietly.

Dick struck the horses with the ends of the lines. Already restless over the unaccustomed hour, the sight of fire, and the smell of frost, they plunged into their collars. The cart lurched up and down on its single axle, then settled to a steady jogging. The rumble of the big wheels filled all the night.

As she sat on the floor beside her father, Maggie turned her head for a farewell sight of their own place. The buildings shone dimly in the moonlight. She picked out each; the mill, with the water silver in the little pond beside it; the barn with its log walls; the house.

They had left the candle burning in the kitchen. For a little way after the horses had trotted into the woods she saw that square of yellow light beyond the leaves.

❧ 8 ❧

FLIGHT

DRIVING with no light, they had to trust in the horses' knowledge of the road. Dick kept them at a slow trot. They had twenty miles to go, unless it happened that Adam Dingman had already started up from the Falls, and that seemed unlikely.

For the first mile the road went southeastward out of Black Creek Valley, at a slight angle to the creek; then it swung almost due south across the uplands. Here the woods dwindled into scrub growth, poplar and soft maple, and occasional ragged birch clumps. As the road became more level, the stones disappeared from the wheel tracks, and Dick pushed the horses into a faster pace.

The moon by now had sunk low in the west, lying almost on the tops of the trees, and giving them little light. There were only the stars overhead. As she sat in the bottom of the cart, Maggie could see Dick's head and shoulders, jigging past them to the motion of the cart.

Her father lay without speaking. It was impossible to tell whether he was awake or had fainted or gone once more into that deathlike coma. In any case, there was nothing that she could do.

With Cobus, it was different. The little fat boy had crept close up to her and nestled himself against her arm. At first he whimpered when a particularly hard jolt hurt his arm, and she stroked his round cheek with her free hand. Now and then she felt tears on her hand and heard him sniffling softly, and she lowered her face close to his ear and whispered, "That's a brave boy, Cobus. That's a fine brave boy."

"Yes," he said. He lifted his face suddenly and put a wet kiss on her cheek, and she was so moved that she kissed him back, bumping her nose as the cart bucketed into a pothole in the sand. He snuggled down then to hide his face in her lap, blushing, though it was too dark for anyone to see him, because he thought, "Now I've gone and kissed a girl!"

Still muttering, he fell asleep.

Along the first straight stretch, Dick screwed round, first glancing down into the box of the cart, then staring back. Looking up at his thin face, outlined darkly against the sky, Maggie tried to read his thoughts. But that was hard in the darkness, with the jiggling of the cart.

"Do you see anything, Dick?" she asked.

His face bent down.

He whispered, "I think they've set fire to your place, too."

"Oh, no!"

"I can see two lights and they look too far apart to both be on our place."

It was not that she had had any idea of their coming back to Black Creek so much as the memory of all they had had to leave behind that so dismayed her.

"Shhh! Don't let him hear."

"I'm afraid it's true, though, Maggie."

"Why?" she cried. "Why do they have to do it, Dick?"

"Why'd they have to kill George and Henry?" he asked stonily.

"Oh Dick!" After a little, when he had turned back to watch the road ahead, "Maybe they didn't kill them, Dick."

He didn't answer her.

She put Cobus carefully down beside her father and pulled herself erect, standing unsteadily, even though she grasped the side of the box with both hands.

Their progress seemed quicker when she could see the road unravelling behind the wheels, instead of the treetops against the sky; and the spot of redness in the north looked far behind them. But there was another spot now, close to the left of the first. So close, indeed, that she could hardly believe it came from their own clearing. And she said so.

Dick replied softly that if both fires were on the Mount place, the two spots, at that distance, would look like one. They must be quite a way apart, therefore, and what other place was there to be burnt?

Maggie felt that what he said was true.

It was strange to think how Mount and her father had cut this road out nearly four years ago. How everything that made their clearings home, how they themselves had traveled in along this route that they were fleeing over. The tools, the cows, the saws and mill machinery, the seeds, and, just this fall, the two stones for the gristmill. Gordon and Mount had brought them in less than two months ago; now they would never eat any of their own gristing. By this time all the wheat on Mount's place would have been burned. There would be nothing left, except in two years, maybe, raspberries would be growing in the clearings. But there would be nobody to pick raspberries.

"Dick?"

"Yes," he said.

"Do you think your Pa and Ma will be coming back?"

"I guess Adam will have seen them down in Little Falls. He'll tell them."

She moved cautiously forward so that she could lean her arms over the back of the seat.

The horses had begun to sweat. Dick eased them down to a walk for the next quarter of a mile. The slowness of the pace got on Maggie's nerves. She kept turning her head.

"Do you think it's all right to walk them so long?"

"Old Blackie's breathing too hard. I never thought he had sound wind. You can see he hasn't."

"Yes, but Dick. They might be coming after us?"

"I shouldn't wonder, if they figure out what a short start we had," he said.

She looked back for a long time. There was nothing to see except the dim straight line of the road, with its point of vanishment that steadily followed their progress.

"Twenty miles is a long way," Dick said.

Maggie did not comment again. But after a little she began to count. She would count up to a hundred slowly, she thought, then she would suggest again that the horses trot — if Dick hadn't started them by that time.

She reached a hundred, and looked up at him. It was still

hard for her to speak of it. He made her a little afraid of him, the way he sat, so set and quiet, on the seat.

"Dick," she said finally.

"Yes."

"Don't you think Blackie's rested enough now?"

He turned his head to her upturned face.

"Who's driving? You? Or me?"

She lowered her face, feeling almost as if he had struck her.

"I get so scared," she whispered.

"Do you think I ain't?" he demanded harshly. He gave a small, cracked-sounding laugh.

"I get the feeling when we walk the horses that they're close behind us."

"So do I. Maybe they are. But there's no sense breaking down the horses. *He* can't walk, you know," Dick said.

"I know, but . . ."

"If you want to drive, say so. Get up here and take the lines."

"I don't want to drive, Dick. You know a lot better than me. Honest you do."

"Well." He sounded slightly mollified. "I'll let them go again when we get through the holler."

The small heads of the team dipped down and the cart wheels whispered through deep sand. They pitched into the blackness and forded a tiny brook. They could not see the water, but they heard the horses splash through, and then the team dug into their collars and heaved up the further bank, their heads working up and down like hammers.

"All right," said Dick. He clucked his tongue and shook the reins and the team trotted willingly.

For a way there was only the tread of hoofs and the steady trundling of the big, loose wheels. The air was quite frosty.

Maggie muffled her shawl close round her neck. Her face peeped out from it, pale and appealing, beside Dick's shoulder. He was conscious of its nearness, even while he kept his eyes glued to a point between the horses' ears. He could see little enough, but he tried to look for potholes. There was one bad one, he knew from what his father had said, between the gully they had just come through and Reeber's Settlement. It had come into the sand since the last time he himself had been over the road, and he wished now mightily, that he had paid closer attention when his father mentioned it.

Maggie could only make out the willing backs of the horses, but she felt her heart warm to them. They went so honestly. Surely it seemed that they would fetch the cart through to the Mohawk.

"Dick," she said softly, "have you thought what your family's going to do?"

"No."

"You don't think they'll go back to Jerseyfield, do you?"

"Not if it's burnt. Pa'll have to go to work. They say work's hard to come by now down there." He paused. "I reckon," he added, "I'll have to go to work, too."

"I don't know what we'll do," said Maggie. "Dad won't be able to do much of anything for quite some time, I think."

"Maybe you could stay with us," he said, shyly.

"Oh, thank you, Dick. But we don't know yet what's going to be."

"No," he said moodily.

"It seems as if I was dreaming," Maggie said.

"I know. It's going to be queer not having George and Henry."

"Yes," she whispered, "Poor things."

She felt him shiver.

"What's the matter, Dick?"

His voice was painfully low.

"I just recollected about Turp," he said. "I never thought of him at all."

She caught her breath.

"Poor Turp."

"He never was any good for anything. He was even smarter than Cobus when it came to dodging work. But he never done any harm beyond taking things, and he couldn't just help that."

"Yes, I know. I heard him telling your Pa once — there were the blueberry tarts, and there was his stomach with the hunger in it just for blueberries. And his hands just did it 'fore he knew."

"Let's not talk about him, Maggie."

"All right, Dick."

They were silent for another mile, then Dick slowed down the team again.

"You'd better take a look at your Pa, hadn't you?"

When she bent down she realized how stiff she was from standing in the cold. She could not see her father, so she put her hand on his chest, lightly, feeling him breathe.

"Hello, Maggie," he said.

"You're all right, Dad?"

"Yes, but hush. The little lad's asleep."

Cobus, lying on his unhurt side, was snoring in a muffled sort of way, his nose against Gordon's coat.

"How far've we come?" Gordon whispered.

"I'll ask Dick."

Dick answered, "I don't know. I think about four miles."

"We ought to be out of reach of them, anyway," Gordon said.

"I guess so, Mister Gordon. But I'll feel better once we get past Reeber's."

"Dick!" said Maggie.

She hadn't thought of that.

Gordon agreed with Dick. "Yes, I've been thinking that's the first place Suffrenes Casselman would head for."

"Pa says that all the people there have gone," Dick said. "But Casselman wouldn't know that."

Gordon fell silent. And Maggie stood up again, to lean on the seat beside Dick.

"Dick, what will we do, if they're there?"

"I don't know yet. There's no road around we could take the cart through. Maybe they won't be there."

She felt that he was lying to her.

"You think they will, though, don't you?"

"I don't know," he said crossly. "What's the use of talking?"

She thought his voice had a teary sound, unlike himself. It made her understand how much more awful things must seem to him.

"Oh, Dick," she said, "I'll bet you'll get us through all right. I'm not worried myself at all. With you along." And she added what was the plain truth in her heart, "Just think of how it would have been for me and Dad without you to look after us."

He didn't answer; but now that the fact had occurred to her, she began to remember how she had thought of Dick as just a boy. She remembered what she had said to him that afternoon in the creek, when they were waiting for their fathers to bring home the millstones.

"Dick," she whispered. "Do you remember what I said to you once, about you being 'most a man'?"

"You didn't think I'd forget that, did you?"

It was hard to say what she wished to, and she felt her breath flutter a little.

"I'd like to say, Dick, that outside of Dad, I think you are the best man I ever heard of."

He sat quite still, as if he hadn't heard her at all. For a minute she was sure he hadn't.

"It's true," she said in a hot small voice, "the way you came around looking after us, and helped us with our wheat, and killed that pig for me. I never noticed," she said wonderingly. "I didn't think, I guess. And then the way you got us out of there tonight."

"Well," he said, in a voice that belied all her saying, "I ain't any older than I was, respecting you."

But Maggie was too convinced, too proud of him, as if she had just discovered who he was, to pay attention.

"I don't think how old a person is has anything to do with what he really is himself."

Dick spoke to the horses, because he could think of nothing to say to her.

"Don't you think I'm right, Dick?"

"I don't know. I don't see how you can talk all the time, now, anyway."

She thought he must be thinking of George and Henry, and she felt ashamed of her self-preoccupation. But with a remnant of her father's stubbornness she said, "I just wanted to tell you, Dick."

After a while, he said, "Thanks."

But she kept silence, feeling a little hurt, and feeling also that she had been wrong, and that any way he treated her now would be fair punishment.

The result was that they hit the pothole at full trot; the horses, without Dick's attention to the lines, never saw it at all, until Blackie struck the soft spot with his nigh forehoof, went down on his knees in the sand, kicked himself up with a lurch against the collar just as the wheel went down. The cart veered sickeningly over and bounced out, almost losing the wheel in the process. Cobus woke screaming under Gordon, and Dick, held on only by Maggie's instinctive grabbing of his belt to save herself, yanked the team savagely to a halt.

He didn't need to treat them roughly. Old Blackie had gone dead lame. Once he stopped, he could not set his nigh forehoof to the ground.

Dick jumped out of the cart to look him over, and Maggie, after reassuring herself about her father and Cobus, climbed down and joined him.

He was standing close to Blackie with his forehead against the horse's withers.

"How is he, Dick?"

"He's gone dead lame."

She could scarcely hear his voice.

"I don't believe he's broke his leg, but he can't use it at all."

"What will we do?" she whispered.

"I don't know."

In the cart Gordon heaved himself up to a semi-upright position, and leaned over the edge of the box.

"What's the trouble, Dick?"

"Blackie hit a sinkhole, and he's spoilt his nigh foreleg."

Her father did not comment. Dick looked miserably at him, and Maggie looked at Dick.

Little Cobus stood up on the seat and looked down at everybody. In the dark he might have been his father turned into a gnome.

"I'd call it dumb bad driving. Gosh, Dick, what was you thinking about? Or was you just plain crazy in the head?"

Dick let his temper go at last. He did not look at Maggie, as he stepped towards the cart. "You hush up right now, Cobus, or I'll *handle* you."

Cobus shrank back.

"You can't," he said. "I been hurt by Indians. You can't do that."

"You hush your mouth then."

"I will," said Cobus with unusual judiciousness.

Gordon said, "I can't get down by myself. So I'll stay here while we decide. One thing's sure, we can't take the cart. Even if Prince could handle it, there's no way to rig it to his harness in a hurry."

"I know," said Dick. "If I'd just been paying attention to

156

the road, I'd seen him go down and might have hauled him up in time."

"It was my fault," said Maggie.

He whirled on her.

"It's no use talking that way."

"No," said Gordon. "None at all. There's just one thing to do. You drag me into the bushes for a way, and I'll lay low. Then you three youngsters get on Prince and ride for all you're worth." He drew his breath. "When they find the cart and see the tracks, they'll figure out what's happened and won't look around any. You can tell Adam or anybody coming up where I am."

"I'll stay with you, Dad," said Maggie.

"You'll not."

"No," said Dick, "she'll not. And I won't go if she does stay. So there's no sense arguing, Mr. Gordon. You'll get on Prince with Cobus and Maggie and we'll light out that way. I'll tie you on. And Maggie can help steady you. Maybe it's just as well. Maybe we'll have to get round Reeber's in the woods, and then we'd have to leave the cart anyway."

Maggie said, "Yes, Dad. We couldn't leave you." It seemed to her that Dick thought everything out.

Gordon said, "You're a good lad, Dick. All right. I'll take orders. Bring Prince round here."

Dick unhitched the pair, but he left Prince's harness on. It offered Maggie and Cobus things to hang to, and it would make tying Gordon's legs easier. While Maggie held the horse's head, he helped Gordon off the cart onto the animal's back. Then he tied Gordon's knees to the bellyband and joined the ankles underneath with one of the reins.

He gave Maggie a boost up behind her father. She put her arms round his waist and took the reins.

"It's like an armchair," Gordon said. "Wait, Dick, could you hop into the cart and get my little satchel? Where is it, Maggie?"

"Right at the top of the trunk."

Dick opened the trunk and, after some fumbling, found the satchel.

"It's all the money we have in the world, Maggie. Hold it safe."

"Yes, Dad."

She passed the strap over her head and felt the weight of the bag against her side. It amounted, she knew, to nearly thirty pounds in English money.

Dick stood for a moment in the cart, staring north.

"I guess we'd better go," he said. "Look back."

Maggie wheeled the horse for her father to see also.

From one of the conical hills way back near Black Creek a fire had been lit. It seemed to rise and fall, in a thin tongue of light. First high, then low, then just a spot, like a low-lying star, then up and down. Finally it burned in one long flare, relapsed, and disappeared.

"Indian fire," Dick said. "They're signaling. I guess there's people down in Reeber's."

They took the road.

Behind them the cart stood over the ruts, its near wheel yet on the edge of the pothole. In it were all their best possessions, even to Maggie's brand new stockings. She thought of these for just an instant, realizing that she had never really worn them. Probably now it would be years before they could afford another pair. And her mother's wedding dress, the Bible, and the box of trinkets, and the locket.

"There's one thing," said Gordon. "Don't you think we ought to get rid of Blackie?"

"He can't follow us," said Dick. "His leg's no good."

"He'll try, and he'll nicker. And Prince may nicker back."

"I just couldn't do it," Dick said. "They'll probably kill him anyway. But let him have his chance."

"All right," said Gordon.

And Maggie felt better.

Prince, with that understanding all honest horses seem to have, went conscientiously, even under the unaccustomed burden of three riders. Dick walked beside his head, the musket on his arm. He had had to leave his squirrel gun in the cart.

Looking over her shoulder, Maggie saw the shadowy figure of the old black horse beside the cart. For a minute he stood still with his head lifted. Suddenly he whinnied. The sound was piercing, and to Maggie it seemed heartrending. She saw him try to limp after them.

Under her, Prince stopped; but Dick caught hold of his headstall and yanked him forward. He did not whinny back, and after a little way, none of them could hear the old horse limping.

The road appeared to be much darker, now that they went at a walking pace and did not have the racket of the traveling cart wheels in their ears. There was nothing at all to hear except Dick's footfalls, the steady tramp of the horse, the small squeaks of harness, and their own breathing.

Between her arms Maggie could feel the effort her father made to keep himself upright without throwing his weight on her, or on the little boy, who was perched ahead of him on Prince's withers. For nearly an hour he managed to hold himself up. Then, with what sounded like a sigh, he slumped between her arms.

At first it did not seem impossible to hold him, but gradually she began to feel her back aching. She had to pull tighter and tighter on the reins to keep her hands from letting go. Prince's head came up, and after another half a mile he stopped.

Dick, who had been trudging a few yards ahead, came back. "What's the matter, Maggie?"

"I just can't seem to hold Dad up any more," she answered.

"You'd better walk then. I'll get up for a while."

He jumped up behind her and she slid out through his arms as he steadied her father. She picked up the musket, and they went that way for nearly two miles more.

Then she fell back to walk beside Dick.

"What time do you think it's getting to be, Dick?"

"I don't know. I think it's getting on to five o'clock." He was watching the east. "I'd hoped we could get past Fairfield before daylight."

"Is it much farther?"

Walking, she could not see as well as he could.

"I think we're getting to it, Maggie. I guess it's about a half a mile to the top of the hill." He looked down at her. "Think you could take a spell with your Dad?"

"Yes."

Somehow Cobus was managing to keep himself on the horse, even though he slept.

Dick held Gordon on with one hand after he had dismounted and with the other made a stirrup for Maggie's bare foot.

❧ 9 ❧

DESTRUCTIVES AT REEBER'S

THEY WENT on a little way as they had before, until, without any warning, Prince's head shot up, and they reached the first downward part of the road. They knew that they were coming out above Reeber's.

In another ten minutes they reached the lip of the hill, overlooking the scattered settlement. The horse stopped instinctively.

To the east, the first faint shimmer of daylight gave an inkling of the vastness of the view; but now the length of the great valley lay in a well of darkness. Dipping into it, the road went out of sight. But a little way ahead, where Reeber's was, they saw a gathering of fires.

There must have been ten buildings burning altogether. When the fires had been at full height, they would have lit the valley for miles. By the time the two Gordons and the Mount boys came in sight of it, the timbers had all fallen in, and each house and barn was defined by masses of coals that seemed to lie in small rectangular pits. Over them smoke coiled slowly into the frosty, windless air.

Here and there among the fires, so far below as to appear like midget presences of men, were moving figures. Some rooted back and forth among the foundations of the buildings. One or two carried burning torches, like fireflies. Beside a well two or three men were drawing water, drinking.

Neither the men nor the place looked real. And yet the red glow under the smoke showed Maggie things she recognized — the fences edging the fields, the course of the road through the settlement, from darkness into darkness, an orchard, a safe shanty.

It all seemed senseless, without order, thought, or purpose. Just the red fires and the slowly moving figures. No sound, from where they stood, not even the smell of smoke.

Dick was breathing steadily, making a little rasping noise that Maggie could hear over the horse's breathing.

"They've burned everything," he announced. "They've even burned the woodpiles."

"Why do they do it?" Maggie asked.

"I don't know. It's crazy."

Maggie felt hushed.

"Dick," she whispered, "was your father sure all the people had gone away?"

"Yes. They'd all moved south," Dick said. "Fairfield will be

the next place. There are some people of the right party there, too." He let his breath out sharply. "Ain't they *never* going to send nobody up from the Falls to stop them?" And he turned to look at her, "I don't know how we can get past," he said. "How's your Pa?"

"Just the same," she answered wearily. "I'm getting so I just don't hardly feel I can go on anymore, Dick."

"You've got to." He turned back to the valley. "We can't go down the road, though. If that was a fire back of us, and they seen it, they'll be watching the road."

Maggie suddenly seemed to freeze.

"Dick! What's that they've got?"

"Where?"

"There by Reeber's house." She spoke of it as if it still stood.

Two men were prying something out of the coals with two long poles. Twice they heaved it out partway and twice it fell back with a little burst of sparks.

"You see," she said in a tightening voice. She felt ready to scream. "It's two legs."

Dick stared, as pale as she was. "I see it." There were always Indian stories. Then all at once he could tell and, he said, "It's a cow! They're roasting a cow, Maggie." And when she burst out crying, he felt the sobs climbing his own throat. It was almost funny, wanting to cry.

Yet because of the thought that they had first had, they were spellbound by the sight. One of the men who had helped drag the charred carcass out now blew a whistle. The note, so distant, was eerie-thin, with a brightness and clearness that suggested the silver that formed it.

The men left off their rummaging of the fires. Others trooped into the zone of light from south and north, where, obviously, they had been watching the road. They gathered round the carcass, worked on it with their knives, and then sat down together, in a fraternal kind of ring, like people gathered at a picnic.

"Come on," said Dick. "This is the best chance we've got."

He took hold of Prince's bridle and led him down the road. When they came to the first pasture he pulled the rails down and turned into it, skirting the woods.

They seemed to be going down into the valley in steps, of which the pasture land and fields were the treads, and the risers were marked by strips of woodland. On the lower edge of each piece of woods they halted while Dick went ahead and scouted the next field.

To Maggie, left alone in the darkness with the horse, her father, and the little boy, hours seemed to pass each time before he returned. Her ears quickened to hear his steps, her eyes to see the first vague silhouette of his head along the fence.

When they finally reached the level of the settlement, he

left her for a much longer time in a large grove of trees. At first she did not know where she was, then it came to her that this was Moyer's sugarbush and that she was not over three hundred yards from where the schoolhouse used to stand.

This time she did not see or hear Dick's return.

He said, "Maggie, it's me," in a low voice and then slipped up to the horse.

"I must have been bearing eastward without knowing it," he said. "I think we've got too close to move. I've been out to the road, and there's a man just come outside. He's standing just beyond the fence there now. He'd hear us sure if we moved."

"What will we do, Dick?"

"We've got to stay, that's all. You might as well get off, Maggie."

"What'll we do with Dad?"

"We'll have to leave him on. It would be too much of a job to get him up again. But we'll take Cobus off."

When he reached up for his brother, the little fat boy gave a murmuring teary sound. Dick clapped his hand over his mouth, and whispered in his ear.

Maggie felt herself turn cold, as a man's voice said incredibly near by:

"Did you hear that?"

"No," answered a second man. "What did it sound like?"

"Like something crying."

"You've got notions. Most likely it was just a cat owl."

"Maybe it was."

There was another pause.

The second man then said, "You might as well go back and get you something to eat. The old cow's tough, but she's tastier than hedgehog."

"Suffrenes told me to stay on the road."

"He won't know. The Indian's down below you, anyway. Come along."

It had sounded like Murray's voice. Maggie held her breath to listen. She heard their feet tread back along the road, then as they went, she felt sure it was he. He began to whistle:

> 'Twixt the water and the willow tree
> There stood. . . .

The second man swore. "Can't you learn no other tune?"
Murray laughed easily.

Even in the pitch-dark, Maggie felt Dick's eyes on her. But she could not keep herself from bending forward and starting to cry. She did not make any sound, but in her complete exhaustion of heart and body, it seemed to her that she cried for everybody. For her father, on the looming figure of the horse; he had tilted forward on the neck of the beast, and lay there unmoving. For little Cobus, with his hurt arm; for George and Henry, and the little black Turp. For their two homes and all the people of Reeber's Settlement. For herself and David Murray, and even for old Blackie.

And after a minute, when she felt Dick put his hand on her shoulder in a tense, shy way, she cried for him, more than anyone. Dick did not say a word; but she put up her hand to catch his, and clung to it.

The horse stood still, as if he understood as well as they did the necessity for being quiet. Over their heads the branches of the old maples gradually took dim shape against the sunrise.

It was nearly half an hour after they had discovered their whereabouts when they heard a whistle blow from the settlement.

Dick went away, then, but he returned shortly to say that a

party had come in from the Jerseyfield road. "They're standing round Casselman, talking. I guess they've heard about us."

Maggie said nothing. She had gained control of herself
finally. While they stood listening, trying to hear what was
happening beyond the trees, they heard a man running swiftly
from the south. They had one glimpse of him in the half-light,
an Indian, in leggings and skirt. They could see the blotches
of paint on his face and the feather dangling from the wooden
hoop round his head.

In a few minutes more they heard the whistle again. Three
sharp blasts of it.

"I'm going out again to see," Dick whispered.

He slid silently away, trailing the musket. Maggie could
make him out now in the gradual lightening among the old
trees. His back bent tensely. He looked so thin.

As the light gathered, she heard him call her softly, and she
stole forward to the edge of the sugarbush.

"They're going, Maggie."

She was surprised to see how light it had become beyond the
trees. There was the promise of a fine day in the sky. The
fields lay before them under a heavy wash of dew. A little
beyond, on the other side of the road, where the settlement
used to stand, there was nothing at all to see except the two
upright posts from which the school bell still hung. The
school itself had burned to the ground.

Dick was pointing.

"There they go," he said.

Maggie saw them, a knot of twenty men or so, she could not
tell how many. They were heading north, up the Jerseyfield
road her father and Mount had made. They kept close together. Now and then one would look back. They had their
rifles on their shoulders or cradled in their arms, or they

carried them at trail. Their hunting shirts were blackened with soot and smoke. A little ahead of them two or three men carried blankets over their bare shoulders. One or two of them had feathers on their heads. The feathers hung limply over their ears. At the very rear, half a hundred yards behind them all, a lanky man with broad round shoulders walked. It was he who turned back oftenest.

"I guess that's Casselman," Dick said. He lifted the musket to his shoulder and took a bead on the figure. "Gosh," he said. "I wish I dasted."

He was glad that he hadn't just a minute later, for a stout, half-naked Indian trotted paunchily out of the woods a little above them, entered the road, and overtook Casselman. He did not wear a feather, but an old black hat with a pointed crown. He and Casselman stood together, looking back on Reeber's. For an instant they were still in the rising light, and Maggie saw the white man's eyes move, with the light across them, so that they seemed opaque, and gray, like blind eyes. She saw his thin mouth move. Then he turned with Hess and followed the others.

As the sun warmed over the fields, the road lay empty. Only the woods rose up and up in their long slopes towards Jersey-field.

Dick set the musket down. "They've gone," he said.

They had not made a sound, their flight seemed as senseless as the burning had been.

"They've got a long march to Canada," said Dick.

More than a hundred miles, however they went. Probably to Oswego, he thought.

Maggie turned her white face to his. Her hair was wet with dew, her cheeks smutted from crying. Her eyes stared almost foolishly.

"Why did they go, do you think, Dick?"

He laughed a little.

"I guess somebody's coming up at last."

Both their voices sounded queer, singing in their ears. They walked a little dizzily back to the horse, found Cobus sitting on the ground, examining his bandage; Gordon lying forward on the horse's neck, his eyes open.

They led the horse out to the road, and took Gordon down. They laid him on the ground. He could not move or speak, but he smiled at them both.

"Dick says there's men coming up the road," said Maggie, as if because Dick had said it, it was true.

The men did come.

There were thirty of them, behind Adam Dingman and a man in a brown coat with white belts crossed over his chest. His name was Ensign Petrie, from German Flats. He was the only man in uniform. The other men wore farming clothes; but they carried their guns like people who knew how to use them.

At the rear came George Mount in his cart. He had left his wife behind. He stared at Dick and then at the blackened heaps of smoldering coals, as if he didn't understand.

"Where's George and Henry and Turp?" he asked.

Dick said he didn't know. He expected they were dead.

"What did you leave them for?" demanded George. "What's the matter with Rob?"

Little Cobus looked his father in the eye. "He's sick as all get out," he said. "But I got shot."

Adam Dingman stared into Dick's drawn white face. He glanced at Maggie and her father. Maggie felt that he understood everything that had happened.

"You must have done a pretty good job, Dick," he said.

Maggie looked at Dick. All the men were looking at him. Most of them were farmers. There was a kind of heaviness in their faces, their eyes looked sleepy still, and as if they did not believe the things before them.

But one thin, ratty, black-eyed man behind Adam said, "That's right, son. Do you know who they was?"

"Casselman," answered Dick. "And Hess and Cataroque. At our place. They're the only ones I knowed."

Maggie moistened her lips.

"There was one I knew called David Murray," she said. "And a man named Ike."

The ratty man turned quickly to her.

"What did he look like? Kind of a measly, thinnish man like me?"

"He did look something like you. He had a bad eye."

"That's Ike all right. Ike Bonny." He cursed the man. "Excuse me, Missy. He's my brother."

Dick said wearily, "They all cleared north a little while afore you got here."

"We'll go after them," said Adam. "Put Gordon in Mount's cart with the girl and the boys and send them all home in it. We'll go on."

"I want to take my cart," said George. "I want to bring out stuff."

"What do you expect to find there?" Adam asked him.

A dullness came over George Mount's eyes, and his face twitched.

"I hadn't thought. I guess you're right."

The ensign then detailed two men to drive the refugees back to the Falls.

❧ 10 ❧

LITTLE FALLS

THEY DIDN'T REACH the Falls till afternoon. On the way they passed through Fairfield; but none of the farms had people on them. An air of desolation hung over the country; the houses were ghosts of houses, with their windows shuttered like blind eyes. A lone abandoned gander, walking from behind a barn to hiss at them, was like a ghostly bird.

But at Snyder's Bush people came out to see them and ask frightened questions; and as they heard the story a half-incredulous and almost hostile expression showed in their eyes, as if they blamed the Mounts and Gordons for this new fear. Several turned to glance at the new stockade fort they had built. It gave the settlement solidity. It had seemed to promise safety and permanence. But now that the Mount boys had been killed and the settlers had left Reeber's and come in from Fairfield, the people at Snyder's Bush saw that they had become the last outpost north of the Valley. The wilderness had moved suddenly much closer to them. The stockade was all they had between them and the Indians now and it no longer looked so strong.

The sky became overcast as the cart moved over the last long hills and headed downwards towards the Falls. A cold wind that had begun blowing from the west tossed the horses' manes forward about their faces and tugged at Maggie's skirt as she stood behind the seat.

She felt her spirits rising. They had already passed three carts along the way, and now there came two small boys driving a calf. The boys stopped to stare at them, mute and curious, and the calf chose that instant to jump into the woods. Maggie did not mind the boys' staring. It was so wonderful to be traveling where people passed you. Only those who have lived at the end of a long road know what loneliness is. Even in the next house to the last, one can look out and see a person passing once in a while. Here, though few houses were immediately in sight, Maggie had the feeling of people living all around. It was to her a settled country.

The cart went creaking down until the wind no longer blew on her, but was a voice above her head. Then, beyond the trees, the noise of the river tumbling on the Falls became audible, and presently their road turned into the broader highway that was called the Kingsroad and ran all the way to Albany.

Now Dick pointed out the mill to her, and they saw a huge wagon drawn by four horses. One of the militiamen said it was a military wagon and would be hauling flour for the Continental Army. It moved down the carrying road beside the Falls, the wheels chained to help the horses hold back; yet even so, they ended galloping.

Maggie glanced at Dick and saw him follow the departing wagon with shining eyes. "He wants to go, too," she thought, and she wondered what would become of them. . . .

Mrs. Mount was staying at Frank's Tavern, but there was no room for Maggie and her father. The house was filled to the last inch, for the garrison of soldiers guarding the carrying place were quartered there. Conrad Frank, the proprietor, said that Dick and Cobus could make themselves comfortable in the haymow of the tavern barn; but he explained that, even if room could be made for the Gordons, it would not be a good place for a sick man, with all the daytime noise and sometimes people rousing the house at night. He thought, however, that some people named Eyseman had extra room in their house and would probably take the Gordons in.

The Eysemans did. They were elderly people, living on a small place back from the Kingsroad, above the Falls and on the edge of the Burnetsfield Patent. They said they had two rooms the Gordons were welcome to use. Maggie soon found out that these rooms had belonged to the Eysemans' two sons, one of whom had been killed in the battle of Oriskany and the other lost.

"I hope he was killed," Mrs. Eyseman said. "I wouldn't want him captivated by the Indians. I've heard some things they did to our people there."

She was a frail woman, with white hair and stilled blue eyes that looked at Maggie without seeming to see her. She often appeared to go into a kind of trance, as if she lived entirely in her thoughts; and yet it was she who, once Gordon had been got to bed, suggested that Mr. Eyseman go fetch Dr. Petry from German Flats.

The doctor came next morning, riding up the road along the brook on an old white horse. He did not hold the reins. It looked more as if the horse were fetching Dr. Petry.

The doctor grumbled to himself as he examined Gordon, asking questions now and then of Maggie over his shoulder. He finally told Gordon that he would probably get well; but once outside the room, he took Maggie's arm and led her out of earshot.

"I do not know," he said, shaking his head slowly. "But he must not be disturbed."

"Do you think he's going to die?" Maggie asked after a moment.

"I do not know," the doctor repeated almost harshly. "How can I tell? He must stay quiet a long time."

He named his fee of fifty cents for the eight-mile ride he had made and went on to Frank's to see to Cobus's arm. He also had a scalp case over the river, Mrs. Eyseman explained.

"But you must stay as long as you want," she said to Maggie. "You must not worry. It's nice to have a young person in the house again."

Dick walked up to the Eyseman place on the second day, and when Maggie saw him coming along the road, she ran out to meet him. She had seldom felt so happy at seeing anyone; his presence there helped to take away her sense of being a stranger in a strange community, and a wave of shyness went over her when she saw that he had some of the same gladness. For a moment they just stood mutely looking at each other, while the cloud shadows passed over them and raced away across the hills beyond the river.

He asked for Gordon then, and when she told him what Dr. Petry had said, he was silent again for a long time. She didn't interrupt his thinking. She was glad just to have him there. And then he said, "Pa's got back."

"Oh, Dick . . ." She was suddenly unable to continue her question.

He nodded. George and Henry were dead.

He waited a moment before going on in a dry, matter-of-fact voice.

All the militia had found was ruins, he said. Everything was burned to ashes — mills, barns, houses. The cow was dead. There wasn't anything. Even lame Blackie had been tracked into the bushes and killed, and the cart had been burned in the road. It was as if the destructives, as the militiamen spoke of them, had set out to obliterate every last human vestige north of Fairfield. And they themselves, of course, had had too great a start to be overtaken.

George and Henry, Dick said, after another pause, had been scalped and hatcheted outside the barn. When the militia got there that was all they saw, but a few minutes later they had found Turp hiding on the edge of the woods. The Indians hadn't harmed him and when they were busy burning down the buildings, he had just slipped off into the woods and hidden himself. The reason was, Dick explained, that a Negro's hair wouldn't fetch any money from the King's High Governor of Canada.

George Mount had sworn he would never go back there to live.

"Pa's through," Dick said. "He wants to get away. He's going back to New Jersey. I came up to see if you'd come and say good-bye to Ma. She'd like it."

"Oh," said Maggie. "When are you starting?"

"Pa says tomorrow."

She couldn't take it in. "Tomorrow?" she repeated. She had expected the Mounts would settle somewhere else. She had never thought of their going all the way back to the Jerseys.

"If you'll wait a minute, Dick, I'll tell Dad where I'm going and I'll come with you now."

All the way down to the Kingsroad and then along the river to the Falls, she felt a strange, lost feeling growing in her. She felt obliged to hide it by talking, and she tried to imagine how nice it would be for them in New Jersey. He made it hard for her; he did not answer or even appear to hear. And suddenly, as they came opposite the rapids under the upper fall, he stopped short.

"I'm not going with them," he said.

"Stay?" she cried.

"Yes. I told Pa I wasn't going with him."

"But didn't he object?"

"Yes," Dick said quietly. "But it didn't do any good." She drew a long breath and stood utterly still, with the roar of the broken river rising up all around her in wave after wave of confused sound. But suddenly she realized that she was seeing Dick clearer than she ever had before. It was as if he had suddenly grown past her, and she was proud. "Dick," she said, letting the pride show in her eyes.

"I've been talking to Adam Dingman," he went on. "Adam thinks maybe I can get to join the rangers. They haven't many who know the north side of the Valley and the Creeks. I'd be on his patrol, if I got in. And they pay fifty-three shillings a month — York money."

"That would be wonderful," she said, but she looked down, thinking of the long patrols. He seemed so young, compared to Adam. And then she realized that being young had little to do with it; they'd gone past the time when they were young.

When she looked up again, she found him watching her.

"Dick," she asked, "do you want to go back to Jerseyfield?"

"I don't know if I want to go back there. There's better farming land. But I don't want to get chased away from here. If everybody started clearing out, pretty soon it wouldn't be safe even in Jersey. I want to stick around until it's safe for even kids like George and Henry to be left alone on any farm that's mine or anybody else's."

"That's what I want, too," Maggie said.

She knew it was true. Even if Gordon died, she knew she would stay in the Valley. And she felt in her heart that when the war was over, Dick would still be close to her, as he was now.

TWO LOGS CROSSING

NOBODY in High Falls had ever put much stock in the Haskell family. They were poor, even in a backwoods settlement like High Falls, where living came hard. People said that the Haskells were shiftless. "They don't get anywhere," they said. Charley Haskell had never stuck to anything, and now it looked as if his son, John, was going to turn out the same way.

He was getting tall for his age. He had outgrown his shirt and his hair needed cutting, but now, as he came along the village road with a string of trout slapping against his bare legs, it didn't occur to him that people might disapprove of him. He had been up the Moose River for two days, fishing the runs below the clefts, and the fish in his string were big ones. When he noticed the people eyeing him, he thought it was because they felt envious of anybody who could bring in fish that size, and he let them slap a little harder against his legs as he approached the store.

There wasn't anything to take him into the store, so he kept on towards home, figuring that he would get there in time for his mother to use some of the fish for dinner. He passed the last house and then the road began to peter out until it was no more than a track in the grass along the riverbank.

The Haskell place stood at the end of it, and the house and barn had a kind of miserable, tumbledown look, even for a poor town like High Falls. About their only advantage was that you could see over the river from the yard between them to Judge Doane's place — if that was an advantage when the roof leaked and the pig fence broke and let the pig into the woods. But John didn't take notice of the looks of the place. His two sisters were on the porch as he came up and he held up his fish for them to see, and when Lissa, who was the next oldest to him, said their mother had been wondering when he would get back, he hung his pole under the porch roof and went inside to the kitchen where their mother was getting dinner.

The brush had been allowed to grow close up to the windows, so the kitchen was kind of a dark room, but with the fire going it seemed all right to John, and he was glad to be home. He slapped the fish on the board beside the dishpan and said that the biggest would go all of three pounds. His mother said they were fine fish and called Lissa in to help fix them.

Lissa kept swinging one or other of her braids back over her shoulder to keep it out of the way. She was getting almost womanish-looking, John thought, as he sat down beside the table to watch her and their mother cook dinner. Then his brothers came piling into the house to see his fish and ask questions of where he'd got them. Morris said he wanted to be taken along next time, and John said he would take him when he got big enough to walk the ten miles in without sitting down to rest every ten minutes, just the way John's father used to tell him when he was Morris's age.

Then his younger sister, Mary, brought in a load of wood in her plump arms and dumped it in the wood box, and Nat, the baby, woke up and started yelling in the ground floor bedroom, and the cat came out of the bedroom with his tail up, and walked through the kitchen without even noticing the fish and went outdoors, probably looking for a quiet place where he could sleep.

Sitting there with all this business going on around him, John thought his father must have felt the same way at times. It gave him a pleased feeling, like being the head of the family. And then he noticed that his mother was watching him over the heads of the others, and he had a disturbed idea that there was something she expected of him.

"John," she said. "After dinner I want to have a talk with you."

When Charley Haskell had died that spring, he had left his

widow with six children, the four-room house and the rickety barn, the old cow, and a dollar owing from Judge Doane for the sale of a calf.

Mrs. Haskell was a plain, honest, and fairly easygoing woman. She worked hard enough in the house to keep it and the children's clothes pretty clean, but for outside things she had depended on her husband. And for a few weeks after his death, she had gone on in her old way, letting things ride. But now she had seen that wasn't going to be enough for the family to get along on, and when John came back she knew she would have to have a talk with him.

John was the oldest boy. Morris, who was seven, was the next. In between were the two girls. Mrs. Haskell told John, therefore, that it was up to him to take his father's place towards his brothers and sisters. They looked to him for support, she said, and she depended on him. Then she kissed him a little tearfully, wiped her cheeks with her apron, and took up her existence again exactly where she had left it off when her husband died — as if by a few words she had settled it in the accustomed grooves for an indefinite time.

The sight of her unexpected tears, however, sobered John. He went out of the kitchen and stood a while on the porch. He looked up at his fishing pole once, and then he looked across the yard, where the brown hen and her chickens were picking around in the pigweed, and then he had the idea of going out to look at the cornpatch.

He found it full of weeds. It was an unusual thing for him to get the hoe without being told to, but he did, and after he had cleaned the first row, he found that it looked much better when you could see the corn.

By the time he came in to supper that night, he had a quarter of the field hoed. He called his mother and sisters out to see what he had done and listened with pride as they said it looked nice.

It was while his mother was looking at the corn that she remembered that they had never collected the dollar from the Judge for the calf. She told John that he had better get it that evening.

John said quickly, "I couldn't do that, Ma."

But Mrs. Haskell said he would have to.

"You're the man of the family now," she said. "You've got to tend to the business."

John was frightened at the idea of going to the Judge's house. In 1830, compared to the small houses in the village, the Judge's big stone house across the river was like a palace. John, for one, had never seen the inside of it, but he had seen the lace curtains in the windows and the oil lamps when he went by at night — two or even three of them in the same room, for Judge Doane was the great man of the district. He owned a vast amount of timberland and held mortgages on most of the farms and had been a representative of the county.

John's mother had brushed his coat for him, but even so it looked very shabby and frayed and outgrown as he knocked on the front door and asked the hired girl if he could see the Judge. He had the feeling that it was an impertinence to ask a person like the Judge to pay a dollar, even when he owed it to you. He thought that probably the Judge would have him thrown out of the house. But his mother had said they needed the dollar for flour and that at least he had to try to get it.

The hired girl left John standing in a front hall that was big enough to put half of the Haskells' house into entire and disappeared down a long passage towards the back. After a while, though, she came back for him, led him to the Judge's office, opened the door, and closed it behind him. John stood with his back to it, holding his hat in both hands, a lanky, overgrown boy, with a thin, rather pale face, and brown frightened eyes. Compared to the Judge, he looked like someone made of splinters.

The Judge's eyes looked cold under the heavy black brows, and he regarded John for a full minute before he said, "Hello, John. What do you want with me?"

But his voice sounded not unfriendly, so John managed, after a couple of attempts, to say that he had come for the dollar for the calf.

"Oh yes," said the Judge. "I'd forgotten about that. I'm sorry."

He heaved himself up from his leather armchair and went to his writing desk and took one end of his gold watch chain from the pocket of his well-filled, speckled waistcoat, and unlocked a drawer. While his back was turned, John was able to see the room, with the impressive lace on the curtains of the windows, the silver plate hung on the chimney piece, and the fire on the hearth, where the Judge burned wood just for the sake of seeing it burn.

The Judge relocked the drawer, replaced the key in his pocket, and handed John a dollar bill. He was a heavy man, and standing close like that, he seemed to loom over John, but in a moment he went back to his chair and told the boy to sit down for a minute. John did so, on the edge of the nearest chair.

"How are you making out?" asked the Judge.

"All right, I guess," answered John. "I wouldn't have bothered you for this, only we had to have it for flour."

"That's all right," said the Judge slowly. "I should have remembered it. I didn't think of it because your father owed me money anyway."

"I didn't know that," said John. He couldn't think of anything to say. He only looked at the Judge and wondered how his father had had the nerve to borrow money from a man like him.

The Judge made an impressive figure before his fire. He was a massive man, with a red face, strong white hair, and uncompromising light-blue eyes. He was looking at John, too, rather curiously.

He nodded, after a while, and said, "He owed me forty dollars."

That was what John had wanted to know, but he was so shocked at the amount of it, that all he could do was to repeat, "I didn't know that, sir."

"No," said the Judge, "probably not. He was a kind of cousin of my wife's but we neither of us said much about it. And after Mrs. Doane died he didn't come around much." His brows drew bushily together and he stared into the fire. "How old are you, son?" he asked.

John replied that he was sixteen.

The Judge went on to ask about the family, the age of each child, and what Charley Haskell had got planted that spring. John answered all the questions and as he did he felt a little more confidence. It seemed odd that anyone living in the High Falls settlement could know so little about anyone else. Why, he knew a lot more about the Judge than the Judge did about him. He told how high the corn stood. He said, "It stands as high as any I've seen around here, excepting yours, Judge. And now I've started looking out for it, maybe it will catch up."

The Judge said, "Hoeing is the best garden fertilizer in the world. And sweat is the next best thing to money."

"Yes, sir," said John. It made him feel proud that he had hoed so much of his corn that day. Tomorrow he'd really get after the piece.

"You can't live on potatoes and corn, though," said the Judge. "What are you going to do?"

John was awed to be talking so familiarly to a man half the town was scared of; a man, it was said, who had even talked out in legislature down in Albany. But his face wrinkled and he managed to grin.

"Work, I guess, sir."

The Judge grunted then, and stood up and dropped his quid into the sandbox.

"You do that and you'll take care of your family all right. Maybe you'll even pay back the forty dollars your father owed me." He held out his hand, which John hardly dared to take. "When do you suppose that'll be?"

John got white.

"I don't know, sir."

The Judge smiled.

"I like that a lot better than easy promises, John."

He walked beside John into the hall, his meaty hand on John's shoulder.

"Good luck to you," he said from the front door.

During the summer John managed to get work from time to time, hiring out for as much as forty cents a day, sometimes as often as three days a week. At first he didn't have much luck getting jobs, for though he was a good deal stronger than he appeared to be, and worked hard, people remembered his father's prejudice against work and preferred getting other help when they could. Besides, in the eighteen thirties, there weren't many people in High Falls who could afford to hire help, even at forty cents a day. So, by working in the evenings and on Sundays also, John had ample time to take care of their corn and potatoes and the garden truck he had planted late.

It used to puzzle him how his father had ever been able to take life so easily. He himself hardly ever found time to go fishing that summer. And once or twice when he did have the time, he thought of the forty dollars he owed Judge Doane and he went out and looked for work instead. He even found occasional jobs at Greig, five miles up the river, and walked back and forth every morning and evening.

Little by little, the forty dollars became an obsession with John, and while at first he had given all his earnings to his mother to spend, he now began to save out a few pennies here and there. When, at the end of August, he had saved out his first complete dollar and held it all at once in his hand, he realized that some day he might pay off the debt; and from there his mind went further, and he began to see that it was even possible that some day he would be able to build a decent house for his mother. Perhaps he'd have his own place, too, and get married; and when the settlement became a town, as they said it would, perhaps he might even get elected to the town board.

By the middle of October, John had saved up enough money to see the family through the winter, as he calculated it, for besides his secret bit, he had persuaded his mother to lay by some of what he gave her. Further, she had been moved by the sight of a decent garden to preserve some beans and also some berries that the girls had gathered, especially since it was the first time in several years that she had felt able to buy sugar ahead of the immediate demand. The potato piece had yielded forty bushels of potatoes; and the corn, which John had sold, had brought in a few dollars more.

The day before he finished cutting the winter wood supply, John counted up his money and decided he would make the first payment on the forty-dollar debt to the Judge that night. It amounted to five dollars, even, but to John that seemed a great deal.

He went up to the big house when he felt sure that the Judge would have finished his supper; and he had the same business of knocking and waiting in the hall while the hired girl took his name in. He found the Judge sitting as he had found him the first time, only the fire was about two logs bigger.

"Sit down, John," said the Judge, "and tell me what I can do for you."

John obviously did not know how to begin his business properly, so, after watching him under his brows for a moment, the Judge continued in his gruff voice, "I may as well tell you I've kind of kept my eye on you this summer, John. I like the way you've taken hold. I'm willing to admit, too, that I was surprised. And I'll be glad to help you out."

John flushed right up to his hair.

"I didn't come to ask for anything, Judge." He fished in his pocket and pulled out his coins. His hands were stiffly clumsy. Some of the coins fell to the floor and one rolled musically all the way under the desk. As he went on his knees to retrieve it, John wished he had had the sense to tie them together, instead of jingling them loosely in his pocket all the way up. He couldn't bear to look at the Judge when he handed him the coins.

The boy said, "I wanted to pay something back on that forty dollars, sir. It's only five dollars, even." The Judge cupped his two hands. "Maybe you'd better count it, sir." But it didn't look like so much in the Judge's hands.

The Judge, however, said, "Quite right, John," and counted up the money. Then he went to his desk, put the money in a drawer, and wrote out a receipt, which he gave to John.

"Yes, sir," said John, wondering what it was.

The Judge looked grave.

"That's a receipt, John. It says you've paid me back five dollars."

John wondered.

"Why," he said, "it's kind of like money, ain't it?"

"In a way," said the Judge, shaking hands. "What are you going to do this winter, John?"

"I don't know, sir. I tried to get a job from Brown at the hotel, splitting firewood, but he's hired Ance instead. Mr. Freel's got all the help he needs at the tannery." Those were about the only winter jobs a man could hope to find in High Falls.

The Judge nodded, and said, "I'd offer you something, if it didn't mean getting rid of someone else, John. I couldn't rightly do that."

"No, sir," John said, and started home.

But somehow, he felt so happy all the way home that when he reached the house and found his mother sitting up in the kitchen, he couldn't help telling her the whole business. He blurted it all out, the way he had saved a little now and then until he had actually got five dollars. And then he showed her the receipt.

His mother didn't say a word as she looked at the receipt, but her head gradually bent farther and farther forward and all at once she started crying. John could not understand at first. He thought it might be because she was happy. But she did not cry like a happy person. Finally she lifted her face to him.

"Oh, John, why did you do that?"

"I wanted to pay off that debt Pa laid up," he said, uneasily. "Ain't that all right?"

"I guess it is, John. But why didn't you tell me first?"

"I kind of wanted to surprise you," he mumbled. "I didn't mean for to make you feel bad, Ma."

"It ain't that, John."

"But ain't I give you enough?"

"I didn't tell you either," she said, almost smiling. Then she started crying again. "I'm going to have another baby, John. And I was so proud of you, I didn't say."

"Baby," said John. "Gee, Ma, I didn't know."

She went right on crying.

"But ain't we got enough?" he demanded.

"Oh, yes. You've done fine, John. But the way you've been working has made me feel kind of better. I got to thinking people talked to us different now. I never thought about that before. Sure," she went on, lifting her face. "I'll be all right now. Only when you showed me that about the five dollars, it made me think I could have had a baby that wasn't on the town. I've never had. I don't want to say anything against your father, I loved him. But I never realized before what it would be like to have a baby not on the town. You see," she finished, quite dry-eyed, now, "five dollars would have paid Dr. Slocum and Mrs. Legrand. Two for him and three for her."

Even so, John did not quite understand his mother, except to see that he had taken something desperately precious from her.

As he thought it over during the next two or three days, John felt all torn up in his chest. He began to see that by starting to be respectable, he had done more than just work for himself. He had done something to his mother, too. And now, by paying back the Judge that extra money, he had put her back where she used to be. It did not seem logical, but that was how it was.

Perhaps he would have fallen back then and there to his old ways of letting the world slide, if he hadn't met Seth one evening at the blacksmith's where he had gone to get the big cook kettle mended. Seth was having Jorgen do some work on a few of his beaver traps.

Seth was an Indian. In summer he worked in the sawmills, when it occurred to him to do so, but in the winter he went into the North woods. People distrusted Seth. They did not like the way he smelled. Even in the forge you could smell him, greasy-sweet, through his thick tobacco smoke.

Seth said he was planning to go north in about two weeks.

He was late, but the winter looked slow. He thought the furs would be coming up pretty quick, though. Better than last year. Last year he had cleared only two hundred dollars.

Two hundred dollars, thought John. He wondered how a man like Seth could spend all that. All he knew was that the Indian took it to Utica every spring. He supposed there were places in such a big town that an Indian could go to. Two hundred dollars.

He turned shyly to the Indian.

"How much does a man need to get traps and food for the winter?" he asked.

The Indian turned his brown face. He wasn't amused, or he did not show it if he was.

"Seventy-five dollar, maybe. You got a gun?"

John nodded.

"Seventy-five dollars," he thought. He knew only one person who could stake him that much.

The Indian asked, "You going?"

"Maybe," said John.

"You come wit' me. Good range over mine. Plenty room us both. I help you make a cabin."

"I'll see."

It was almost ten-thirty at night when John reached the Judge's house. He had made up his mind he would ask the Judge, if there was a downstairs light still on when he got there. If not, he wouldn't.

The house was dark on the town side, but when John went round to the office window, his heart contracted to see that the Judge was still up. He tapped on the window. The Judge did not start. He got slowly up and came to the window and opened it to the frosty night. When he saw the boy's white face and large eyes, he said harshly, "What do you want?"

"Please, Judge," said John, "could I talk to you?"

"It's late," said the Judge, staring with his cold blue eyes, for a while. Then he shut the window, and presently opened the front door. He was looking a little less threatening by then, but he wasn't looking friendly.

"Be as quick as you can," he said, when they were back in the office.

John was as white as a person could be. His tongue stuttered.

"I — I wanted to ask you something, Judge. But if you don't like it, say so plain. It's about me and getting to trap this winter on account of that five dollars I paid you." He couldn't think decently straight.

The Judge barked at him.

"Talk plain, boy. Begin at the beginning. What's the five dollars got to do with it?"

John began to talk. He repeated what had happened with his mother, how she felt, how odd it seemed to him, but there it was. The Judge began to sit less stiffly. He even nodded. "Women are the limit," he observed. "You want to take back that money?"

"No, no, *I* don't," John said desperately. "But people don't like giving me work yet, and I want Ma to feel respectable. I thought if you could make me a stake to go trapping — "

"How much?"

"Seth said seventy-five dollars," the boy almost whispered. "But I guess I could get along with fifty. I'd get the traps and some powder and ball, and I could go light on the food. I don't eat a great lot and I'm a handy shot, Judge."

"Seventy-five dollars," said the Judge. "You're asking me to lend that much to a boy, just like that?"

His red face was particularly heavy-looking.

"I'd make it on fifty," said John. "But it was just an idea. If you don't think it's all right, I won't bother you anymore."

"Then you want the five back, too, I suppose — makes it forty again. Forty and seventy-five is a hundred and fifteen dollars."

"It would be ninety dollars, wouldn't it, if you give me fifty?"

"Shut up," barked the Judge. "If I'm going to stake you, I'll do it so I'll have a chance of getting my money back. It won't pay me to send you in with so little you'll starve to death before spring, will it?"

John could only gape.

"How about this Seth?" asked the Judge. "He's a drunken brute. Can you trust him?"

"I've met him in the woods," said John. "He's always been nice to me."

The Judge grumbled. He rose and took five dollars from his desk and gave it to John.

"You bring me back that receipt tomorrow night," was all he said.

When John gave the money to his mother it made her so happy that he felt wicked to feel so miserable himself. It seemed as if all his summer's work had been burned with one spark. And he was frightened to go next night to the Judge's house. But he went.

The Judge only kept him a moment.

He took the receipt and gave John another paper.

"Put a cross in the right-hand bottom corner," he directed; and when John had done so, "That is a receipt for seventy-five dollars. Here's the money. Don't lose it going home."

He walked to the door with John and shook hands.

"Good luck. Come here next spring as soon as you get back."

"Thanks," was all John could say.

The Judge made a harsh noise in his throat and fished a chew from his pocket.

"Good-bye," he said.

John got Seth to help select his outfit. The Indian enjoyed doing that. And John felt so proud over his new traps, his powder flask and bullet pouch, and his big basket of provisions, and he felt so grateful to the Indian that he offered to buy him a drink out of the two-shilling bit he had left.

"No drink," said the Indian. "Next spring, oh yes."

He shared his canoe with John up the Moose River and they spent two weeks getting into Seth's range. They dumped his stuff in the little log cabin and moved over the range together to the one Seth had selected for John. There they laid up a small cabin, just like the Indian's, and built a chimney. They had trouble finding clay to seal the cracks, for by then the frost was hard and snow coming regularly each afternoon.

Then Seth took John with him while he laid out his own lines, and after two days went with John, showing him what to start on. After that the Indian spent all his spare time making John snowshoes. He finished them just before the first heavy snow.

John learned a great deal from Seth that fall. First of all he learned that an Indian in the woods is a very different person from an Indian imitating white men. He had always liked Seth, but he had never suspected his generosity and good humor.

Seth seemed to understand how lonely it could get for a boy

living by himself, and during the entire winter he never failed to pay John a weekly visit and ask him back to his cabin in return.

John never figured out which was the best part of that exchange of visits — the sight of Seth coming down the brook shore on a Saturday afternoon, or his own trip the next day over the trail between the cabins. In one way he liked this second part better, for it meant that when he got to Seth's he had nothing to do but sit down and be fed.

It was a six-mile walk that took John up along his own creek for a mile and a half to a low pass between two mountains. Then there was a beech ridge where the bucks had scarred the trees with their horns and fought long battles in the fall. From this ridge the trail went down into an alder swamp and crossed it on the remains of a beaver dam that Seth said had been there when he first came into the country. Why the beaver never returned was a mystery, but the dam was there, an enormously long, curving dyke above the swamp. Only it no longer held water. The stream it used to dam flowed through its ancient course and only the dead stubs of spruces, gray and broken, like old teeth in the alder growth, remained as evidence that once there had been standing water.

From the swamp John climbed another ridge and picked up a small brook on the far side that led him down a long easy grade to the small lake on which Seth's cabin stood. And when he came out on the ice, John would see the smoke rising up from the fringe of cedars, a clear blue finger against the evening sky.

The cabin itself was hidden under the trees, but when he yelped he would hear Seth's yell in return, high-pitched, and far carrying, and a little wild-sounding, especially when the echo came back off the ridge where the pines towered. Then, presently, he would see Seth, brown and shapeless in his old coat, come out on the ice, lifting his arm in greeting, as John approached, grinning round the stem of his old pipe, and taking it out long enough to say, "How, John?" before they shook hands. Then they would go into the cabin, which seemed solid with heat and tobacco smoke and the smell of cured pelts and the steam from the kettle of broth that Seth had on the fire.

Seth was always making broth of some kind — it might have a rabbit in it, or black squirrel, or partridges or even odds and ends, like muskrat, that John would have found it hard to like if he had known of them beforehand, but that seemed all right to Seth. Generally, though, it was a mixture of a good many things and thick and strong, and after his walk through the cold it tasted good to John.

He would admire it, giving Seth great pleasure, and the old Indian would sit back and beam, his broad face suddenly squeezed into innumerable fine wrinklings.

Afterwards they would look at some of Seth's pelts, and talk about their traplines, and wonder how much money they had made, until it was time for John to start back.

At first he had arranged his visits so that he could get started before dark, but as the winter went on he became so familiar with his route that he often tackled it after sunset. His snow-shoes had packed a hard footing it was easy to follow, even in the dark. The snow had a faint luminance to shape the trees. The night would be full of frost sounds, or he would hear a fox barking on the high slopes, or an owl would hoot him over the pass, and he would occasionally see its dim shape, noiseless as a snowflake in its passing, a dark blot against the stars. The owl lived there all winter and seemed to feel a kind of famil-iarity towards the boy — as if it looked for his coming. After he got over the first eerie sense of being followed by the disembodied, invisible voice, John came to look for the owl in his turn.

Occasionally he would pick up the sound of his own brook, muffled under the deep snow, and hollow-voiced, where it made small falls between big rocks. This sound of running water came and went beside him until he reached his own cabin under the thick stand of spruce. He would feel his way in and stir up his fire, climb into his bunk and pull his blanket over him, thinking it would be a full week now before he would hear Seth's yell echoing down from the pass and he in turn would go out and wait for the brown figure to come down along the brook.

But that was for the end of the week. Every day John would run one or other of his traplines. Except for the one he called his home line, that ran down the brook, taking in a couple of beaver colonies, and came back round the small hill, these lines would keep him out till dark, walking hard all the way, when he wasn't resetting his traps.

It never occurred to him to worry about anything happening to him and he was lucky. He didn't get sick, except for one heavy cold and that came near the end of the week and Seth showed up to look out for him. Seth rigged blankets over a kettle to make what he called a steam lodge. He made John sit naked under the tent of blankets while he dropped hot stones into the kettle from time to time until the steam had the boy pouring sweat. Then the Indian took him out in the snow and rubbed his bare skin with it and dressed him and put him in his bunk and covered him. After that he made him an infusion of some tree bark and roots; he never told John what it was, but it tasted bitter and black and John went to sleep suddenly, his last sight being one of Seth sitting on the floor before the fire, poking wood into it, and smoking his pipe, the smoke of which was sucked into the chimney where it joined the fire smoke, and the creeping, lichenlike fringes of sparks.

Once in a while Seth would give a day to go over one of John's traplines with him, showing him how to reset this or that trap; whereabouts at the top of a slide to set for otter; how to bait for marten; the best way to make deadfalls. John learned how to build pens for beaver under the ice and sink fresh twigs for bait and when the younger beaver swam in, to drop the closing pole and let them drown.

He learned a lot about foxes, both about their habits, so that he could use their own intelligence to trap them, and also how they could be poisoned. Foxes were vain animals. They could not resist leaving a mark on any isolated pole, and one trick was to set your pole up in the ice of a lake. The fox had to come out to cock a leg, and afterwards he felt so proud he would eat anything and he would crack down the bait right away without a thought.

One thing John never became good at was still-hunting fisher. He shot one, but that was a fluke. The rest of the time he spent trying it was just wasted.

But Seth told him not to worry. Either a man could still-hunt fisher or he could not; there was no shame in not being able.

There were days, of course, when John came in without a single skin, but generally he had something to keep him busy in the evenings. And sometimes he would work by the firelight until he fell asleep and the cold waked him later, when the fire was just a handful of embers, so dim his own shadow did not show against the log wall. It was lonesome for a boy then, and one night he was so cold and stiff it hardly seemed worth trying to move and he let his eyes close again.

But suddenly he came wide awake in a kind of panic and found himself standing up. He never knew what waked him; but years afterwards, when he was an old man, he told one of his grandchildren that every man at least once in his life, anyway, comes close to death, and maybe that was the time.

It was hard work, running traplines. It was hard work just to live alone in the woods and keep working, even when you have a friend only six miles cross-country. But John did well. Early in March his bale of furs had mounted up so that he had Seth make a special trip over and appraise them. The Indian said that John had more than two hundred dollars' worth. It would depend on the market. By the end of the month he might have two hundred and fifty dollars' worth.

John dug into his flour and made soda biscuits for the Indian. They ate them with a little sugar he had left and Seth spent the night in celebration. They talked a long time about how John would be fixed up to pay off the Judge, not only the stake but also the debt, and even have some money to start the summer on. Next winter he would make a clear profit. He would put money in the bank.

Seth did not understand what you put money in the bank for — not even when John explained that it was by saving money and laying it up against the future that a man got rich like the Judge. Seth agreed that it was a wonderful thing to have a house like the Judge and hire help; but he still did not see the point of having money you did not use up. Besides, as he said, the Judge didn't like him. "Don't like Indian. Don't like me drunken brute."

"That's it," John said. "You spend your money on likker, Seth. Then you haven't got anything at all."

For a few minutes Seth looked both enlightened and sad. But then he smiled at John.

"I lose money," he said. "Well, then maybe I get some more."

It came to John then that the future meant nothing to Seth. He worked and made money and drank it up and worked again, but it all meant nothing. He was just passing his time that way.

It didn't bother John much, though. Seth was a good friend.

The snow went down quickly. When he woke one morning, John was aware of a faint ticking sound all through the woods. He went out of his cabin and looked round but there was nothing to see. Later, however, the drip from the branches began to dent the snow in the black part of the spruce woods. Seth said maybe it was the frost working out of the trees, or the first creeping of sap. It came every spring. You didn't know. Maybe it was the little people under the earth getting ready to push the grass up. Or maybe it was just something you heard.

Whatever it was, John began to get restless. He was eager now to leave. He wanted to show his furs; he wanted to sell them, he told Seth, on a young market. Seth nodded. He knew how John felt, and he agreed that if John went now there was a chance he could get across the Moose River on the ice somewhere. But he begged John to wait. There was still two weeks for the fur to hold up well, and he had sometimes made some lucky catches in March.

But John's heart was set on going. He couldn't put his mind on trapping any more. He had done so well already. So finally Seth agreed to come over and help him pack his furs and traps. They had a big feed on about the last of John's grub.

In the morning the boy set out. The Indian walked with him to the end of his own south line, and shook hands.

"You one good boy, John," he said unexpectedly. "You come again next year."

"I will sure," promised John. "Thanks for all you've done for me, Seth. Without you, I wouldn't have done this." He hitched the heavy pack up on his shoulder. "I guess next the Judge, you're about the best friend I ever had."

The Indian's brown face wrinkled all over beneath his battered hat. He made a big gesture with his hand.

"Oh sure," he said. "Big country. Nice company. Plenty furs us both."

He held John's hand.

He said, "Now listen to Seth. *If creeks open, you cut two logs crossing.* You mind Seth. You cut two logs. One log roll. Two logs safe crossing water."

"Yes, sure," agreed John. He wanted to get away. The sun was well up by now."

" 'Bye," said Seth.

John walked hard. He felt strong, that morning. He felt like a grown man. The weight of the pack, galling his shoulders, was a pleasure to carry.

Every time he eased it one way or another, he thought about what it was going to mean. He thought about coming home and telling his mother. He would buy her a new dress. He would make a purchase of some calico for his sisters. Make a purchase, when you said it that way, was quite a word. He'd never even thought of it before.

He would see the Judge. He imagined himself walking into the Judge's office and dropping the pack on the floor, and looking the Judge in the eye. He realized that this almost meant more to him even than doing things for his family.

He remembered the way he had started the winter. He had asked Seth to estimate the worth of each first pelt. When they had figured up on forty dollars, he had made a bundle of them. They were still packed together in the bottom of the pack. It seemed to him that getting that first forty dollars' worth was twice as much of a job as all the rest afterwards had been.

The snow was a little slushy here and there, but it held up well in the big woods and John made pretty good time. Nights he set himself up a lean-to of cedar and balsam branches, and sitting before his small fire, he would think ahead a few years. He could see himself some day, pretty near like the Judge. He even figured on teaching himself to read and write, write his own name, anyway. No matter how you looked at it, you couldn't make a cross seem like John Haskell, wrote out in full, with big and little letters in it.

Mornings, he started with the first gray light, when the mist was like a twilight on the water and the deer moused along the runways and eyed him, curious as chipmunks. He walked south down the slopes of the hills, across the shadows of the sunrise, when the snow became full of color and the hills ahead wore a bloody purple shadow on their northern faces.

Now and then he heard the first stirring of a small brook under the snow in a sunny place and he found breath holes under falls wide open.

John had grown taller during the winter, and he seemed even lankier, but his eyes were still the boy's eyes of a year ago.

He crossed the Moose River on the ice about where Mc-Keever now is, just at dusk one evening. He had not made as good time that day. The snow had been a good deal softer and his legs ached and the pack weighed down a bit harder than usual. But though the ice had been treacherous close to shore, he had found a crossing place easily enough.

That night, however, as he lay in his lean-to, he heard the river ice begin to work. It went out in the morning with a grinding roar, and built a jam half a mile below his camp.

He saw it with a gay heart as he set out after breakfast. It seemed to him as if it were the most providential thing he ever had heard of. If he had waited another day before starting, he would have found the river open and he would have had to go back to Seth's cabin and wait till the Indian was ready to come out. But as it was, now, he would have only brooks to cross.

There were a good many of them, and most of them were opening. But he found places to cross them, and he had no trouble till afternoon, when he found some running full. They were high with black snow water, several of them so high that he had to go upstream almost a mile to find a place where he could fell a bridge across.

Each time he dropped two logs and went over easily enough. But each time the delay chafed him a little more. By late afternoon, when he was only a few miles from High Falls and began to recognize his landmarks, he came to what he knew was the last creek.

It was a strong stream, with a great force of water, and it was boiling full. Where John happened on it, it began a slide down the steep bank for the river, with one bend and then a straight chute. But it was narrow there, and beside where he stood grew a straight hemlock, long enough to reach across.

Hardly stopping to unload his pack, John set to work with his axe. The tree fell nicely, just above the water. There was no other tree close by, but John thought about that only for a moment. It was the last creek, he was almost home, and his heart was set on getting there that night. Besides, he had had no trouble on the other crossings. He was surefooted and in every case he had run across one log.

He gave the tree a kick, but it lay steady, and suddenly he made up his mind to forget what Seth had said. He could get over easy enough and see the Judge that evening.

With his furs on his back, his axe in one hand and his gun in the other, he stepped out on the log. It felt solid as stone under his feet and he went along at a steady pace. The race of water just under the bark meant nothing to John. His head was quite clear and his eyes were on the other side already, and he thought, in his time, he had crossed a lot of logs more rickety than this one.

It was just when he was halfway over that the log rolled without any warning and pitched John into the creek.

The water took hold of him and lugged him straight down and rolled him over and over like a dead pig. He had no chance even to yell. He dropped his gun and axe at the first roll and instinctively tugged at the traps which weighted him so. As he struggled to the top he felt the fur pack slip off. He made a desperate grab for it, but it went away. When he finally washed up on the bend, and crawled out on the snow, he hadn't a thing left but his life.

That seemed worthless to him lying on the snow. He could not even cry about it.

He lay there for perhaps half an hour, while the dusk came in on the river. Finally he got to his feet and searched downstream, poking with a stick along the bottom, though he was hopeless. The creek ran like a millrace down the slope for the river and the chances were a hundred to one that the traps, as well as the furs, had been taken by the strength of water and the slide all the way down to the river.

But John continued his search till nearly dark before he gave up.

By the time he reached High Falls, John had managed to get back just enough of his courage to go straight to the Judge. It was very late, but the office light was still burning, and John knocked and went in. He stood on the hearth, shivering and dripping, but fairly erect, and in a flat, low voice, told the Judge exactly what had happened, even to Seth's parting admonition.

The Judge said never a word till the boy was done. He merely sat studying him from under his bushy white brows. Then he stood up and fetched a glass of hot water with some whiskey in it.

Though the drink seemed to bring back a little life, it only made John more miserable. He waited like a wavering ghost for the Judge to have his say.

But the Judge only advised in his heavy voice: "You'd better go on home. I understand you have a new sister. You'd better start hunting work tomorrow." His voice became gruffer. "Everybody has to learn things. It's been bad luck for us both that you had to learn it like this."

John went home. All he could remember was that the Judge had said it was bad luck for them both. It seemed to him that was a very kind thing for the Judge to say.

John did not see anything of the Judge that summer. He worked hard, planting corn and potatoes and the garden, and later he managed to hire himself out. He seemed to get jobs more easily that summer. But his family seemed to need more money. People had been impressed by Mrs. Haskell's having the doctor and Mrs. Legrand for her lying-in, and now and then they visited a little, and that meant extra money for food and tea. By working hard, though, John found himself in the fall about where he had been the preceding year.

He had put in a bid with the tannery for winter work and had had the job promised to him. Two days before he would have started, however, the Judge sent word for him to come to the big house.

The Judge made him sit down.

"John," he said, "you've kept your courage up when it must have been blamed hard. I've been thinking about you and me. I think the best thing for us both, the best way I can get my money back, is to give you another stake, if you're willing to go."

John felt that he was much nearer crying than he had been when he lost his furs. He hardly found the voice to say that he would go.

For some reason that John never understood, Seth had decided to move west in the state, so the boy had to go into the woods alone. The idea worried his mother, but he told her that in a way it would be better for him. He would be able to use Seth's cabin and work both their ranges.

But on the second day of his trip in, lying alone by his campfire, with all the miles of woods he still had to travel into, he knew that it wasn't better for him: and when at last he reached the little lake and saw Seth's cabin, he would have swapped both their ranges together for a sight of the broad brown face and the shapeless figure coming along the shore with the deceptive stride, which, like a bear's, seemed slow and shuffling but which carried him along so quickly.

He settled into Seth's cabin because it was better than his own; but there were times during that winter when he would start up because he thought he heard Seth's wild-sounding yell echoing off the pine ridge, and he would go outdoors in the darkness to listen. All through the winter, he never quite got rid of the notion that somehow Seth was going to turn up; but he never did. John never saw him again as long as he lived; but he never forgot him.

The cabin had been shut up tight. Porcupines had whittled here and there round the outside, but there was little to interest them. Seth in the woods left the ground round his cabin looking as if he had never been there. The inside of the cabin might appear to be inhabited by a pack rat, for the litter that jumbled it. But the woods Seth never spoiled the way a white man would — even John, who had picked up habits from the Indian, never learned the full art of it. Seth could spend the night and move on in the morning, and only an Indian would have known a man had slept there. It was so around his cabin.

John laid his lines out early and when the freeze came he was ready to start trapping. He followed two of the Indian's lines and laid out two new ones on his own, and after a month or so these two began to earn as well as the two others. He kept learning more and more about animals, and now and then, when he did well, he would think that Seth might have said, "Good!" the way he used to, and he could almost hear the quick laughter.

The hardest part of living alone was the Sundays without company. It was then that he realized how much Seth had done for him. The storekeeper had given him an almanac and every night before John sat down to supper, he checked off the day. That was the first reading he did, learning the look of the days of the week in print. He spent long hours puzzling over the other words and symbols and studying the picture at the head of each month. For December there was a picture of a family sitting down to dinner at a table with a white cloth, and John sometimes fancied himself as sitting in the place of the man. When things got too lonesome, he would get out that picture and think about it.

There were deep snows in February, but after the crust formed, John suddenly had a run of luck with his traps, better than anything he had had the year before, so that sometimes it was past midnight before he had finished cleaning the skins. But even so, he stayed right through to the end of the season, and then his pack was so heavy that he had to leave his traps behind.

The morning he decided to go, there was a mist over the ice on the lake and the trees were like clouds in it. Somewhere back in the woods he heard a deer flounder in the heavy snow.

Then in the ensuing complete silence, he seemed to hear Seth's voice: "You mind Seth. *You cut two logs crossing.*" But John didn't need to be told.

The Moose River was open when he reached it, so he had to build himself a raft. He spent a full day working at it. And from that point on, he took plenty of time, when he came to the creeks, and dropped two logs over them, and made a trial trip over and back without his fur packs. It took him three days longer to come out of the woods than it had the year before, but he brought his furs with him.

The Judge saw to it that he got good prices; and when the dealer was done with the buying, John was able to pay the Judge for both stakes and for the forty-dollar loan as well. The year after that he made a clear profit for himself.

John did well in the world. He found time to learn to read and write and handle figures. From time to time he visited the Judge, and he found that the Judge was not a person that anyone needed to be afraid of. When the Judge died, in

John's thirtieth year, John was owner of Freel's tannery and one of the leading men in High Falls.

Going to the Judge's house, that day, to help settle the affairs, he thought of how scared he had been the first time he went to visit and, strangely, he remembered Seth. Without the two of them, he might never have got started in life.

It is a simple story, this of John Haskell's, but it is not quite done. When the Judge's will was read, that afternoon, in the big house, it was found that the Judge had left the house to John, together with a good share of his timberland. There was also a sealed letter for John that the lawyer handed over.

That night in his own home, John opened the letter. It was dated the same day as the one on which John had received the money for his first pack of furs and paid the Judge. It was just a few lines long and it contained forty dollars in bills.

Dear John,

Here is the forty dollars, and I am making you a confession with it. I liked your looks when you came to me that first time. I thought you had the stuff in you. It was a dirty thing to do in a way, but I wanted to make sure of you. I never liked your father and I would never have lent him a cent. I invented that debt.

Good luck, John.

TOM WHIPPLE

◀ I ▶

TOM AND HIS MOTHER

ON A LATE OCTOBER MORNING in 1837, just after sunrise, a woman and a lanky boy, approaching the Cortland Street wharf, asked a deckhand if that was the steamboat for Albany. When he said it was, the boy turned to the woman.

"See, Ma. You didn't miss it anyhow."

"Yes, Tom." Her voice was timid. "I was only feared the Amboy boat had made us late. I'd be feared to stay all day in a big city like this one. Washington City was big enough for me." She cast an anxious glance over her shoulder. New York was waking up and the frosty streets echoed with the clatter of drays and water carts. "Hadn't we ought to get onto the boat, Tom?"

"Might as well."

Beside her small bent figure, he looked tall. He was a big boy anyway, with the flesh on him not yet grown up to his bones. He was carrying a small satchel and a bundle rolled up in a cotton print and his hands hung well below the cuffs of his shabby coat, showing the wrist joints.

Choosing a corner behind the stove in the main saloon of the steamboat, they stowed the satchel under the seat, and the woman sat down. "This here's real nice," she said, looking up at her son. "I think it's pertier than the other boat, don't you, Tom?"

"Yes, Ma."

He was looking out of the window that faced south. He

could see the bay beyond the river's mouth, the white gulls against the sky, and a ship sailing past the Castle Garden.

She watched his face for a moment, thinking, perhaps, that it favored her own more than his father's.

"You can put your bundle side of mine, Tom," she said, gently. "There's room for you to set here, too."

"Yes, Ma," he said. But he stood still, looking away from her, and she saw him swallow. Then he turned to her and fixed his eyes on a nail in the wall about two feet over her shawled head. "You ought to get home all right," he said.

"*We* ought to," she said sharply, as if she had been seeing into his mind for some time. "You don't mean . . ."

He nodded and said, "Yep."

She said then angrily, "You know I'm feared of traveling alone. It ain't right of you to leave me here, Tom. This way. In this big boat." She saw that she was getting nowhere. "Ain't it enough for you to go see Washington City? Didn't we traipse all the way over to that Mount Vernon? And we rode on the cars. Ain't many boys done that much. Not even Supervisor Utley has rode on railroad cars. Besides, how'm I going to run the place without you there?

He was still looking over her head. His face was blank as only a boy's can be, defensive, and stubborn. She took the end of her shawl to put it to her eyes. "When Pa moved us from New Haven way out into York State he promised I was to have a home permanent in Westernville. And then he died and I calculated you would grow up there and take care of me. Remember how you promised Pa? What will I say to the Utleys?"

"Tell them I aim to see something of the world," Tom said. "I aim to look me around a spell. I'll come home, maybe in the spring. You'll be all right. You got your widow-pension off the government, didn't you? You can hire help now."

"Yes, I suppose so." She sniffed two or three times. "Oh, Tom," she said, "where'll you go to?"

"I don't know," he said, shuffling his feet. "Maybe Europe. Maybe I'll go to China."

"But oh, Tom, how'll you get along? You ain't got money. You ain't never been nowhere."

"That's it. I ain't been nowhere," he said. "I want to look around a little before I get home. I calculate I'll get along."

Passengers were coming onto the boat, their feet cracking sharply on the deck outside. She saw that his face was set, and she looked at the freckles as if she wanted to count them over before he left her. His father had been just as stubborn; you couldn't turn him; wasn't anything more stubborn, she thought with a little twinge of pain and pride, than a Whipple man when he got dead set.

"Kiss me, Tom," she said.

He cast a look around and saw that they were partly screened by the stove. He bent down awkwardly to kiss her.

"Good-bye, Ma," he said. "See you come spring, I guess."

The warning bell began to toll as he stepped off the boat.

❧ 2 ❧

SIGNING ON THE
FLORA BASCOM

"WELL, BUB," said the man with the hedge of black chin whiskers, "what do you want?"

"You're hiring help, ain't you?" asked Tom Whipple.

The man shoved the stiff-visored cap back on his head and put his feet on the box he had been writing on. He had a square face, the skin like red leather on his cheeks. His eyes were piercing, gray, and hard. "Yep," he said. "What can you do? Milk perty good, hey? Pitch hay? Say, maybe you can make butter, too?"

"I could," said Tom. "I ain't done much, but my ma makes dandy butter. We sell ourn to Supervisor Utley."

"Yew deaow, hey?" The mate got a big laugh from the men in the three-cent gin shop where he was signing on the crew. "Now that's real handy of yeaow."

Tom Whipple stared at him. He said, "I calculate you must come from Massachusetts State."

This time Tom got the laugh and the mate's eyes narrowed. But though he let it go, anybody could see he wasn't going to let Tom Whipple out of his hands after that. His voice was even and cold.

"Ever been to sea?" he asked.

"No," said Tom.

The mate turned to the saloon keeper for sympathy. "By Lucifer, Jeff, did you ever see a crumbier bunch of lubbers?" He wheeled round again on Tom. "This is a ship, not a farm. You'll get eleven dollars a month but you don't milk cows. We don't lay eggs either, not the kind you boil," he said, looking down at his square fists. "But we make a ship sail, see?"

"Yes," said Tom. "That's what I want. I want to travel."

"You'll travel all right with me." The mate smiled thinly. "Name?"

"Tom Whipple."

The mate's pen squeaked.

"Born?"

"New Haven." Tom stared round. "But I live in Westernville in York State. It's just north of Rome."

"I don't care two cents where you live. You're going to do your living on the *Flora Bascom*. Now," the mate said evenly, "sign your name, or if you can't write, make a mark."

"I can write pretty fair," said Tom, and bent to take the pen from the mate. His face became intensely serious. He had never learned to make a first-rate W. But you could read it.

"All right," said the mate. "Next man."

"Just a minute," Tom said. "Where's the ship sailing to?"

"It's none of your business," said the mate. He rose behind his box. "My name is Mr. Bullett," he said evenly. "I don't want remarks from you. I don't want questions. But when you speak, I'm *Mister*. Understand?"

"All right," Tom said, good-naturedly.

He didn't know what happened. The mate did not move from behind his box, but his fist hit Tom between the eyes.

The next Tom knew he was lying on the floor, and Mr.

223

Bullett was saying "MISTER!" and breathing gently on his knuckles.

"Mr. Freel," he said, "take him aboard and see if you can pick some of the straws out of his ears."

A thick-shouldered man yanked Tom to his feet and shoved him towards the door. "Come along, hayfoot," he said.

He smelled of tar and plug tobacco and gin and a peculiar kind of hair grease. Half a dozen of the other new hands came after them; but their laughter stopped as they emerged into the rumbling clatter of South Street.

"The mate's a bully, ain't he?" one asked.

"Not too bad, if you look sharp and jump when he spits," replied the second mate. "Besides, he's found himself a toy."

He nodded at Tom, who was giddily trying to avoid a cart horse.

⚬ 3 ⚬

BOUND FOR RUSSIA

TOM SPENT all that day trying to do what he was told, along with the other men. The idea seemed not so much to get work done as to keep the hands busy, and there were moments when Mr. Freel looked hopefully towards Mr. Bullett for ideas.

At noon and at four o'clock the men were allowed ashore for an hour, but Tom was kept on board, for Mr. Freel had an idea he might clear out. He told Tom that somebody had to keep watch on the ship. Tom didn't know his rights, of course. Nobody informed him that the one-armed old fellow smoking a clay pipe amidships was the shipkeeper, hired according to law.

Tom was glad enough to stay on board and take the hour admiring the vessel. Mr. Freel brought him some scraps of food from the captain's table. Mr. Freel, it appeared, did not eat in the cabin but, like other second mates, lived a kind of ghostly existence halfway between the forecastle and the cabin. And because Tom had proved handy with the ropes, he acted friendly. One of the first things he asked was whether Tom had any money.

Tom said no, but he expected to have plenty when they docked across the ocean. Eleven dollars a month was good pay for an apprentice, he thought.

Mr. Freel, whittling plug tobacco into his horny palm, grunted. "You'll need clothes," he said. "Sea boots and a pea jacket. You'll have to buy them from the slop chest." He tamped his pipe with a blunt thumb. "And you'll pay the master a hundred and fifty per cent profit on the transaction," he added.

Tom thought about it for a while before he said, "That don't seem honest."

"Maybe not," Mr. Freel said shortly. "But it's regular. He keeps good stuff in the slop, which is more than some do. You won't have much of a fortune, though, when you reach St. Petersburg."

Tom cleaned up his beans and said, "Where's that, Mr. Freel?"

"Russia. And a shivering cold place, they say."

"Ain't you never been there?"

"No. And I ain't got much desire to go. But I couldn't get a second mate's berth on another ship and I got to have the pay.

I got a wife and two children in Liverpool, and a third ready to berth."

"My," said Tom, "that's dandy."

"It's dandy as long as you're a second mate," said Mr. Freel.

Tom lay on his back and looked up into the rigging. The sun and the wind put a kind of shine on the spars; and with the clouds passing the blue sky beyond them, he could just about imagine that the ship itself was moving. "I'm glad we're going to Russia," he said. "I've had a fancy to see that place. Maybe I'll get to see the Emperor. Have you ever seen an emperor, Mr. Freel?"

"No," said Mr. Freel. "Captain Stath is emperor enough for me. Him and Mr. Bullett. What do you want to see the Emperor for anyway?" he asked.

"Oh," said Tom. "I'd kind of like to talk to him. When you want to find out about something, Supervisor Utley says you want to see the top man."

❧ 4 ☙

ON THE YARD ARM

TOM WHIPPLE had the bunk in the peak of the forecastle where the air still smelled of the sick Portuguese sailor who had occupied it on the preceding voyage. When the crew laid aft to be chosen into watches, he was taken by Mr. Bullett. The choosing was done under the eye of Captain Stath, a clean-shaven man with a calculating face. He was short with the first mate and he did not speak to the second except to give orders; but he took the ship down the river in fine style and they dropped Sandy Hook astern a little after noon.

Tom Whipple felt the *Flora Bascom's* forefoot take the heave of the Atlantic, and he saw the dirty green of its restless waste meeting a steel-gray sky. The cries of the tagging gulls lost heart and dwindled. By evening the brig was a lonely box on the waves with eighteen men and a spotted cat, and America was a place on which the sun had set. Tom was sick, and the cold bit as the sun went under, and Mr. Bullett, who had been driving him since the *Flora Bascom* dropped Castle Garden, ordered him aloft with a ball of marline for the boatswain.

"Stay up there till he tells you to bring it down," said Mr. Bullett. "Maybe the wind will blow the hayseed out."

Tom took the ball in his right hand and worked himself onto the shrouds. He could hear the hiss of the water under him, and the cross ropes pushed against his chest. But he went up, and the only time he looked down he could see Mr. Bullett and Mr. Freel both looking up at him and Captain Stath coming out of the cabin. Mr. Freel looked anxious, the Captain showed nothing on his face at all, but Mr. Bullett was smiling that usual thin smile of his.

"Consarn him," Tom said to himself. "I'm just as good as he is off this ship." He didn't stop again. He felt the back wind off the sails against his face; the curve of them made dingy feather beds to lure a man to let go; but he went up.

He saw, after a while, the noncommittal face of the boatswain leaning over the yard. The boatswain's feet were like glue, and his hands were careless, and he laid a long line of tobacco spit level on the wind. "I've see a snail go up a bush," he shouted. "But he got there, too, Bub."

It wasn't praise, exactly, but it made Tom feel easier. He found the yard a comfortable pressure at his waist. He let it carry his weight, gingerly, then with more confidence. In a minute he tried looking down and saw the hull slitting the water like a needle that a bug might straddle.

"It's bigger than it looks," shouted the boatswain. "But don't look at it too long, Bub. You'll see plenty of it when you're down."

So Tom looked out, while the boatswain worked. He saw the night on the Atlantic; the great heaving mass of water was leveled from that height, and he felt himself swoop over it, a little like the motion of a gull. But a gull didn't fly in the squeak and crash and booming of rigging. A gull had feathers to silence the wind.

Out there was Russia, Tom thought, and back of him was Westernville. His mother would be home now, telling Mrs. Utley and the Supervisor what had become of him. She would say he was on a ship, maybe for Europe, maybe for China. He could imagine her crying and saying, "He didn't have any money. He didn't want any. You know how Tom is. Always going round with his pocket full of nails and things he picks up, thinking he is as good as the richest man alive." She would think of him asleep in bed possibly. She would never imagine him up alone in the wind, with the yard pressed against him and his feet balanced on a spider thread. And the Supervisor would clear his throat and say, "Pshaw, Mrs. Whipple," and ask where his supper was.

Thinking of supper at the Utleys' made Tom hungry. For the first time since the brig had met the Atlantic swell he felt his stomach take a rational shape. "By thunder," he said to himself, "I'm all right."

Then the marline ball was slapped against his palm and the boatswain said, "Get down, Bub. And take it easy. Any man can climb."

He went down easy, and when he hit the deck, the roll met his feet squarely. He could smell pork in the galley vent. Mr. Bullett came stamping aft along the deck. His eyes had not changed and he was still smiling thinly. But all he said was, "Take the marline back to Mr. Freel."

🙌 5 🙌

TOM INTERRUPTS THE CAPTAIN'S WALK

AFTER a week or so, Tom was getting along well enough with the officers. But the fact that he was planning to see the Emperor was too much for Mr. Freel to keep to himself, and once the foremast hands got wind of it they talked about it all the way to Russia.

It didn't bother Tom a great deal, though. He himself didn't know how he was going to get to talk with him. He didn't even know what the Emperor's name was, and nobody in the forecastle was able to tell him. They were a pretty mixed crew: mostly Britishers, a couple of Scandinavians, one Dutch, one French, and two Italians. Tom was the only genuine American citizen in the forecastle, except a man from New Orleans, and he wasn't hardly what Tom thought of as a Yankee. He saw they didn't mean harm; they had to have something for their minds to chew on; but he thought they plain didn't understand how a man could get along. He wasn't worried, except about finding out the Emperor's name.

The bosun told him that Russian names didn't count. You couldn't pronounce them anyway. And the carpenter said they didn't have last names in Russia at all, the names all ended in *sky,* which meant son-of, which started some of the hands laughing, and the cook said why didn't he ask the Old Man. So Tom said maybe he would.

But he didn't make up his mind to it till the *Flora Bascom* had worked her way across the Baltic Sea and was heading in for the Gulf. At the wheel was the dim-witted Swede; but he could steer a ship like a brooding archangel. It was Tom's turn at polishing the brass work and he was rubbing up the binnacle when Captain Stath came on deck for his morning constitutional. All the time Tom worked he could hear the smart crack of the Captain's heels on the frosty deck, measuring out his exact rectangle. It was easy to tell that the Captain was feeling brisk. So Tom gave the shining brass a last flourish of the rag and caught the Captain on his twenty-third quarter turn.

He touched his forelock smartly with the knuckle of the hand holding the brass polish and said, "Excuse me, Captain. Could you tell me the name of the Emperor of Russia?"

The Captain wheeled like a speared sturgeon, and roared "WHAT?" in a t-gallant bellow that brought the entire crew up standing.

Tom saw that he had put his foot in it; but he had to get out the question now, so he asked it again.

The Captain's face was no warmer or more enlightening than the Baltic itself. His voice cut like the ice spray as he shouted for Mr. Bullett. The rest of the crew all grinned, for they had been awaiting this minute; only the Swede didn't change face, but he wiggled his ears for a moment, as if he felt a shift coming in the wind. The sight of them didn't help the Captain. By the time Mr. Bullett came up he was in a state of frenzy.

"Do you know what's happened, Mister?" he demanded, leveling his voice.

"No, sir," said Mr. Bullett.

"I've been interrupted on my own deck by one of the watch. YOUR watch, Mr. Bullett. And do you know what he wanted to know? He wanted to know the name of the Emperor of Russia, Mr. Bullett! . . . Are you going to stand there like a blasted gaping marble image, Mr. Bullett? Ain't you going to do something?"

Mr. Bullett did. He hailed Tom down amidships and had a couple of seamen hold him over a barrel, and he put a rope's end on his bare back twenty times.

"Interrupt the Captain's walk," he said. "Emperor of Russia," he said, and he kept repeating it, *"Emperor of Russia! . . ."*

When he was through, they rolled Tom over and emptied buckets of sea water over him and told him to put his shirt on and get to work. Tom felt sore, inside as well as out; the Captain had taken up his walk at the exact point at which he had left off, and the only time he watched the flogging was during the short space when he was coming forward and crossing to starboard. The crew thought it was a prodigious joke, discussing it in the forecastle when the watch was off. It

was the carpenter's opinion that none of the officers knew the Emperor's name.

Somehow the word of that got aft and the rest of the voyage became pretty brisk for all of them and Tom wasn't sorry to jump the brig as soon as she berthed in Kronstadt.

ᵉ 6 ᵖ

ST. PETERSBURG

BUT BEING ASHORE Tom got to feeling better, even though he couldn't talk to anybody. The people all looked foreign to him anyway and some of them had a queer fat smell that made him think of a sheep's carcass hanging in the cool room. The men were almost all bearded and wore sheepskin hats. He was immensely excited by the things he saw and spent days walking the streets, looking at the strange churches and the great palace, and the very fine horses the military rode.

New York, he thought, or even Washington City, wasn't in it, for strange sights. He saw all sorts of different-appearing people, and they didn't all talk one language either; even a stranger could tell that. He could see it was a big country, and the urge to find out about it got more and more intense, and he felt surer than ever that the only way to do that was to have a talk with the man at the top, the Emperor.

He tried two or three times at the palace, and he kept watch at the gates, until he began to realize that to get next to the Emperor he would have to have letters or something of that sort.

He didn't know how to get hold of letters, and he had been there two weeks, and his money was about gone. He was feeling a bit low that afternoon, standing outside a pub, when

he saw a sailor ambling down the street and looking as footloose as himself.

Tom hadn't dared to go back to the port in all this time, for
fear of being picked up by Mr. Bullett. But he could see that
this sailor was as strange in the city as himself, so he hailed
him, and they shook hands, like two white men meeting up in
Indian country; and Tom, fingering the few coins he had left
in his pockets, asked the sailor if he couldn't buy him a drink.

"I don't know what they've got in there. I guess it's just a
potlikker," he said. "But Supervisor Utley says even potlikker
warms a man when drunk between friends."

The sailor turned out to be off a British ship and he was
sympathetic to Supervisor Utley's opinions. He had Tom's
drink and then he bought Tom one, and when Tom said he
didn't rightly drink, the sailor drank it for him, apologetically,
and they got so friendly that Tom told him how he had been
trying to get to see the Emperor, but didn't know how to go
about it.

The sailor said it appeared to him like a difficult problem.
"Can't your Minister help you out?" he asked.

Tom said, "My Minister?" And the sailor said, "Yes, the
Minister of the United States."

Tom said he hadn't been to see him. He hadn't thought of
it, he said; as a matter of fact, it hadn't even occurred to him
that there could be such a job — he didn't like to say he didn't
understand what the job was. But it made him feel that the
United States was a pretty fine country to send a minister all
the way to St. Petersburg. He felt considerably better just to
think of it; it was the next best thing to seeing a picture of Old
Hickory himself on the wall.

Well, said the sailor, why didn't Tom go to see the Minister? Taking care of the interests of American citizens in Russia was what the American Minister was paid to do.

"He's got to look after you same as the British Minister has to look after me," he said. "That's what they collect taxes off us for."

Tom said he would go. The sailor offered to lend him the money to hire a sled with, but Tom declined. He didn't care to be beholden to a man he didn't know well, and a foreigner at that. So he said good-bye and started off for the American Embassy.

He had an idea of the direction, because there happened to be a Frenchman in the pub who said he knew, and he had heard Supervisor Utley say once that all Frenchmen were democrats, and democrat was a good American word, no matter which way you voted on election day.

❧ 7 ❧

THE AMERICAN MINISTER

WELL, the Minister lived in a mighty fine big house with the American flag flying over it, and when he saw it Tom Whipple felt good and wondered how he had never happened on that street before. He took careful note of the house, comparing it with the other fine houses along the street, and as far as he could see, it was just as fine as any of them.

While he was standing looking at it, a man came walking

235

from the other direction and he was dressed in a good American coat; you could tell it a mile. He had a sealskin cap on his head, with the flaps up, pretty near exactly like the one Supervisor Utley wore when he got into the cutter behind the bays and drove down to a Sunday dinner in Rome.

But even without those garments, Tom could have told he was an American by the way he walked. He was coming right along, and you could see he meant business. So Tom stepped across the roadway, dodging a couple of droshkies with their jingling bells, and touched his hat to the American and asked whether the American Minister was home.

The man looked Tom up and down, from his worn felt hat and pea jacket to the old pants and the sea boots. He looked at Tom's freckled face, and his young turkey neck and his raw-boned wrists, and he gave him a smile.

"No," he said, "the Minister's not home yet, but he will be in two shakes. Come in and let me see what I can do for you." He took off his hat, so Tom took his off and they went in the outer door.

"My name's Dallas," said the man. "I'm the Minister."

"Whipple," said Tom. "I'm pleased to meet you."

Well, when they came to the inner door, the Minister stood to one side to let Tom in first, and then a couple of Russian-dressed servants came up and one took the Minister's hat and coat and one took Tom's hat and his pea jacket. Mr. Dallas and Tom went upstairs together to where the Minister had a kind of office. There was coal burning in a tiled stove; there were books on the walls; and there was a table, something like a dresser, laid out with about every kind of bottle there was.

Mr. Dallas pointed to it and asked whether Tom would have anything to drink. But Tom declined. "There ain't nothing I'd like now except a glass of fresh buttermilk," he said. "I ain't been able to find none anywhere, Mr. Dallas. I can't figure out the Russian for it either."

Mr. Dallas smiled. He said he hadn't thought of buttermilk himself but if there was anything that would taste good to him at that moment, buttermilk was what it would be. So he pulled a velvet rope hanging on the wall and a servant came and went, and pretty soon he came in with two big glasses on a gold tray. Mr. Dallas took one and Tom the other. Mr. Dallas raised his and said, "Your very good health, Mr. Whipple."

So Tom raised his and returned the compliment and they took chairs and drank the buttermilk. Tom thought it wasn't near as good as what came out of his mother's churning, but he didn't like to say so. And after being so long without it, he had to admit it tasted pleasant.

The Minister talked plain to him. He asked how the U.S.A. was getting along and Tom said that money was awful tight. He told how he and his mother had been to Washington to get her pension and how he had seen President Van Buren go by down the avenue. He said he had gone over to Mount Vernon. And then he told about putting his mother on the Albany steamboat and how he had signed on the *Flora Bascom*. He hadn't known she was coming to Russia when he did it, but he was mighty glad when he learned, for he had heard about the Russians licking Napoleon Bonaparte, so he knew it was a great country, and he had made up his mind to see the Emperor. That, as a matter of fact, was what he had called on Mr. Dallas about. He would like to get a letter from Mr. Dallas, saying who he was and that he would like a little conversation with the Emperor.

Mr. Dallas looked at him for a moment before he said, picking his words, "You know, Whipple, the Emperor's a pretty hard man to get to see." Then he tried to explain how it was in an empire as compared to a democratic country. Tom thought it over, but he shook his head. He said he couldn't see it that way. He could see it might apply to a Russian farmer, in a manner of speaking; but he was a United States citizen. Martin Van Buren, now, he could see the Emperor, couldn't he? Mr. Dallas nodded his head; that was true. Then why couldn't Tom Whipple?

Well, they sawed away at it for a spell, and Mr. Dallas was

as friendly a man as you could ask to argue with. But Tom got the best of him at every turn, and finally he agreed to write a letter to the Imperial Court Chamberlain for Tom. But he said there was one thing: it was the custom when you went to call on an emperor to take him a present.

Tom hadn't thought of that but he could see how it would be, and he stuck his hand in his pants pocket to fiddle the junk he carried, the way he always did when he was puzzled, and his fingers closed on an object he'd hardly thought of since leaving Washington City. Holding it, he thought how lucky it was he hadn't dropped it anywhere, like up on the topsail yards of the *Flora Bascom,* driving off Finisterre.

"All right," he said. "Tell him I got a present I'd mighty like to give the Emperor and that I figure the Emperor is going to be mighty pleased to have."

Mr. Dallas looked at Tom's face and he wrote the message down without asking what the present was. Then he sealed the letter inside and out, prettifying it like anything, to Tom's way of thinking. He gave it to Tom, telling him to come around in the morning and he would send a man with him to be sure he got in to see the Chamberlain. Then he asked Tom if he would have supper. He had to go out himself, he explained. His family was going with him, but he couldn't offer to take Tom, as it was a formal court dinner. But, if Tom didn't mind eating alone, he could have dinner here.

So Tom ate alone in the dining room, with five men to wait on him, not one of whom could talk good English. And after dinner, to save money, he found himself a stable and slept in the hay.

It meant a good deal of picking and dusting to get clear of the hay in the morning, but he turned up at the Minister's house on time and was sent off with a clerk. Mr. Dallas came down to shake hands with him and said for him to come back when he was ready. He would see that Tom got a berth on a ship to go home. Tom thanked him and said he would.

He could tell that Mr. Dallas didn't expect he would get to see the Emperor at all, but he didn't hold it against him. Mr. Dallas had been as neighborly as any man could be.

❧ 8 ☙

THE COURT CHAMBERLAIN

THE CLERK was a dapper man. Tom could tell at first glance he wasn't the quality of man Mr. Dallas was. As soon as they got round the corner, he asked Tom whether he had the Minister's letter. Tom slapped his coat pocket to show he did, and the clerk said, "Well, come on, then."

It amused Tom some to see how walking alongside of him made the clerk uneasy. He didn't talk, and he kept pressing forward, as if he was trying to leave Tom behind; but he couldn't walk worth a duck. It didn't bother Tom. He could imagine how the clerk would look setting out to pitch hay.

But the clerk knew where to go and who to speak to. Inside the palace, he kept whispering to Tom not to make such a hooraw with his boots; but you can't help making some noise with sea boots on a tile floor, so Tom went the quietest he could without tiptoeing, and let it go at that. He knew people were looking at him; they in their Russian costumes and him in his pea jacket made kind of a mixture, he could see. But it didn't bother him. They liked to wear those kind of clothes, and he liked his own.

When they got to the Chamberlain's room, the clerk gave his message to a flunky of some sort, though he might have been one of the military, too, and pretty soon this man came out and told them to go in through the inner door.

Tom had supposed that the clerk would go in with him to see the Chamberlain, but the clerk was through. He said, "In there," to Tom, as if he were driving a pig to a sticker, and turned on his heel. Tom let him go. He didn't feel that the clerk would have been much help anyhow.

In the Chamberlain's office there was a handsome, bearded, elderly man sitting at a desk. He got up and bowed when Tom entered, and Tom handed him Mr. Dallas's letter, and the Chamberlain said he was honored, in very unsteady English, but understandable. He read the letter, and then he looked at Tom for a spell.

"You know the Emperor is a very busy man, Mr. Whipple," he said.

"I calculate he must be, running a country this size and without no congress either, so far as I know," said Tom.

The Chamberlain bowed.

"For instance, today he has five audiences in the morning; then an hour of state papers to sign and the Imperial policies to consider. Then he has to go to a military review. Then he eats with the Empress. Then this afternoon he receives a delegation of Cossacks, and must inspect the Palace Guard, and decorate a Grand Duke, and in the evening he has to appear at the Opera. You see, he is busy."

"I expected he would be," Tom said. "But I don't aim to take a lot of his time."

"Well," said the Chamberlain, "using my influence, I might be able to arrange an audience with him next April."

But that didn't suit Tom's book at all.

"It's this way," he said. "I ain't got the money to stay here that long. In fact, if I don't see the Emperor in the next day or two, I'll have to just take ship without seeing him at all. I'd hate to do that. You tell him, seeing he's so all-fired busy, I won't take any of his time. I'll just give him my present and wish him luck and clear out."

"Well," said the Chamberlain. "I will see. But perhaps you would give me the present to present it for you."

"I wouldn't," said Tom. He wanted to be polite, though, so he added, "I got this present in America, Mister, and I'd like to give it to the Emperor with my own hand."

Well, the Chamberlain hadn't ever come up against a genuine Yankee, and he couldn't make him out. He looked baffled, biting the inside whiskers of his mustache, as if he'd like to turn Tom over to a squad of Cossacks, maybe. But there was Mr. Dallas's letter in his hand, so he couldn't do that. And after a couple of minutes of thinking, he made up his mind.

"I'll take your letter in to the Emperor now," he said.

"That's fine," said Tom. "Just put it up to him. It's a fair proposition."

❧ 9 ☙

THE EMPEROR OF RUSSIA

WELL, in about ten minutes, back came the Chamberlain and along with him was a fine tall man. From the way he walked, Tom saw he was a man who didn't have to fiddle with this and that but marked his first chip and axed right to the line.

He was a good deal bigger than the Chamberlain and he had a bold sharp eye. He wasn't dressed as fancy, but he didn't have to be dressed fancy to tell a person he was somebody. There wasn't any doubt he was the Emperor. And then Tom realized he didn't know the man's name.

He hesitated a moment, and then he decided, even though he was younger, the thing was up to him so as not to embarrass the man. So he took three steps forward and held out his hand.

"My name's Tom Whipple," he said. "I'm from the U.S.A. I ain't been in your country long, but it seems like a fine country, and before I left I wanted to give you a present."

The Emperor looked at him a minute. His eyes went all over Tom in a glance and rested on his face. Then he smiled and held out his own hand and they shook.

"Hello, Tom," he said. "My name's Nicholas. I'm glad to welcome you. I wish you'd come to see me sooner."

"Well," said Tom, "you're a mighty hard man to get to see, Emperor. I tried half-a-dozen times."

"That's the trouble with being an emperor," said Nicholas. "They run in all the people you don't want to talk to, and they keep out the people you do."

He had an easy way with him; he seemed neighborly to Tom; he wasn't a bit like the Chamberlain. He said, "Now you've got here, though, we'll have a talk. You come with me, Tom."

But the Chamberlain interrupted in Russian and from the way the Emperor talked back it sounded like something pretty terrific. The Chamberlain stepped back, and the two of them walked out on him. As soon as they were outside, Nicholas laughed and put his hand on Tom's shoulder. "I told him to throw out everybody," he said, "and he doesn't like it much. But he's got to do it. That's one of the good things about being an Emperor, even if there aren't many."

Well, he took Tom to another room as big as a convention hall, to Tom's eyes, which he said was his own snug place where they wouldn't be disturbed, and the first thing he did was ask to see his present. Tom was glad he had thought of it, then. He pulled his hand out of his pocket and then he opened it and he showed the Emperor an acorn resting in the palm of his hand.

The Emperor looked at it and then he took it and said thanks in a friendly way, but Tom could see he was a mite puzzled. It made him grin.

"Shucks," he said. "I wouldn't bring you no ordinary acorn, Emperor. I picked that up in Mount Vernon. That was the place George Washington lived and died at. This nut's right off one of his own personal trees."

Then he felt a little bashful, so he added, "I thought you'd appreciate it, being as it comes from the home of the greatest man of the U.S.A., greater even than Old Hickory."

"I do, Tom," said the Emperor. "I've studied the history of

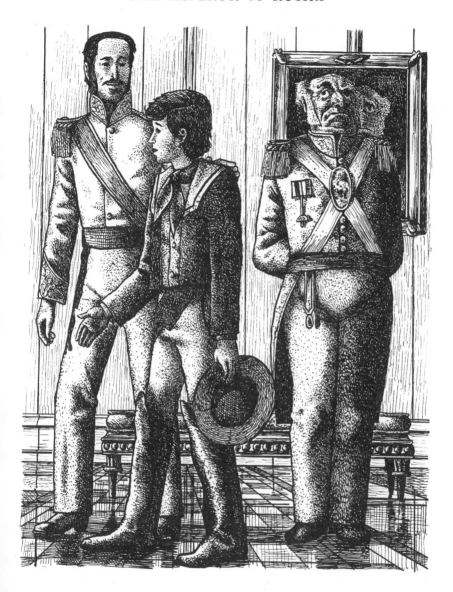

your country, and I admire General Washington more than about any man I know of.''

"Well, you ought to," said Tom. "And over there we admire you folks, too. The way you licked Napoleon Bonaparte. I calculate that took some doing, too."

"I value this acorn a lot, Tom," said the Emperor, "and I'll tell you what I plan to do. We'll have a good talk till the day warms up some, and then we'll go out and plant this acorn. I'll have them thaw out a piece in my own palace garden, and you and I'll plant this acorn there together. An American and a Russian."

"That sounds just proper to me," Tom agreed.

"And then we'll have lunch with my wife and family," said the Emperor, just as Supervisor Utley might have said it. "But now you sit down."

❧ 10 ☙

WASHINGTON'S ACORN

WELL, the Emperor put Tom right through the business. He wanted to know all about America. He was most interested in the railroads and the schools and the steamboats, and Tom was mighty proud he had been through grammar school and had rode on the railroad cars. He could tell the Emperor a lot he didn't know.

Then they talked about tight money, and the Emperor told him about a famine he had had. It seemed in Russia you didn't have a money panic at all, you had a famine, which was simpler in a way, but Tom thought it amounted to much the same thing for the people who were hard up to start with.

They kept at it till noon, and Tom gave the Emperor some of Supervisor Utley's ideas about banking, which interested the Emperor a lot. He wanted to know about Mr. Utley, so Tom told him what a good job the supervisor did running things in Westernville, and he went on to tell the Emperor how Supervisor Utley had starting working there under General Floyd.

General Floyd was one of the signers of the Declaration of Independence, and Tom said it was a wonderful thing to live in the same town a man like that had lived in. He didn't know how to make the Emperor understand that; it made him homesick thinking of it, for you could see the General's grave from the front porch of the Whipple house. But the Emperor said he understood.

Then he got up and suggested that they go out and plant the acorn. There was a squad of Cossacks standing around, but they kept out of the way. The Emperor wondered whether the acorn would grow, and Tom didn't see why not. It was a sound nut from a sound tree, he said.

So then they took a turn around the palace grounds and a couple of big spotted silk-haired dogs, kind of like greyhounds, joined up with the Cossacks. They looked at some horses, which Tom could see were dandies, and he asked where the Emperor kept his cows. He was mighty keen to see a Russian milch cow, he said, but the Emperor told him he would have to go out of the city for that and he said he would send him out tomorrow. He couldn't go himself, because an Emperor might kick over the thills once in a while, but he had to keep on the road, too, by and large, to get along, just like an ordinary man.

❧ 11 ☙

VISITING WITH THE FAMILY

WELL, they had their food in another apartment of the palace and the Empress turned out to be obliging. She talked English better than the Emperor did and she wanted to know all about housekeeping in the U.S.A. Tom told her all he knew, which wasn't so much, since his mother took care of that end of their lives. But he told her how they made butter, and maple sugar, and mincemeat, and cornbread, and she called a servant and had it all written down, just as he said it. Then she said she guessed she was right in thinking that there wasn't any servants in America. And Tom had to laugh at her and said she must have been reading Mrs. Trollope's book. He hadn't read Mrs. Trollope's book himself but he had heard Supervisor Utley talk about it enough to know the kind of nonsense that was in it. The Empress admitted she had, so Tom told her that while poor folks did their own work and weren't ashamed to, either, rich people in the U.S.A. were just like other folks, and had servants and plenty of them. But the Empress said you didn't call them servants, but *help,* and Tom said that was so, but it always appeared to him like a good idea.

The Emperor seemed pleased by the conversation and he made one of his daughters go out for some crochet or some kind of fancywork she had been doing, and Tom admired it.

The Emperor's daughters were fine girls, modest and well-mannered, but shy of him. When he praised the fancywork, the girl that had made it colored all up and made him a curtsy, and then asked him if he would take it back to his mother as a present from her.

That made Tom blush, but he said he would. He hadn't felt so much at home since he left Westernville, and he made up his mind he would have to show the crochet to Mr. Dallas.

Well, they talked all through the afternoon and the Emperor called in some Russian dancers to show Tom how they danced in Russia and Tom, turn about, tried to show them a square dance, but only the girl who had given him the fancywork and the Emperor himself seemed to catch on. The rest weren't handy at it at all. But he put that down to their being bashful and foreign and it didn't bother him.

Then the Emperor said he would have to get back to work, but he asked Tom where he was staying so he could send around a sleigh for him in the morning to go see the cows. Tom told him he was getting hard up so he was sleeping in barns, but would meet the sled at the palace door. The Emperor wanted him to stay at the palace, but Tom wouldn't. He said he could take care of himself, and wouldn't put anybody out, so the Emperor shook hands with him and said to see him after he had looked at the cows.

⟐ 12 ⟐

TIME TO GET HOME

Tom LOOKED at the cows next day. He went out in a sled with
three horses and a fine fur robe over him and a squad of
Cossacks ahead and another behind. He saw the Emperor the
next day and told him he had a nice barn and that he had
milked a couple of the cows and thought they were a fair-to-
middling good breed, and there was one of the springers he
downright fancied. The Emperor said he was glad of Tom's
opinion; he had never been able to judge a cow himself. Then
he asked Tom whether there was anything else he wanted to
see, and though Tom didn't like to ask so much, he finally
admitted he would like to look at Moscow where Napoleon

was licked. So the Emperor sent him to Moscow, and this time Tom traveled with all the luxuries and stayed in the palaces and the best hotels, and the officer who went with him took him to the theater and gave him supper in a different hotel every night.

Tom found it hard to keep going, not being used to so much high life, and he had to admire the Russians for the way they could keep it up. But he enjoyed it, too, and he had to tell the Emperor he was sorry to think of leaving for home. "But I got to get back and get to work," he said. "Ma's expecting me." And he pointed out that even an ordinary man had to work like an Emperor.

The Emperor said he was sorry to see him go. But if Tom had to get back, he would have to go down into Europe to France, for the gulf was frozen over and no ships were leaving. To Tom that seemed like putting the Emperor to a lot of trouble, but he told Tom to think nothing of it. If a man had to get to work, he had to. So they shook hands, and Tom said good-bye to the Empress and her girls, and he called on Mr. Dallas, who was surprised and interested to hear his story. Then the Cossacks took Tom out of Russia.

✿ 13 ✿

SUPERVISOR UTLEY

Now, though Americans have always been great ones to travel and to look around, when one of them begins to think about getting home, his mind sticks right to the one idea; and that was how it was with Tom Whipple.

He had more than one country to cross before he got to the port of Havre, where Mr. Dallas had told him he would find the quickest vessel to take him back to the U.S.A.; but Tom didn't pay much attention to what there was to see in crossing them. He wanted to find that ship. And when he got down to the docks, the ship that seemed to him to be the largest, handsomest, and cleverest to look at was flying the American flag. He went right aboard her and got himself a berth before the mast for the voyage home.

She was bound for New York, the *Francis I,* Captain Cast-off, of the Union Line of packets, and she was a great vessel compared to the *Flora Bascom.* The crew told Tom that she was a fast ship, too. And so she proved, for the Captain drove her every inch and it was still early in April when they sailed up New York Bay.

New York looked fine to Tom, but he couldn't spare the time to look it over again. He had to get to Westernville, and when he reached it, walking up the road from Rome, the

creek was full of snow water, and the boats were just coming
down the canal. He was mighty glad to be home. All the way
across the Atlantic he had kept thinking of maple syrup and
buckwheat cakes; and sure enough, his mother had them for
him when he sat down that night to supper.

After supper they went up to the Utleys', and there he told
them all about the trip. The women could hardly credit the
wonders Tom had seen till he pulled out the fancywork the
Emperor's girl had sent to Mrs. Whipple. Then he showed
them a big watch and chain with a ruby stone hanging to it
that the Emperor had given him in return for the acorn. It
struck its own hours and half hours and was made of gold.

But even then it seemed like a fairy story to Mrs. Whipple
— the great people treating her Tom like a prince — and she
remarked on it so often that Supervisor Utley was obliged to
say, "Pshaw, Mrs. Whipple. Any American lad, like Tom
here, can get along anywhere on earth."

CADMUS HENRY

❧ I ❧

THIS HAPPENED when General George B. McClellan was beginning his Peninsular Campaign against Richmond. He had over ninety thousand men, and gunboats on the York and James rivers to protect his flanks, and a park of artillery that seemed a wonder of the world to the eleven thousand Confederates who had to hold him off till General Johnston could bring down his army from the Rappahannock. Their defense line ran twelve miles across the Peninsula, from Yorktown, along the Warwick River, to Mulberry Point, and their little force was commanded by General John Bankhead Magruder.

There never was another general like Magruder when it came to getting the breath of gallantry and battle into his dispatches. He would send off as many as four or five in a day by special couriers, all the way to Richmond, each with the last instant's news. "I have just left my saddle," he would begin, "and hasten to make a rough sketch of the day's action." This in a thousand words would tell how he had ridden over to confer with Lafayette McLaws, while the booming of cannon announced the opening of action in front of Yorktown. And then how he had ridden back, stopping at Wynn's Mill pond to chat with Colonel Winston, who held the position with "three regiments, a small battalion and two batteries well posted, and the men in fine spirits." No doubt the men cheered him there in the gray rain in the woods beside the deep-green water. It was all a part of making war, to Bankhead Magruder, but in Richmond General Lee must

sometimes have wished that the man didn't have such a fac-
ulty for galloping on horseback, as long as he felt obliged to
write about it mile for mile. General Lee had once even
suggested that it wasn't necessary for Magruder to include all
these details, but the suggestion was gently made, for General
Lee would never willingly have hurt the feelings of any man
who was wholehearted in the cause.

Cadmus Henry, however, admired these reports, and as he
made clean copies of them in the adjutant's office, he thought
that any reader must feel as if he too had ridden with the
General, and for himself, he considered it a wonderful privilege to serve under such a commander.

2

TWO MONTHS AGO, when Cadmus Henry rode in to General
Magruder's headquarters, the young aides and couriers loung-
ing outside the door weren't much interested. All they saw
was a long-legged young man who hadn't yet turned eighteen,
with light-colored hair and solemn dark eyes in a narrow face.
But they took a second look at the brown mare he was riding.

She was a parting gift from his Great-Uncle Eppa Tatum.

"You might as well have her," the old man told him. "I'd
planned to breed her to McGehee's Trinket, but of course the
scoundrel had to take the horse with him when he went to
war."

It took a horseman to see her, but those boys had been

raised to use their eyes, and a couple of them started questioning Cadmus about blood lines. But he excused himself and asked to be taken in to General Magruder, who greeted him cordially, after he had read Eppa Tatum's letter, and told Cadmus he would be glad and honored to accept him as a volunteer aide.

That meant, of course, that Cadmus held no commission, and you might think it would have bothered him not to be able to wear braid on his sleeve. But it didn't. It merely heightened his sense of dedication. He didn't mind being addressed as "Mr." Henry. All he wanted was a chance to distinguish himself. So when he was turned over to Captain Bryan in the adjutant general's office, and Captain Bryan said, "Let's see how you write, Mr. Henry," Cadmus set out to do as good a job as possible. He took pride in his writing, and he felt pleased at the gratifying reaction it earned from the captain. The writing of the other gentlemen, the captain said, looked more like crows' prints tracking through a hen yard than anything in the English language. He said Cadmus could consider himself as permanently attached to the adjutant's office.

He was not only attached; it seemed to Cadmus that he was cemented to it. As time went by, the idea was formed in his mind that he was going to fight the war fraying out successive sets of cuffs against the edge of a desk. The only active work he did was when the general shifted headquarters. Then he packed papers in one place and unpacked them in another and rode between the two places in the interval. Once he got up the nerve to talk to Captain Bryan, he started asking for another job, but no matter what he said, Captain Bryan wouldn't hear of letting him go.

When a couple more volunteers turned up, Cadmus tried

to get them shifted into his job; but the word had got around what happened when a man could write a fair hand, and those two young men, seeing the horrible example Cadmus made, did things to simple spelling and orthography that an ordinary man would never have supposed possible.

It wasn't that Cadmus didn't find some interest in his work. There were times, as he sat and opened dispatches coming in and made copies of those going out, that it seemed as though he had his fingers on the pulse of the whole Peninsula defense line. The simple ruses by which Magruder made his little army appear five times its actual size delighted Cadmus. One day General Early would make a sortie into Palmentary's peach orchard in front of Yorktown with the Florida and Mississippi regiments. And the next day a Georgia regiment would be marched at intervals across a woodland road from one side to the other, crossing back again when it was out of sight of the Federal scouts, to repeat the operation until the Federals started frantically throwing up fieldworks to protect their flanks from this threatening concentration. It was almost like a game, and the younger officers made fun of McClellan and the brag guns he was dragging up to demolish Yorktown with and said how they would drive the whole eternal Yankee army into the rivers, once Joe Johnston got down from the Rappahannock.

Cadmus knew that General Johnston was on the way, and whenever he looked out of the window at the hitch-rail and saw a courier's horse there, steaming in the rain, a revulsion would rise up in him. He hadn't volunteered for office work. He didn't see any sense in his being outfitted for a soldier and given one of the best mares in Henrico County if all he was going to do when the offensive started was to go on sitting at his desk like a lawyer's clerk in term time. He hated to think what his Great-Uncle Eppa would say if he could see him now.

His Great-Uncle Eppa had been mighty particular about Cadmus's clothes. He saw to it personally that they were in the best military style and the correct shade of gray; and he had had his own bootmaker all the way down from Richmond to make Cadmus a pair of boots. "If I give him a letter to Bankhead Magruder, I can't have the boy discrediting me. You can always tell a gentleman by his boots. They're important," the old man said, "especially in a war. A man has to stand up to fight."

The boots were beautiful things when they were done, and they fitted Cadmus like a second skin. He was mighty proud of them; but they required all of his strength, dexterity, patience and powers of prayer to get off. Every night when he wrestled with them he would think of the old man bundled up in coats and blankets on the riverside verandah the day he went to say good-bye.

Great-Uncle Eppa looked him over carefully. "Now anybody would know you came of good people," he said. "We'll have a drink together, and then you'd better start."

He rang the bell by means of a string that was attached to the arm of his chair. The bell had a mellow sound you could hear all over the house grounds and it would still be humming in its throat when the butler brought the toddies through the doorway. The old man had a way of adjusting his voice to the note of the bell.

"Circumstances have put me *in loco parentis* to you, Caddy. I suppose, if your father was alive, he'd tell you one or two of the things you ought to know. I'll have to try." But he bogged down in silence, with the bell still humming over his head like a bee wing-deep in a foxglove, and when the toddies came, he took the glass thoughtfully and held it where his eyes could rest on it. "Tatum men," he began again, "are hairier than bears, but their women are beautiful. Look at your mother and you'll see what I mean."

Cadmus would always remember him as he sat there, pushing the toddy glass towards an invisible orifice in the tangle of his whiskers and gently tilting his head. When he took the glass away, the hairs stirred and shifted and moved around as if a gradual subsidence of forces was taking place somewhere below. He breathed heavily for a moment, waiting before he made another try.

"Caddy," he said, "the fires of war are apt to touch men and women and even horses. You'll have to watch out for them. I want you to be careful of that mare. I wouldn't want her lined by any bush-bred, slat-ribbed peddler's hack." He emptied the toddy glass and then startled Cadmus by standing up. "Anything else I ought to tell you we'll let pass. A colt worth his salt learns to take his own fences anyway." He held out his mottled old hand. I can't go with you, my boy, so you'll have to do my shooting for me. When things get good and hot, you say to yourself, 'This one's for the old man,' will you?"

It made Cadmus feel ashamed to think of Great-Uncle Eppa. When he had turned the mare at the end of the drive between the gateposts with the urns on top to have a last look back, the old man was still standing in front of his chair, and while Cadmus watched, he turned his hand into a fist and delivered three shaky blows against the air. Cadmus, letting the mare dance on between the gateposts, had repeated these symbolic blows to show that he would not forget.

ᘓ 3 ᘖ

Now with the thin white sunlight slanting in across his desk, Cadmus looked down at his fist and at the pen in it and the ink stain on the knuckle of his thunb, and there was a bitter scorn in him — the kind of scorn only a young man can feel and that is bitterest when he feels it of himself — as he read the words he had just copied down.

The spade and the ax have been no less familiar to their hardy hands than the musket and the sword.

On the eighteenth of April, by General Johnston's order, the Army of the Peninsula had been merged with the Army of Northern Virginia, and General Magruder, instead of exercising independent command, was assigned to the right wing of the army. The paper Cadmus had been set to copy was his farewell message to his former troops. It covered two full foolscap pages and it was resonant with phrases like "the frowning fortress of Monroe . . . immense legions of the enemy . . . roar of your artillery . . . unaided efforts of our little band." A month ago Cadmus would likely have admired it, but now it only meant another shackle to bind him to his desk.

Outside the door the voices of the couriers and aides exchanging news made a low, continuous murmur in the pale sunlight. For the past twelve hours headquarters had been

swarming with rumors of the coming offensive. Even the paper under Cadmus's hand hinted at "the great drama about to be enacted on this Peninsula." But Cadmus had begun to feel that when it came he would still be making copies of this proclamation. "We'll want ten copies, Mr. Henry," Captain Bryan had said. "Keep right at it, will you?"

Captain Bryan had a desk at the far corner of the room, and if there was a sympathetic glint in his eye, it did not show from where Cadmus was working. The captain was a hard man; he had an office to run; and now that he had found himself a decently useful clerk, he intended to hang onto him. Being a wholehearted man in his work, moreover, he had no time to spare for catering to what he considered the purely senti-mental ambitions of Mr. Henry, or of any other young aide or officer, for that matter. So Cadmus had gradually become convinced that Captain Bryan had about as many human attributes as a muleshoe.

Cadmus was grimly beginning his third copy when the

captain had to leave the office. As he legged it through the door, he called back something about starting on the dispatches, "if you finish with that proclamation before I get back." Cadmus didn't pay much attention for it didn't signify anything except the captain's dislike of leaving anybody in circumstances in which they could conceivably find an idle moment. Considering the length of the proclamation, he thought bitterly, there wasn't much chance of that.

But it wasn't his temperament to stay bitter, and after he had been alone for five minutes he realized suddenly that this was probably as close as he would ever come to being adjutant; for Captain Dickinson, the other assistant adjutant, had gone over to Yorktown to straighten out a difficulty with General D. H. Hill over a 32-pounder columbiad, and that left Cadmus in sole charge of the office.

He enjoyed the sensation. He kept reasonably hard at his work till there were four copies left to be made. At least he had the privilege of giving himself orders. "I said *ten* copies, Mr. Henry. Keep at it, my boy." Still, being in charge, he didn't feel obliged to burn himself up at the job, either; and he kept an ear open, also, for any excitement that might develop outside. That was how he heard the courier coming.

The courier took his time. There was something almost drowsy in the jingle of his spurs as he walked in and remarked in a soft drawl that he carried a dispatch from General Johnston's headquarters.

"I'll sign for it," Cadmus told him.

The courier looked at him out of drooping eyes, but made no demur about taking a receipt from a civilian. He pocketed the slip and let himself walk out.

Cadmus picked up the dispatch. He could leave it till Captain Bryan returned; but, on the other hand, as he was in charge of the office, maybe he ought to open it to see whether it was important. After a brief hesitation he persuaded himself he ought to open it; but the dispatch was not important. It was no more than a request from General Johnston to General Magruder for a qualified observer. The man, General Johnston wrote, would need a thorough knowledge of the Peninsula and a good comprehension of the general situation, and he was to report to General Johnston before nightfall.

Cadmus felt cheated. He had half hoped there might be an emergency and that he could take some part of it. He got up drearily to take the message across to the adjutant's desk, but as he laid it down there, his eyes went over the wording of the message and suddenly his heart skipped a beat. General Johnston hadn't asked for an officer; he had merely asked for a qualified observer.

It didn't take Cadmus more than a second to make up his mind about it; just long enough to step to the back window. The coast was clear, so he went to find General Magruder, who was at his own desk in the act of composition. The general wrote, Cadmus thought, a little the way he rode a horse, at full gallop. "Come in, Mr. Henry," he said with the faint lisp that came curiously from such an imposing figure of a man. "Just let me finish this sentence." It must have been a good one, for it covered more than nine lines before it hit a period and the general dropped his pen and reached out his hand with almost a single motion.

"Let's see what you have, Mr. Henry."

"It has just come in, sir." Cadmus couldn't keep the excitement out of his voice. He could feel the shakes getting a hold on him, and he froze onto them like a bird dog working up to a point. "I thought I'd better bring it in now."

The general looked up.

"It's not very important, you know, Mr. Henry."

Cadmus had stopped himself shaking, but he was so stiff that for an instant he didn't think his jaw was going to open. When it did, his voice came out louder than necessary. "I'd like to volunteer for the job, sir."

There were some people who thought Bankhead Magruder was a fool and others who considered him pompous and a show-off, and there were a few who wondered if he had ever quite grown up. He said now, with a sober face, "I suppose you've consulted Captain Bryan."

"Captain Bryan was out, sir." Cadmus looked at the handsome, florid face framed in the elaborate whiskers and suddenly he took his courage in both hands. "He'd never allow me to go," he blurted out. "He wants to keep me clerking the way I've been since I got here. I can't fight this war at a desk, sir. I've got to get out of that office. I've just absolutely got to."

He stopped himself short and swallowed hard. He had the dry swallows. He hadn't meant to raise his voice that way, but General Magruder didn't appear to have noticed.

"I know how you feel, Mr. Henry. We all of us get taped down in different ways, but you've had a dose of it. Do you think you're qualified for the work?"

"I know the Peninsula, sir. Before my father died he used to take me round with him on his calls. He was a doctor. He was a good one," Cadmus said with the pride in his voice he had first learned from his mother. "I've seen most of the papers going through the office, too, and I know where our people are, pretty well."

"Well," the general said, "you're very young. But I'll give you a letter to General Johnston. If you can convince him, you can have the detail." He wrote a few rapid lines and handed the sheet to Cadmus. "There you are. I wish you luck, Mr. Henry." He shook hands with Cadmus and said casually, "That's a fine pair of boots you have on. Would you mind letting me have the name of your bootmaker?"

Cadmus gave it. His estimation of Great-Uncle Eppa's knowledge of the world had been considerably raised. He saluted the general and went out of the room as happy as a fiddle string. He could even feel a twinge of conscience when Captain Bryan finally returned; he could afford to now, for there was nothing Captain Bryan could do about his leaving.

But the captain made no attempt to stop him. He merely grinned sardonically. "You go right along, Mr. Henry. You go right along. If you're going to become a hero, you might as well become one now as later. I doubt if General Johnston will take you, anyway. You're too young for the work. But if he does, you'll probably get into hot water. Mighty hot," the captain added, rather as if he hoped so.

❧ 4 ❧

CADMUS didn't put much dependence in what the captain said. He thought Captain Bryan was just jawing because he was mad. It didn't seem likely that General Johnston would turn him down when he came with General Magruder's personal recommendation.

It wasn't any distance over to Lee's house where General Johnston's headquarters were, but Cadmus got out the brown mare. He took her down toward the river road a piece and let her travel, for she was fresh as paint with all her idle days, and he told her to have her fun — she was going to have work soon enough, he told her.

The sun was setting when he turned back. The color from it came through the trees and picked out threads of light in the water-filled ruts. A section of a battery was having a slow time with the mud and the men looked up from the two guns and hooted as the mare danced into the ditch to get by. "One of Magruder's little boys," they yelled after him. "Look out you don't spoil them nice new clothes." There was a kind of anger, too, in their voices that made the blood rise uneasily in his face. They looked as if they had been a long time in the rain; their faces had the color of mud, and the teams were irritable and uncertain. But then he had the road to himself and the twilight started coming into the woods and he realized that he had better get back in a hurry. The mare was willing, for the Union batteries were opening up all along the line and there was a new deep undertone over toward Yorktown, as though some heavy guns had got to work. Now and then, too, there would be outbreaks of musketry that suddenly fused to a single point in the line and then quickly faded out. None of the shells reached in his direction, but it was an unearthly feeling to be alone on a woods road with all that racket going on; and the mare went like a blown leaf.

Cadmus arrived at Lee's house like someone with important news, but the sentry wasn't impressed. He sent in for an officer, and a young lieutenant came out and took Magruder's letter. It was several minutes before he came back for Cadmus and led him inside. They stopped at the door of an inner room, which the lieutenant opened for him.

There were two men in the room and Cadmus didn't have

to be told which was Joe Johnston. The other introduced himself as Major Rhett, but Cadmus hardly noticed what he looked like. The general's eyes held him. They were gray and penetrating and they gave nothing away.

"How old are you, Mr. Henry?" he asked, and when Cadmus told him, he said sharply, "He's too young"; and Cadmus didn't like the twist of his thin lips. It looked to him as if Captain Bryan would prove to be right, and a wave of humiliation went through him.

But the major said, "You can hardly blame Mr. Henry for his age."

General Johnston had already picked up some papers. But he put them down and lifted his head again, and as he studied Cadmus's face, the bitter lines of his mouth softened.

"No," he said. "I don't suppose we can. Sit down, Mr. Henry, while I ask you a few questions."

There were only a few, but it seemed to Cadmus that the general had found out from them most of what there was to know about his life and his experience with the army. He hadn't realized before how little there was to the sum total, and when the general finished, he expected to be told to get out; but instead General Johnston said, "Bring me the big-scale map," and while the major fiddled with some map cases, the general started clearing the papers off a big table at one side of the room.

Cadmus saw that he had probably squeaked by the first part of his examination, and he took heart from it. He made up his mind to do better with the map.

"Take a good look at it, Mr. Henry," the general told him.

It showed the whole end of the Peninsula up nearly to Barhamville. Roads had been marked out, and the better farms, and the defense lines penciled in.

"What are you looking at?" the general asked suddenly.

He was standing next to Cadmus, and he was short enough so Cadmus could look right over his head.

"I was looking at Lee's house; it's marked there," Cadmus said.

"Why?"

"Because that's where I am."

The general was very erect. He had sloping shoulders but he had a wiry quality about him. Once in a while you'll get a little rooster, and he'll dodge and turn and run off and make motions, but when he sets to fight he's wicked as perdition. That was how Joe Johnston looked to Cadmus. In the candle-light his eyes took on some of the hard, clear brightness of a bird's.

He started asking questions about turnpikes and woods, roads and farms and the places where there were fords. Cadmus could tell him almost all those things and even show where the map was wrong. Most Confederate maps of the Peninsula at that time were pretty inaccurate. The Union generals weren't any better off on that score, though, of course, Cadmus couldn't know that.

Then the general made Cadmus go to the far side of the room and he asked him a few more questions when he didn't have the map to help him out. But Cadmus was sure of himself now, and he answered as fast as the general asked him, and after only a minute or two the general stopped and rolled up the map and looked across it at Cadmus with an unex-pected twinkle in his eyes.

"I wouldn't have thought Bankhead Magruder had it in him."

"Had what in him?" asked the major, who had gone back to some work of his own.

"Sending us the right man. I think Mr. Henry's going to be all right. You'll have to show him the kind of report we need and what sort of information we're after," said the general. "And make out a special order assigning him to the balloon."

Cadmus felt his heels shove suddenly against the floor. He thought for a minute he hadn't heard straight. Then he knew he had, for the major had reached for a clean sheet of paper and dipped his pen. It was getting dark and the panes in the window had turned to mirrors and in one of them he could see himself standing with his mouth half open.

"Balloon?" he said.

General Johnston had started toward his desk. He stopped short and looked sharply at Cadmus.

"Did you say something, Mr. Henry?"

Cadmus swallowed.

"I said, 'Balloon,' sir."

"Well?" It was a cold word.

"I thought I was going to scout for you, sir. I don't know anything about balloons."

"Mr. Henry." The general raised himself slightly on his toes. His cheeks darkened. "I requested General Magruder to send me a qualified observer. You were assigned. You will accept the duty. Major Rhett will tell you when you are to make an ascent."

Cadmus said, "Yes, sir."

Major Rhett saw him out.

"It might be a good idea if you went to the balloon camp in the morning and had a talk with the crew. You'll have to learn about signals."

He spoke kindly and Cadmus said, "Yes, sir," like a grateful dog. Only he didn't actually feel grateful. He felt trapped.

The Federals had some balloons and whenever one of them

went up, the Confederate gunners always tried to shoot it down. Cadmus remembered seeing one of them go up behind Wynn's Mill, and every Confederate cannon within range let go at it. One shell burst close enough to make the balloon rock crazily and Cadmus had cheered and laughed with the rest.

He realized now that that had been a wicked thing to do.

ઢ 5 ૐ

CADMUS FOUND the balloon camp in a small opening in the woods, about a half mile behind the lines. But he hadn't come to make any preliminary visit. He was going to go right up. And perhaps that was a good thing in a way, for he hadn't had time to get more than just about scared to death.

At six o'clock that morning he had been brought orders to report to General Johnston's headquarters. There Major Rhett had supplied him with a notebook, pencils and a powerful pair of glasses. "We want you to mark down all the enemy troops you can see. Take your time, and identify them by organization, if possible. Estimate the numbers. Also mark down any moving troops, and any new batteries. You'll want to go high enough to get a look back as far as Howard's Bridge and Deep Creek." He dropped a hand on Cadmus's shoulder. "I'm sorry to call on you so suddenly. But you ought not to have any difficulty with signals and things. The crew has had experience. It would be a good idea though to keep the strap of those glasses round your neck all the time. They're valuable."

He shook hands.

"They'll be expecting you out there. Good luck, Mr. Henry."

It was an almost idyllic spot for a camp — that is, if you were camping there. The fine running spring, the stand of pine trees that left the ground free of underbrush and the good green grass meant nothing to Cadmus. All he saw was the apparatus that used up most of the open space.

It consisted of a long iron flue resting on bricks. One end of the flue was bent up and passed into the mouth of the balloon, while the bag, like the dead body of a slovenly monster, enclosed in the net of cordage, sprawled out on the grass beyond. A rope was attached to the cordage, from which it reached to an enormous windlass; it made several turns round the windlass and then continued off into the woods in coil after coil. To Cadmus's desperate eyes it did not seem possible that so much rope could exist in the world, let alone in the Confederate States of America.

The balloon crew must have heard him coming, for one of them was building a fire under the flue, while a round-shouldered Negro brought up pine knots and turpentine. Two other men were standing near the windlass and they, with a fifth man, who appeared to have charge of the crew, watched Cadmus ride up.

The fifth man was a gangling individual with an intermittent flutter in his left eye. He was wearing what might have passed for a military cap at some earlier stage of its career.

"You Mr. Henry?" he inquired in a soft, slow voice.

Cadmus allowed he was.

"The boys will have her ready for you right quick," he said. "My name's Norment, Blaney Norment, Mr. Henry. I'm glad to be of service any time." His eyelid nearly closed and then slowly and fascinatingly fluttered open. "Mebane," he shouted, "you come here and take Mr. Henry's horse."

A second Negro came shuffling out of the woods, a little man with grizzled hair and a thin line of whiskers. When he saw the brown mare, his hands cupped a little, and he made a humming sound. The mare, who usually was leery of strangers, dropped her nose and made a faint whickering over the little man's head. When he led her off into the woods she went as slow and shuffling as he did.

"Something about Mebane," Norment said. "Horses like it. I don't know what it is."

Cadmus said something polite, but he didn't know what. He was watching the way the big Negro had begun slinging turpentine at the growing fire. The flames almost exploded upward and the roar of burning found an echo in the iron flue, as if the flames had hands to beat it with. He was conscious of the speculative stares of the men, but he didn't pay much attention. He was finding it hard to make his knees keep upright.

"That's a lot of rope, Mr. Norment," he said, because he had to say something.

"Maybe half a mile. It has good long splices. Mink makes good splices. He was a sailor."

The big Negro lifted his head. He looked at Cadmus briefly, and then threw another armful of knots on the fire. The man who had started the fire now came over to where Cadmus and Norment stood together. He looked like an Irishman and somewhere he had picked up a Zouave's red hat.

"She ought to start swelling pretty soon now, the danged old beast," he said, glancing at Cadmus from the corners of his eyes. "Will I get the gentleman the flag?"

"Yes," said Norment.

Neither he nor Cadmus had anything to say while the Irishman went for the flag. Cadmus wondered momentarily whether it was a Confederate flag, to be attached to the balloon. His attention was absorbed by a sudden swelling of the bag, just beyond the point where the flue entered it. It made no sound; or if it did, the roar of the fire covered it. He watched while the swelling grew. The fabric began to lift uncertainly, the center of heat shifting slightly as the draught through the flue gained or lost momentum. Whenever the last seemed to be the case, the Negro, Mink, threw on turpentine.

As the bag distended, Cadmus observed that it was made up of a great number of irregular pieces of cotton cloth, originally of varying colors, but now faded into an approximate uniformity. The cotton had been coated with some sort of waterproofing to make it airtight, but in places the coating had cracked, and the entire contrivance looked pretty dubious to Cadmus.

The Irishman returned with a small square of red bunting tacked onto a short stick. The man Norment took it from the Irishman.

"Here's the flag," he said. "When you want to go up, you wave up with it. When you want to go down, you wave down. It's easy to remember."

"How can you tell which way I'm waving?" Cadmus asked.

"Oh, we can figure it out," said Norment. "When a man wants to come down, he leans farther over the edge. Hooley, here, has good eyesight. Now when you're going up or going down either one, and you want us to hurry up, you shake the flag. The more you want the boys to hurry, the harder you shake it. When you want us to leave off whatever we're doing, you wave."

Cadmus said, "I should think it would be plainer if you had two flags of different colors. That would tell you everything. Red to come down, blue to go up."

"We had a yellow one."

"What did you do with it?"

"Nothing. It got lost." Norment regarded him with a thoughtful expression. Suddenly his eyelid fluttered.

Cadmus looked away. The bag of the balloon was increasing enormously. Nearly free of the ground, it had definitely formed its spherical shape. Printed in huge letters around the side was the name PIZZINI.

Seeing that Cadmus was looking at the name, Norment looked at it also.

"Was my brother," he explained. "That was his professional name. Professor Pizzini. He dropped the flag and tried to grab it."

Hooley said, "What goes up must come down." He studied Cadmus out of the corners of his eyes.

Cadmus looked away. His feet didn't feel right. They could have walked out from under him and he wouldn't have known it.

Norment said, "I never sent up a balloon on this kind of business. Only for my brother Pizzini, to make a civilized ascent. Likely they'll shoot at you, Mr. Henry. Those Union people over there, they shoot at anything. Shoot, shoot, shoot, all day and all night till I get tired. But there's one thing about it, they can't shoot only so high, so when you get up far enough, they can't touch you. That's one thing about it, all right."

Cadmus tried to grin.

"But you have to come back down through it."

"What goes up must come down," Hooley said again.

"You shut your mouth with that business," Norment told him, in an utterly toneless voice. He walked over to the windlass, and then back along the coils of rope. "You boys got the end of that rope around something?"

They said no.

"You, Mink," Norment ordered, "you go tie that rope around a tree. Can't never be sure about anything in ballooning unless you're tied down to earth somewhere," he said to Cadmus. "Suppose a cannon shell dumped in here and killed us all when she was still skinful and hot — that rope would ravel through that windlass like a tax collector's soul. And the man up there wouldn't know a thing about it till he found himself riding in the hand of God. We don't want that to happen, Mr. Henry. There's a time for all things. I guess the old bag's about ready for you."

Cadmus saw that it was so. The two men over by the windlass had laid hold of the handles and now the balloon had drawn free of the flue, and swung suddenly straight above the windlass, picking up its cords as it went. It poised there, a great sphere blotting out half the woods, a monstrous thing to grow in a quiet place, swinging a little, the cords slatting loosely together.

Norment respectfully touched his elbow.

"You want to get in right quick, Mr. Henry. The quicker you do that, the more hot air you've got to lift you."

"When will I know it's getting too cold?" Cadmus asked. "So I can signal you."

"You don't need to worry about that; we'll know."

"Yes," said Hooley, with his sidelong glance. "We'll know."

The Negro, Mink, came up to them. "Mist' Norment, you all ready for the basket?" There was a peremptory note in his deep voice.

"When Mink says it's time to go, it is," Norment told Cadmus.

The suspension lines that connected the basket with the concentration ring tightened as the men at the windlass eased up on the brake handle. It seemed to Cadmus that he could see a tremor in the rope. He was conscious of the big Negro's glance, which was almost contemptuous. Mink's eyes seemed to take in everything, and it ocurred to Cadmus that he probably had more to do with the actual management of the balloon than Norment.

"All right," he said. "I'm ready."

Mink turned a serious glance on him.

"That's good," he said. He steadied the basket with his great hands as Cadmus climbed in.

⋙ 6 ⋘

CADMUS stood holding onto one of the suspension lines with one hand, and grasping the small red flag in the other. He looked around on the good green grass and the line of woods from the shade of which the horses were watching him. The sunlight had a fine warmth. There was hardly a cloud in the sky. But he could feel the tremor in the great envelope as it came down through the net of cords into the suspension line his hand had hold of. He looked up and saw it over his head, looming against the blue sky like the belly of eternity. Underneath, the appendix, by which the hot air had entered this vastness, dangled incongruously, like an elephant's tail.

A slight jerk made him turn to see what the men at the windlass might be up to. But instead of the men, he saw the middle branches of the trees. The balloon was rising, and Cadmus was shocked to realize that he would have to look down if he wanted to see the clearing. The men at the windlass were working the handles; Norment had moved back, resting his hand on his narrow posterior and arching his back to look upward. His mouth was open. Hooley stood off to one side by himself and Mink was watching the uncoiling of the rope. It all seemed very simple and easy, now that he was underway. In fact, Cadmus thought, as he straightened himself in the narrow basket, there was practically nothing to it. He felt almost casual as he glanced out across the treetops.

Lee's house looked closer than he would have imagined.

The line of the Warwick River came quickly into view. He
made out the dams, the two mills and the Union earthworks
on the far side. He could see the troops moving about behind

them, the dark blue uniforms almost black, and the men standing on the ends of their shadows. Then he picked out a battery in a meadow beyond Dam No. 2. The guns were placed in a line with the caissons close up. He could even see the battery teams in an elbow of the meadow, behind some trees. It gave him a curious feeling of detachment to look down on the enemy, as they went about their morning chores, oblivious of his eyes.

But then he noticed that men had started running to their guns. They looked to him like a smart outfit; and they must have had a serious alarm to react so sharply. He wondered what his own people might be up to. He couldn't see any signs of activity in the nearer woods, however, and he looked back at the battery to find an officer busily elevating one of the guns. The muzzle rose and kept on rising, and then it stopped, and Cadmus was seized by a horrid comprehension of the battery's excitement. They had seen the balloon. They were about to shoot at him.

A puff of smoke leaned out of the gun's muzzle and drew to one side, and in the same instant, it seemed to him, a shell burst on his left. In the next instant the entire surrounding sky was filled with bursting shells. They kept on bursting. He felt completely naked there, and tried instinctively to crouch down behind the basket rim; but the basket was made too small for that. He could neither sit nor kneel.

Then he remembered the red flag. It was still in his hand. Reaching out, he signaled frantically for speed and then ducked back again as a shell passed, cutting a kind of whistle out of the air. He shut his eyes and started praying and heard a thunderous explosion somewhere below. Then another, also below; and still another; and gradually he realized that all the bursts were below him. But he couldn't get up or even open his eyes. He kept crouched as he was, with his heart hammering and a drenching sweat all over him.

A moment later the firing stopped entirely. He felt silence sweep over him, and when finally he opened his eyes, he was surrounded by the sky. Without looking down, he waved the flag from side to side to stop the ascent, and for a little he stayed still, just staring at the blue sky or at the bag over him, with its ridiculous, restless appendix. He had a strange and fanciful impression that the balloon, instead of being attached to earth by a straining rope, was suspended from some tackle in the sky. He could feel a stir of the air passing him. It was a little like resting in a fabulous swing.

His confidence came back to him with a rush. There was nothing those blue people could do to him now. As he thought of it, he came to the conclusion that none of their shells had burst anywhere really close. So he hoisted himself slightly and looked over the edge of the basket.

The Peninsula now lay like a cloth in gray and green and earth color, stitched and seamed with roads and rivers and fences. It was a clear and beautiful day. The lower waters of the James and the York were blue as the sky itself and to the east he saw the wide shine of the Bay.

All over the land below, and back toward Big Bethel, he made out units of enemy troops: some moving along the roads with what seemed infinite slowness; others in tented villages new-white on the green meadows. Houses and farm buildings cast bold shadows; and the shingled roofs of Yorktown were black and white. Three crows went by below, cocking their heads at him and raucously discussing this phenomenon of a man in the sky; and he had a sudden notion that perhaps they regarded his presence as a usurpation of the rights of crows. It made him grin. He pulled out his notebook and glasses and got to work.

It was a more difficult job than he had supposed, for no sooner had he started sketching in the Union positions, than the balloon, with a kind of comic perversity, started slowly to revolve; and Cadmus would no sooner have the line of a fieldwork started than it would have slipped past the orbit of his vision. The basket was too narrow for him to keep continually shifting, so that he had to wait till the continuing revolution brought him round again. But he had good eyes, and the crudely sketched map began to fill up rapidly with the letters I or C or A, to indicate the branches of the service, and the numerals beneath them indicating Cadmus's estimate of their strength.

He had begun with the battery that had fired at him and worked outward and eastward from that point. When finally he finished his work, he turned his glasses back to it again, and saw with a feeling of complete horror that the Yankees had practically filled the field with guns. There must have been three complete batteries brought up while he was working, and more guns were struggling through to roads for neighboring vantage points.

He leaned way over to look down at the balloon camp, which now seemed very far away. He could not identify the men from that distance, except for the Irishman Hooley, whose red cap stood out against the grass. But when he turned the glasses on them, he saw all of them looking upward, and the Irishman made a gesture with one hand, as if he repeated his favorite phrase.

He had to go down, whether he liked to or not, for the balloon would not retain its buoyancy indefinitely. He unfurled the red flag and waved it.

Long before he reached the danger zone, single guns had begun feeling out the range. The moment the balloon came low enough, the Yankees opened with all their batteries. The shells came in salvos: four, six and eight guns firing at once. Cadmus thought he could hear the shells rumbling from the instant of leaving the cannon's mouth until they burst. They burst in one continual, uninterrupted and enormous blast.

The balloon, which had started down with what had seemed to him a suicidal quickness, now hung floating with tantalizing and vagarish slowness. He had once heard a minister with the preaching gift deliver what Great-Uncle Eppa had pronounced a mighty sermon on the gaping jaws of hell. To Cadmus, the sounds and agonies described by that preacher were a trifle to what he was now passing through himself. He kept on signaling for more speed, and he said prayers at the top of his voice. And then, miraculously, he had passed through the thunder; he was behind the shelter of the trees; and the bombshells were passing overhead.

The balloon crew stood as they were, just staring at him, as if they didn't believe the evidence of their own eyes. The two men last at the windlass continued leaning on the handles. One of these was the Negro, Mink. His bowed shoulders were drenched with sweat and his chest labored heavily. But there was a kind of pride in his face as he looked at Cadmus, as if he now had a share in his existence.

"He wouldn't give up his handle, once you got in among them bombshells," Norment explained. "But the other boys took turns on the other one."

When Cadmus climbed out, the earth shifted under him and he had to hang onto the rim of the basket. A shivering was coming down the suspension lines. Looking up, he saw a puckering in the under side of the patchwork bag, as if the balloon too shared in the general exhaustion. Then abruptly the Yankees gave up shooting. Silence blanketed the clearing, and through the silence, shuffling slowly towards them and mumbling some kind of jargon about the Promised Land into her attentive ear, Mebane came leading the brown mare.

It was easier for Cadmus in the saddle. He looked down into the men's blank faces and tried to find some words to say to them. But he couldn't.

The flutter in Norment's eyelid was translated to the envelope of the balloon. It began to settle.

"We all wish you luck, Mr. Henry. Maybe we'll see you again some time. But it won't be this place, I reckon."

Norment looked regretfully round their comfortable camp-site.

Cadmus tried to sound casual.

"I probably won't be going up again. But what makes you think you'll have to move?"

"Them Yankees," Norment said drearily. "Now they've missed the balloon, they'll be bound to try and hit us in this camp. Shoot, shoot, shoot. It makes me tired."

As if to second him, a Hotchkiss shell howled gaudily across the trees and exploded with a sudden thump a hundred yards or so back in the woods.

❧ 7 ❧

THAT SHELL made the brown mare light out of there as if she
intended to get shut of balloon camps and ballooning for the
rest of her natural days, and Cadmus had no inclination to
dispute her. He reckoned he'd have to go back to the adjutant's office, once he had made his report; but the way he felt
just then, even considering the remarks Captain Bryan was
bound to throw at him, he wasn't exactly sorry. In fact, he
could see important features to clerking that hadn't been
apparent to him before.

There was a whole mess of officers and couriers cluttering
up General Johnston's headquarters that morning when he
galloped in; and though, like most men, they showed some
interest in the mare, they didn't bother to look twice at
Cadmus. Therefore, it raised something of a stir when, within
three minutes of the time he had sent in his name, an aide
came calling for him. A brigadier and a couple of colonels got
pretty hot-eyed about it, but there wasn't time for him to hear
what they said before the aide shut the door at his back and
General Johnston said, "Come in, Mr. Henry. I'm glad you've
got here, sir."

He stepped forward with his hand out, and by daylight he
looked more grizzled to Cadmus. In a way he looked tougher
and more stubborn. But his eyes were bright and sharp and a
half smile played round his mouth.

"Mr. Henry doesn't look as if he felt too sorry himself, eh, Rhett?"

Major Rhett grinned. They had had a report, he explained, that the Yankees had done some shooting at the balloon. Cadmus admitted to some. It was even possible to feel amused now, with these two older men showing their friendliness. They put him at his ease, and he made a clear report. He had a good visual memory. When he looked down at the big map, with his notebook open to check by, it was almost the same thing to him as looking down again from the basket of the balloon. Only this time he didn't have to worry about the Union battery. It was only a mark in blue ink, with the letter A traced under it by Major Rhett.

They asked him a few questions, and when he had answered them, they told him he had done well. That seemed like a good time for him to take his leave, so he held the glasses out to Major Rhett and said he'd better be going.

"Going?" the major echoed blankly, and General Johnston turned from his absorption in the map and fixed Cadmus with his birdlike eyes. The atmosphere of the room changed. It didn't exactly chill, but it filled with questioning, and Cadmus found himself stammering.

"I — I thought I ought to get back to General Magruder's," he said, and he added, after a pause, "as long as this job's done. They're mighty shorthanded there, sir."

"Who said it was done?" Johnston demanded harshly. "General Magruder has more people hanging around and doing nothing than a guinea chicken has spots. Let them do his clerking. You forget that you're the only experienced aeronaut in the Army, Mr. Henry. I can't spare you."

So Cadmus was stuck with the balloon job tighter than a tick in a sheep's ear; and, as far as he could see, there wasn't an earthly thing he could do about it. He had managed to get out of clerking in the adjutant's office by escaping upstairs, so to speak, where Captain Bryan couldn't come after him; but the only upstairs there was to this job was where the balloon went. He used to think at times that Captain Bryan was a hard and unrelenting man, but the captain's eyes had never showed anything remotely like the degree of frost that could come into Joe Johnston's. There was something about Joe Johnston that didn't leave a man much room for leeway.

Of course, Cadmus gained a kind of notoriety. You couldn't call it fame, exactly, for though the army admired the idea of having a balloonist on their side, they thought that Cadmus must be crazy in the head. It didn't take any great experience in aeronautics for a man to see, even from a considerable distance, that the balloon PIZZINI was a different grade of fish from the Union craft. They would go floating up into the soft April sky, big and steady and sort of silver-smooth. They moved up and down with almost arrogant assurance, and if nothing was happening to distract him, a man in the rifle pits could lie back and watch them all day long. But when PIZ-ZINI made an ascent, it went up "steady by jerks," the way Paddy went to Heaven, and it wouldn't have surprised any man to see one of the odd-colored patches let loose from the fabric, like the knee off a worn-out pair of pants.

It would have surprised Cadmus even less. Up there, underneath the sag of PIZZINI's antique belly, he sometimes thought he could hear the stitches in it talking back and forth, and they sounded mighty tired to him. The breeze off Chesapeake Bay blew in against the dry old cheek of the balloon to set it slowly turning, and as it revolved, it made a kind of rustling whisper, as though it said, "Poor Pizzini, poor Pizzini."

He became accustomed to it after a while, and when it was time to go down, he allowed himself a few extra minutes, just to look at the blueness of the sky and the whiteness of the clouds and the sunlight like a golden wine spilled from the bowl of Heaven. Yet even there, with the cool wind blowing through the basket weave of the balloon car, he couldn't forget the shape of the world below and the war upon it.

A turkey buzzard came sailing down a long incline between some distant clouds, not moving a wing, but letting the wind work for him, and swung over close beside the balloon. Cadmus could see that he was making his own inspection of the armies, and in the course of it, the bird turned his naked head and had a look at Cadmus, too, and then looked back at the opposing lines; but there was no choice in his small round eye. They sailed awhile there together, Cadmus half kneeling and looking over the edge of the car, and the bird holding the wind in his wings as he judged the earth with his bird's brain, and together they looked down with their naked eyes.

It was what Cadmus had been doing all the time of his

observation; but now it was different. There was the great fleet of transports gathered in the York River — two hundred and fifty ships and five hundred bateaux, enough to move a division, and he had the count in his notes. But now he saw how they threatened the whole Confederate position.

He didn't see it exactly as a general might in his reports. He saw instead the men in the rifle pits or working behind the guns. Some men close to the river were standing out their hours of duty in water over their knees. Others were digging a faint line along the edge of some woods, and a gun crew, bringing up a gun behind them, were struggling in the deep Peninsula mud, and they were like ants about a task that, to a mortal eye, seemed far too great for them, but they kept right on with their business. It was like a map beneath him, and yet it wasn't either, for shell holes don't keep appearing on a map. There a skilled hand traces a line in colored ink and establishes a theoretical fact; but from the balloon car Cadmus was having a vision of the infinite toil by which that easy stroke of the pen must finally be translated to the earth.

And suddenly, looking down as it were with the bird's eye, as they sailed there together in the wind, he could see no real difference in the appearance of the two armies, except for the way they faced and for their size. And afterwards, when Cadmus heard officers talk about the difference between Confederate and Union soldiers, he was to remember this moment looking down on the Peninsula lines. Even then a small doubt about how easy it would be to drive the whole Union army into the river had begun to crawl around inside his mind, though, of course, then and for a long time later, he had no doubts about how the war was going to end.

The turkey buzzard twisted his head to have another look at Cadmus, and in the next instant he had swept himself away, still without a movement of his wings, and upwards and up until he was no more than a speck in the topmost edge of blue, and so was gone.

Once more alone in the wide solitude, Cadmus groped for the red flag and gave the signal to go down.

❧ 8 ❧

No BALLOON ever returned to earth quite as PIZZINI did that day. One minute it had started down in what appeared to be its usual slow and jerky progress; and the next it was dropping like a rabbit whizzing down a bolt-hole. The Yankee gunners never had a chance to get in a second round. Even the Confederate troops were still laying bets on whether the old bag would make it when she dropped entirely out of sight. They thought she must have been hit, and a lot of Confederate soldiers paid out money and some never found out they had been cheated.

Cadmus himself thought something had gone wrong; but when he looked over the edge of the car the explanation was simple enough. Instead of cranking him down, the balloon crew had hitched a team of artillery horses to the anchor rope. Mebane, like an old but active lunatic, was galloping them full pelt down the road. Parked nearby in the ditch was a Parrott gun, its wondering crew gaping up at him. Then he saw Mink, standing with upstretched arms, saw the ground rush at him with a hideous force, heard a deep roar of "Whoa!" from Mink and an indescribable shriek of "Whoa, hoss!" far down the road from Mebane, and the next instant the car struck the grass with a jolt that rattled his teeth and pitched him bodily out onto the ground.

He lurked there on his hands and knees with a dizzy feeling that he could eat grass, until Norment came over to help him up.

"Never saw anything come down faster in my life," Norment was saying with admiring flutters of his eyelid. "Not even Pizzini himself didn't ever come down faster, it seems like. And it didn't hurt the balloon any at all. Just only one little jounce of the car." He turned to the officer who was in charge of the gun. "We're mighty obliged to you for the loan of your team, Mr. Lieutenant."

"Not at all," said the lieutenant, coming forward to shake hands with Cadmus and introduce himself. "Proud to be of service. I must say, though, that Negro of yours can handle horses."

Norment nodded casually.

"Something about Mebane when it comes to horses. It was Mink's idea we could do it, but I wouldn't have tried it without Mebane. Might have tore that bag right through the windlass."

It became a legend as the lieutenant told the story: "Had my team running like crazy," he said. "Just like crazy down the road, with the little Negro using everything he knew on them. And then the big Negro yells, 'Whoa' and that little black midget stops those six big running horses just like that. I give you my word. And the bottom of the basket no more than kissed the ground. Just bent the grass, you might say, sir. And that aeronaut steps out cool as a straw in a julep. I never saw such a cool man in my life. He seemed to think nothing of it. Not a thing, sir."

Maybe the lieutenant had a touch of Homer in him. But whether he did or not, he had a bard's instinct not to let his lyre rust from want of use. Before he had worked out the details of that landing to his satisfaction, half of the Confederate army had heard the story and were telling it themselves. It tickled them wonderfully to think of the Yankees being outfoxed at one of their own games. They started making brag talk about "our balloon" and "our aeronaut," as if Cadmus could see more and act slicker in one trip than any Union observer could in ten. There was hardly a soldier who didn't keep his eye peeled for the next ascension, hoping to be near enough to get over and see for himself how the thing was done.

As events turned out, plenty of them were on hand, for the next flight took place on the night of May third, when the Confederates were evacuating their lines along the Warwick to fall back on the Richmond defenses. Magruder's command had marched at dusk along the Hampton Road, and Longstreet's followed them, while D. H. Hill's troops took the Telegraph Road out of Yorktown. Cadmus was ordered to make an observation of the Union concentrations and report to General Johnston in Williamsburg.

The balloon camp had been moved back along the Telegraph Road to Burwell's Mill, and Cadmus had a hard time reaching it. The roads were filled with slowly moving lines of men and guns. It was long after dark before Cadmus, dismounting, turned the brown mare over to Mebane and Mink touched off the fire under the slanting flue. As the glare rose blindingly through the dark, the swelling bag caught the light like a ball of molten fire and the soldiers broke from the ranks and came flocking from all directions like moths to the flame.

There must have been hundreds of them crowded round the fire in their mud-caked boots and pants, standing with their hands clenched on their muskets, and their eyes staring curiously out of their sweat-streaked faces. As the light rose higher, still more drifted in among the trees where the coils of rope loomed in fabulous anthill shapes. And a Mississippi battalion, stalled by the breakdown of a wagon up ahead, lined the roadside fences and made joking comments on this almost supernatural dilation.

It was difficult for the balloon crew to find room to work in, for the troops were continually getting underfoot and asking questions. Some members of a Georgia company that had lost its regiment and didn't much care either, wanted to know if the thing was likely to explode, and why the air didn't come out the hole it went in at, and whether it attracted light-ning. There were also a few who, when they saw the balloon close up, felt definitely skeptical. Among these was a gaunt man with a pendulous nose and a tired voice. He was dogged by a partner who carried two hens in a bag made out of a flowered petticoat. After they had watched the balloon swell up for a minute or so, they announced that there was nothing in it and went off to lie down in the woods.

Hooley, the Irishman, soon gathered an admiring following who were eager to pick up some of the finer points of the science, which he freely dispensed. But Mink was uneasy. He didn't like the looks of things at all. "Cain' keep track of nothin', Mist' Norment. When I says for them to please keep back, they pay no attention to me."

He spoke in the soft voice of his race, but there was a dark scorn in his eyes as he reared back his head to stare at the thronging faces round him. Maybe, he suggested, they would heed Mr. Henry, if he spoke with them about it. But Cadmus only laughed.

Nothing could go wrong, he said. The Yankee gunners wouldn't spot him at all in the night sky, and even if they did, moonlight made for tricky shooting. Probably they'd be mov-ing their batteries anyway. He wasn't afraid of anything with Mink handling the windlass.

It made Mink look proud for a minute, but he couldn't shake his sense of trouble coming. He didn't know what it was, but it was coming, he knew that. There was sweat all over his face and arms. In the heat of the fire they shone like dark, polished wood. And he said to Hooley, "Got to go slow. You'n me got to handle that windlass, Mist' Hooley, and watch every foot of that rope." But all he got from Hooley was a wink and grin.

Cadmus was now in the car, and the hush that had come over the troops was interrupted by a deep, unanimous sigh as Hooley threw out the pinion and the car lifted suddenly from the ground. It was followed by a surge of voices and quick, loose laughter, as the natural wits in the crowd struck fire. The men saw the balloon receding like a gigantic spark as it moved out beyond the firelight. In a little while it was only a gray blur at the far end of the rope.

There had been a little confusion back along the rope but everything now seemed to be going smoothly. Hooley was explaining the value of the brake by telling a man it was harder to crank the balloon up than crank it down, when the tension on the rope suddenly increased and it changed its slant to the drag of an upper draft of wind. Mink fought it with the brake for a while, but as there seemed no harm in letting the balloon have a little more head, he relaxed his pressure on the lever and the rope began to snake through the windlass at a sharply accelerated pace.

It was then that the outcry started in the woods. At first it was just a confused jumble of sound; but this was immediately succeeded by the screams of a man in mortal terror. Others, too, began to shout, but the screams rose through those voices with a dreadful soaring quality that chilled Hooley to the marrow of his bones. He turned, leaving Mink alone at the windlass, and went to see what was up.

Mink also was rocked by ancient terrors that even Hooley knew nothing of. He stuck to his post, but he couldn't keep his eyes from roving backward towards the outer dark. And then, like the blessed word, a new voice became articulate above the screams and the shouting. "It's all right. It's all right. I fixed it."

In spite of himself, in his overwhelming relief from the he-

297

didn't-quite-know-what, Mink closed his eyes. He didn't need to see, really; he could tell the speed by the pressure of the brake shoe coming up the lever into his hands from the spinning drum. And then, just as a new shouting broke out behind him, that vibration was gone. It wasn't there, it wasn't there at all. He opened his eyes and felt them swell in his head. The windlass drum was empty.

A weird sigh issued from the upturned faces of the troops. The balloon was no longer visible. It had simply vanished from the earth.

In the silence, Hooley returned, bringing the gaunt and skeptical men who had announced that there was nothing in it. He had gone to sleep on one of the coils of rope, which had wrapped around him like a boa constrictor and started to drag him towards the windlass. The man's partner, waked by the screams, had grabbed the camp axe and severed the rope with one wild blow and would have continued praising himself for his cool-headedness had not an even cooler-headed man in the meantime made away with his two hens.

"I hollered," Hooley explained. "And then I tried to catch up with the rope. I figured you couldn't see its end with all these hooligans around you. But I couldn't burst them out of my way."

Norment, resting his hands on his narrow posterior, still hopefully looked upwards. He sighed.

"It wasn't your fault, Mink. I reckon it wasn't nobody's fault."

But Mink was shamed. He was shamed before all the white men. He didn't hang his head or look aloft either, with foolish, straining eyes. He knew that Mist' Henry had regarded him as the real pick and boss of this balloon crew, and instead he had been plain no account. He heard one of the soldiers asking Hooley where he supposed the balloonist was by now, and Hooley answered him, "I guess he's in the hand of God."

To Mink it was a fact.

Lawd know how high, he thought. *Lawd know how high.*

~ 9 ~

To CADMUS it seemed like the end of the world. One minute he was rising smoothly over the trees — perhaps two hundred feet high, because he could see the big fires that D. H. Hill's rear guard were keeping up in Yorktown to fool the Yankees. The balloon was entering a level of cooler air, with a breeze blowing gently up the Peninsula; the big bag had started its slow turning and Cadmus could hear the old dry voiceless whisper of its wrinkled skin. And then the thing happened.

It felt as if an enormous force had snatched the balloon into eternity.

When Cadmus came to and could begin to breathe once more, he was hashed down in the narrow car like wet clothes in a wash-basket. There was a ringing in his ears and his heart was pounding hard enough to spring his ribs. He couldn't move, not even to stir a finger. He could only stay cramped down in the car, and stare up at the huge, shadowy shape of the balloon against the sky.

The stars were marching solemnly round its rim, and a spot of silver from the moon traveled the patchwork fabric as it revolved. Cadmus became aware of a new chill in the air —

and of the stillness. It was an incredible stillness. There wasn't even a whisper of the wind's drag through the suspension lines. But the silence went beyond any mere absence of sound. It flowed in upon him from every part of the surrounding sky. He seemed to feel it on his skin, soaking in through his pores, so that he became a part of it himself and was lost in an immensity of silence.

The thoughts that passed through his mind were mere snatches of ideas and recollections — a little like the broken images a man's mind carries when he is waking from a troubled sleep. Most of them were related to sound. He seemed to hear the humming of the bell over Great-Uncle Eppa's chair on the front veranda and then the soft, slow slapping of the butler's thin-soled shoes as he came along the deep hall with the toddies. But somebody else seemed to be saying, "Whatever goes up must come down," and that made no sense because the brown mare was thudding along a dark and leaf-blown road, and off beyond the woods was a thundering cannonade.

Then Cadmus remembered the big guns that had been sounding off in Yorktown, where D. H. Hill was keeping up a show, and he wondered what had happened to change the sound of them. They seemed far away, though now that he was listening for them, the beat of each explosion came with a dry and light distinctness. At the same time, while he wrestled with this difference in the sound of the guns he had an irrational recollection of Great-Uncle Eppa Tatum saying, "A man has to stand up"; and he started working himself out of his cramped position.

It wasn't an easy thing to do. There was hardly room enough ordinarily for his feet in the bottom of the car, and the way he had been jammed down left him no means of leverage.

But finally he struggled up and seized two of the suspension lines and looked over the edge.

He did not immediately comprehend what had happened to him. The shape of the Peninsula was immeasurably small beneath, but he could see it clearly enough, for the moonlight put a silver shine on the bay and the two rivers. He could even pick out Yorktown, though the great bonfires he had noticed on his way up were now the merest specks of light. He was far too high to make any detailed observations. It secmcd to him that he must be two miles up in the air, and he couldn't understand how Mink had come to give him so much rope. Leaning farther over, he tried to locate the balloon camp.

He could make out the pinpricks of fires all along the roads reaching westward from Yorktown and Lee's Mill, but it was impossible for him to distinguish between them. Staring down at them, however, he began to have a strange feeling that the Peninsula was moving out from under him. The motion was barely perceptible; he wasn't at all sure of it; and he crouched down in the car to steady himself and measure the motion against the basket rim. As he did so, the anchor rope came into view.

It swung into the moonlight below with a long and sinuous motion, pausing far out, with the end hung cleanly in space. And then it slowly swayed back under the car again, mysterious and silent and deadly as a blacksnake sliding over silver moss.

For a time he still couldn't grasp the meaning of what he had seen. Then his hands clamped on the rim of the car and the shakes took hold of the rest of him. For there was nothing he could do. He didn't know the first thing about a free balloon. He didn't even know how soon he could expect it to start going down. He didn't know whether it would settle gradually or just fold up and drop when the time came. All he could do was stand in that narrow basket, sweating out the time, while he waited for whatever was to happen to him.

❦ 10 ❧

THEY SAY that a man's whole life will pass through his mind when he sees his end confronting him. But nothing as dramatic as that happened to Cadmus Henry up there in the higher sky during the long minutes before he noticed that the balloon had begun to settle towards the earth. Possibly his life had not been long enough to turn his mind to such backward glancing thoughts.

At first he was mostly concerned about what would become of the brown mare if he failed to get back to the balloon camp in time. He had confidence in Mebane, of course. Mebane wouldn't forget or neglect a horse. It wasn't that angle that troubled him; it was the fact that one old Negro would have small hope of keeping possession of a valuable animal like her if a white man laid claim to her. The brown mare was the kind to raise the natural unscrupulousness in any horseman; and in the confusion and turmoil of that nocturnal retreat a man wouldn't have a bee's chance in a frost of tracing a missing horse.

Then, as he stared down at the tiny pattern of the land beneath him, where the whole Peninsula looked less than the thickness of his little finger, his own fearful remoteness over-

came him. Cadmus stopped worrying about the mare, and it
was then that, for an instant, his mind employed itself with his
own unearthly situation. There was nothing connected about
the thoughts and impressions that occurred to him. He didn't
think about dying in terms of death either. But he thought
about the setter dog he was planning to field break in the fall;
and he thought about the way his mother used to come into
his room at night when he was small, with the shine of her
candle stealing in before her; and he also thought of Great-
Uncle Eppa's asking him to get in one shot with his name on it.

There was a kind of irony in that. Shooting anybody, even a
Yankee, was about the last thing in the universe that looked
like a useful objective where Cadmus was; and it seemed
impossible that he could ever have found anything admirable
in the idea. Indeed, at that moment, he wondered fleetingly if
any of the important people, like General Joe Johnston, or
General McClellan, or any of the higher officers, drawing
their bold strokes on the maps, had stopped to figure out what
they were fighting about, or whether it was worth the effort, or
what exactly that effort meant in terms of trouble for an
ordinary man in the front lines. But as he looked up at the
curve of PIZZINI's antique belly against the shining sky,
Cadmus had a lonely conviction that even supposing they had
done so, their reckoning wasn't likely to include a volunteer
aide in a free balloon, two miles high in the air, and heading
the Lord alone knew where.

There was no sense of motion. For all the monstrous bulk
of its seamed and patchwork bag, the balloon hung in the
night sky as lightly as a thistle seed. On previous ascents, when
the rope anchored them to earth, there had always been the
pull of the wind and the sway of the leaning car and the
rushing air to give an illusion of flight. But now the air against

his skin had a cold, thin touch, and an utter stillness. How long it was before he realized that the balloon was moving he could not possibly have told.

He first became aware that they were going down when he observed that what he had till then casually assumed to be a single large fire was in reality a cluster of many small ones. A regiment, he thought, or perhaps even a brigade, must be bivouacked there, and an irrational anxiety to identify it took hold of him, as if in knowing where the men came from he could gain a closer contact with the earth. At that height, through the darkness, he could not identify details of the terrain; a threadlike shine of water told him nothing. But while he studied the fires, he saw that they were moving appreciably beyond the basket rim. Then, with a sudden sense of shock, he realized that the balloon and not the encampment had been moving.

It was altogether a ghostly business, and Cadmus found difficulty in accepting the fact of his own passage through the night. It almost seemed that PIZZINI, soundlessly and stealthily, had filched a little of the mysterious power of the stars and now, with them, could hang in the sky and watch the small and distant turning of the earth. Cadmus tilted his head to look at them; but the balloon's huge belly blotted out a great section of the sky. Underneath it, within the funnel of suspension lines, he could just make out the dangling appendix, which seemed to be twitching in a rather flaunting manner; and, watching the passage of the bag across the cold pattern of the stars, he saw that it had begun to circle.

It had swung a short way south of the James River; but now, as it settled, it began drifting back over the Peninsula once more and hovered for a while over what looked to Cadmus like the mouth of Skiff Creek, though he couldn't be sure, for he was still mighty high, and the moon did tricky things to the outline of the shore.

There was a slight haze, too, and a bank of clouds had built up over the horizon; but the fires showed plainer and Cadmus could now hear the thudding of the cannon over by York-town. It sounded good to hear a human noise — even can-nonading.

11

To CADMUS, PIZZINI seemed to be hovering in the neighbor-hood of Skiff Creek, if it was Skiff Creek, for an interminable length of time, though actually it was only a few minutes. But during them the balloon performed a variety of maneuvers: first rising fifty feet or so, and then settling; then heading inland maybe a quarter of a mile, only to come back over the same spot where the break in the James River shore indicated the creek mouth; and doing all this with a kind of skittish uncertainty, like an apprehensive old woman trying to make up her mind to cross a crowded street on a rainy day. It got on Cadmus's nerves. He had no idea how much longer a hot air balloon could be expected to stay in the air, particularly on a cool night, and this apparent attraction for the James River was a disturbing thing.

But when it started down again, it was taken in a draft of air that carried it steadily eastward, and now, as if to make up for its former indecision, it moved over the land with surprising speed. In practically no time at all Cadmus saw that he had crossed the lines and was over Union territory.

All the roads were marked by fires. There was a big one at every crossroad, and even as high as he was he could see the long files of Union troops moving forward. The whole country was alive with them.

The bag kept going down all the time, and so fast that it looked to Cadmus as if he was bound to drop in enemy territory. He wondered whether that would mean spending the rest of the war in prison, for it didn't seem likely that military men would show a great deal of interest in exchanging a mere voluntary aide. But he thought that if he were lucky enough to drop away from the roads and could only get clear of the balloon before he was seen, he might be able to work his way back through the lines without getting captured. So he started keeping track of the main concentrations of Yankee troops and tried to fix landmarks in his mind.

But a few minutes later it all looked like wasted effort. The balloon had stopped settling. In fact, it even lifted a little as it suddenly started off on a new, northeasterly slant and at an even more rapid rate. Before he grasped the full possibilities of this new maneuver, Cadmus saw Old Point Comfort and Fort Monroe sliding past off to his right. The place was stacked with Yankee shipping and he was so impressed with the amount of it that it took him a minute to realize that if the balloon persisted on this course, it would carry out over Chesapeake Bay. But that, with a cussedness that he had supposed mostly confined to pigs and frightened hens, was exactly what PIZZINI did.

The bay was like a piece of darkly gleaming silk, with a silver stripe reflected from the moon. The waves on it made a smooth and lovely rippled pattern; and two vessels, coming down from the north, were stitching out arrowhead seams with their side paddles as they crossed the moonpath.

But Cadmus found nothing beautiful in the sight. He had never been much of a swimmer, and the idea of getting drowned when he had just made up his mind to face the chance of being a prisoner of war, enraged as well as frightened him. It became obvious that, from its initial leap into the sky, through every subsequent, and apparently aimless, move, the hideous old bag had been animated by pure malice. Realization of this swelled Cadmus's anger to such a pitch that he forgot to be scared, and he started vehemently telling PIZZINI exactly what he thought of it.

Under ordinary circumstances, berating something the size of a balloon, when you are hanging under the bulge of it by nothing more substantial than a few cords attached to a frail wicker basket and the appendix of the thing keeps twiddling unconcernedly fifteen or a dozen feet above your eye, would not appear an effective, nor an especially gratifying, occupation. But it cleared Cadmus's mind wonderfully to let loose that way, and the total of his condemnations, anathemas and imprecations would have made even such an enriched old fire-eater as his Great-Uncle Eppa sit up and take notice.

Whether it was the heat of Cadmus's maledictions or the very thorough accounting he cast up of his grievances against PIZZINI, or whether it was merely a shift in the wind, the balloon started circling back. It went for shore even faster than it had left and headed in towards the Poquoisin River, crossing over land about by Ship's Point. It was now so low that Cadmus could see little things like fences and garden plots and outhouses. He hadn't realized how steadily the balloon had been dropping; but the fact couldn't escape him any longer. By the time it reached Cockletown, PIZZINI wasn't much over five hundred feet high; Cadmus could see that it was also losing speed; and the prospect of falling inside the Union lines once more confronted him.

After leaving Cockletown, however, the balloon veered again and drove slowly up the Peninsula, passing the Brick Church on one hand and Howes's Sawmill on the other; and everywhere under him Cadmus saw the Union army filling the roads: infantry and artillery and wagon trains — he had never dreamed of wagon trains as long as these — all moving up, like flood water thrusting into new channels. He was so low now that he could pick out little, insignificant details of their advance. Beyond a grove of trees he caught the faint, sinuous shimmer of bayonets as a regiment marched along a winding road; he saw a sutler's wagon turn into an orchard in which a company had fallen out, but there wasn't time to see whether the sutler did any business; then he came on a gun stuck deep in a hole with the gun crew laboring like ants about it while the stream of troops along the road behind them choked slowly to a halt; and in one place he sailed right out over a field of white tents. They belonged to a brigade, as near as he could judge, and he was close enough to hear the blur of noise the troops made. They were breaking camp; it seemed extraordinary that none of them looked up to see the old balloon drifting through the night sky.

But none did, and the balloon continued, sinking all the while, with a kind of flutter coming now and then into its flight. At such moments, looking up, Cadmus thought he could see deeper puckers coming in the bag and peculiar puffs of mustiness surrounded the car. They would drift into the clear air again; but each time it looked to Cadmus as if they had lost another piece of altitude. He wondered what would happen if the balloon came down in the woods, whether the car, catching in the treetops, would spill him out or whether he would have a chance to seize a limb and so climb down to earth. He began studying the ground again with an eye to landing, and it was after two minutes of this that his heart gave a great bound; for in the moonlight he could see where two shadowy lines of earthworks came together in a V and he recognized it as the point where the Confederate and Union lines approached each other south of Yorktown.

As if to make up for all its previous antics, PIZZINI sailed almost tranquilly across these lines.

❧ 12 ❦

It was surely wonderful to be back over Confederate territory again; his heart swelled with relief. The balloon was following roughly the course of a small woods road; and as Cadmus looked down, he could see a regiment straggling along it in the deep shadows and the thought came to him that these men were his friends and if he had been low enough he would have liked to lean out and shake hands with them.

They were making pretty fast time, he noticed though. Half the men were running, and they kept shooting continually. He could see the flashes of their muskets under the trees; but he was puzzled by the apparent lack of answering fire. It was hard to figure out what they thought they were doing, running hemmed in by the woods on each side of the road. One would have expected them to take to cover with the enemy that close.

He was still exercising his brain over the problem when the balloon car jerked as one of the suspension lines parted. Cadmus realized that the regiment wasn't concerned with an enemy on the ground. The men were shooting at him. He leaned over to yell at them that he was Confederate, too; but they were yelling so loud themselves as they pounded along the road that they probably didn't hear him at all, or if they did, they weren't convinced. They chased him for half a mile before they would give up. By then the balloon was nearing the Telegraph Road over which all of D. H. Hill's division was withdrawing from Yorktown; and when Cadmus looked down on the mud-bound, crawling mass of men, wagons, and guns that clogged it, the thought of what would happen to him if they reacted to his passage as the men in the woods had, made him close his eyes and pray. But apparently no one saw him; there was no shooting; in a few minutes he was safely across and the balloon was drifting down Philgate's Creek.

At least, that was where Cadmus supposed they were, for just as he picked up the gleam of water the clouds caught up with the moon and it became suddenly dark. It was no longer possible to tell how high he was or which way he was heading except by the fires he had left behind. But after a few minutes he heard something splashing down below.

It was a queer sort of sound. It seemed to keep following him. At first he thought it might be the paddles of a steamboat on the river beyond the creek mouth, but the beat was not regular nor steady enough for that. Then the moon appeared through a gap in the clouds to give an instant of light.

The balloon had come out over the York River and was now so low that the trailing anchor rope kept dipping down to slap the surface of the water. Cadmus saw he didn't have much time left aboard PIZZINI.

He tried to be cool about it. Though he had never swum a quarter of a mile in his life, and the river hereabouts was better than two miles wide, he didn't intend to drown like a cat in a meal sack. He hadn't any idea of how the car might be expected to behave once it struck, but he thought it ought to give him time to get clear if he was ready to jump.

The anchor rope had stopped splashing, so he reckoned that it must be trailing in the water. The drag of it had markedly slowed the balloon's progress, but at the same time the fact that a part of its weight had now been removed lent the bag a little extra buoyancy. This gave him just about enough leeway to get rid of his clothes.

He took off his coat and threw it overboard. Then his shirt. Then he tried to get out of his boots; but he couldn't do that. Back in camp it took his whole strength and a bootjack to accomplish the trick, and the balloon car was so narrow that he couldn't even get the toe of one foot properly behind the heel of the other. He didn't have proper room to really get at it when he raised his leg and took hold of the boot with both hands; and when he tried, it set the car rocking so he had to grab hold of the lines. For the first time in his life he began to entertain doubts of Great-Uncle Eppa's judgment. But he wasn't left a chance to indulge in speculation.

The car hit the water with a long dragging splash. It filled at once and went down, and then, with a strange, vast, rank, oilcloth breath, the envelope collapsed on the river. Cadmus struggled through the lines and cordage. He thought for an instant that he was going to be dragged down, but he kicked loose and struck out for shore. He made only half-a-dozen strokes before his knee hit bottom and he stood up in water to his waist.

The shores were pitch-dark; no lights showed anywhere; but the persistent growl of the batteries in Yorktown reached out of the darkness like summer thunder from a distant sky.

Cadmus stood listening to it in the inky shadows of the river bank. The cold ripple slapped against his short ribs and the mud sucked at his feet. He was afraid to move. An enormous feebleness had taken hold of him. Now that the flight had ended and he was safely out of the balloon, he felt tired and frightened. The empty darkness of the river appalled him. He knew that he must get to shore and find a house and beg a horse to carry him to General Johnston's headquarters. But it wasn't going to be easy to walk up to a strange house and say he had just come out of a balloon — not outfitted the way he was, with no clothes on above his belt except for an adjutant's field glasses. The fact that he was alive ought to have been enough for him and, at almost any time during PIZZINI's free ballooning, it would have been; but now that he was safe, he took a more demanding and worldly view of human privileges and it seemed a profound injustice to him that no one should come along to solve his difficulties.

He started finally to wade towards shore; but he went only a few steps before the bottom shelved under his feet and he realized that he had been standing on some sort of bar. Though there was probably shallow water somewhere between him and the bank, finding it was likely to be a slow and difficult business. He stood there listening, shivering a little with the touch of the night air on his skin and feeling desolate. Suddenly he was aware of silence. He could no longer hear the guns in Yorktown. As he listened for them, the small sounds of darkness crept into the stillness on the river, and somewhere among them was a quick, light beat of oars.

13

THE OARS came nearer. Now and then they would stop, as though the rower paused to listen; but in the interval Cadmus heard the ripple on the moving boat. And suddenly a voice called softly, "Hello! Hello, the balloon! Are you all right?"

His own voice sounded strange to him. It seemed a long time since he had used it to speak to a human being.

"Over here."

The oars made a few tentative strokes. The boat slid across the water, and then scraped gently into the waterlogged fabric of the balloon. The rower gave a slight, half-suppressed gasp. Cadmus had an absurd impression that the person in the boat was a woman.

"This way," he said impatiently. "I'm towards shore."

The oars obediently resumed their beat and a moment later

the shadow of a skiff moved out of the darkness. Cadmus saw that there was only one person in the boat. He said, "Right here."

The rower braked with the oars and started backing water toward him. In a moment the gunwale was in Cadmus's hand and he was floundering aboard. The boat rocked, but the rower offered neither comment nor advice.

"It's lucky for me you came along," Cadmus said gratefully. "I've got to get back to General Johnston's headquarters as soon as possible. Do you know where I can find a horse?"

"Yes," the rower said in a grave voice. "I reckon I do."

Turning the boat, she started rowing towards the middle of the river. By now there was no question in Cadmus's mind about the matter of her sex. He sat on the stern seat with the night breeze pouring over him, trying to see her better without being obvious about it. And then, as if to help him, the moon came through the clouds.

He thought, from the oval of her face, that she was young, but he could not see her features. Her eyes and mouth were dark shadows. She was bareheaded, and in the moonlight her hair was like ink — so black that he could trace the smooth line of the part in it. She rowed well, as if she had done much of it, and her small shoulders had a capable squareness.

The clouds overcame the moon once more, and in the darkness there was only the swirl and drip of the oars, and the ripple on the boat.

Then out of the silence she said, "I saw the balloon floating over the river. I thought something must have gone wrong with it."

Cadmus said, "I don't see how you managed to get here so soon."

"I was out in the boat, anyway," she explained.

"Alone?"

It seemed strange for a girl to be out by herself like that at night on the river.

"Oh, I'm often out alone," she said. "I was listening to the guns. They seem nearer when you're on the water."

That was a queer thing, too; and Cadmus said, "I shouldn't think you'd want them to sound any nearer." He couldn't quite keep a note of disapproval out of his voice.

She didn't answer; but after several minutes she said, "They've stopped. What do you suppose it means?"

"Probably that our troops have left Yorktown."

"I thought it must be that," she said quietly.

She rowed steadily, apparently without tiring, and the boat made good way. When she reached the middle of the river, she turned downstream at a wide angle to the shore. It was evident that she was completely familiar with the river, but when Cadmus commented on the fact, she merely said, "Yes."

He felt rebuffed. Her appearance out of the darkness, alone in her boat, had seemed romantic to him; and his heart warmed to imagine her as she spied the balloon falling through the sky and determined instantly to row to the aeronaut's rescue. Few people would have done it so unhesitatingly, let alone a girl. He wanted to find out who she was and where she came from and especially why she went out on the river alone; but he could not decently press her with questions if she did not want to talk, and he relapsed into the same silence until quite suddenly she broke it.

"Are you cold?" she asked softly.

"A little."

"We won't be much longer," she said.

He felt an increased urgency in her strokes as the boat slipped along, close to the shore. No lights showed anywhere nearby, and he wondered where she was taking him. He didn't like to ask, for he did not want her to think that he mistrusted her. But he was almost certain that they had passed a plantation jetty a little way back.

As if she were aware of his uneasiness, she said, "That's the Willis place. They've all gone away. I'm going to take you down to Osbornes'."

Again, he thought it was strange that she hadn't taken him to her own home. But she explained that, too, in part, by adding a moment afterwards: "I'll have to stop at a place before we reach Osbornes'." She seemed to speak a little hesitantly, as though she were feeling carefully for her words. "I have to leave something. I — I was taking it when I saw the balloon coming over the trees. But I won't be long, and maybe I can get you a coat there."

Cadmus had noticed a pile of stuff, covered by an old blanket, in the bottom of the boat; and he supposed she referred to that, though what it was and why a girl should have to deliver it at night, as if it were contraband, was beyond his comprehension. She didn't sound in the least like someone who would be running contraband. Her voice was warm and friendly; it had a plain, direct quality that he didn't recollect having heard often in girls' voices; it didn't sound just the way he was used to thinking of girls' voices anyway; and all of a sudden he realized that she didn't exactly sound like someone who had been raised in Virginia. Once he thought about it, it became very plain; and he couldn't understand why he hadn't noticed it before.

Then, out of the darkness, she asked, "Are you an officer?"

He explained, giving her his name, that he was a volunteer. But he hoped to get a commission. "Now the balloon's done for, I'd like to join a good regiment," he said.

She wanted to know how long he had been an aeronaut before he joined the army. It made him laugh, and when he told her how he had become one, she laughed with him, but broke off after a moment to say in her grave voice, "But I think you must be brave, just the same."

He said that there was no question of bravery. It was a matter of orders and General Joe Johnston's eyes.

"I should think it would feel strange, being so high and looking down on both the armies. Don't you get mixed up sometimes over which one's which?"

Cadmus admitted that it was confusing at first and some of the feeling he had had when he and the turkey buzzard looked down on the armies together recurred to him. They went along for a few moments without talking, and the faint splash of the oars echoed off the bank. And then she said, "My brother's a private."

He started to remark that there were lots of good men in the ranks, but checked himself. He had a feeling that she might regard it as patronizing, though he did not know just why. Instead he asked, "Is he down there?"

He tilted his head, forgetting the dark; but she understood. "I don't think so."

"Don't you know?"

"He's not much of a letter writer," she said.

"I'll look him up for you," Cadmus offered, "if you'll tell me his name and regiment."

"His name's John Heath." She hesitated. "But I don't think you're likely to meet him."

There was something odd in the way she said it, as if she smiled inwardly at him; and his uneasiness, which had momentarily blown away while they were talking, came back to him. But at that instant she turned the boat sharply in to the shore. All at once reeds scraped against the sides and the smell of swamp and woods enclosed them. Then they were in open water again, and the girl let the boat drift. Looking up, Cadmus saw the tops of the reeds against the sky close on either hand, and farther ahead the blacker line of the woods. They were lying in the marshy mouth of one of the little, steep-sided creeks. Probably the entrance didn't even show from the river. It was a lost place, and it seemed a wonder that she could find it in the darkness.

She said now, with a note of earnestness in her voice, "I have to row up the creek a way to the landing. I'll go ashore, but you mustn't come with me. Will you wait in the boat, Mr. Henry?"

The uneasiness that had been creeping into him crystallized. He felt afraid. He said, "What is this place, anyway? Why can't you take me straight to Osbornes'?"

"Be quiet," she said sharply, and then, "Please be quiet. You might frighten my friends, and they wouldn't like it. They may be listening there, right now." She waited a minute. "I'd have taken you straight to Osbornes', but my friends have been waiting. It will be all right if you'll just keep quiet and stay in the boat."

He didn't answer. He was thinking that there was no way in which he could get at the oars. If they didn't overset the boat, the commotion would attract her friends, whoever they were — it was hard to imagine people living in a lost spot like this. If he jumped and tried to get ashore, there would still be her friends. He felt the back of his neck prickle like a dog's.

"It will be all right if you'll wait in the boat, Mr. Henry," she said, with the warmth back in her voice. "I'll only be a minute or two. Will you wait in the boat?"

He wanted to believe her; and there didn't seem to be

anything else for him to do. He told her he would, and she
started rowing ahead with a gentle dipping of the oars. The
crescent drip they made was the only sound, until the bow of
the boat slid onto a low bank and the girl stepped out with the
rope in her hands. He did not see her walking in the darkness,
but he heard her going up the bank.

Somewhere above him a murmur of voices began.

"Who dar?"

The girl answered and a door squeaked as though it hung
on wooden pins. The door squeaked again as it closed, and the
resonant Negro voice was shut off with the girl's. It seemed a
long time to Cadmus, alone in the boat and slapping mos-
quitoes, before the door swung open with its protesting creak.

This time a faint light showed him the girl standing before
a crazy little shack set among trees whose moss-hung branches
swept low across the roof. The girl had some clothes in her
hands, and as she turned back to the door her face came
briefly into the light, giving Cadmus an impression of a round
forehead and a curving mouth and dark eyes under strong,
arched brows. An old Negress, wearing a man's coat and
slouch hat, stood in the doorway.

"Whyn't you let 'm drown?" she demanded.

"*Sh-h-h,*" the girl said. "You don't mean that, Harriet."

"You don' know what I mean," the old woman said in her
deep and resonant voice. "Nobody know what I mean, till
they been out on the long road in the rain, or hidin' in the
swamp with the dogs runnin', or jus' stayin' where they was
bawn when their family's sold down into Egyp'."

She stepped out of the cabin, brushing past the girl, and as
she did so the faces of several more Negroes appeared behind
her, their eyes staring against the darkness with a fear as
palpable as one feels in the wild things cornered in a rabbit

319

drive. It reached Cadmus like a cold wave, and instantly he knew that the girl too had been touched by it. He could hear it in the enforced calm in her voice.

"I could have taken him on first," she said, "but I knew you had to have these things. If you take them now, you can be gone long before he could reach anyone, even if he wanted to trouble his head about us."

"How you know whut he gwine do an' whut he ain' gwine do?" the old woman asked. "I ain' los' none of my people on the road yit, an' I ain' gwine lose one now. You men," she

called sharply, "git down theah where the boat is an' don' let 'm go."

The Negroes had all edged out of the cabin. At her command, three men broke from the hesitant group and plunged down the bank to lay hold of the boat's bow. If he had thought of it sooner, Cadmus might have backed the boat out into the creek; but it was too late for that, and he stayed still, feeling helpless and slow-witted and trapped. He knew now what the shack was used for and why the Negroes were waiting in it. He had heard his Great-Uncle Eppa and their neighbors blowing

off steam about the Underground Road by which Negroes were run off. These people were escaping slaves; the cabin was a daytime hideaway; and it must have been to bring them supplies that the girl was on the river.

The three men at the bow kept very still. He could almost feel their tenseness. He had no wish to turn them in; all he wanted was to get back to headquarters; but he had sense enough not to talk. If they had any trust in the girl, it was better for her to speak to them.

"I've helped you before, Harriet," she said, still quietly. "I've helped other people coming through here. I promise you won't come to harm through him — you'll be behind the Union army in two hours anyway. If you like, Mr. Henry will give you his promise, too."

For an instant the old Negress's voice softened.

"I know that, Missy," she said; but then her voice grew harsh once more. "An' I know white folks does two kinds of promisin' in Egyp'. If it's for white folks, that's one kind. But if it's for black folks, when the time comes they forget it."

A whispered murmur of agreement came from the little group behind her.

"Even mine?" asked the girl.

"We know you keep yo' word. But you caint promise for him."

"Suppose he gives his word to me."

"What he care for that?" the old woman said with cutting scorn. "Better we leave 'm so he don't have to make no promises."

There was an instant of complete silence. Then the girl said so quietly that Cadmus had to strain to hear her, "You can't do a thing like that." She no longer addressed merely the old woman but included them all. "Your freedom won't be a good

thing for any of you if you get it that way. I'd be ashamed all
my life for ever helping one of you."

Again, a thin murmuring came from the group. The old
woman, however, gave a short, hard laugh.

"Don't have to kill him, if that's what scares you. We can
just leave him here. You can come back for him when we're far
enough away."

"No," the girl said. "I said I'd take him where he could find
a horse. We'll stay here till you've started, if you like. But
you'd better get my bundle out of the boat and Mr. Henry
better come up and get into this coat."

The men at the bow of the boat hesitated a moment; then
one reached in for the bundle and they waited for Cadmus to
get out. They kept close to him, climbing the bank, and
though they did not touch him, he was very conscious of the
fear among them — theirs and his own — and of the threat of
violence it contained. He tried to keep all thought of it out of
his mind, and when the girl held out a coat as he came into the
light from the doorway, he took it from her and put it on as if
the two of them were there alone. But the old Negress came
between them, thrusting her face close to his and studying
him with narrowed eyes.

She might have been just any old Negro woman. Her bent
shoulders and weathered skin gave her the look of a field
hand. But there was a strange shrewdness in her eyes.

"You in the ahmy?" she asked abruptly, as if she were surprised to find how young he looked. Then she asked his name
and where he lived, and when he told her she called to one of
the Negroes to come forward and identify him.

"That's where you come from," she said. "You know 'm?"

"Yes. It's Doctuh Henry's boy." The speaker was a dark,
strapping, youngish woman. Cadmus had no recollection of

ever having seen her before, and it must have showed in his face, for she smiled. "When he little, he ride everywhere with his Pa," she explained, "and everybody know who Doctuh Henry is when he livin'." And after a pause she added, "He was a good man."

She smiled again at Cadmus before stepping back into the shadows and left him with a sense of pride. He remembered his father often saying, when his mother expostulated about his going out again at night, that black folks could feel just as sick as white folks, and just as scared. Praise from a Negro now seemed fitting and natural to him, and he felt himself relaxing and was aware that the tenseness had gone out of the Negroes — even the old woman, who now ordered the men to open the bundle they had carried up from the boat and parcel out the food and clothing it contained. Then she turned back to Cadmus.

"You ain' gwine tell nobody about us?" she asked. "You promise that?"

He gave her his word, explaining that all he had ever wanted was just to get back to his headquarters. In any case, there would be no point in telling anyone about them or their hideout, for both armies would have passed beyond it in another day.

The old Negress nodded. She said she and the others would start off at once.

"You won't see me no more," she told the girl. "I reckon 't's the last trip I make down into Egyp'. After this, all my people free."

She sent one of the women into the cabin for the lantern, and when it was fetched out to her, she extinguished it. In the darkness she thanked the girl for the bundle; then, calling her followers together, she led them away down the creek.

"They have a boat below," the girl said. "We'd better wait

till they've had time to get started. Is the coat all right?" she went on, speaking rapidly, like someone trying to make conversation. "It's pretty worn, I'm afraid, but at least it's dry."

Cadmus said it was fine. It seemed a queer thing, his being brought here for a coat intended for a fugitive slave. It seemed a queer thing altogether, the shack, and the Negress in her men's clothes, and now being alone here with a girl he had never seen before tonight — whom he had never seen properly at all, if it came to that, except for brief glimpses in the dim light before the cabin door.

Cadmus had never felt much interest in girls; but now, somehow, he was aware of a shyness in her and became shy himself. For several minutes neither spoke a word. Then, in the stillness, the sound of oars came faintly to them and the girl said with a quick, bright accent of relief, "We'd better get back in the boat now and I'll row you right down to Osbornes'."

❧ 14 ❧

ONCE on the river, she seemed to feel easier and talked to him about the old Negress who, she said, had been a slave and had escaped. Once free, she began to think of leading others of her people into freedom. So she had started coming back and this was her nineteenth trip. Altogether she had led off some three hundred. "And whatever you think," the girl said earnestly, "she's brave and good. You mustn't mind what she said about you. She's not usually like that, but perhaps she's touched in the head the way some people think." She explained that when the Negress was still a young girl a drunken white man had clubbed her off a fence. "Sometimes she remembers that."

There was little Cadmus could think of to say. It had turned out all right, though it might not have; but to make the girl feel better he told her that he hadn't troubled his head about it; and if he had, it wouldn't make any difference now, if only he could borrow a horse at Osbornes'.

"They'll surely have one you can take," she said. "And we'll be there in a few minutes . . ."

A little pier ran far out from shore to the edge of the deep water. The girl swung the boat neatly to meet it and caught hold while Cadmus stepped out. She did not immediately push off. Cadmus had a quick feeling that she, like himself, was hunting words.

He looked down, trying to see her through the darkness. But there was only the indistinct pale oval of her face.

"You've been mighty kind," he said at last. "I can't rightly thank you. But I wish there was something I could do for you."

"You needn't thank me. I'm just sorry it took so long to fetch you here."

"I'd like to look your brother up anyway," he said. "But you didn't tell me his regiment."

"Oh," she said. She had given a little shove and dimly Cadmus saw the water come between the boat and the pier. "His regiment's the 21st Massachusetts."

So the reason for her helping run off Negroes became clear. He had heard Great-Uncle Eppa say that Massachusetts was a great place for Abolitionists, though Great-Uncle Eppa never confined his statement to such few or simple words.

Cadmus said, "You're not on our side. How'd you come to live here?"

"My mother married a Virginian. I go by my stepfather's name. But my brother stayed up North."

"I don't see why you helped me then."

"I wouldn't let a white man drown, any more than I would a Negro," she said. "I wish you luck, Mr. Henry."

Cadmus heard her turn the boat with quick strokes, and the water bubbled under the stern as it swung away from the pier. There was a faint lightening of the sky downriver, but a mist moved in towards shore. In a moment Cadmus could not see even the shadow of her boat.

He hadn't learned her name, nor where she lived. And he felt that she wouldn't have told him. So there was nothing for him to do except to take himself up the pier to the house.

Then, through the mist, he heard the beat of her oars stop, and her voice carried back across the water.

"The house sits a little way up from the river. You won't have any trouble finding it."

As if to corroborate her, a dog started barking.

"You mustn't mind the dog," she called. "He's friendly. He just barks."

❧ 15 ❧

THE BARKING continued as Cadmus walked the length of the pier and then it materialized into a white setter dog which shepherded him hysterically to the house. By the time he reached the carriage block, other dogs, kenneled out behind, had taken up the alarm. The house was roused; a sleepy

Negro stood waiting in the portico; and Mr. Osborne himself, with the tassel of a striped silk nightcap dangling before his nose, leaned over the banisters. Behind him Cadmus made out the shapes of children, and when he had explained his need and given his name, a woman's voice cried from somewhere out of sight entirely, "It must be Dr. Henry's boy. Eppa Tatum's great-nephew."

Most of the furniture in the hall was covered over. Trunks and packed hampers stood near the stairs. It was obvious that the Osbornes were on the point of leaving home. But they gave no sign of it in their behavior. They insisted on Cadmus sitting down to eat a breakfast while the stable hands were being roused and a horse saddled for him. Mr. Osborne provided him with a respectable shirt and coat, and Mrs. Osborne, in a purple garment dignified by enormous quantities of lace, took a genealogical canter through his family connections and returned with a cousinship that would pass muster, so that all of them began to feel very much at ease with each other. The small children eyed him from doorways and corners, and a near-grown daughter, who made her appearance miraculously toileted with every curl in place, declared that she had twice seen his balloon from the upper forty. It reminded her of a bird — a hawk or an eagle — the way it seemed to soar, she said, turning her fine eyes on Cadmus. She was a handsome and high-spirited girl. She had even taken time to put on scent.

They wanted to hear about the war, of course — but not in relation to their having to leave home. They treated that as if they were about to set out for a summer at the springs. The fact that General Johnston was retreating and letting the Yankees overrun their soil was solely due to his looking for the proper place and time for wiping out the entire Union army.

They never doubted that. And one good thing the war had done was to bring Cadmus to their door. Mrs. Osborne hoped he would come back some day and get a happier impression of Roseacres.

They all escorted him to the porch. As they stood in the doorway, Cadmus thought they made a picture of exactly the kind of people the war was being fought for. The older daughter stood a little apart, waving a lace handkerchief.

He looked back once more from a rise of ground and saw the house white against the wide marsh, and the river a deepening blue beyond it. The pier was like a thread stretched over the water, and as Cadmus watched, a white speck that must have been the setter dog trotted out along its length.

He was reminded of the girl in the boat and her assurance of the dog's friendliness. She must have visited the house more than once to know the dog so well. She hadn't had anything to say about birds or soaring; but she had been easy for him to talk to. He remembered the way she had laughed with him and a kindness he had heard in her voice, and it didn't seem to matter that he knew she wanted the Union to win, though he knew that it ought to.

▞ 16 ▚

IT IS HARD to describe exactly how Cadmus felt on his long ride
into Williamsburg in the early morning. He should have been
dead beat, but he wasn't, for there was a kind of exaltation in
him.

For one thing, he was seeing the earth again the way the
Lord designed the human eye to see it, and it looked better to
him than he had ever known before. It crossed his mind, also,
that a man never really understood what it was to have a good
horse between his legs until he had ridden in a wicker basket a
mile high in thin air.

The cool wind in his face had a taste of the river mist in it,
and he could smell the green fern as he crossed the little runs
with their dark water and deep banks. When he scared a
rabbit out of the roadside brush and she went bucketing along
the ruts ahead of him to whip back into the next thicket, he
laughed and shouted, "Good luck, Molly!" after her. He was
just a healthy young man with an ambition to make a name
for himself, and he realized that morning that he had accom-
plished something beyond the common run.

It took him back to the time he had come home with his
first brace of wild ducks, remembering the calm glance of
pride his mother had bestowed on Great-Uncle Eppa, and the
old man's protests that it went to show the boy was mostly
Tatum, after all. He sounded gruff, but after dinner he had

taken Cadmus back into the office and, opening the gun cabinet, had given him the double-barreled Webley to use, instead of the heavy, antique muzzle loader that was so long in the barrel it was impossible for a boy to fire it and simultaneously get any part of his anatomy in front of the business end. "I reckon it's time you got promoted to a real man's gun," Great-Uncle Eppa had declared.

That had been a tremulous moment for a boy, and some of the same sort of feeling came over Cadmus now. He thought it likely they would give him a commission for the night's work he had put in, though it didn't seem to matter now the way it would have only a day ago. It was mainly that, like the brace of ducks, it would be something to take home and show the old man and his mother, and he did not think of it as something in the military sense at all. He wasn't much concerned with the war that morning, or the course it was likely to follow. If he had thought about it, he would probably have agreed with the Osbornes that it was merely a question of finding the time and place to whip that Union army. With the horse cantering under him, it was easy to forget the miles of road he had passed over, packed with Yankee troops. And he had no idea yet of the real meaning of retreat.

But he began to understand a little when he came into the streets of Williamsburg. The advance elements of Longstreet's troops were just working into the town from the east. They were moving with a dreadful slowness. Men's faces were drawn; their minds appeared confused; they did not walk as people ordinarily do, but as though each man had a weight to carry in his mind besides the weight he carried on his back. Something of the same uncertainty showed even in the horses, worn out by their struggles with the heavy going. It had not rained that night for the first time in days, but the rains that had gone before had left the ground sodden and after the passage of the first few heavy guns the roads turned into troughs of mud. Mud caked the fetlocks of the horses. It clogged the spokes of the wheels. It was heavy on the men's boots.

There was little order in the ranks, or anywhere else as far as Cadmus could see — no camps, no food. The commissary appeared to have completely broken down and a bitter look was growing in the eyes of harassed officers, a look that was to grow still more bitter in the years ahead. But the army kept on coming, in companies, in regiments, and now a whole brigade, and then a section of artillery, or a halting string of wagons, or a handful of stragglers, sheepish, cocky or just plain bewildered. They made a slow, dull, heavy, plodding sound that filled the streets. There was nothing for them to do but keep on to the west side of the town and hunt among the sodden roadside fields for a space in which they could lie down. It was some time before Cadmus found a man among them who could tell him where General Johnston's headquarters were.

17

IF JOE JOHNSTON was confused, he did not show it. A kind of irritable relief sounded in his voice, as though he was glad to be moving back up the Peninsula and had never liked going down it to begin with. He stood up while Cadmus talked, his small body with its sloping shoulders strung as fiercely as a gamecock's.

"It looks as if McClellan's planned to move," he said to Major Rhett. "If they drive Stuart in, we'll have to fight him here tomorrow."

He turned back to Cadmus.

"You've done well, sir. I'm glad you're all right. But we shan't need you anymore. Report back to General Magruder."

He walked quickly to his desk and picked up a sheaf of papers.

"There's nothing yet from D. H. Hill," he said.

That was all there was to it, but it took a minute for Cadmus to realize the fact. A sense of deflation hit him. He hadn't known exactly what to expect. Whatever his expectations were, they made no difference now. A feeling of drugged tiredness had got into his legs and started working upward. He found it hard to walk, and then, as he reached the door, Major Rhett called after him, "Just a minute, Mr. Henry."

Cadmus turned hopefully, to see the major in the doorway, smiling slightly and holding out his hand.

"I believe you forgot to return my glasses," he said pleasantly, and then added, "you'll find your division a few miles out on the New Kent Road, Mr. Henry."

Cadmus didn't know exactly what he had expected from the major; but the latter's words left no alternative except to report to Captain Bryan, who would inevitably put him back on the eternal grind of copying dispatches. A footloose idea came into his head that in all the world there was no more useless or unwanted being than a balloonist without a balloon, and for the only time in his life Cadmus had a kindly recollection of PIZZINI.

He felt utterly dispirited. For a long time he just stood in the crowd in front of headquarters and watched the slow stream of men and horses go by; and in the end something of their tiredness seeped into his own brain, and he thought that he might as well climb on his horse and join them.

Though the rain had held off all day, there was a threat of showers to come in the watery sky. The pale sunlight slanting across the pink brick walls of the town and the fields beyond had little warmth. The men in line ahead of Cadmus moved with a slow dejection, their shoulders hunched in their blouses as though they felt cold. They did not bear much resemblance to the brightly uniformed units that had marched out of Richmond almost a year ago behind their noisy bands; they carried no extra equipment now; and in their long night march they had absorbed the color of the universal mud. Townspeople who stood along the sidewalks to watch the troops pass showed little inclination to cheer. More often their faces betrayed their fear and bewilderment. To them the army looked more like a beaten force in full retreat than one merely withdrawing to a more favorable position, according to General Johnston's plan. Or perhaps there was a prophetic sense abroad in Williamsburg that day, as if the ghost of the army they would become marched for a while with the troops.

But Cadmus was too deeply absorbed in his own disappointment to feel concern for other people's troubles. Most of the natural optimism had gone out of him and the future, whenever he had the nerve to turn his mind to it, looked intolerably bleak and full of problems.

Here he was, riding back to a job he loathed, with no real recognition for the work he had done, in borrowed clothes and on a borrowed horse, both of which would have to be replaced before he could return them. That meant finding money to buy a horse, if he didn't recover the brown mare. When he thought of the confusion he had looked down on in his flight, he didn't see how he could possibly find out what had become of the mare; and if he couldn't find her, he didn't see where he could find the money to buy another horse; and worst of all, he didn't know how he was going to break the news to Great-Uncle Eppa.

Like any youngster, he had taken the gift of the mare pretty much as a matter of course; but now he began to realize how much the old man must have valued her and remembered how he had cast his mind over all the blood lines in Virginia in planning her breeding and that of all her future foals. In fact, Great-Uncle Eppa firmly believed that maintaining the superiority of Virginia horseflesh was almost as great a social obligation as preserving the standards of her first families; and the former process interested him a good deal more. The mere idea of the brown mare in another man's hands, and possibly a Yankee's at that, would be enough to blow him up entirely.

Cadmus now saw that he ought never to have accepted her at all.

⋘ 18 ⋙

ABOUT TWO MILES out of town, after nearly two hours of intermittent progress, a hullabaloo up front heralded trouble of some kind, and the troops ahead of Cadmus came slowly to a halt. His horse stopped with them, slinging one hip resignedly, and gradually the whole long line of men and animals behind them stopped also and waited with the deep mud sucking at their feet. Cadmus felt no interest in the cause of the disturbance; there had been too many similar halts; but when a foot soldier asked if he could see what was going on, he looked ahead obligingly.

A wagon was being hauled off the road. As Cadmus watched, it lurched across the roadside ditch into the open field. A group of soldiers who had been shoving let it go. It rocked crazily a few feet more; then a rear wheel seemed to buckle; the box teetered crazily and crashed to the ground; and the team, a half-starved, rack-ribbed pair, stopped dead and abandoned all further interest in progress.

"It's just a wagon lost a wheel," Cadmus told the soldier.

He would have forgotten all about the incident except that at that moment his eye was caught by the driver of the wagon, as he climbed down from the seat. The man had on a red Zouave's hat, and something in his attitude as he stood back to view the wreckage was familiar. When a second, equally ram-

shackle wagon, though possessed of all its wheels, also left the road and joined the first, Cadmus did not need to read the remaining gilt letters along its weathered sideboards to know that they had once spelled the name PIZZINI. As he came abreast, he turned his horse into the field and, riding up behind the lugubrious pair, spoke Norment's name.

The balloon boss turned to stare incredulously at Cadmus.

"Praise the Lord!" he exclaimed. "It's Mr. Henry!"

For the moment he seemed to forget all about his wagon troubles, but just stood in gangling wonder, staring at Cadmus, while behind him the slow-moving lines of men kept going on along the road.

He wanted to know where the balloon had landed, and when Cadmus had given a brief account, he said, "We seen her go. And Hooley there, he thought he saw her coming back. But the moon was gone, and she might as well have been a cloud."

Hooley said, "So she was drowned."

Cadmus nodded, and the three of them stood there in front of the broken wagon, not speaking, but thinking what may have been a farewell thought; and, as if in requiem, from back to the east of Williamsburg, cannon started barking.

The men listened to them.

Hooley said, "The Unions must be catching up." And Norment nodded drearily. "All the time they shoot, shoot, shoot. You'd think that sometimes they'd get tired of it, too."

After a pause Cadmus asked what had become of his mare.

"I don't know," Norment said in his tired voice. "Mink and Mebane has her somewhere. They took her off. They had an idea you wasn't dead and reckoned consequently that you'd want her back. They cleared out when we broke camp this morning. Wouldn't come with us, and I had to let them go.

They're both of them free Nigras," he explained with a faint flutter of his eyelid. "Wasn't anything I could do to stop them, once that Mink made up his mind. I ain't that kind of interfering man."

They stood awhile in silence, listening to the development of cannon fire. The first lone gun had been quickly joined by another and a third, until it sounded as if a whole battery were in action. Now, after holding steady for a few minutes, the sound was again growing louder, and Cadmus wondered if Stuart's rear guard was being driven in. He didn't much care; he was willing to let the war go its own way just then.

Norment said, "Mink did say something to Hooley about you might show up at Magruder's headquarters, if you showed up anywhere on earth. Maybe they'll be near there."

Hooley nodded with a sidelong glance, and Cadmus said good-bye to them. Norment wished him luck as they shook hands.

"I'll kind of miss our ballooning together," he said. "Though all that Yankee shooting used to make me tired."

Both men returned disconsolately to their inspection of the broken wagon, and when Cadmus looked back from the road he saw them still bent over the broken wheel, while their three scarecrow horses watched the proceedings without enthusiasm.

✌ 19 ✎

IT WAS RAINING when Cadmus finally arrived at Magruder's headquarters, and he was wet through. He had had a hard time getting there. All afternoon he had worked his way along the road, from one unit to the next, asking directions. Men were scattered everywhere, in miserable bivouacs in half-flooded fields, or populating whole groves of trees with their makeshift shelters. But even after he began to find elements of Magruder's command, no one was able to tell him exactly where headquarters was. No one seemed to care much either. The cannon fire east of Williamsburg had faded out with the waning daylight, and now the only concern the soldiers had was their nearly hopeless effort to keep dry. In only one or two small units were rations being served the men; the rest were going hungry, and many of them made it plain that it wasn't going to break their hearts if one of the general's staff boys had to spend a night out in the rain.

Darkness had closed in when Cadmus at last walked up to another lighted doorway to ask if anyone could give him directions to General Magruder's headquarters.

"Why, yes. Just walk right in."

Captain Bryan looked up from the small table on which his field desk rested, and when he saw who it was, he half rose in surprise, while the two aides simply stared.

"Good grief, it's our aeronaut!" The captain surveyed Cadmus with sardonic eyes. "Reporting back for duty, I suppose?"

"Yes, sir."

"Well, welcome home. Or perhaps I should say, welcome back to earth. We heard that the balloon had broken free and apparently carried you straight up to Heaven. I gather that you didn't quite qualify." And rather unexpectedly the captain grinned at Cadmus. "It's stirred up quite a ruckus, though. Apparently some of General G. W. Smith's troops accused ours of stealing their rations during the excitement. Something about chickens. General Smith's headquarters sent over an unofficial memorandum suggesting the need of better discipline in this division, and General Magruder thought it impugned the honor of his command. He wanted to make an issue of it but he was taken ill and we have General Jones commanding. General Jones doesn't care a hoot who steals what. He says he'd steal rations himself if he could get them for our troops that way. There's hardly enough to feed a company in the whole division, and nobody seems to know what's become of the commissary. But you wouldn't know about it, Mr. Henry. You were above all that! Tell us what happened to you."

So Cadmus gave them an account of the flight of the balloon, and he could see a kind of awe in the faces of the two other aides, particularly in young Brashear's. Tired as he was, he rather enjoyed himself. It was pleasant talking to the three of them there in the lamplit warmth, with the downpour of the rain outside. His story became vivid, even to himself, and if a skeptical glint at times crept into the captain's eyes, it didn't really matter.

Cadmus did not mention the girl in the boat, or their encounter with the fugitive slaves, but only said that after he got ashore he was fortunate enough to find the house of some hospitable people named Osborne, who had fed him and lent him a coat and shirt and a very good horse. The two aides, Boyce and young Brashear, displayed quite an interest in his description of the eldest Miss Osborne, but Captain Bryan merely said that he was acquainted with the family and that they were fine people.

A remnant of his smile still showed in his eyes as he returned to his papers.

"I've saved up some work for you, Mr. Henry. But it will have to wait. The division will march again tonight, as soon as General McLaws comes up with Toombs's and Semmes's brigades. You'd better get some sleep — if there's any to be had. Mr. Brashear will show you where to go."

Brashear led Cadmus through a back door, explaining that the aides were quartered in the stable. An orderly had already stalled the Osbornes' horse there, and as Cadmus had bread and bacon and milk in the tack room, with the companionable sound of the horse crunching his oats outside the door, he thought it was as good a meal as he had ever had in his life.

Brashear was full of talk about the army's withdrawal, giving Cadmus highly colored accounts of vanishing units and his own rides round the countryside in search of them. He had never managed to find a single one and, as a result, he said cheerfully, he was in very low standing with Captain Bryan. But that wasn't exactly a new situation for him, either, and, anyway, the whole division had turned up in Williamsburg during the morning.

There was a good deal of speculation also, he went on, as to just what Joe Johnston had in mind by this withdrawal. Quite a number of people disapproved of falling back so close to Richmond without fighting. But the way Brashear himself looked at it, it was better to have a victory close enough to Richmond so one could attend the balls and parties afterwards. And if General McClellan merely scratched dust and no battle came off, why it would be a pretty unimaginative aide who couldn't find ways of getting a few free hours in the city now and then.

When Cadmus at last got a word in edgewise, he asked if Brashear had seen or heard anything about his mare, and the latter was instantly contrite.

"Yes!" he exclaimed. "I ought to have told you. There was a Negro here earlier in the afternoon. A big, round-shouldered fellow who wanted to know if there was any news of you and one of the orderlies came in and got me out to talk to him. He looked pretty disappointed when I said we hadn't the faintest idea of what had become of you, but he said if you did show up, to tell you Mink had your mare all right and was taking care of her. I told him to fetch her in here so we could bring her along with the spare staff mounts. But I don't think he liked the idea much. Anyway, he didn't come back."

"Oh, I reckon he's hanging around somewhere close by," Cadmus said. "And he'll bring her in, once he knows I'm back."

"I doubt it," Brashear disagreed. "I had a couple of men scout round for him when he didn't show up, but they couldn't find hide nor hair of him. If you ask me, he figured you'd been lost and thought he might as well clear out with the mare. He probably expects he can sell her without too many questions asked, if he picks the right man. It would be a mighty big temptation."

To Cadmus it seemed much more likely that the two Negroes had been scared off entirely when they found they were being looked for. He didn't think Mink would try to sell the mare, and he took a blanket and went up to the haymow with a half idea that they'd probably wake him up to tell him there were a couple of Negroes waiting down below with his mare.

◆₰ 20 ₷◆

WHEN the orderly woke him, however, it was to say that headquarters was already moving out and he had better hurry. So Cadmus, mounted on the Osbornes' horse again, found himself riding out into the pouring darkness, amid the muffled, slow, uncertain sounds of the army straining to move itself along a road the rain had long since turned into a river of mud. During his balloon observations, Cadmus had gained an inkling of the enormous amount of drudgery required of the man in the ranks; but until that night he had never realized the sheer, back-breaking and exasperating effort it cost to make a night march in the rain, and it made little difference whether the commanding general called it a withdrawal or a retreat.

But neither on that night nor in the days that followed, when the division bivouacked at the Diascund Bridge, moved up to Barhamsville in support of General Smith, fell back on the Chickahominy and finally crossed that river to take position on the left of Johnston's army before Richmond, did Cadmus receive any news of the two Negroes or the mare. It was a strange, unhappy time. Discipline had grown ragged; stragglers swarmed through the countryside between the two armies; there was a disturbing sense of uncertainty in high places, and this, oddly enough, seemed to be increased by the very slowness with which the Union army came up to them.

An inward restlessness infected Cadmus, as it did many others in those trying days, though in his case it did not come from any want of work. There was plenty in Magruder's headquarters to occupy the time of half-a-dozen clerks. After his momentary illness, General Magruder had become embroiled in a controversy with Gustavus W. Smith over a dispatch whose arrival had waked the latter general at an inconvenient hour. The ensuing series of exchanges were so biting that they resulted in General Magruder's first being relieved of his command, then ordered to a new one beyond the Mississippi River, and then reinstated at the head of his former troops, all in a sequence of moves so sudden that his own headquarters wondered dizzily what would happen next.

As Cadmus made copies of these heated missives, the splash and gusto of the general's literary style, which he had formerly admired, began to seem vaguely ridiculous. He could not have explained why this was so. General Magruder was always kindness personified to all his staff. But the bird's-eye view Cadmus had had of the movement of the two armies had brought with it some comprehension of the size of the impending battle, and it seemed a strange performance for two general officers to waste their time and that of other people over a dispute about the sleeping habits of one of them. It did not seem to Cadmus that a war could be won that way, and he wanted to be done with it. He had no very clear idea of what he did want to do. The prospect of personal glory did not concern him in the same way it had before; he had had his own taste of glory and found it an overrated word. But he did feel a simple need of serving more directly in the war and among people who were less preoccupied with their personal rights and dignity.

The trouble was that he did not know how he could properly resign, and he might have continued as General Magruder's voluntary aide through all the fighting round Richmond if it had not been for a letter from Great-Uncle Eppa Tatum.

21

THE OLD MAN had never taken very readily to the process of writing, his main activity in that line being entries in his stud book or occasional letters to the Richmond papers, which, since they were nearly indecipherable, were very seldom published. But when Cadmus opened the folded sheet and saw the crabbed lines erratically traced across the paper, a sudden warm recollection of the old man, hunched over his desk with a toddy glass placed perilously close beside the inkwell, almost overwhelmed him with a desire to be home. And that, it appeared after some concentration on his part, was what Great-Uncle Eppa wanted, too.

Dear Caddy,

Your Mother has just reminded me that You will soon be 18 yrs which will Bring you under this new Conscription law the necessity of which is a Blot upon the honor of our Confederacy. As no man with Tatum or Henry blood in him would ever consent to enter a compulsory Service you are no Doubt designing to Enlist & as that will have to be for the duration of this Struggle it seems important to me that you select the Arm best suited to your inclination and talents. I mention this Because your Mother seems to think from your letters that you are not Altogether satisfied in your present situation. It might be well if you came home for a day to talk this over Provided you can be spared in the Present military situation. You might show this to your superior Officer or Gen'l Magruder, to whom convey my compliments. A visit from you would give your Mother pleasure & myself also.

Yr Great Uncle, Eppa Tatum

Then, as he turned the letter over, marveling how anyone could render writing so illegible, Cadmus discovered a postscript faintly traced in the inner fold, as though to insure **its** being seen by no one. It was headed by one of the old man's few known words of Latin, which he never failed to use:

Postscriptum — There has been a Negro man here asking for you but would not stay to talk to me or state his business.

With a sudden lifting of his heart, Cadmus thought it must have been Mink, and the fear that he and Mebane would not stay long enough for him to reach them made him doubly anxious to be gone. But he did not consider it either just or wise to ask any unsuspecting man to cope with the peculiarities of Great-Uncle Eppa's handwriting, so he made a fair copy of the letter before applying for his leave.

It turned out to be much easier than he had dared expect.

"Mr. Tatum's right, of course," said Captain Bryan. "If you were my son, I'd look at it the same way. I see no reason why you should not start home the first thing tomorrow. How far is it?"

Cadmus told him that the house stood about eight miles south of Richmond, on the James.

"On this side of the river?"

"Yes, sir. We're a mile or so above Chaffin's Bluff."

"You'd better plan to spend the night, and report back here by sunset the day after. You'll need a pass. They've begun picking up soldiers in the city. The streets are full of people without leave." The captain wrote out a pass and handed it to Cadmus. "I hope you'll want to stay with this headquarters, for you've done a good job here. But if you decide to go anywhere else, I'll be able to see your point. I don't doubt I'd have felt the same way at your age. But," and the captain gave Cadmus one of his dry grins, "there's always a penalty hitched to every good thing, and I want the 'out' basket cleaned up before you quit tonight."

Cadmus had to stick to his desk till well on towards midnight. He was dog-tired when he finally reached the tent he shared with Brashear, and he felt that he would never be able to wake in the morning. But it is always easier to make an early start when you are heading home, and Cadmus had bolted his breakfast and was on his way while it was still dark.

He reached the city just at dawn. Mist hung over the lower streets as he trotted in from the straight Mechanicsville road. Far away he could hear the rattle of market wagons, but where he was there was only the brisk echo of his horse's hoofs. As he came into Main Street, however, and turned east into the eye of sunrise, he heard the city begin to stir behind him, and the sound of it was like the harsh breathing made by any living creature just before it wakes.

⤆ 22 ⤇

THE CASUAL VISITOR who finds the country below Richmond flat and uninteresting does so because he has not taken time to know it. For the main roads, which fork from the city like fingers from an open hand, follow the higher ground, and there the fields that border them do lie flat or, at best, only gently rolling. And the woodlands are folded into the creases of the land in a manner that disguises their extent. One must walk into them to know the true height of the trees and the dark, wandering courses of the streams, with their marsh-stained, secret flowing water. The woods are like the shadows of an older land, from whose borders the community of wild life — the foxes, the rabbits, the belly-crawlers, and the birds — has from the beginning kept close watch on the human community, working the fields for crops that may or may not be fruitful for the watchers, or merely traveling the roads as Cadmus did on that May morning.

He had to stop once to show his pass where the raw earth-works of the defense line crossed the Osborne Turnpike south of Rocketts, but after that he had the road to himself, except for a lone farm wagon, drawn by a sleepy mule and driven by an old and even sleepier Negro, which he encountered at the turn-off of the Wilton road. Always afterwards, whenever Cadmus thought of going home, it was in terms of that lonely morning ride, with the level sunlight filling all the river mist and the breakfast smokes from farmhouses and Negro shanties, rising unwaveringly in the still air.

Just after breakfast time he came out past the southwest corner of the Wilton woods and saw ahead of him the familiar gateposts with their urns and beyond them the house, with its long porch facing the river; and as he turned through the gateway, he saw the front door open and Great-Uncle Eppa come out with the butler behind him, carrying a blanket for the old man's knees.

Cadmus halted his horse just inside the gate to watch the ritual of the old man seating himself while the butler put the blanket round him and tied the bell cord to the arm of the chair; and when everything had been arranged and the butler had gone back into the house, Cadmus walked the horse slowly up the drive and dismounted at the block below the step.

Great-Uncle Eppa greeted him quietly, showing no surprise, though Cadmus could see his eyes behind their tangled brows going over the Osbornes' horse.

"Hello, Caddy," the old man said. "I'm out a little early, but I had an idea you might be coming home this morning. How are you, boy?"

He reached for the cord and over his head the bell's note sounded, carrying back into the house, with a gentle echo of it humming softly into silence under the porch roof.

"You'd better go in and see your mother," he said, as the butler came to the door with exclamations of surprise and welcome home. "She'll want to see you right away, but after that come back out here and tell me what you're doing with that horse there, and why you haven't the mare."

But in the mysterious swift way in which news spreads through a big plantation household, the word of Cadmus's

349

arrival had already reached his mother, and when he turned to the door he saw her coming down the hall to meet him. All the time she was greeting him, asking him how he was and searching his face with anxious eyes, Great-Uncle Eppa hunched motionless in his chair and stared accusingly at the Osbornes' horse. Cadmus knew that the best way was the quickest way, so he sat down beside the old man, with his mother on his other hand, and, like Ulysses, began to tell the story of what had happened to him. From time to time his mother made soft exclamations of wonder or distress, but Great-Uncle Eppa never uttered a word or moved or turned his eyes from the Osbornes' horse; and so fixed was his stare that when two stable hands came round the house to fetch the animal, they did not dare to lead it away but stood like graven images at its head till Cadmus interrupted himself to wave them off.

"You see," he said, "this girl that picked me up was taking food to a hideout of some runaway slaves, and I thought perhaps you wouldn't want them to hear."

The whiskers over the old man's mouth shifted and stirred but settled back in place again without anyone's hearing what it was he said. So Cadmus went on with his account, ending with his receipt of Great-Uncle Eppa's letter.

"When I read the postscript," he said, "I thought it must have been Mink who came here asking for me. Do you know where he went?"

The old man shook his head.

"He just cleared right out," he said. "If he's around, though, he'll hear you've come back and show up. That is, if he really wants to see you. But I don't believe he has the mare, Caddy. A Negro could never get around the country without somebody noticing an animal like that and stopping him. And you hadn't given him a letter or anything."

"I didn't expect to land in the York River," Cadmus said defensively. "I thought I'd be coming right back to the camp."

"I know. But he must have lost her, Caddy, and he doesn't know how to tell me about it. It's not likely any Negro would have the nerve to do that anyway."

For a few moments in the sunlit silence the harsh sound of the old man's slow and heavy breathing was like grieving. He kept looking out towards the river, over the home pasture, as if in his mind's eye he could see the mare there. But after a little he turned his head and his beard went through a series of upheavals and he smiled.

"It wasn't your fault, Caddy, so you mustn't feel bad. And you've got to expect to lose horses in war, just about like men. But," and his voice grew heavy and a kind of glare came into his eyes, "it goes to show what happens when people start doing things like using balloons in war. It's not right. It's against nature and the human race. What did you see when you were up there, after all? Just the way a lot of Yankees look to a turkey buzzard. And if you hadn't been mighty lucky, you'd have ended up seeing how the bottoms of Yankee gunboats look to a pokefish. And what good that would do anybody, I'll be . . ." the old man champed his whiskers a few times and looked sidewise at Cadmus's mother before continuing ". . . I'll be blessed if I can see. The way to win a war is to get right up close to the enemy and shoot him before he can shoot you. I'm surprised a man like General Johnston would waste his time agreeing to anybody's using a contraption like that, and I don't give a leather dollar how many balloons the Yankees use or whether they start carrying cannon in them to shoot down kitchen chimneys and scare the women. If we can't whip the Yankees on the ground, we might as well pull in our horns right now and quit. And as for you, Caddy, the sooner you get through with such kinds of doings, the better I'll feel, and I daresay your mother will, too."

So they got onto the subject of whether Cadmus was to stay with General Magruder's headquarters or not and Cadmus tried to explain the feelings that had been coming up in him. Not only how he was just tired of writing copies of proclamations, and high-sounding orders, and doing ink and paper chore work. It wasn't just that, he said, if it was useful work and it must be, or generals wouldn't keep at it so much of the time, and General Magruder had been more than kind to him. He began to fumble for his words as he tried to tell Great-Uncle Eppa the way it was when you looked down on both armies — the size and might of all the men and batteries and cavalry and gunboats that the Union army had, and all these people and wagons and cannons and guns moving up into the land he'd been through with his father at one time or another and which was home country to them and to other people who had never done anybody damage; and yet, when you saw the two lines set one close against the other, they looked pretty much the same, and from that high part of the sky you might have had the armies shifted without seeing any real difference; and there didn't seem much purpose in what the generals did with their moving regiments and brigades here or there and making bold lines on their maps that ordinary men had to whittle out of the raw face of the earth with their sweat and aching backs. Cadmus said when he started his ballooning he'd hoped it was going to mean a commission for him, because he knew it would please his folks. He felt that way when he was coming back, before he had reported in to General Johnston. But now he wasn't sure he felt that way at all. He didn't know what had changed him. Maybe it was meeting the girl with the slaves, or maybe because nobody seemed to care what happened to a balloonist, once his balloon was gone. He didn't know, but he had the feeling that the real people in the army were the people who carved the work out in the lines and did the marching and got shot at if necessary. He didn't want to get shot at; he'd had his taste of it in the balloon and he didn't like it at all; but that was how he felt . . . He floundered and broke off. His mother had gone in to see about their luncheon and he and Great-Uncle Eppa were alone.

It was a long time before the old man moved, but when he did Cadmus saw the eyebrows had come up and the old man's shrewd eyes were looking at him.

"I think I understand the way you feel, Caddy." Something of Cadmus's own hesitation and diffidence seemed to have crept into the old man's voice. "It occurred to me you might want to do that, though I thought you'd want to go in the cavalry. That's why I let you have the mare."

"I know. I'm sorry," Cadmus said.

"Don't think about her now. If you join an infantry regiment, you'll be a foot soldier, and that's different; a lot different from what you've been doing. It's tiresome, dirty work. There's mighty little comfort in it, Caddy. And every night it rains your mother's going to start worrying, and that's going to be hard on me."

"I reckon she worries anyway," Cadmus said, grinning, "even with me in a tent."

"Well, perhaps she does," said Great-Uncle Eppa. "But if you're bound and determined to go into the infantry, you ought to pick a good regiment. Have you thought about that?"

Cadmus said he had, a little. He'd thought about the 38th Virginia.

The old man nodded. "They have a lot of people we know," he said. "Who's commanding?"

Cadmus said that Colonel E. C. Edmonds was, with Lieutenant Colonel Powhatan B. Whittle second in command. The latter, he said, had led the regiment in the Williamsburg battle.

"I know Colonel Edmonds," the old man said. "He'll be glad to welcome any blood relation of mine." He broke off a moment, his eyes apparently lost in the far distance beyond the river. Then he went on with fiery emphasis, "But whatever you join up with, Caddy, you'd better cure yourself of this fool idea about the people on both sides being pretty much alike. A turkey buzzard might look at it that way, but no real Virginian could — not while there's an armed Yankee left above ground in Virginia."

Cadmus knew that he hadn't explained his feelings clearly, and he realized that perhaps they were not quite clear in his own mind. But there was no use in arguing them out with Great-Uncle Eppa, who belonged to the old school. Like a great many Virginians, he had been strongly against secession, but once war came and the Union army moved onto Virginia soil, he had become rabid in his loathing of all Yankees.

The old man seemed as willing as Cadmus to drop the subject, and so they left it that way for the rest of Cadmus's stay. At lunch, when they went into the cool, quiet house, it was as if he had never been away, and, except for his gray jacket, as if no war had even been, and the nearest they came to it was a discussion of the best way of returning the Osborne horse. Warm contentment welled up in Cadmus's heart. He felt that this was to be his real departure to the war and that all that had happened to him was a purely fantastic business, like the business of dreams.

The loss of the mare still bothered him, because of his great-uncle; but even that he could put by.

Then, as they sat there with the meal finished, talking family things in the leisure he had forgotten could exist, the butler came softly in and said there was a Negro outside asking to see Mister Cadmus. The same big man, he said to Great-Uncle Eppa, who had been there before.

◆⋵ 23 ⵚ◆

IT WAS MINK, right enough. He was standing below the steps with his head uncovered, and a brief smile lighted his face when he saw Cadmus.

"I'm certainly glad to see you, Mist' Henry."

"I'm glad to see you, too, Mink." Cadmus could not quite bring himself to ask about the mare, so he said, "How's Mebane?"

"He's all right," Mink said. "He'd have come over with me, except he didn't want to leave the mare. We got her camped out in the woods."

"Why didn't you both bring her right in?" asked Cadmus.

Mink looked troubled.

"Well," he said, "we wanted to make sure you was here, Mist' Henry, before we brought her in. You see, if a couple of men like us takes a horse like her round the roads, they likely to get stopped. So Mebane he had to fix her up so nobody'd pay much 'tention to her. Mebane wouldn't trust her to

355

nobody else, not even to Mist' Norment. That's why he fix her so. But he cain't unfix her quick, and he's scared to have the ol' man see her like she is." Mink glanced uneasily towards the house. "Mebane say if you'd come out, then we could all fetch her back together and it'll be all right."

Cadmus agreed, and turning at once back down the drive, Mink led the way straight across the Wilton road and through a bordering field towards a long arm of the woods. There was no visible trail, but he seemed to be entirely familiar with the lay of the ground and strode on ahead till they struck an overgrown wagon track and followed this to a small, steep-sided ravine where the two Negroes had pitched camp.

A small fire burned in a screening hollow and tending it was Mebane. He hunkered down close to the flames, the limp brim of his hat hiding most of his weazened face as he studied a blackened tin propped up against the fire. Close by stood a ramshackle wagon and under a piece of canvas tied between four trees, with an old gray-muzzled mule for company, was the brown mare.

Only she was no longer brown. Some sort of dye had been

used on her, leaving her sleek hide streaked and mottled, and the dye, especially about her head, had been used to give her the appearance of a much older animal. She had been recently groomed, but Cadmus saw at once that, with the dust of the road on her and her mane and tail left matted, she would have looked pretty much like the ramshackle kind of horse you would expect to see tied to the tailgate of a Negro's wagon. All except her gait. She had always moved stylishly and that, combined with her bedraggled exterior, would surely have given her away. But when Mebane led her out, she seemed to move awkwardly and Cadmus asked the old Negro what had happened to her.

Mebane muttered and mumbled something in reply but so unintelligibly that Mink was forced to interpret it to Cadmus.

"He put some heavy shoes on her to make her walk lame. It was hard on her, but he say she'll be all right in a little while, leavin' her out on pasture without no shoes on. But he say the color won't come off her for a month. That's why he skeered for Mist' Tatum to see her."

The older Negro nodded vigorously, shooting quick, anxious glances at Cadmus's face. But Cadmus, thinking of all their ingenuity and all the worry and trouble they had gone to, was hardly able to do more than thank them. He offered them money, but they wouldn't hear of it; Mink was almost sharp in his refusal and there was a moment of difficult silence, which Mebane's mumbling finally broke.

Again Mink had to explain what he had said.

"Mebane askin' what happen to that old balloon. He say can you tell us while he hitchin' up the mule?"

So for the second time that day, Cadmus described his free flight in PIZZINI, and when he had finished, Mink's stiffness

357

had vanished and he asked, "You couldn't use a servant, could you, Mist' Henry?"

Cadmus was touched. He thanked Mink but explained that joining an infantry regiment as a private made it hardly possible for him to keep a body servant, even if he could afford to pay Mink wages.

Mink looked down at the fire.

"I'm a free man. But they won' let me get in the army. They say I can be a servant, that's all. They say a Negro cain't fight with a gun in this here war. Don't matter if he's free."

His voice was strident. It filled the hollow where the camp-fire was. But there was nothing Cadmus could think of to say to him. He turned unhappily to watch Mebane fish the mare's bridle from under a nest of rags in the wagon box. The old man brought her forward and put the reins in Cadmus's hands, making a kind of little bow and mumbling something in an undertone so softly that once again Mink was obliged to interpret for him.

"He say he guess that our ballooning days is done."

Cadmus found it hard to speak. It seemed to him that in his army experience he had found no truer friends than these two Negroes. He stood uneasily by while they took down the canvas that had sheltered the mare and harnessed the old mule to the wagon. Mebane climbed up to the seat and as he lifted the reins the mule's ears drooped in comic duplication of the old man's limp hat brim. One of the rear wheels squeaked as it started turning, and Mink said, "We'll go along to the road with you, Mist' Henry. And then I guess we'll say good-bye."

He seemed vague as to their plans. He said they would probably look for work in Richmond. There was plenty of work for a strong hand there. Perhaps there wasn't much for someone like Mebane, but he didn't need a great deal, after all, to keep on living, and Mink could make enough for both.

Cadmus couldn't leave it that way. He wanted them to come back to the house with him and meet his great-uncle. Mink shied at the idea, but Cadmus finally persuaded him by saying how badly the old man would feel if he didn't have a chance to thank them himself.

So, with Mebane leading in the rickety wagon, they went up the drive together and stopped below the steps, under Great-Uncle Eppa's eye. It carried an unfavorable glint when it took in the mare's appearance; and when the old man heard how the mare had been made to walk lame, he demanded to have the shoes put in his hands. Mebane fetched them up to him, muttering one of his incomprehensible explanations; but Great-Uncle Eppa understood him without difficulty, and holding the shoes for a moment and examining them, he gave a grunt of approval.

"Well, you knew what you were doing, all right."

Mebane made one of his little bows, and the old man grinned at him. It was obvious to Cadmus that the two had already established a communion that went beyond the mere mechanics of language. After a moment Great-Uncle Eppa addressed himself to Mink.

"When people do as much for anyone as you two men have done for me and Cadmus," he said, "there's no use trying to thank them. All you can do is ask them to do more. I'd feel glad if you two men would stay here and work with my horses. The man I had's been taken by the army. Besides, I'd like to feel there was a good man here to get that brown mare back in shape."

There was no question about Mebane's acceptance. He went straight down the steps and took the mare's bridle rein from Cadmus's hand. Whatever hesitations Mink might have felt seemed to melt away as he saw Mebane's obvious satisfaction; but Cadmus sensed an inner reservation. And this was borne out next morning when he had said his good-byes in the candlelit dusk of the hall just before dawn and, riding down the drive, wheeled his horse at the gateposts for a last look back at the house, dimly seen through the river mist.

He had a strong sense of the future before him, as if this moment and not his previous departure were his final severance with his boyhood, and even his service with PIZZINI appeared for the instant to be fading with the house. It

seemed strange, then, that the image of the Abolitionist girl should come so clearly into his mind. He saw her as she stood by the door of the little shack, holding out the shabby coat for him, with the hostile faces of the Negroes surrounding them. He did not know the name she went by — she had said it was her stepfather's — but he had a presentiment that their paths would cross again.

Then, as the river mist rolled thickly in, so that even the

nearer trees were lost in it, he heard light feet on the gravel and a mule came drifting up to him with shadowy, upraised ears, and Mink's voice said, "I'm coming along with you, Mist' Henry. Now Mebane's got himself settled, I reckon I can come along and see some of this here war. Mist' Tatum's given me a letter so I can take back that Osborne horse when you jine the infantry, so I'll have to be gone that time. But after that I'll be back with you."

"I told you," Cadmus said, "that I can't keep a servant."

"I know that," Mink answered. "But I reckon I can just keep track of you for Mist' Tatum."

That was the way it turned out. For Cadmus there was still a period of uncertainty, as there was for many men, before, out of the confusion that ended in the bloody muddlement at Seven Pines, an army was forged by another hand than Johnston's. Once it came to feel the steadfast purpose of its new leader, this same army, in the terrible battles of the Seven Days, learned to fight under Lee as few other armies ever fought.

Cadmus survived those battles and went on with the 38th Virginia to fight again in all the battles that culminated finally at Gettysburg. Sometimes he saw Mink, but more often, for long periods he did not. Yet it was Mink who found him in the field below Cemetery Ridge after the third day at Gettysburg and stole a wagon from a Pennsylvania farmer to bring him back in. But that, and his meeting with the Abolitionist girl again, would be another story.

WATER NEVER
HURT A MAN

HE TRUDGED with his hands tight fists in his pockets, his head bowed to the wind and rain. Ahead of him in the darkness, so that he could hear the squudge of their hoofs, the towing team bowed their necks against the collars. He could not see them in the darkness. When he lifted his face, the rain cut at his eyes; and when lightning split the darkness he shut his eyes tight and pulled his head closer into his coat collar, waiting blindly for the thunder. Once in a lull he looked back. He could barely make out the bow-lantern and the arrows of gray rain slanting against it. Between him and the light he caught glimpses of the towrope, dipped slightly between the team's heaves, and the roughened water in the canal. Somewhere behind the light his father stood by the rudder-sweep, his beard curled and wet, his eyes slits, sighting for the bank. John wanted to go back, wanted to tie-by for the night, wanted to be in the bunk with his head buried in the friendly, musty smell of the blanket, where the storm could not reach him. He had gone back once, but his father had reached for his belt, saying, "Go on back. Watter never hurt a man. It keeps his hide from cracking."

John had gone back to the team. They did not need his guidance. But it was his place to keep the rope from fouling if a packet boat coming their way signaled to pass. He was afraid of his father at night, afraid of the big belt and strong hands with hair on the fingers over the knuckles. He caught up with the plodding horses and let the rain have its way. At each stroke of lightning his small back stiffened. It was his first year on the canal and he was afraid of storms at night.

He had been proud that spring when his father said, "John's old enough to be a driver-boy; he's coming along with me and the *Bacconola*." He had showed his dollar to his brothers and sisters, first pay in advance, and his father had bought him a pair of cowhide boots from the cobbler when he came to the village. Later, when the frost was out of the mud, John would go barefoot.

He was proud of his father. In Westernville, with other small boys, he had heard the dock loafers talking about his father, George Brace, bully of the Black River Canal. In some strange way they had news of every fight his father fought a day after it happened. "George licked the Amsterdam Bully Wednesday mornin'. Lock fifty-nine. It tuk nineteen minits only." "George is a great hand. Them big ditch bezabors is learning about George." A stranger had said, "Wait till Buffalo Joe meets up with him." There was silence then. Buffalo Joe Buller, he was bully of the western end of the Erie. A pea-souper, a Canadian, he fought the Erie bullies down

one by one, and when he licked them he marked them with his boot in the Canadian style. It had a cross of nails to mark the beaten man's face. "You wait," said the stranger.

Little John, listening, felt shivers down his back. But now, with the wind and rain, and the lightning tumbling the clouds apart, he forgot. They were on the long haul westward, to Buffalo, with ploughs aboard, full-drafted in Rome. They had had to leave three-hundredweight on the dock.

He felt his muddy boots slip in the towpath. He heard the squelching of the horses. Squelch-squelch, a steady rhythm as they kept step. Once the lightning caught his eyes; and he had a clear view of trees beyond the canalside meadow, their budded twigs bent down like old women with their backs to the storm, and the flat, sharp wall of a canal house sixty yards behind him. He had not even seen it as he passed. The rain was finding a channel down his neck. It crept farther, bit by bit, with a cold touch. He could feel his fists white in his pockets from clenching them. His legs ached with the slippery

going. They had had supper at six, tied up by the bank, and John had eaten his plate of beans. He had felt sleepy afterward, barely noticing his father's big body bent over the dishpan. It was warm in the cabin, with the little stove roaring red-hot, and his small hat hanging beside his father's cap on the door.

He had been almost asleep when his father's hand shook him roughly, then tumbled him from his chair. "Get out, John. Them ploughs we've got has to get west for spring ploughing. We'll pick up Bob in Syracuse, then we'll have a better chance to rest. Get out now," and he had reached for his belt.

What did John care for the old ploughs anyway? But it hadn't then begun to storm, and he had gone, with a tired sense of importance. One had to keep freight moving on the old Erie. The old *Bacconola* always made fast hauls. He had been proud and shouted in a high voice to the tired horses and kicked one with his new boots.

But now he did not care about the ploughs. He wished the crazy old *Bacconola* would spring a leak in her flat bottom, so they would have to stop till the hurry-up boat came along and patched her up. He thought of her now, bitterly, with her scabs of orange paint. "Crummy old blister," he called her to himself and made names for her, which he said aloud to the horses in a shrill voice. He was only twelve, with all the bitterness of twelve, and the world was a hateful thing.

"God-damned old crummy bitch of a tub . . ." But the lightning caught him, and his throat tightened and he wanted to cry out under the thunder.

A water rat went off the towpath with a splash, and a frog squeaked.

He glanced up to see a team on the opposite towpath

heading east. "Hey, there!" yelled the driver in a hoarse voice; but John was too tired to answer. He liked to yell back in the daytime and crack his whip. But he had dropped his whip a while back. He would get a licking for that in the morning. But he didn't care. To hell with the whip and the driver and Pa!

"Hey, there!" shouted the other driver, a voice in the rain. "All right, all right, you dirty pup. Eat rain, if you want to, and go drown." The rain took the voice, and the boat came by, silently, noiseless as oil, with its bow light a yellow touch against the rain. The steersman gave a toot upon the horn, but the sound bubbled through the water in it, and the steersman swore.

They were still on the long level, alone once more. It must be midnight. If only the lock would show. In Syracuse, Bob would come. He took turns driving and steering and cooking — a little man with a bent shoulder who had dizzy spells once in a while.

At the lock John could sit down and rest and listen to the tender snarling at his sluices while the boat went down, and heaving at his gate-beam, while John's father heaved against the other. He was crazy, the lockkeeper was; all lockkeepers were crazy. John's father always said so. John had seen a lot of them in their week of hauling, but he did not see why they were crazy. They looked no different even if they were. He hoped the lockkeeper would be asleep, so it would take a while to wake him.

Squelch, squelch-squelch, squelch. The horses kept plodding. Suddenly John caught a break in the rhythm. One foot sounded light. He pushed his way up beside them against the wind and laid a wet hand against a side. He could not see, but the side felt hot and wet, and he got a smell of sweat. Yes, he

could feel the off horse limping. Hope filled him. He waited
till the boat came up where he was, a small figure, shrunk with
cold. The boat's bow, round and sullen, slipped along, the
bow light hanging over and showing an old mullein stalk in
silhouette against the water.

"Pa!"

His voice was thin against the wind.

He saw his father's figure, rain dripping from the visor of
his cap, straight and big, almighty almost, breast to the wind.

"Pa!"

The head turned.

"Hey, there! What you doin'? Get on back, or I'll soap you
proper!"

"Pa! Prince has got a limp in his front foot. Pa!"

The voice turned hoarse with passion. "Get on back, you
little pup! Fifty-nine's just round the next bend. Take your
whip and tar him, or I'll tar you proper."

John sobbed aloud. For a bare moment he thought of
staying still and letting the boat pass on. He would run away
and join the railroad. He would get run over by an engine
there, just when things went well, and they would be sorry.
He started to draw himself a picture of his body coming home
in a black box, and his mother crying, and his father looking
ashamed and sorry, and then the lightning made a blue flare
and he saw the straight figure of his father ahead, on the
Bacconola, which seemed struck still, a pillbox in the flat
country, and he was afraid and went running desperately,
hoping he could get back to the team before he was missed.

He caught the horses on the bend and, lifting his face to the
storm, saw the lock lanterns dimly ahead. And even then his
ears caught, coming up behind him, the harsh blast of a tin
horn.

He looked back and saw a light, two rope lengths behind the *Bacconola*. Even while he watched over his shoulder, he saw that it was creeping up.

"John!" His father's voice beat down the sound of rain. "Lay into them brutes and beat into the lock!"

He could imagine his father glaring back. If only he had not dropped his whip. He would have liked to ask his father for the big bull whip that cracked like forty guns, but he knew what would happen if he did. He shrieked at the horses and fumbled for a stone to throw. But they had heard and recognized the note in his father's voice, and they were bending earnestly against the collars. A sudden excitement filled John as his father's horn rang out for the lock. The wind took the sound and carried it back, and the other boat's horn sounded a double toot for passing. John yelled shrilly. The horses seemed to stand still, and there was an odd effect in the rain of the canal sliding under them inch by inch laboriously, as if with his own feet he turned the world backward.

Minutes crept at them out of the rain, and the lights of the lock did not seem to stir. Then John heard the squelching of the team behind his back. Little by little they were coming up, past the *Bacconola,* until he could hear them panting through the rain, and saw them close behind, behind dim puffs of steamy breath. He watched them frantically. Then the lightning came once more, a triple bolt, and the thunder shook him, and when he opened his eyes once more he saw the lock lanterns a hundred yards ahead.

At that instant the driver of the boat behind yelled, "Haw!" and the following team swung across his towrope and they were snarled.

The horses stopped of themselves, shuddering. They were old hands, and knew enough not to move, for fear of being

thrown from the towpath. The boats came drifting on, plac-
idly as waterlogged sticks. The light of the following boat
showed a dark bow coming up. John heard his father roaring
oaths, and saw by the bow light of the other boat a tall, clean-
shaven man as big as his father, crouched to jump ashore.
Then both boats came in by the towpath, and both men
jumped. They made no sound except for the thump of their
shoes, but John saw them dim against the lantern light, their
fists coming at each other in slow, heavy swings.

The strange team was panting close beside him, and he did
not hear the blows landing. There was a pushing upward in
his chest, which hurt, and his fists made small balls in the
pockets of his trousers. The other boater and his father were
standing breast to breast, their faces still, cut, stonelike things
in the yellow light, and the rain walling them in. He saw his
father lift his hand, and the other man slip, and he would have
yelled, for all his cold, if the lightning had not come again, so
blue that his eyes smarted. He doubled up, hiding his face,
and wept. . . .

A hand caught him by the shoulder.

"A little puny girly boy," said a voice. "I wouldn't lick you
proper! Not a little girly baby like you. But I'll spank you just
to learn you to let us come by!"

John opened his eyes to see a boy, about his own height, but
broader built, squinting at him through the rain.

"Take off your pants, dearie," said the boy in a mock voice,
digging in his fingers till John winced. "Joe Buller can handle
your captain smart enough. Me, I'll just paddle you to learn
you."

John, looking up, was afraid. He did not know what to do,
but without warning his hands acted for him, and he struck at
the square face with all his might. A pain shot up his arm,
making his elbow tingle, and the boy fell back. John could

feel the surprise in that body stock-still in the rain, and had an instant of astonished pride.

Then panic laid hold of him and he tried to run. But the other boy jumped on his back. They went down flat in the mud, the older boy on John's shoulders, pummeling him till his head sang, and forcing his face into the track, and crying, "Eat it, you lousy little skunk! Eat it, eat it, eat it, eat it!"

John could taste the mud in his mouth, with a salty taste, and he began to squirm, twisting his head to escape the brown suffocation. He heaved himself behind, throwing the boy un-expectedly forward, twisted round, and kicked with all his might. The boy yelled and jumped back on him. And again they went down; this time the boy bent seriously to business. And this time John realized how it was to be hurt. At the third blow something burst loose in his inside and he screamed. He was crying madly. The other boy was heavier, but John squirmed over on his back, and as the brown hand came down

on his face he caught it in both his own and bit with all the strength of his jaws. The hand had a slippery, muddy taste, but in a second it was warm in his mouth, and there was a sick, salt wetness on his tongue. The boy struck him once in the eyes and once on the nose, but John held on and bit. Then the boy howled and tore loose and ran back. There was another stroke of lightning, and John saw him doubled up, holding his hand to his mouth; and he got stiffly up, turned his back to the thunder, and saw his father bent over the other boater, taking off his shoe.

John walked up to them. His father's face was bleeding a trickle of blood from the right eye into his beard, but he was grinning.

"I'll take his boot for a souvenir," he said. "How'd you come out, Johnny?"

"Oh, pretty good. I guess that other feller won't bother us no more," said John, examining the fallen man. He lay half-stunned, by the water's edge, a smooth, big man, with frightened, pale eyes. And one crumpled arm was in the water. John's father looked at the man and then at the boot he had in his hand.

"I'd ought to mark him by the rights of it; but he ain't worth the work, the way he laid down. Who'd ever know his name was Buller?"

Buller. . . . John gazed up admiringly at his big father and studied how the blood ran from the outer corner of the eye and lost its way in the black beard, which the rain had curled. His father had licked the western bully proper.

"Hey, there!"

The hail came in a thin, cracking voice. Turning, they saw the lockkeeper, white-bearded, peering at them from under the battered umbrella he held with both hands against the wind. The tails of his nightshirt whipped round the tops of his boots.

"Hey, there, you. There'll be some down boats by pretty quick, so you want to hurry along now, while the level's right."

John was aware of his father standing looking down at him.

"Shall we tie-by where we be?" asked his father.

John felt pains coming into the back of his neck where he had been pummeled, and his knuckles ached.

"We can stay here a spell," said his father. "The storm's comin' on again. There'll be bad lightnin', I make no doubt."

As he spoke there came a flash, and John whirled to see if the other driver-boy was still visible. He was proud to see him sitting by the towpath, nursing his hurt hand. John did not notice the thunder. He was elaborating a sentence in his mind.

He made a hole in the mud with the toe of his boot, spat into it, and covered it, the way he had seen his father do at home on a Sunday.

"Why," he said, in his high voice, eying the old *Bacconola,* "I guess them poor bezabor farmers will be wantin' them ploughs for the spring ploughing, I guess."

"Me, I'm kind of tuckered," said his father, raising his shoulders to loose the wet shirt off his back. "And the rain's commencing, too."

John said importantly, "Watter never hurt a man; it keeps his hide from cracking."

His father jumped aboard. He took his horn and tooted it for the lock. John ran ahead and put back the other boat's team and cried to their own horses to go on. They took up the slack wearily, and presently little ripples showed on the *Bacconola*'s bow, and the lantern showed the shore slipping back.

On the stern, George Brace blew a blast for the lock. The old lockkeeper was standing by the sluices, drops of water from his beard falling between his feet.

The boat went down, and the horses took it out. Ahead, the team and the boy left the lantern light and entered once more the darkness. The rope followed. And once more the *Bacconola* was alone with its own lantern.

Presently, though, in a stroke of light, George saw his son beside the boat.

"What's the matter? Hey, there!" he asked.

"Say, Pa! Will you chuck me your bull whip here ashore? Them horses is getting kind of dozy. They need soaping proper."

"Where's your whip?"

"I guess I left it awhile back. I guess it was in that kind of scrummage we had. I guess it needs a heavier whip anyhow. I guess a man couldn't spare the time going back for it."

"Sure," said George.

He reached down and took it from its peg, recoiled it, and tossed it ashore. The boat went ahead, slowly, with a sound of water, and of rain falling, and of wind.

UNCLE BEN'S WHALE

WE SAWED the last cut on the last tree and sat down side by side on the log. John got out a wad of Happy Days, when he saw that I was lighting my pipe, and stowed it away in his right cheek. His eye was taking in the river valley, with the canal beyond. Some plover were calling down the river, but he did not hear them. And then, just as I was getting back my wind, he swung his eye round at me. "Say," said he, "did I ever tell you about my Uncle Ben?"

❧ I ☙

MY UNCLE BEN MEEKUM was kind of a dingy old coot. They say in his early days he was a pretty fast kind of a spark; but when I first remember him he'd married Aunt Em, and the two of them made just about the most respectable sort of home life a woman could want. Uncle Ben would load his boat, and him and Henry Plat, who done his driving, would keep the old boat going, along with the aid of Ben's mules; but inside that boat Aunt Em ruled the roost.

It was kind of hard on a man, after he'd run a boat to suit his own notions for forty years to have the bad luck to get married to Aunt Em. You couldn't spit out of the window or knock out your pipe on top of the stove or have a drink in your own cabin (or anywhere else for that matter), and she used to make him and Henry, who was bothered with soft feet, wash 'em every night before they come to supper. It was a pitiful sight to see them two old coots setting up on the roof of the cabin on a cold night and easing their toes into a basin. Every time he felt the touch of the water, Henry'd say he was going to get loose and leave, but Uncle Ben'd beg him to stay.

Henry'd never actually have gone off and left Uncle Ben defenseless. Them two had been boating it together ever since Uncle Ben'd got his boat, and Henry was just as scared of Aunt Em as Uncle Ben was. If he'd have left, he'd have been scared clean crazy of her coming after him.

I don't say Aunt Em was a bad woman, but she was too big to live in a boat. She'd always been heavy and her blood pressure generally kept going up on her. Quick-tempered! And she could have taken on both of them old men at once if she'd been a-mind to, and she probably did when she got restive.

You see, she belonged to my family, and Uncle Ben only got in by marrying her. His name was Meekum, and he had to take about everything that was coming to him.

He used to talk to Pa about it and ask what a man had ought to do, and Pa'd tell him, "Strop her up and if that don't work, use the hone." But Uncle Ben'd shake his head and say Pa was a young man. Then he'd give Pa some of his own dauntless early history until he'd start off home with active ideas. But the minute Aunt Em'd get her eye on him, he'd lose his nerve.

It went on that way till the time Uncle Ben made a big deal in New York. He'd often thought before that of sneaking out on her; but she'd put all the money he used to keep on the boat in a bank in Boonville in her own name, because Uncle

Ben couldn't read nor write, and she took the money the boat earned off of him as quick as it come in.

Well, sir, Uncle Ben finally did bust loose, and this is the way it happened.

❧ 2 ❧

IN THE SPRING of the year Uncle Ben and Henry had loaded up their boat with ice at Forestport and picked Aunt Em up at Boonville, where they spent the winter in her mother's house, and they all started off down the canal for New York.

They made a regulation haul to Albany and left their mules in the round barn and got into a tow on the Swiftsure and had the ride down the Hudson River. All the way Uncle Ben kept considering what he'd get to haul back. Fertilizer would have made him a good haul, and he thought the trip to New Jersey after it might be pleasant. But Aunt Em wouldn't consider it. She said it would make the boat smell too strong.

She took a lot of pride in that boat, even if it was Uncle Ben's. She'd had it painted up a good bright yellow with a white trim and she had the cabin fixed up dainty with curtains at the windows and the best geraniums on the Erie Canal. She was a good hand to cook and keep house, and the best meals I ever ate I ate right there. She could make a pie to bring the watter to a man's eyes. And the boat did look nice. It was all painted blue inside, with the cupboards white and the stove black and the pans always hanging in the same place. She had a little brass clock, too, that struck the hours with a bell. It didn't keep very good time, always being slow; but the way she polished it you would have thought it had come from the factory in the morning mail.

The boat's name was *Louisa* and you can see it laying in that set-back below Hawkinsville today, what's left of it.

So Aunt Em'd said there'd be no fertilizer, and Uncle Ben had to agree. Him and Henry had had it all figured out, but most of the time Henry was riding on one of the other boats traveling down the canal and river, where it was more peaceful, so Uncle Ben got to New York without knowing what he was going to haul back.

Well, they tied up in the East River dock the same as usual, waiting for a calmer day to get the boat across the harbor, and they hadn't more than got to the Swiftsure office to pay off before the clerk handed Uncle Ben a letter for Aunt Em. Uncle Ben was an ignorant old bezabor when it come to civilized ideas. Pa used to say he'd been born with just as much sense as anybody else, but that he'd lost progress since then. When the clerk explained who the letter was for, Uncle Ben paid off, and him and Henry went back to the boat.

Uncle Ben walked right up the gang and down into the cabin. Getting a letter that way made him feel important.

"Wipe your feet," says Aunt Em.

"To heck with my feet," says Uncle Ben. "Here's a letter, Em."

"For me?" she asks, and Uncle Ben says, "Yes, sir."

She dropped the potato she had commenced peeling into the wrong pan and grabbed that paper. It took her just a minute to figure it all out and she turned kind of pale.

"Ma's sick," she says. "I got to get right home. It says that she's real sick again with the sugar diabetes."

"I don't wonder," says Henry from the door, "the way she eats it with her coffee."

But Aunt Em didn't notice it. She was all dithery.

"I got to start right out," she says.

"And me unload this ice into the river?" asks Uncle Ben.

"Stupid!" she says. "Do you think your cheap mules can get me home in time? Poor Ma, with such a son-in-law! It's a lucky thing she's got a daughter."

"Well," says Uncle Ben, "if you want to beat out the *Louisa,* you'll have to take a train of cars."

And that's what she done. She got out her old satchel and her hat and she put off with them for the station as tight as she could make it.

"You come right home the minute you've got rid of that ice," she says.

"Yes, Em," says Uncle Ben.

"And you make Henry mop out the floor every other day and don't you set down after eating till you've done the dishes. And don't you dasst to use that new china set."

"No, Em," says Uncle Ben.

"And you put the money in the box when you get paid and don't you touch a penny."

And then the train took her off.

◄ 3 ►

THERE AIN'T ANYBODY to tell how Uncle Ben commenced getting his old spunk back. But he kept setting a pretty good pace right along till he and Henry got back to the boat. Well, they took the ice across the harbor, and it was the first time in

ten year Uncle Ben hadn't got sick making the voyage. He stood on the cabin set-back, holding the sweep with his shirt unbuttoned and the spray slopping against his wishbone, and every time a gull hollered he'd look up against the sun. And Henry Plat, he lay on the deck, looking up at Uncle Ben, full of admiration.

Well, sir, they unloaded that ice and they took a tow back to the East River dock, and halfway across they seen a lot of boats

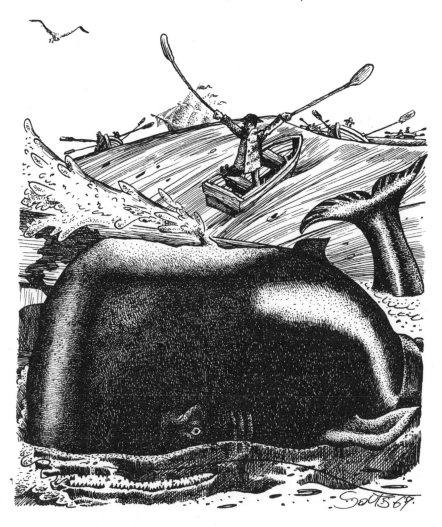

rowing to beat the nation and right ahead of them the scaredest whale that ever got mixed in the traffic of New York. There was a lot in the papers afterward about how that whale got into the city anyway, and they had pictures of it, and a picture of Uncle Ben a-standing on the *Louisa*, holding a skipper's cap in his hand and looking modest. After it was all over, Uncle Ben had bought him a secondhand hat with gold braid in a slopshop and let on how he'd been around the Horn in his early manhood.

But what happened was that that whale seen the old *Louisa* butting her stummick on the waves and I guess he thought she was another whale.

Uncle Ben seen her coming and yelled at Henry to look and tell him what in tarnation was coming and Henry looked and just hollered. Uncle Ben was always quick in a tight situation and he grabbed his horn and let out a good one on it, but the whale run up alongside of him and squirted the boat with watter and blood and Uncle Ben lost his temper and grabbed his boat hook and jammed it against the whale to keep her off and stuck her right in the eye. I guess the old brute was pretty near exhausted because she just raised a fin and died right there.

Well, the other boats come up, and the men in them claimed the whale was theirs; but Uncle Ben had his boat hook well set in the brute's eye and he wouldn't listen. Seems as he made a great impression and they laughed and asked one another what they would do with a whale anyhow, and pretty soon they asked Uncle Ben would he buy out their share. And he smacked his hand on his wallet and fishes out the money, and what with counting and the motion of the waves and Henry Plat he had only just enough left to pay for a tow up the river and get his mules out of the barn in Albany.

❧ 4 ❧

WHEN the *Louisa* got back to the dock again and the watter got calm, Henry Plat rose up and commenced taking notice.

"What," he says, "are you going to do with that whale, Ben?" And then he remarks, "How Em's going to make you squeak when she finds out what you've spent your money on!"

But Uncle Ben was too set up with his new importance to be scared.

"Shut up, you poor jellyfish," he says. "Em hasn't got nothing to say about this whale."

"No," says Henry, "I guess not."

Well, right then a lot of reporters come aboard and they begun asking questions. Uncle Ben got him his hat with gold braid and a shiny visor and had his picture took. And just after the whole of them had left, along comes a boat with a chesty bung in uniform that comes aboard and wants to know how long Uncle Ben aims to keep his property in New York harbor. Well, Uncle Ben says he'll get it out of the way pretty quick and treats him handsome and that was that.

But he still had Henry Plat to talk to before he could get any rest.

"What am I going to do with it? What am I going to *do?*" and right there he got his idea. "Why," he says, "I'm going to load that whale aboard the *Louisa* and take her up the Erie."

"Be you, Ben? What are you going to do that for?"

"I'm going to show her for a nickel."

Henry sneered. "How much money will that make when anybody can look at her from the towpath for nothing?"

"You shut up," said Uncle Ben.

He'd got more up-and-coming every minute since Aunt Em had gone back to Boonville, and he wasn't going to let no bezabor like Henry Plat gum his fun. He just walks up the dock and goes off to the public library. Now he'd got a whale, he wanted to know all about it. So he walks in and says to the lady, "Please show me your whales, Miss." Well, that caught her attention and she was a pretty girl and in two minutes had got the whole business out of Uncle Ben. "I want to find out what kind of a whale it is," he told her, "and all about it."

Well, she took him through a lot of books, and they discovered about fourteen different kinds of whale. Finally they got Uncle Ben's whale sorted out as number eleven.

⊷ 5 ⊶

WHEN UNCLE BEN come back to the *Louisa* about supper time, Henry asked him again what he aimed to do with his fish.

"Fish? That ain't no fish. Gosh, Henry, you're a ignorant bird, all right. Why that's a mammal!"

"What," asks Henry, "is a mammal?"

Uncle Ben just looks him up and down.

"Henry," he says, "your mother was one."

"Do you want to fight?" asks Henry.

"No," says Uncle Ben. "You've been upset by this business, Henry. Of course, it's been different with me. I've been around the Horn in my young days. In my day I've speared more'n a hundred of this identical variety. I've got sperms, and speared narwhales, and blowed the very guts out of a killer oncet at three hundred yards with my old thirty-eight."

"What's the name of this variety?"

"It's a cash-a-lot."

Henry looks at him kind of wondering. "Honest?"

Uncle Ben nods to him. "Honest," he says.

"Golly," says Henry, "maybe there is money in her after all.

"Listen, Henry, did you ever hear about a feller named Jonah?"

"Sure, he got swallered by one of them animals."

"That's right, and then he got spit up. Well, look here, Henry. Anybody that wants to can look at the outside of this whale for nothing, but them that want the whole works is going to have to pay me fifty cents."

"How're you going to show them the whole works, Ben?"

"I'm going to dig em out and make a room in his inside!" Uncle Ben looks proud.

"But Ben," asks Henry, "if you dig them out, where in Sarah are you going to put them for people to see?"

"Gosh, Henry, can't you think of nothing but inwards? I'm just going to have a room there and a bar — no, I guess I'll just have a kind of refreshment parlor — then I'd ought to get the ladies and children, too."

"That's an idea," says Henry, and it was.

6

UNCLE BEN and Henry got the whale hoisted onto the *Louisa* next morning with her nose on the cabin roof and the rest of her laying along the pit beams and the stable and her tail hanging over the front end. Then they joined their tow and started back for Albany.

Well, the old *Louisa* was the first boat in that line; but along about Spuytenduyvil the wind changed to the north and the rest of the boats made the Tug change the line to put her on the back end. They'd thought at first a whale was a pretty handsome thing to examine, but about there Uncle Ben and Henry had got through the outside layer of fat. You could see them any time, burrowing in like a couple of beagles digging out a woodchuck. They had little shovels, very sharp, and they certainly made progress.

At first Uncle Ben was real mad at being stuck onto the back end of the tow, but Henry pointed out it would be

handier getting rid of the insides of the whale so he didn't argue very hard. He was having too good a time. Henry wasn't so well fixed. What with digging back of Uncle Ben and getting the throwout, he was so danged greasy that he wouldn't dasst to scratch a match along his back end. No sir, and what's more, he wasn't fitted out for hard work and he couldn't keep up with Uncle Ben. That old coot was just about possessed. He'd got a dish towel tied around his beard and cotton in his ears and even at that, about every ten minutes he had to walk out and let himself dreen over the edge.

Well, about the second day they got pretty well into the core of the whale. They'd mixed themselves a mess of beans down in the cabin and Henry wanted to lay down on his bed, but Uncle Ben hadn't time. He kept explaining, "I got to get the outfit in afore we get to Watervliet." So up on deck he went and walked into the whale and the first stroke he took he went through between two bones and the yell he let out come right out of the whale's mouth and Henry come a-running.

"Where've you reached to, Ben?" he asks.

Uncle Ben didn't know. He was kind of puzzled, inside and looking out.

Henry looks around too, and says, "I don't see where that feller Jonah managed to get along. I don't believe he was a

whole week down inside like us are here. It ain't got no ventilation, hardly at all."

"You poor twerp," says Uncle Ben. "This ain't the same whale."

"I don't see what that's got to do with it."

"No, you've never been around the Horn. But I have and I've seen whales blow out the bad air fifty feet high."

"If there was that much pressure of bad air, I don't see how Jonah lasted out a minute."

"Well, maybe he was that kind of a feller," says Uncle Ben.

Well, when they got the insides into the river, Uncle Ben begun to fashion out a room. "Right here," he says, "is going to be the refreshment tables for the ladies. I'll get them in Albany. We won't need so many cheers, with what we got in

the cabin. And then," he says, "seeing as how the lighting ain't very good, I'll arrange a winder on each side." He stood there looking around kind of pleased and wondering. "Henry," he says, "what kind of curtains do you think would go best with these walls?"

Right then some blubber went into the back of Henry's neck and got the best of him.

"You're going to need something waterproof to wall this room," he says.

"Nonsense," says Uncle Ben, but it was a hot day and he discovered for himself there was a leak in the roof. But his ideas had got pretty well formed, and by the time he'd showed the outside of his whale in Troy for fifteen cents he'd got the inside all fitted out. And when the *Louisa* hauled out of the Basin for Lock Number One, the whole contraption did make a display.

First, the two mules, a couple of scrummy old screws, had had their harness blacked and tassels and rings hung out to hide the bare spots in their hides till they sounded like a circus parade. And then the towline had a twist of yeller cloth on it and a big ribbon bow. And then come Henry Plat. Uncle Ben had rigged out the poor bezabor in a secondhand coachman's outfit, and he had a top hat with a ribbon bouquet on it and a coat with tails — and Henry's back end wasn't the kind to carry tails, it stuck out between — and white pants like knickers and a pink weskut, and then there was the boots with flesh tops. Henry had tried them out in Albany, but they pinched him so that he hollered and argued till Uncle Ben allowed him to go back to the old boots he always wore and the red socks Aunt Em had knitted him for Christmas. But even then the poor twerp's whiskers and little eyes looked kind of wistful, as if the clothes had got him and was taking him somewhere where he didn't want to go.

But then come the boat. They had kind of washed her outside but she looked a little greasy; but as Uncle Ben said, everybody had seen a bullhead boat anyway. It was the whale they'd look at. And sure enough, there was the whale stretched out on the boat, looking Uncle Ben right in the eye where he stood steering. She had a door in her side opposite the gang, and a flag stuck into her nose hole saying CASH-ALOT in green letters. And over the door was a sign saying "Be a Jonah for fifty cents." And underneath it said, "Complete equipment.

And that wasn't all. Getting familiar with the whale the way he had had made Uncle Ben feel kind of affectionate towards

her and he wanted her to look her best; so he'd got a pair of glass eyes off an oculist in Albany which was as big as apples and he'd arranged them in her, which gave her a real active appearance. He got himself a sailor's coat to go with his gold-braided hat and a new tie and done the steering. Every time he come to a village he blew on his horn and put into the dock. And the whole town come down. And danged near everyone would go inside the whale. It certainly was rigged out.

Uncle Ben had built a regular room out of matched lumber and he had a winder on the far side opposite the door, and a chair and table in the front end, and a bunk and a stove running through a double pipe, which he didn't never get up his nerve to light. And on the shelf in the back end he had a

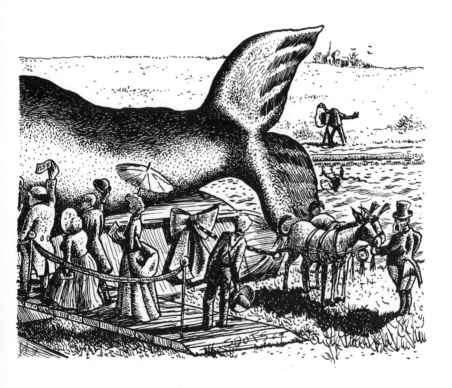

cupboard with all Aunt Em's best china set out. And as he told the people, it was all real shipshape and very actively arranged. A lot of those farmers commenced to take the Bible seriously after that. But they thought all whales was rigged out the same way.

Well, the first day Uncle Ben paid all his expenses, and every day he went along he made more money, because the word got into the papers and there was the picture took of him in New York and a picture of the complete whale, and even of the mules and Henry Plat. Farmers come from fifty miles away to intercept the creature and get a look at his insides.

❧ 7 ☙

BUT what was more important, Uncle Ben began to get more owdacious every day. By now he had killed whales in his early days with his bare hands, this one he'd fixed with his boat hook — you could read it in the papers — but of course he was getting on in years, and the number he had shot with his old thirty-eight was financially extraordinary. He showed you the thirty-eight to prove it and the notches he had cut in it for woodchucks became whales. You'd never have guessed he'd ever have been married to Aunt Em.

You won't believe it maybe, but that old coot had made over a thousand dollars before he got to Rome. And by now the Utica papers had the whole story and described the boat and the china and remarked on the pattern, which was in forget-me-nots and roses, and Henry Plat begun to wonder if it wasn't about time they heered from Aunt Em.

But by the time they got to Rome there had been a week of hot weather and the whale had swollen some and on the last day Uncle Ben had to do some trimming to get her under the bridges. And when he done that, even though he'd been living in that whale for two weeks, he had to admit that she was getting higher. And every day after that, the more he trimmed her, the higher she got, and at Rome for the first time, the price of admission went down a quarter. But Uncle Ben had become a regular Wall Street wizard and he bought out two perfumery peddlers and did a handsome business in that line.

⊰ 8 ⊱

BY THIS TIME, too, Henry Plat had become used to his uniform and was beginning to regret that the smell was getting so bad it threatened to stop the show. He hadn't ever had such light hauling to do in his life before. His breathing system had got used to blubber. But he felt real apprehensive, just the same, when, sure enough, there was Aunt Em on the dock, in front of the crowd, with her bag in her hand and her hat over her eyes, looking half as big as the whale and more than twice as powerful.

She'd been reading the papers. She didn't even look at the mules or Henry Plat or the yeller bow on the towline, and if her nose was working, she didn't even show it.

She waited till the boat had tied up and the gang come out and then she marched right aboard.

Uncle Ben come down the gang walk.

"Hullo Emmy," he says, and Henry was real startled to hear him so cool.

She stopped right still and kind of shivered.

"You runty little spider," she was always naming him by an insect, "is this the way you spend our money? Is this the way you hurry home to the bedside of your poor sick mother-in-law?"

Uncle Ben sounded patient.

"I was detained on business," he says.

"Business?"

Henry Plat kept feeling little cold winds climbing up the inside of them white pants. But then he seen Uncle Ben wink.

"Well, old girl," he says very loud, "welcome home. I'm surprised you was so long gone, but, now you're back, you're welcome."

He must have had that speech all figured out, I guess.

The crowd let out a cheer. Here was the whale killer being met by his loving wife. Crowds like that kind of thing. If there'd only been a baby on hand for Uncle Ben to use, he could have collected a dollar, instead of twenty-five cents.

Well, Aunt Em took a look at the crowd and went below without talking.

In a minute up she come hollering mad. "Where's my chiney?" she yells. And outside of the condition of the blankets, the fat had come through onto her crocheted tidies and the brass clock was running about forty-two hours a day with the oil that had got into it and striking faster than a man could wind it. Her curtains was streaked and the geraniums looked kind of sickly, and there hadn't been a dish washed in two weeks.

But she couldn't make no headway into that whale, it was jam full of humans, and when she finally did get in, she slipped on the floor and set down.

Uncle Ben helped her onto her feet and begun to explain the inside workings of that cashalot. And when he come to the money in it, Aunt Em was impressed. Even she could see that Uncle Ben was the killer of a whale, and wasn't scared of a woman anymore, and so she commenced to cry.

"Look at my chiney, look at what you have done to my pretty boat," she says. "How can I expect to live in a cabin full of a smell like that?"

"If you don't like it, Emmy, you can go home," says Uncle Ben.

But there was too much money involved. She stayed, and when she complained again, Uncle Ben told her to go home if she didn't like it. She got mellower and mellower, and when the price of admission had to drop to two for a nickel, she didn't even open the winders; and when they had to sell the whale for fertilizer in Rochester, for eighty cents, and Uncle Ben said to her, "This smell of fish is kind of strong. You'd better give the boat a good clean up," she didn't say a word but got right to work. Even when Henry Plat come in with his boots on, she didn't say a word.

And Uncle Ben just set in the cabin looking on, and gazing from time to time at them two glass eyes hung up where the geraniums used to set. He'd put his money in a bank himself, and his heart had gone with that whale, and Aunt Em wanted to keep what was left. Once he'd showed himself a man, she turned out a fond woman.

They worked the *Louisa* back through hogs and potatoes to

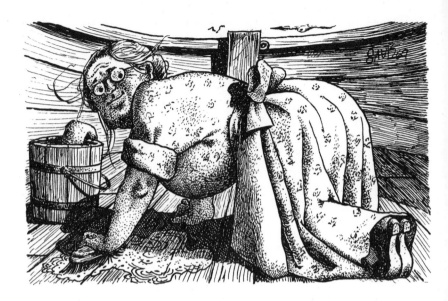

grain until she was as nice as ever. But Uncle Ben had become a kind of old mariner, and Aunt Em continued a changed woman, and if you want to see them glass eyes, my Pa has got them in his house.